You are travelling to another dimension.

A dimension not only of sight
and sound, but of mind.

A journey into a wondrous land whose
boundaries are only that of the imagination.

You are entering The Twilight Zone.

**New Line Television unleashes the seminal classic
series into a modern incarnation featuring all-new
tales from The Twilight Zone. This awesome book
features two stories with a sting in the tale that
will draw fans into a world of fantasy and
suspense like no other!**

Burned

When agoraphobic real estate agent Scott Crane hires an
arsonist to burn down a building, he causes the death of two
innocent children. Then when ghostly phenomena starts to occur
in his own house, Crane must face the possibility that the dead
really can return to take their revenge on the living.

One Night at Mercy

A young doctor meets a man who claims to be Death incarnate.
When Death insists he wants to stop his killing ways, the doctor
is forced to contemplate what life would be like without death.
Unfortunately he doesn't have to contemplate it for long when
Death takes a break for 24 hours and... no one dies.

THE TWILIGHT ZONE™

BURNED ◆ ONE NIGHT AT MERCY

Novelization by Christa Faust

BLACK FLAME

*Thanks again to Maria, VG and Mr C Natural.
Also thanks to Comrad Nathan (workers of the
WORD unite!), DJS and Dr Jay Slater.*

A Black Flame Publication
www.blackflame.com

First published in 2005 by BL Publishing, Games Workshop Ltd.,
Willow Road, Nottingham NG7 2WS, UK.

Distributed in the US by Simon & Schuster, 1230 Avenue of the
Americas, New York, NY 10020, USA.

10 9 8 7 6 5 4 3 2 1

ISBN 13: 9781 84416 179 9
ISBN 10: 1 84416 179 X

A CIP record for this book is available from the British Library.

Printed in the UK by Bookmarque, Surrey, UK.

BURNED

Based on the Teleplay written by
Seth Weisburst and Daniel Wolowicz

ONE

They say revenge is a dish best served cold. But Scott Crane will learn that vengeance can just as easily be delivered up red hot, compliments of The Twilight Zone.

Ten year-old Dimitri Pamchenko sat on the curb in front of his tired and sagging apartment building on Heliotrope Street, watching the last of his neighbors hustle their meager belongings into a sorry-looking rental truck. The building had been cheaply built in the optimistic postwar boom of the Fifties and the ensuing decades had not been kind. Its patchy, gray stucco hide was scrawled with graffiti, greasy with pollution and grime. It was the tallest building on its block and seemed somehow ashamed of that fact, as if it were stooped in an attempt to avoid drawing attention to itself. It stood beside a large and formerly grand house that had been divvied up into apartments and an older bungalow style apartment complex. Dimitri had been living there with his mother and sister for five years. He barely even saw the building anymore.

It was Christmas Eve, dull gray Los Angeles December, not cold enough for snow, just cold enough to make Dimitri wish he had a new jacket. He shifted his chilly butt on the concrete step and pulled last year's scrappy old jacket tighter around his body, hating its too-short sleeves and worn out elbows. He was a skinny, awkward kid with big feet and a face like a kick-me sign. Sensitive and intelligent brown eyes behind crooked glasses. A grade-school bully's dream date. He had a thick library book open in his lap—a complex, speculative science fiction novel, but he wasn't reading. He was looking anxiously down the street, waiting for Nellie Wallace.

Nellie lived around the corner with her grandmother, her aunt and her aunt's boyfriend, four of her aunt's kids and the pregnant fourteen year-old girlfriend of her aunt's oldest son, currently doing time for armed robbery. Nellie's real name was Chanel, a preposterously glamorous name that didn't really suit the intense, peculiar girl who had slowly, almost inexplicably become Dimitri's best friend.

The first time he met Nellie was a warm spring morning just like any other. He had been leaving for school and was walking down the path in front of his building, fretting over an upcoming math test, when an urgent female voice had called out to him from high above.

"Look out!"

There was a loud splat as something landed on the concrete path scant inches from his feet. When he bent to examine the thing, it proved to be an odd, handmade construction of Popsicle sticks and strips of foam rubber. Raw egg was leaking out between the struts, pooling on the cement.

When Dimitri looked up, he saw a furious black girl charging down the path towards him. She was a little taller than him and maybe a year older, all bones and angles. She had an intense, feral face, high cheekbones and sharp, golden-brown eyes like the eyes of a hunting hawk. She wore an awful, over-sized orange jacket that looked like something a city worker would wear to prevent being hit by a car while picking up trash alongside the freeway. Her hair was pulled up into two fuzzy puffs like mouse ears and her thick eyebrows were knitted in intense consternation.

"Shoot, shoot, shoot, shoot, shoot," she said, squatting beside the leaking contraption and pulling a battered green notebook from her jacket pocket.

"What is it?" Dimitri had asked, staring down at the tiny curls on the back of her long brown neck and then looking quickly away.

"That's the third broken egg," she told him, as if that explained everything. "The third."

With sudden clarity, he realized what she was trying to do. She was attempting to create a protective capsule that would prevent a falling egg from breaking on impact. A simple experiment in physics. He watched her scribbling away in the little notebook for a long minute before he got up the nerve to speak.

"What about water?" he said softly.

"What?" She looked up at him with a hostile glare.

"I mean..." He looked away. "Maybe water-filled compartments would provide more adequate cushioning and then..."

The hostility evaporated and she grabbed his arm.

"Come on," she said, hauling him back into the building and up to the roof.

He missed the math test that day, but it was worth it when, four days later, their combined design for an egg-protection capsule was ceremoniously flung from the roof and retrieved from the bed of dying rose-bushes with a perfectly unharmed egg inside.

They had spent nearly all of that summer together, combing the junkyard for spare parts to make model rockets, wandering through the local Radio Shack and drooling over complex electronic components they would never be able to afford. Nellie wore that same ugly jacket every day, even in the killing heat of summer, and it wasn't until August that Dimitri finally got up the nerve to ask her why.

The story came out in a fast, whispered gush. When Nellie was a baby, her mother had been smoking crack and had accidentally set the bed on fire. Nellie's mother and older sister had both died in that fire but a fireman had pulled baby Nellie out of the blaze just in time. Nellie's right arm and the whole right side of her torso had been terribly burned.

That night, on the roof of Dimitri's apartment building, Nellie had shyly pulled back the cuff of her jacket to reveal thick swirls of scar tissue coiled like melted chocolate around her skinny wrist. Dimitri had felt some huge crush of emotion in his belly that he couldn't name. He wanted to say something but his mouth felt full of glue. Instead he reached into his knapsack and pulled out the present he had been saving for her birthday the following week. A new blast deflector for her model rocket launchpad. When she saw it, she threw her arms around him and he thought his heart would burst in his chest.

That night he found himself lying awake in his bed and imagining that he was the fireman rescuing Nellie from the burning building, not as a baby, but just like she was that day. The fantasy didn't really have any conclusion beyond her throwing her arms around him like she had on the roof, but it made him feel hot and anxious and he found himself repeating it over and over in his mind.

When he woke up the next morning, there was an eviction notice on the door of his apartment. The landlord was kicking everyone out of the building, claiming that it was no longer safe to occupy. They'd had three months to move, but the deadline to vacate the premises had come and gone and Dimitri's mother still had not found any place for them to go. All of the other apartments that she was able to find were far too expensive, and with his sister Sonia's never-ending medical bills, there was no chance to save up enough money for a deposit. Every single month was a desperate struggle to just barely get by. Dimitri had no family in America and his mother flat-out refused to take her children back to Russia.

Dimitri was so lost in his thoughts that he didn't even see Nellie until she kicked the toe of his sneaker.

"Hey," she said.

"Hey," he replied.

"Merry Christmas," she said, dropping a brown paper bag into his lap.

He wrapped his hands around the bag and looked down, blushing deeply.

"Well?" She kicked his toe again. "Aren't you gonna open it?"

He put his hand in the bag and felt around dramatically as if trying to guess the contents. Finally, he extracted a slick little package labeled ALTITRAK. He turned it over in his hands until the purpose of the curious object became clear. It was a tracking device to measure the altitude achieved by model rockets.

"So we can finally prove once and for all that my rockets will always go higher than yours," Nellie said, grinning broadly.

"You think so, huh?" Dimitri said, letting her grin infect him for a moment. Then he looked down at the crumpled paper bag between his feet. "I don't have anything for you."

"Don't worry about it," Nellie said, shrugging. She looked up at the weary old apartment building behind them. "Your mom find a new place yet?"

Dimitri shook his head.

A long, awkward silence unspooled between them. The two of them watched the neighbors climb up into the rickety truck and drive away, leaving a large pile of junk behind on the curb. When the truck disappeared around the corner, Dimitri pulled an envelope from between the pages of a library book and quickly handed it to Nellie as if it were hot. He felt a little nauseous watching her open it.

Inside was a card he had made himself. It was made from red cardboard he'd saved from school and folded in half. He had cut out pictures of rockets and the letters to spell "Happy Holidays" from various magazines and carefully pasted them on the front. But the inside had been the hardest part. He had rewritten the message a dozen times, but in the end it just said:

"Dear Nellie, Will you be my girlfriend? Love, Dimitri."

He watched her open the envelope with his heart in his throat. He felt sure he was going to puke or pass out. She stared at the front of the card for way too long and Dimitri felt like yelling at her to open it already, but he couldn't because he was holding his breath. She finally opened it and there was a long pause in which Dimitri felt as if he might collapse or run screaming down the street. Then, she laughed and punched him in the arm. "Stupid," she said.

He looked away, drenched in shame and wishing that a hole would open up in the sidewalk and swallow him. She'd laughed at him. What the hell was he thinking, imagining that a geeky loser like him stood a chance? Now he had ruined everything. He stood up too fast and the ALTITRAK tumbled from his lap. Nellie caught it neatly before it hit the cement.

"Don't you get it?" she asked, handing his present back to him. "I already am your girlfriend, dummy."

She leaned in and kissed him on the cheek, tucked the card into her ugly jacket and turned away.

"Gotta run," she said. "Aunt Sharee'll be pissed if I miss her big Christmas Eve dinner. She's got everybody in the universe coming over and guess who'll be stuck doing all those dishes." She rolled her eyes. "Anyway, I'll come by tomorrow if I can."

He stood there, dumbfounded, watching her walk away.

"Okay then," he was finally able to say when she was more than halfway down the block, "I guess I'll see you later."

Dimitri had no idea how long he stood there, staring off into space with the feel of that swift little kiss tingling on his hot, pink cheek. He didn't even notice his sister's stubby, yellow school bus pulling up to the curb until the driver honked at him, shattering his reverie.

Dimitri headed down to the curb, struggling to shake his goofy stupor. The driver got out and helped Sonia maneuver her wheelchair into the lift. The machine wheezed and clicked and slowly lowered Sonia to the level of the sidewalk. She reached her arms out to Dimitri and Dimitri hugged her tiny, bird-like body close to his.

Sonia was two years younger than Dimitri and painfully beautiful, the spitting image of their mother as a child. Delicate, with almost elven features, dark, almond-shaped eyes and a pointed chin, Sonia might have grown up to be a model or an actress if it weren't for the cerebral palsy that twisted her tiny body into a useless joke and slurred her words into nearly unintelligible mush. People often thought Sonia was retarded because of her voice, but in truth she was gifted and brilliant, in the same grade as Dimitri and at the top of her class.

"Bye bye kiddo," the bus driver said, patting Sonia's scrawny shoulder. "Don't you be doing no more drag racing, you hear me?"

Sonia grinned and used the back of her right wrist to toggle the control that swung her chair around in a tight circle. The burly bus driver laughed and climbed back behind the wheel.

As the bus pulled away, Sonia thumped the pocket of her sweatshirt with one twisted hand. "Guess what," she said, though no one but Dimitri would have understood. "You'll never guess."

"What?" Dimitri reached into her pocket and pulled out an envelope. The return address read: CHA—Canine Helpers of America. "They got your letter?"

"Just read it," Sonia commanded.

It was a reply from the president of the organization, informing Sonia that her story had personally touched him so deeply that he not only approved her application to receive a canine helper—a beautiful lab/shepherd cross named Luka whose photo was included—but he also wanted to feature her on a new TV special about dogs that assist the disabled. For this, she would receive five hundred dollars, a lifetime supply of food for Luka from Wellness pet food and a full scholarship to a prestigious boarding school for gifted kids.

"Wow," Dimitri said, but his brain had already wandered back to Nellie kissing his cheek.

Sonia said something else but he wasn't listening so she socked him in the belly.

"HEY!" she said.

"What?" Dimitri said.

"She said yes, didn't she?"

He blushed and said nothing. Sonia laughed and started chanting. "Dimitri and Nellie sitting in a tree, Kay—eye—ess—ess—eye—en—gee."

"Shut up, Sonia," Dimitri said.

"First comes LOVE, then comes MARRIAGE—"

"I'm warning you," he said.

"Then comes Nellie with the BABY CARRIAGE."

"All right already," he said, unable to get really upset about her teasing. In fact it was nearly impossible to think of anything but Nellie.

Sonia turned her head toward the pile of trash and unwanted items left behind by the fleeing neighbors. There was an old sofa and broken folding chairs and a crummy, stained, twin-sized mattress with a pattern of rockets and stars; an ancient television with a cracked gray screen; wire hangers and old videotapes and crumpled, dusty curtains.

Sonia reached out one of her twisted hands and touched Dimitri's arm with the back of her wrist. "Neighbors are gone, huh?" she said.

Dimitri nodded silently.

"We'll be gone soon, too," she said.

Dimitri looked up sharply and then down the street at the corner where the sorry-looking rental truck had disappeared. What if their mother moved them far away, to another neighborhood or even another city? He might never see Nellie again. But that thought seemed too vast and scary to hold on to. Best not to think about that. Best to let this warm, dumb euphoria keep his mind on better things. Together, he and Sonia went inside.

Their apartment was on the top floor. Dimitri hated the elevator, a tiny, piss-stinking closet that shuddered and shimmied all the way up. If Sonia hadn't been with him, he would have taken the stairs. When the elevator finally dragged itself up to the sixth floor, Dimitri quickly scuttled out and pushed Sonia down the dim hallway to their apartment.

The lock had been picked, messed with and broken so many times that it now required a complex series of maneuvers bordering on voodoo in order to get it to open. His mother must have complained to the landlord a dozen times, but he still had not replaced it. Now he probably never would. Dimitri fished his key out of his pocket and slid it into the lock, carefully lifting the key inside the tumbler and pressing to the left while simultaneously pressing down on the doorknob and then shouldering the door open. It took two tries before the door finally opened for him.

The apartment was dark and tiny, but immaculately neat. Dimitri was very proud of the job he did cleaning and straightening things up every day. It wasn't easy cleaning by flashlight. He stepped inside the apartment and lit the brace of cheap candles on a small table by the door. The electricity in their apartment had been turned off three weeks before, but Dimitri didn't mind the candles. It was sort of cool and old fashioned and the flickering orange light smoothed over the worst of the stains and cracks in the walls. This place wasn't much, but it was still home, and in a way, Dimitri was going to be sad to leave.

He and Sonia shared the one bedroom while their mother slept on the couch in the living room. Every night Dimitri would carefully lay out her blanket and pillow before he went to bed so they would be ready for her when she got in at around three am. In the mornings when he was on his way to school, she would turn over on the couch and beckon him to come and kiss her. She'd tell him and Sonia that she loved them more than anything and would be asleep again before they made it out the door. That sleepy morning kiss was the only time he had seen his mother in nearly six months, so when she came home at seven that night, Dimitri and Sonia knew right away that something was very wrong.

She had a bag of hamburgers and fries from McDonalds, and they sat together around the candlelit table for the first time in over a year. Sonia told her about Canine Helpers of America and, much to Dimitri's chagrin, about Nellie. Their mother smiled weakly and hugged them both tight, telling them to read for a little, while she had a quick shower. After that, she said, there was something important that she needed to tell them.

Both Dimitri and Sonia could tell something was wrong, but neither said anything. They both had books, but neither one read. They just stared at the tiny, plastic Christmas tree with its coiled green string of dark, useless lights, quietly listening to the soporific sound of the shower.

When their mother came out of the bathroom, she was dressed up in a short tight skirt and low cut blouse. Her hair was down and her face heavily made up. She slipped her feet into high-heeled shoes and sat down on the couch next to Dimitri, taking one of each of her children's hands.

"I am going to see an old friend from Russia tonight," she told them softly. "If we are lucky, he will help us."

Dimitri's eyes went huge. "Not Sadko Zajic?"

Their mother frowned and looked away. "He's been very generous towards us in the past. When Sonia's father left us..."

"He hurt you," Dimitri said, angry, a strident panic cracking his voice. "You couldn't go to work for three days last time, remember?"

Their mother's face constricted with an emotion too complex for him to interpret and he immediately felt bad for having brought that up. He would never forget that horrible morning when he'd come to kiss his mother and seen her face all swollen and discolored like some cheap Halloween monster mask. There had been a fat roll of bills on the dresser, and Dimitri had been gripped with fierce desire to fling the money out the open window. He didn't, though, and that money had gotten them this apartment and kept the creditors at bay for a few precious months.

"Listen," their mother said. "I don't want this either, but I have no choice. You are young and you cannot understand, but I have no choice. No choice."

"We love you, Mama," Sonia said in her soft, slurred voice.

Their mother stood, carefully pressing a tissue under each heavily lined eye to stop the tears from spoiling her make up.

"I know you do, my darlings, and I love you both so much." She turned away and stuffed the tissue into her pocketbook. "Now be good and don't stay up too late. Tomorrow morning we will go Christmas shopping and you can have anything your hearts desire, okay?"

Dimitri nodded, unable to tell her that what he really wanted was for her to stay home with them. She kissed their faces, leaving smudges of shimmery pink lipstick, and then she was gone.

That was the last time they ever saw her.

TWO

Rick Driscoll sat behind the wheel of his generic rented car, smoking sullenly and watching the mouth of the alley behind the Heliotrope Street property. He was thirty-four and of a slight build, with neat, slicked-back dark hair, a weak chin and pale blue eyes that moved restlessly over everything around him, casing and cataloging and missing nothing. Dressed in loose-fitting, comfortable and inconspicuous clothing, Driscoll possessed a nearly supernatural ability to go unnoticed. He was a fastidious man with clean finger-nails and an intense dislike for trendy modern styles.

He was also a brilliant arsonist.

Driscoll was not a firebug. He did not get uncontrollably aroused at the thought of burning things. He did not wet the bed, sniff kerosene or masturbate while setting dogs on fire. He was not obsessed—he was a businessman. Flame was not his lover—it was his tool. His skill at the creation, management and control of that complex, chemical oxidization, commonly known as fire had once made him one of the most sought-after pyrotechnicians in the motion picture industry.

Those were good years. Driscoll left the dreary, gray Chicago of his dismal youth for the sunny, palm-lined fantasyland of Hollywood, California. He was a hot young gun, a pyro-savant, who could always make the flames bigger, longer lasting and more dramatic. Women seemed to think that his connections in the film industry meant he could get them acting roles and he did nothing to correct that assumption. For nearly four years, he was on top of the world.

Then digital CGI came along and changed everything. It was safer, easier to control and required no expensive insurance. Driscoll found himself bitter and broke, drifting aimlessly from one demeaning, low-paying job to another. He had been working the pirate show in a Vegas casino when he was approached by one of the directors he had worked with back in the good old Hollywood days.

The director, it seemed, had had a beautiful young wife and she'd had this problem with nose-candy. The beautiful young wife had blown her beautiful young head off with the director's ostentatious .357 Magnum, leaving him several hundred thousand dollars in debt. The director had been building a million-dollar love nest in Malibu especially for the beautiful young wife, and now that she was gone, the half completed eyesore was a financial stone around the director's neck. He could not afford to finish it, and incomplete, it was impossible to sell. Wouldn't it be nice, the director had intimated to Driscoll over frozen stoli in the pirate casino's upscale high-roller bar, if something happened to that house. Say, a fire. Accidents happen all the time. The director was well insured. It would be a "win-win situation."

Driscoll walked away from that little accident thirty-five grand richer, and the director had a new house, a new, younger and more beautiful wife, and a mega-blockbuster hit movie less than a year later. Definitely a win-win situation.

Driscoll was not a man burdened by superfluous morals. So long as no one was hurt in any of the fires that he set, what did it really matter? The only people who were really being hurt by Driscoll's fires were the insurance companies. Driscoll paid one hundred and twenty-five dollars a month for car insurance and two-fifty for health insurance. He had never had a car accident, and had been sick enough to need a doctor exactly three times in his life. He figured anything he could do to stick it to those lousy, corporate, rat bastards was making the world a better place.

There was no one in the alley behind the Heliotrope Street property. He had been watching for nearly an hour now, and he'd seen only one homeless guy with a shopping cart about forty minutes ago. The guy was rail thin and bug eyed with ratty, dirt-matted hair crushed down around the crown of his skull, as if he had been wearing a hat for several unwashed weeks and then lost it. Driscoll thought contemptuously that the guy would not have looked out of place in a trendy nightclub with hair like that. It made him nuts, this new style where men went out of their way to look like their boozy mom had cut their hair the day before their freshman class pictures in seventy-nine, and they had subsequently gone on a bender and spent the night in an alley, face down in a pool of vomit. Cowlicks for Christ's sake. Who on earth would deliberately cut cowlicks into their hair? Driscoll himself spent quite a bit of daily effort to keep his wavy hair slicked back and under control, and yet it seemed like every woman he tried to get ahead with was far more interested in some unshaven, polyester jag-off with homeless hair.

The only other living thing that Driscoll had spotted in the alley was a scrappy, stray mutt with gluey eyes and grungy white fur. It had passed by twice in its search for trash or cats or whatever it is that stray dogs want. Driscoll wondered if the lady dogs went for the dirty look as much as their human counterparts. If so, that filthy beast must have sired buckets of puppies. Driscoll checked his Rolex. 11:45pm. It was time.

He slipped on a pair of tight-fitting latex gloves and inventoried his things: the brand new set of keys, given to him a week ago by the landlord along with the first five grand; the roomy black duffle containing a metal gas-can filled with kerosene, a plastic funnel and a padded cloth pouch that hid a clever little device of his own design; and, just in case, the Sig Sauer P226 9mm that fit snugly into his armpit in a comfortable nylon web shoulder harness. He had never been called upon to use the gun, but many of the properties he found himself visiting in the dead of night were located in less than savory neighborhoods. Like this one. He scanned the deserted street carefully and, convinced he was unobserved, he got out of the car and made his way down the alley.

It took him three minutes and twenty seconds to walk the length of the alley to the back door of the property. Just slightly quicker than his last runthrough, but that was not surprising. He was antsy, wound up and moving faster. He made a mental note to slow down and stick to the precise schedule he had worked out in his head.

As he entered the decrepit old building, he took a moment to orient himself in the dark hallway. He never used a flashlight, as it called unwanted attention to his presence, but his night vision was excellent and he had done several dry runs to imprint the building's layout permanently into his mind. In less than thirty seconds, his eyes had fully adjusted and he made his way through the basement to the stairwell.

Even in the dark, the place was a dump. There was the stale stench of roach spray, cheap paint and poverty. The trash and crumpled beer cans on the steps. The graffiti and the wild, malicious gouges in the soggy plaster walls. If ever there was a building that needed the apocalyptic cleansing of fire, it was this sorry old joint.

Driscoll arrived on the top floor and headed to the back. The apartment he had chosen had been abandoned for months. The lock was smashed, kicked in by cops during some drug raid and never repaired. Inside, the place had been used as a party pad, a homeless hideout and apparently, a toilet. There were several important factors that made Driscoll choose this apartment as his point of origin. First off, it was on the top floor. If a fire destroys the roof of a structure, that structure is automatically considered "unusable" and insurance companies must pay in full to rebuild. Second, it had very flammable wood paneling on the walls and was already conveniently filled with crumpled newspapers, old sofa cushions and alcohol-soaked clothing. All wonderful, yummy food for Driscoll's fire. Third, someone had, for their own drug-addled and unfathomable reason, smashed a hole in one wall, into the neighboring apartment. Inside the hole, the wooden bones of the building were exposed and through that rift, valuable oxygen could flow, helping Driscoll's little fire grow up to be something truly devastating.

A week ago Driscoll himself had left the one other key item in the apartment, a cranky old kerosene camp heater there. It was too heavy and unwieldy for him to carry up the stairs in the dark on the night of the fire, so he had brought it up on one of his dry runs and locked it to the existing radiator with a bike chain. If it had been stolen in the days before the fire, Driscoll would be up the proverbial creek, so he was relieved to see it hunkered there by the broken window like a sullen little robot.

A kerosene heater is a fairly simple mechanism. It consists of a removable tank for the kerosene and a shallow reservoir below the constant, active flame. The flow of fuel into the reservoir is controlled by a barometric valve. A partial vacuum exists above the liquid fuel reserve, preventing the kerosene from flowing into the reservoir until it drops below a level preset by the valve. If this vacuum is compromised for any reason, fuel floods the reservoir and overflows, drenching the surrounding area with flammable liquid. That liquid is then immediately ignited by the heater's flame and you have yourself a fire.

The trick to safely compromising the vacuum was not easy, but Driscoll was good. The device hidden in that soft cloth bag was not complicated, but it was elegant and accurate. It was a tiny timer suspended above a linked pair of grape-sized compartments. In each compartment was a chemical that alone had no real power. Together, however, they formed a voracious acid that could easily eat through any metal. Like, for instance, the metal wall of the kerosene heater's fuel reserve. Once released, the acid would also destroy the little device, rendering it into an unidentifiable lump of slag. Driscoll knew that a real go-getter could analyze the lump and discover tiny particles of residue from the acid, but the landlord assured him that he had someone in the department in his pocket and that the investigation would be cursory at best.

Besides, it was a cold night in Los Angeles. Most people from cities that drop below zero on a regular basis have little sympathy, but the dry desert chill of winter nights in Los Angeles can still make people take risks to stay warm. Faulty heaters were the cause of almost a third of winter fires in the city. Homeless people using an old, cracked heater to stay warm was an easy answer: a filed report, a closed case, and the path of least resistance.

Driscoll carefully filled the tank with kerosene, thinking briefly that it would have been funny and ironic to rig something electrical using Christmas lights and that awful, ultra-flammable silver junk his mom always used to put on the Christmas tree. Driscoll hated Christmas. Growing up, it had always been a holiday of stress and suffering. His mother would become totally, almost fetishistically, obsessed with creating immaculate decorations and perfect dinners. Like clockwork, on the day after Thanksgiving, the "holiday spirit" descended upon the Driscoll house like martial law. Little Ricky and his older sister Vanessa were mere accessories to be dressed in humiliating red and green outfits and posed like automatons in front of the perfect Christmas tree. Their father would hide in his study and drink, while their mother tore through the house, putting up tinsel, baking beautiful cookies no one was actually allowed to eat and berating everyone to be cheerful or else. As an adult, Christmas was always a holiday of lonely resentment and last-minute presents that were never quite expensive enough to please whatever woman had accidentally wandered into his life that year. Like the dreaded Valentine's Day, it became a holiday of guaranteed failure, one he could never seem to live up to any more than he'd been able to live up to his mother's expectations when he was a kid.

Once, almost ten years ago, he'd had a girlfriend who hated Christmas as much as he did. She was a big broad with red hair, a sardonic laugh and strong, muscular legs, and she had refused, as she put it, "...to be a slave to the mindless, holiday consumer feeding frenzy." She had taken him out for cheap Chinese food on Christmas Eve and when they got home afterwards, he discovered that she had a red ribbon tied around her body under her clothes. That was all the Christmas he needed.

She left him eventually, like they all did, and Driscoll went back to hating Christmas alone. As he lit the flame on the kerosene heater and clamped his little device to the curved skin of the tank below, he thought this Christmas might not be so bad after all.

Checking his watch again, Driscoll saw that he was within thirty seconds of his projected time. He gathered the scattered newspapers and other flammable items close enough to the heater to be sure to catch, but not so close as to seem deliberate. Checking the airflow through the broken window for the last time, he set the timer on his device for five minutes and hustled out of the apartment, leaving the door open behind him for the fire to follow.

Out in the dark hallway, Driscoll thought he heard something. Something very soft, almost like kids laughing, sharing a secret. His hand went unconsciously to the butt of the Sig in his armpit.

It had to be his imagination. The building was empty. The landlord had confirmed it. The last of the tenants were long gone. Driscoll supposed it wasn't out of the question for neighborhood kids to be playing in the building, but in the dark at midnight on Christmas Eve? He cocked his head, listening intently, but heard nothing more. He was more than a minute behind now and he did not want to be standing here in this stinking hallway, listening for phantom laughter, when the device went off and the top floor of the building was engulfed in flames. Shaking his head, he hustled down the stairs, out into the alley, and away.

THREE

Dimitri and Sonia lay squeezed together under the covers of Sonia's bed. Dimitri was reading out loud to his sister from Madeline L'Engle's *Swiftly Tilting Planet*. It was their nightly tradition. Even when Sonia had been in the hospital for yet another horrible, painful and humiliating surgery they could not possibly afford, Dimitri would climb under the covers with her, clutching his bulky plastic flashlight, and read to her. But that night neither of them were able to concentrate. They were both intensely anxious and worried about their mother. Less than halfway through the chapter, Dimitri trailed off and took his sister's hand. They sat like that for a long, silent minute, staring up at the cute, cheerful characters from the Power Puff Girls all around them on Sonia's sheets.

Sonia loved the Power Puff Girls. The spunky little-girl superheroes were everything that Sonia was not. Super strong, super fast, they fought monsters and saved their city while still managing to be cute as buttons. His sister's obsession with the Power Puff Girls sometimes made Dimitri feel sad in a way he couldn't quite define.

"I wish I had the five hundred dollars now," Sonia whispered suddenly. "I would have given it to Mama and she could have stayed here with us."

Dimitri nodded. He knew that five hundred dollars would not even come close to being enough, but did not want to make his sister feel bad. Instead he reached over and tickled her under her armpits. She giggled and twisted away.

"Don't worry, kiddo," he said. "It'll be all right."

But it wouldn't really be all right, Dimitri knew that it wouldn't and something about that simple placating lie made Dimitri feel what it was like to be a grownup.

That Sadko Zajic was a horrible, horrible man. Sonia was too little to remember him, but Dimitri did. He remembered the first time he met Zajic. It had been near Christmas then too, and this huge man in a gray suit had arrived on their doorstep with a thick yellow envelope filled with money. He gave Dimitri a crisp new hundred-dollar bill and patted the top of his head with one enormous hand. Looking back at that memory, there was nothing in the man's actions that was overtly bad. It was his eyes, cold, grey eyes as unfeeling as concrete. Dead eyes like the cold, silver eyes of fish, piled up on shaved ice in the supermarket. Like the Terminator, only worse somehow because he was real, standing there in their living room with a gun under his jacket. Dimitri was too scared to speak, even when his mother poked him in the arm and told him to say thank you to Mr Zajic for the generous gift. He never forgot the way that their mother had flinched when Zajic kissed her cheek. Dimitri was glad Sonia didn't remember. He put the bookmark in their book, closed it and set it on his chest.

"Do you feel hot?" Sonia asked, cocking her head under their tent of blankets.

Dimitri frowned. He saw that there were beads of sweat on Sonia's pale face, plastering her bangs to her forehead. Now that she mentioned it, it was very warm. Since the heat had been turned off, Dimitri and Sonia had taken to wearing sweatshirts to sleep and combining all their blankets onto one bed. They had gotten so used to the chilly nights, they barely noticed anymore. But now it was warm, really almost hot.

Curious, Dimitri threw back the covers and was immediately choking on thick, stinging smoke. His eyes watered, blurring his vision. He could feel Sonia's frightened fingers clutching at his arm as her sudden, startled scream wound down into a sputtering cough. Without thinking, he grabbed his sister and pulled her down off the bed with him, onto the floor.

Down there, the air was a little clearer, and Dimitri could see a little better. He watched horrified as tongues of orange flame crept out from behind the dresser, flaring bright and sudden and shooting up the wall, boiling across the ceiling. For a handful of endless seconds, Dimitri could not look away. He remembered when he and his mom had had to wrestle the heavy dresser across the room to cover a saucer-sized hole some crazy person next door had made in the wall. He remembered how scared he and Sonia had been that night when they heard that wild, shrieking laughter and rhythmic pounding on the wall, like some horrible monster was trying to smash its way into their apartment. Dimitri had called 911 and the police had come and taken the neighbors away. Now it was as if the monster was back and this time it actually made it through into their room and there was no phone anymore, no way to call 911. Dimitri grabbed his sister around her skinny chest and started dragging her across the floor, staying low like they'd taught him in school and desperately trying to get away from the blistering heat and hideous, mesmerizing beauty of the fire.

The living room was also filled with thick smoke and Dimitri quickly became disoriented. Sonia was coughing weakly and struggling against him and he kept bumping into things, chair legs and bookshelves. When he found a wall, he started following it, dizzy and nauseous with only a cold spiny panic pushing him forward. Finally, he came to what had to be the front door. Cooler air flowed through the crack beneath the door and Dimitri pressed his mouth to the gap, sucking desperately to fill his aching lungs. For a terrifying second, he thought for sure that he was going to black out. But he had to save Sonia, he had to get out of there so he steeled himself, took in another deep breath and hauled himself to his feet.

Standing, it was easily thirty degrees hotter and the stinging, poisonous smoke was unendurably thick. Dimitri fumbled blindly for the doorknob, hands slapping uselessly across the surface of the door. He would not be able to hold his breath much longer, but the doorknob continued to elude him. He was forced to drop down for another precious mouthful of air. Lungs filled, he stood again and finally his fingers found the warm doorknob. It would not turn.

For a second, he just wrenched the doorknob furiously, unthinking and driven by panic. "Locked," the last rational part of his mind whispered. "It's locked, remember?" Lungs screaming for oxygen, he forced his hands to still and move calmly up to the lock above. His fingers encountered the smooth round face of the lock and a horrible realization hit him. The lock required a key to open on both sides. The key was in the pocket of his pants, hanging over the back of the chair by his bed. In the bedroom. The hellish, blazing rectangle of the bedroom door was the only thing visible through the smoke. There was no way to go back in there.

Dimitri collapsed back down to the floor, pressing his mouth to the crack under the door and gasping for air. The air out in the hallway was much hotter now and Dimitri could see a dull orange glow flickering on the other side of the door. For a long string of seconds, panic short-circuited his thought processes and he curled in on himself, sure that it was all over.

Then a single, crystal clear thought sliced like an ice-cold razor through the chaotic madness inside his head: where is Sonia?

She had been right there, less than a foot away on his left when he first stood to try and open the door. Now she was gone, lost in the heat and smoke. Dimitri tried to call her name, but his voice was nothing but a thick, clotted whisper, easily swallowed by the furious animal roar of the flames.

She could not have gone far. Even at the best of times, she was too weak to drag herself more than a few feet without her chair. She had to be somewhere close by. He began to feel along the floor around where she had been, reaching out and forcing her name from his raw, swollen throat. In less than a minute, the door was gone and Dimitri was in the middle of the room somewhere, sick and disoriented.

Was this a chair here beside his face or the leg of the table? Which way was the bedroom? He thought he saw the little plastic Christmas tree tipped over and burning furiously. He continued to crawl across the floor, the only thought in his mind to find and save Nellie.

Not Nellie, Sonia.

But his brain was feeling sludgy and dull and the pain in his chest was becoming increasingly unbearable and he kept thinking of Nellie, Nellie in the burning building, crying, needing him to save her. It was so hot now that his skin felt dry and painfully tight and his hair and clothing were starting to smoke. He thought of deserts and ovens and ants under magnifying lenses and it just got hotter and hotter. His lungs felt like steel wool in his chest and he still couldn't find Nellie.

Sonia. He couldn't find Sonia.

He remembered being seven and Sonia was five and he had forgotten to fasten Sonia's strap after helping her off the toilet. She fell out of her chair while Dimitri was reading and bumped her chin on the floor. His mother had been furious.

"Sonia is your sister. She's counting on you to help her and keep her safe. Nothing is more important. Do you hear me? Nothing. When I am not here, you are all she has."

And now, Dimitri had clearly failed. Sonia was lost in the fire, unconscious or dead, and there was nothing Dimitri could do but keep crawling in woozy, stupid circles, making the shape of her name with his mouth. Then, suddenly his hand hit some hot, crooked thing. He felt lumpy, blistered skin, a scrawny unmoving arm, and he knew he had found her. He grabbed Sonia's wrist and the flesh of her hand slid off in his grip like raw chicken skin. He turned away, shaking and struggling not to vomit.

When he was able to force himself to look again, he saw his sister sprawled out against the wall beneath the window. Dimitri saw with embarrassment that her pajama bottoms had scrunched down around her knees somehow, from crawling maybe, and she lay there in her Power Puff Girl underwear. The plastic bag that held her urine had broken and her clothes and skin were wet with it. The place where the tube went into her body on the side of her belly was inflamed and crusted with dirt and ash. There was black gunk around her nose and mouth. She didn't appear to be breathing.

At first Dimitri was overwhelmed with a desire to cover her. She was always so ashamed of that tube in her side, she would hate for anyone to see her like that. Then that thought and any others lingering in his head were wiped away by a sudden pure understanding that they were both going to die. Rather than panic or fear, that realization brought a cold flood of rage.

He wrapped his arms around Sonia's limp, unmoving body and hauled her slight bulk up with him as he stood. In his mind, a furious wordless negative eclipsed all other thought and he smashed his fist through the window, feeling nothing, no pain, only apocalyptic anger. It wasn't fair. Not when Nellie had just said yes. It just wasn't fair.

There were solid iron bars on the window, blocking off any hope of escape with immovable smugness. Dimitri beat his bloody fists against them, some awful sound spiraling up and out of him. Their mother had begged the landlord a hundred times to put in bars with a safety latch, but, like everything in this dilapidated building, he'd just never got around to it. Now, with the glass smashed, the ravenous fire lunged toward the fresh gush of air, engulfing Dimitri and Sonia in flame.

Pain boiled through Dimitri's nerves like lava, scorching, impossible, and he could feel the fire inside him, charring his lungs and flash-frying the soft tender organs in his belly. That moment of total, overwhelming pain seemed to last forever until all at once, it was gone, flicked off like a switch.

Suddenly, inexplicably, Dimitri was standing out in the hallway. The same awful, trash-strewn hallway he'd walked down a million times, only now it seemed longer and darker, thick with smoke so that it took on a skewed, funhouse perspective. None of the doors to the other apartments had numbers on them. In fact they seemed... fake somehow, as if they were just painted on the walls like some kind of movie set. Dimitri knew without trying the knobs that none of them would open.

Dimitri looked down at his body, suddenly terrified, but he did not look burned at all. When he tried to touch himself to feel for damage, it was like trying to touch a reflection on the surface of water. His feet did not seem to reach the ground.

Down at the very end of the hallway was a glowing sign that read EXIT in blocky, official letters. Dimitri could see that there was somebody standing by the exit: a grown-up, tall and broad and smeared with shadow. Dimitri wanted very much to get to the exit, but he was afraid of that tall, shadowy person. When he felt a strange, distant pressure on his fingers, he looked down and saw that there was a thin white hand holding his. Sonia's hand. She was standing next to him and grinning, and that fact should have bothered him but he couldn't quite remember why.

"Come on," she said in a clear, sweet voice.

She made her way towards the exit and as they approached, they saw the grownup at the end of the hallway more clearly. It was a man, a firefighter in a bulky black raincoat with florescent yellow stripes on the back and sleeves. His helmet was pushed back on his head and his face was smeared with soot and grime. He had a cigarette in the corner of his unshaven mouth. Dimitri thought he looked kind of like an action movie hero, handsome and rough with piercing blue eyes.

"What's your hurry?" he asked, taking a deep drag off the cigarette and squinting at them.

"The building's on fire," Sonia told him. "We need to get out of here."

The fireman nodded thoughtfully. "I can see how you'd want to go," he said. "If somebody set my building on fire I'd want to get out of there right away too."

Dimitri frowned. "Somebody set our building on fire? On purpose?"

The fireman nodded again. "They sure did." He paused and looked down the hall. "And you know what? Now that your house is burned up, that guy and all his buddies are gonna make a million dollars. How do you like that?"

"Really?" Sonia asked.

"Think a guy like that cares about kids like you? He just wants his money. That's not fair at all, is it?"

Dimitri and Sonia both shook their heads.

"If I was you, I'd be awful mad at that guy." The firefighter looked at them both, his blue eyes suddenly hard and fierce. "I'd want to make that guy pay for what he did. Wouldn't you?"

Dimitri was mad. It wasn't fair at all. He thought of Nellie. He thought of his mother, coming home and finding their building burned to the ground. He thought of Luka the dog and the scholarship Sonia would never get. He was furious, but it was Sonia who answered for him.

"Yes," she said, little fists clenched and jaw set with fierce determination. "Yes we would."

The firefighter smiled and stubbed out his cigarette against the sooty wall. "Well then," he said, opening one of the doors to his left. "Right this way."

The door wasn't fake after all, but whatever was on the other side of the door was obscured by thick smoke.

"Come on," Sonia said again, leading Dimitri through the door.

FOUR

Svetlana Pamchenko stood before the full-length mirror in an upscale hotel bathroom, taking inventory. Amazingly, there were almost no bruises on her face, just a little lingering redness on her left cheek and around her neck. That would fade away before the morning. The worst of the external damage was on her breasts, lurid bruises, bite marks and, on the right just above the nipple, a wet pink crater where one of Zajic's "associates" had put out a cigarette. She slipped her arms carefully into the straps of her bra, coldly relieved that the burn was hidden by the edge of the lacy cup. If she concentrated very hard on walking normally and not allowing the deep, thudding pain between her legs to show, her children would never know what she had done for them.

Sadko Zajic. She thought she had been rid of that poisonous reptile years ago. But somehow, she always seemed to wind up back in his lush Hollywood office. A fact that he never let her forget.

The first time had been the hardest. She was desperate and terrified, deeply in debt with nowhere else to turn. She had moved to the United States to marry a computer programmer named Donald Spencer who she met through an international dating service. She remembered sitting on the plane with baby Dimitri in her arms, filled with a kind of terrified elation, as if she were flying into the future. She remembered walking into an American supermarket for the first time and feeling faint at the sight of all that food. Towers of cereal and massive piles of gorgeous, perfect fruit. The programmer's apartment seemed palatial, perfect, and while he was distant and stiffly polite toward her, he was rarely home and Svetlana was cautiously happy. She spent her days with Dimitri in the park, window-shopping and watching American television, and her nights cooking for Spencer and performing her wifely playacting. When she became pregnant with Sonia, Spencer suddenly warmed up to her, doting on her and surprising her with little gifts. He had always been reserved towards Dimitri, but now that his own child was on the way, he started acting almost paternal towards her son.

Then, when Sonia was born, everything changed.

The delivery was difficult and the doctors knew right away that something was not right with the tiny baby girl. When the diagnosis of cerebral palsy was confirmed, Spencer nodded thoughtfully, patted Svetlana on the hand in her hospital bed, and turned to go.

The next day, Spencer did not visit Svetlana and little Sonia in the hospital. There was no answer when Svetlana called home, but later that night, she received a phone call from a neighbor who found two year-old Dimitri wandering alone in the hallway of the apartment complex. When Svetlana checked herself out and rushed home in a cab, she found all of Spencer's things gone from the apartment.

The rent for that lovely, big apartment was fifteen hundred dollars a month. Spencer's health insurance was cut off two weeks after he failed to show up for work, and Sonia was still not home from the hospital. She needed reconstructive surgery on her tiny bladder to prevent her system from filling up with uric acid and Svetlana was alone, terrified of losing her helpless little girl. She struggled and worked two extra jobs, moving to cheaper and cheaper apartments as she was evicted again and again, taking Sonia to new hospitals every few months under an assumed name and hiding from the towering piles of medical bills.

Four years later, when Sadko Zajic walked into the club where Svetlana worked as a cocktail waitress, she was hit with a powerful, childish desire to hide, to run away. She had left Russia to get away from him and now, somehow, he had found her. His smile when he saw her was like the instinctive flexing of teeth exhibited by sharks preparing to attack.

Zajic was a huge, hulking beast of a man, with a concrete jaw line and a close-cropped blond flat-top, his Armani suit bulging with excessive, steroid-induced muscle. When Svetlana first met him he was a fighter in an illegal, no-holds-barred, mixed martial arts promotion. He had connections with the Russian mob and was moving swiftly upward through the ranks with ruthless determination. To Svetlana, he seemed glamorous and tough. To the young girl who had been abused by her drunken, Ukrainian father and raped by thugs as a runaway on the streets of Moscow, he offered protection and safety. By the time she realized the price for his protection, she was in over her head. Leaving the country seemed the only way to escape. Now he was here, in Los Angeles, and Svetlana was terrified.

He seemed to smell Svetlana's distress the moment he walked in the room. He cosseted her and told her he only wanted to help a friend from the old country. He could get her extra work, entertaining his business associates who wanted a friendly Russian girl to make them feel at home. Wear pretty dresses and show them around the city. Anything more would be at her discretion, of course. He would be happy to lend her money that very night to help her get a new apartment. She could pay him off by helping him out now and then, whenever he had out of town visitors. She knew it was a deal with the devil, but what could she do? She took the money and let Zajic take her home that night, to "seal the deal." When he was unable to perform, he beat Svetlana savagely. Afterward, he gave her an extra five hundred dollars. She spat blood in his face and left.

That year she went on thirty-five "dates" with Zajic's associates. She kept a careful record of every transaction and as soon as she had worked off Zajic's loan, plus the outlandish interest, she endured another failed romantic interlude and another beating, and then figured she would never have to see him again.

The look on his face when she came into his office made her feel lower than dirt. That casual, confident smirk that said, I knew you'd come. If she had a gun she would have shot him dead right there, but instead she flattered him and flirted with him and told him everything he wanted to hear. That he was right. That she did need him. She watched herself acting out the scenario like an alien observing the behavior of primates, as if it had nothing to do with her. When he took her out to introduce her to his pals from Moscow, she smiled and was charming. She took every humiliating indignity without protest, making a list in her head of things to buy for her children with the money she would receive that night.

Now it was over. In her life, Svetlana had endured countless beatings and violations, but no matter how bad they were, eventually they were over. Like always, she took the horror of what she had been through and formed a thick protective bubble around it in her mind, burying it deep down with all the others until it became like a story she heard once, something that happened to some other woman on television. She had her children to think of. Nothing else mattered.

She would have splurged on a cab home, but she wanted to save the money for presents instead, so she sat for an hour and a half on the stale, warm bus, staring mindlessly out the window at the passing city. She was exhausted and sore, but cautiously excited. The apartment she had looked at on Normandie was the cheapest she had found so far and they would allow dogs, which would be perfect for Sonia's new canine helper. With the money from Zajic, she might even be able to afford a new sofa, maybe something with a sleeper bed built in.

These bland, simple thoughts filled her mind as she made her way down Heliotrope towards her building. She was so tired and preoccupied that it took several seconds for the police cars and fire trucks to register and nearly a minute for her to realize that they were in front of her house.

Panic stabbed like a long thin needle in her chest and she started to run, clumsy in her high heels. The building was still pouring thick, toxic smoke and flames were shooting through the roof. Black-faced firefighters were staggering out, supporting one of their number who seemed to loll in semi-consciousness between his fellows. There was yellow tape blocking the sidewalk but Svetlana pushed her way through, shaking off the restraining arms of police and stumbling from one person to another.

"My children," she said, gripping the thick rubber coat of a burly, black firefighter. "My daughter, she is handicapped. She can't walk. You need to get them out of there right away."

"I'm sorry, ma'am," the firefighter said, shaking his head and laying a big hand on Svetlana's shoulder. "I'm afraid there are no survivors."

"No survivors?" Svetlana felt her English failing her. That word, survivors, it meant nothing to her. "But where is my Sonia? My son and daughter, please, where are they?"

The man shook his head again and Svetlana whirled away from him with a cry of anguish. She grabbed another firefighter, this one older with a fancy insignia on his hat.

"Please," she begged. "Please where are my children? My daughter... Please."

"We are still in the containment phase at this time," the man said. "The recovery of remains will not be possible until the fire has been fully contained."

He might as well have been speaking Swahili, making sounds that were totally incomprehensible to Svetlana. Frustration coiled in her chest, crushing her heart. She saw that black girl, Dimitri's friend, standing there, staring at the flames with a kind of sleepy horror on her face. She did not seem to take any notice of Svetlana. When a dark-haired police officer took Svetlana by the arm, she fought against him, straining towards the burning building.

"You can not go in there," the police officer said in Russian. "It is not safe."

"You are Russian?" Svetlana's heart leapt. "Thank God. Please help me. My children are in there."

The Russian cop put his arm around her and led her to the open door of a nearby squad car, sitting her down in the passenger seat.

"I am Officer Emelianenko," he said. "What is your name?"

"I am Svetlana," she said, "but listen to me, officer. My Dimitri and Sonia are in there, do you understand? They are in there. My daughter is in a wheelchair. She cannot get out alone. You must help her."

"Svetlana," the cop said softly. "Svetlana, I'm very, very sorry. No one could be alive in there. Do you understand?"

Again, Svetlana had that feeling of detachment, of watching herself from a distance as she flailed out against the cop and struggled, howling, towards the building. She thought she might have been sobbing, screaming, but she was too far away from herself to hear. Someone else was trying to tell her that her children were gone, but that just wasn't possible. It wasn't possible when she had the money for a new apartment right here. She watched herself showing the money to the Russian cop and explaining how they were going Christmas shopping in the morning, but then there was a paramedic there and something in her arm, a needle and some cold liquid speeding though her veins and as the paramedic began to gently examine her, her last thought was that they would see the bruises. She couldn't let her children see the bruises.

FIVE

It was Tom Phillips's first day on the job as a member of the Arson Investigation Unit. He was thirty-seven and powerfully built with a friendly, open face that made him look much younger, like a varsity wrestler or a college football star. He had been a firefighter for sixteen years and when he had finally passed the test to become an arson investigator and received his first assignment, he'd got a lot of ribbing from the boys in the station house.

"So," his friend Beto Velez had said while Phillips was clearing out his locker at the homey, familiar station of Engine Company 103. "I hear you're leaving us for Ice-Panties Graham."

"Christ," Phillips said. "You guys are like a bunch of gossip queens around this place."

"Kate Graham?" An incredulous Korean probie named Milton Kim came up behind Phillips with an armload of gear, ready to take over Phillips's locker as soon as it was empty. "You're gonna be partnering with Kate Graham?"

"Is that right?" Captain Dewey chimed in, lighting up a cigarette. "Let me tell you, stepping up to Saint

49

Jimmy's widow, you're gonna have a pretty big jock to fill."

In truth, Phillips was very nervous about meeting his new partner. Kate Graham was the only female arson investigator in the country, known for her arctic demeanor and her ball-busting intolerance towards newbies like Phillips. Her late husband James T Graham had been one of the most popular fire marshals in the city. The kind of guy you wanted to grow up to be. Handsome, charismatic, and married to the woman everyone wanted, but no one could get near. Everybody in the department was sure he was destined for great things, politics maybe or some plushy, brass setup, so it was a real shock when Jimmy Graham put his pistol in his mouth one steamy summer evening and pulled the trigger, leaving behind a beautiful widow and a thick cloud of rumor and speculation.

Phillips didn't have any opinion about Jimmy Graham's suicide. He couldn't afford one. This was his big chance to move up in the world, to prove that he was more than just hose-hauling muscle. Okay, maybe he wasn't Einstein—the physics and chemistry required to pass the exam had been excruciatingly difficult for Phillips—but he was intuitive and ambitious and he possessed a dogged determination to see things through to the bitter end. And more than that, he was good with people. A crackerjack judge of character, Phillips had a bloodhound-like ability to sniff out lies. People trusted him. Maybe it was his gentle, friendly face or his self-deprecating sense of humor, but people would tell him things they wouldn't tell their own mother. Even when he was just a firefighter, suspects that gave nothing to the cops or the boys from Arson would inexplicably confess to Phillips. It was his wife Lucy who had finally convinced him that he should go for the AI exam, though in retrospect, Phillips suspected she wanted him to move into Arson because it meant he went in after the fire was already out. It must not have occurred to her that being an investigator meant dealing with criminals, making arrests and going door to door in some very bad neighborhoods, asking questions nobody wanted to answer. He was sure she didn't think it would mean being called in to work on Christmas morning.

When Phillips reported for duty at the stuffy, chaotic Arson Unit office downtown, he was immediately sent into the field, to meet the legendary Ice-Panties Graham at the scene of a fatal structure fire on Heliotrope Street.

He arrived on the scene with butterflies in his stomach. The first real fire he had battled as a young probie had been a four-alarm blaze in an upholstery foam warehouse. The huge rolls of polyurethane foam had gone up with terrifying ferocity, hissing and spitting like malevolent, living creatures, but Phillips had been too jacked up on adrenaline to feel anything but urgent excitement as he and his squad worked with picks and axes to ventilate the roof, hauling the lines and fighting to beat back the roaring flames. Now, as he approached the black and dripping husk of the Heliotrope building, he knew the real danger was over, but he still could not shake the chilly anxiety that gripped him. He threaded his way through firefighters in full turnout gear, muscling up the hoses and stowing their equipment. It felt weird to Phillips to step into the dark and char-stinking scene of a fire in his flimsy civilian clothes.

"Hey," a deep, scratchy voice called out from the ruined staircase. "You can't come in here, this is a closed scene."

An older Latino man materialized out of the gloom. He wore a nice sports jacket and expensive shoes that did not belong tramping through puddles of tarry water and melted human fat. He had a gun and a gold badge on his belt.

"Tom Phillips," Phillips said, flashing his own brand new shield and feeling silly and small. "Arson."

The man looked at Phillips as if he were a toddler that had wandered into a strip club. "Arson's robbing the cradle now, eh? They must be desperate for someone dumb enough to work with Graham." He smirked and jerked his chin towards the stairs. "Top floor in the back. Go get her, tiger."

Phillips slipped past the hostile cop and started up the slippery steps, glad he had chosen sturdy work boots with thick chunky treads.

"And don't touch nothing," the cop called back over his shoulder. "This is still an active homicide scene. At least until your new girlfriend says different."

The walk to the top of the stairs was grim and exhausting. There was little real damage on the lower floors, mostly smoke and water damage, but when Phillips arrived on the top floor, he was amazed by the totality of the devastation.

Huge, gaping holes had burned through what little remained of the roof, letting the weak morning sunshine drift down in thin, sooty columns. There were almost no inner walls left, just some charred wooden beams and a vast open tangle of sodden debris. An almost church-like hush had settled over the scene, broken only by the hypnotic sound of dripping water.

At the far end of the mess, back to Phillips, was a tall figure in an old firefighter's regulation coat and helmet. It wasn't until the figure turned and he saw the thick red braid swing free from the collar that he knew it must be Graham. She was tan and fiercely muscular with her coat sleeves rolled up on her strong forearms and latex gloves over her big hands. Her profile was hard and stony but still quite attractive. She looked more like a fitness instructor than an arson investigator. Phillips took a step forward and her head shot up, frozen like a deer, scenting trouble. When she spotted him she turned away without a word, crouching down at the base of a large V-shaped wedge of char extending up the wall and onto what remained of the ceiling. She pulled a small digital camera from an inner pocket and snapped a few shots.

"I'm Tom Phillips," Phillips said to her broad back. When she did not respond he continued, "Your new partner."

She nodded without looking up. She pocketed the camera, pulled a small jackknife from a long, open toolbox beside her and began to poke through the ash, uncovering a few unburned fragments of newspaper beneath what looked like the blackened remains of some sort of heater.

"That the point of origin?" Phillips asked, looking up at the ominous V-shaped burn on the wall above.

"Figured that one out for yourself, did you?" The redhead lifted some of the newspaper up on the end of her knife and slipped it into an evidence bag. "Guess I can retire now."

Phillips frowned, but he was determined not to let Graham's legendary attitude get under his skin. Her coat was unbuckled and he had to concentrate on not looking down at the tan, freckled cleavage displayed by the buttons left open at the top of her shirt beneath. Instead he turned his focus to the heater.

"What have you got so far?" he asked, trying to gently defer to her rank without seeming sycophantic.

She looked up at him as if reassessing her opinion of him, but her dark eyes were too walled off to let him in on what that opinion might be.

"Old kerosene camp heater," she said. "The wall of the fuel reserve was obviously corroded."

She indicated a ragged gap in the heater's curved skin with her knife. "The reservoir burst, allowing the kerosene to overflow and..." She shrugged, indicating the wreckage all around them with a wave of her hand.

Phillips nodded, trying to absorb every detail of the scene. He could clearly see where the fire had spread across the room, across the fragmented ceiling, through the wall and out into the neighboring unit. Its tracks were as clear as the spoor of some big predator in the Serengeti and Phillips felt the first licks of uneasy excitement in his chest. Every book he'd read, every photo he'd poured over, every crumb of information he'd jammed into his head all seemed so small and two dimensional compared to the stark, soot-stinking reality of this, his first real fire scene. He tried to keep his excitement close to the vest and instead looked around for the bodies. There were none that he could see and he wondered if they had already been removed.

"I understand this was a fatal fire," he said quietly.

Graham stood and looked at him again, cautious and skeptical. "The crispies are over there." She gestured

towards a broken window on the far wall. "Two victims—one male, one female. Kids, apparently."

Phillips glanced over at the window she had indicated. He saw the twisted remains of what might have
been a small wheelchair about twelve feet away from
the window, but could not make out anything that
looked even remotely like a body, let alone two of
them.

"Teenagers?"

Graham shook her head. "Kid kids," she said. "Ten
and eight. Mom was out partying all night and left
them alone in the apartment."

Phillips swallowed hard. He had come up against
his share of fatalities in his career as a firefighter, but
the children were always the hardest to take. Not
wanting to show any weakness in front of Graham,
Phillips walked over to the window to take a closer
look.

At first his eyes could not separate the charred,
shrunken corpses from the surrounding debris. One
was nothing but a tiny pelvis, a spine and a skull with
a few shreds of dark red meat like cheap beef jerky
clinging to the bones. The other was larger and more
complete, ribs and most of the legs still attached. The
smell was ghastly, like rotten bacon and old grease
and burnt hair.

Phillips did not allow himself to flinch. He willed
away his nausea and turned to examine the little
wheelchair.

The skeletal metal frame was warped from the heat,
rubber tires burned down to nothing and the seat
cushion destroyed. There was a cluster of charms
hanging from one handle. Most had been reduced to
unidentifiable slag but one was miraculously

unharmed, a thimble-sized figure of Blossom, kid super-heroine from the Power Puff Girls.

A profound wave of sadness swept over Phillips. He could too clearly imagine these kids, trapped in the smoke and heat and chaos. How Dimitri had tried to save his handicapped sister and his fury and anguish when he failed.

That was odd. Phillips didn't remember anyone telling him the name of the kid who died.

Dimitri, he thought. Dimitri and Sonia.

He thought he heard a soft, shuffling footstep behind him and whirled around, jumpy and inexplicably anxious. There was a sound like the faint echo of a child laughing, like something playing on the radio in a passing car, then silence.

When Graham laid a hand on his shoulder, he jumped like a goosed cheerleader.

"Try decaf next time, kid," Graham said, her eyes giving away nothing as she peeled off her latex gloves. "There's nothing more for us to do here. This is clearly just another tragic holiday accident in the big bad city."

Blushing fiercely, Phillips started to follow sheepishly after Graham, when a sudden thought came whole and unbidden into his head, just like the dead kid's names.

"Did anyone get out?" he asked.

Graham frowned. "No, why?"

"Well," Phillips looked over his shoulder at the place where the tiny corpses lay, "the kids were in a different apartment than the point of origin, right? So who was using the heater?"

Graham gave him a peculiar, intense look he couldn't quite read. Looking into her eyes was like looking at one-way glass. All he could see was himself.

"Homeless people, no doubt," she said. "They probably ran when the fire started. People like that don't stick around to talk to the authorities."

"Maybe we need to try and locate witnesses who might have seen people exiting the building prior to the inception of the blaze. Just to be sure. I mean..." He looked into Graham's dark, chilly eyes but had to continue. "Who's to say someone didn't start the heater and run, expecting it to break down and start a fire? After all, it is a top rear apartment, a classic choice for an arsonist's point of origin. What do we know about the landlord?"

"Look," Graham said suddenly, turning on him with sarcasm. "I've been in Arson for ten years. I was putting down cases when you were still a snot-nosed probie wrapping hoses and polishing brass. But if you think you know more about basic scene analysis than I do, by all means, let's start canvassing the block. Let's spend the rest of the day talking to dirtbags and crack-heads who I'm sure will be lining up to tell us every detail about who was in this building before the fire. If we work hard and get lucky, sometime next week we might have ironclad proof of what I already know. Or you can put your little Fire Science 101 hard-on back in your pants and let me do my job."

Graham brushed past him and walked away, down the stairs.

For a long minute, Phillips just watched her go, speechless. There was something going on here, something more than Graham was letting on, but she was so tightly sealed, he had no idea what that might be.

Without meaning to, he found himself looking back at the little corpses by the window. From where he stood he could barely make out the rounded shapes of the two skulls. A sudden vision of the room in flames struck him with brutal, migraine intensity and he flinched back, staggering and nearly sprawling in the wet and treacherous debris.

Then with as little warning, the vision was gone. Feeling weirdly embarrassed, Phillips wrapped his arms around himself and headed down the stairs after Graham.

SIX

In a house high in the Hollywood hills, far away from Heliotrope Street, Scotland Crane sat at a huge, raw marble slab of a desk, popping the lid on and off a bottle of Xanax and talking into a headset. The house, the office and Crane himself were all spare and immaculate. The house was a geometric tumble of white blocks cascading over the edge of the hill, easily worth four or five million. Crane was young for a self-made millionaire, but he had none of that movie-mogul, nouveau-riche bad taste. There was no pool filled with silicone-enhanced models in tiny bikinis. No white tigers or gold-plated Ferraris. Just a tasteful but no-nonsense fence and a cheerless, businesslike security system giving the outside world the cold shoulder. Crane had no interest in seeing anyone, especially not that day. It was early, the sun just barely up, and already the day had gone to hell in a handbasket.

"A terrible tragedy," he agreed, punching the remote that turned on the enormous, flat-screen TV taking up most of one wall.

Of course the local news already had the story, but now it looked like CNN had swooped in and was having a field day with the whole cripple angle. A blonde lady reporter that looked semi-hot, but had probably had a ton of work done was interviewing the head of some kind of dog charity that was supposedly all set to help out the crippled kid before the "...terrible tragedy that senselessly ended her young life." The reporter was petting a big, sad-eyed mutt and making big sad eyes at the camera. The Ken doll in the studio agreed that it was sad. So terrible and sad. Crane shook his head. What a disaster.

"Of course I will be paying for the funeral," Crane said to the perky, cappuccino-fueled reporter on the other end of the line. "It's the least I can do for the grieving family. I will also be making a substantial donation to..." He squinted at the TV screen. "Canine Helpers of America." He scribbled the name of the stupid dog charity on a scrap of paper to pass on to his secretary. "To help other needy children... without dogs."

Now the tearful mother was on the screen. Obviously a hooker, wearing an awful, tacky mini skirt and a slutty leopard print top that left nothing to the imagination, but the news jackals were making her into Mary Goddamn Poppins. As difficult as it was, Crane could have dealt with the kid angle. It was tricky, but hey, kids die all the time, especially poor kids. And from the look of the mother, she'd be out making more before the first two were in the ground. But the cripple thing—that was the icing on the cake, the sweet, sticky sugar that attracted the media wasps to his little picnic.

"Look," he said to the reporter. "That's my other line. I'll need to take this. It may be the funeral director." He smirked. "Yes, it certainly is. A terrible tragedy."

He shook his head and clicked over to the other line. "Crane."

"Merry Christmas, Daddy."

Crane took a deep breath and muted the TV. "Hello, Charlotte." He rubbed his temples. "Did you like the..." He sifted through his inbox to find the receipt from the present his secretary had bought for his daughter. "Barbie's Rollerblade Beauty Parlor?"

"It was nice," she said. "But I miss you, Daddy. Can't you come over for a visit? How about tomorrow? My ballet recital..."

On the television, a photo appeared over the Ken doll's left shoulder. It was Crane in a very unflattering shot that emphasized his bald spot. Under his picture was the caption SLUM LORD. Crane cursed under his breath.

"What?" Charlotte asked. "Daddy, are you okay?"

"Look, Charlotte, I can't talk right now." He turned up the volume on the television. "I'll call you later."

"Well, okay." Charlotte paused. "I love you, Daddy."

"Yeah, right, okay, bye." He hung up.

Now they were interviewing former tenants. Drug addicts and welfare moms and other human waste, all jumping like fleas at the chance to be on TV and complain about him. Some even implied his negligence had something to do with the deaths of the cute little moppets. Like that slut and her gimpy brats didn't have months and months to find someplace else to go. They weren't even there legally. They were practically squatters for Christ's sake. It was their own fault they were still there when the building went up.

Not thirty seconds had gone by before the phone rang again.

"Crane," he said into the headset.

"You bastard," said the voice on the line. It was Risa, his ex-wife.

"I don't have time for this right now."

"I don't give a damn what you have time for. You can't just hang up on your own daughter on Christmas morning."

He could feel the claw feet of a champion migraine digging into the base of his skull. "Risa," he said. "There's been a fire in one of the properties."

"I saw that," she said. "Burning little children to death now, are you?"

"I pay thousands of dollars a month so I don't have to listen to you anymore, Risa. I'm hanging up now."

"Well, you don't care at all about your own flesh and blood, why should it bother you that someone else's children are dead because of you?"

Crane hung up.

When the phone rang again he let the machine get it. It was Rick Driscoll's thick Chicago accent.

"Crane," Rick said. "Crane, pick up, I know you're there."

Crane clicked over. "What is it, Driscoll?"

"Crane, what the hell happened?" Crane could hear the quick inhale of a cigarette through the phone. "You told me there'd be no one in the building."

"How was I supposed to know some hooker was squatting there illegally with her damn spastic, telethon kids?"

"I don't care about that, Crane, all I care about is the fact that I'm now facing double murder charges on a job you hired me to do. Higher risk, higher pay, man. I want more money."

"You think you're getting a penny over the forty-five we agreed on, you've been sniffing too much gasoline." Crane spat, furious. "Don't try to play hardball with me, Driscoll."

"No hardball, eh? How's this for hardball? I'm gonna come over there and burn you alive in that big fancy prison you live in, you son of a bitch. You hear me? I'll burn you alive. You told me there would be no one there and now two people are dead. Two little kids. Christ, Crane. Kids."

For a long stretch of seconds, Crane was speechless with anger. "Are you threatening me?" he was finally able to whisper between gritted teeth.

"Yup, pretty much. And remember, if I get popped, you better believe I'll be rolling over on you like a goddamn circus dog. So don't piss me off. I want double, in fact, make it an even hundred grand, fifty for each dead kid. And believe me, that don't even come close to covering it."

Crane hung up. The little punk had some nerve. He was crazy if he thought he was going to get a penny over forty-five grand. Besides, why hadn't he checked around first to make sure the building really was empty? Crane couldn't be expected to do everything.

Once again, it had been made abundantly clear that no one could be trusted. Crane had made every dime of his money alone, with help from no one. He learned from an early age that betrayal was part of human nature and trust was nothing but an invitation to get screwed.

Crane had trusted his father to take care of their happy little nuclear family and for years, that's exactly what Raymond Crane did. Scott Crane was an only child, loved and nurtured by his mother

Amanda, a retired runway model turned full-time homemaker. Raymond worked in finance, some complex adult thing that Scott did not understand or care to know about. All he knew was that he had a nice house with a pool, a new bike, and tons of friends at his exclusive private school where he was an A student.

Then, when Scott was thirteen, the smooth pretty face was torn off his life and he saw the true shape of the world.

Raymond Crane was arrested for embezzlement and went to jail. Broke and bankrupt, Amanda moved with Scott into a poverty-stricken neighborhood in which they were the only white people. His new school was a nightmare, a grim shabby edifice lined with metal detectors and patrolled by armed security. There were few books and fewer materials for trivial things like Scott's favorite subject, science. The teachers were shell-shocked veterans who seemed less interested in helping the students learn than simply surviving each day without being physically or sexually assaulted. Scott was beaten up by the tough, urban kids in his new neighborhood on a daily basis. Amanda started drinking heavily, staying out later and later, leaving Scott alone to subsist primarily on Wonder Bread and Tang. He would lay awake nights, recreating his old room in his mind with vivid, almost painful clarity. His little TV with his brand new Atari video game deck. His clever loft bed with a cozy little desk beneath where he could sit and do his homework. Posters of the bands he liked on the walls and thin red blinds on the windows, and a rug that his mom had let him choose—a simple red weave that he thought looked very grown up. He focused so clearly on that room that he was able to block out the shabby, awful room he lived in now with its dirty stucco walls and stained yellow carpet like the pelt of some diseased animal. Dreary, thrift shop bed and cheap white veneer on the dresser, peeling already to reveal the particle board beneath. Scott would spend hours laying there, visiting his old house in his mind.

Eventually Scott became afraid to leave the apartment and started cutting school, not to party or hang out with friends, but to hide in his room and imagine a house that he could never be forced to leave. A place that belonged totally to him and no one else. Other people always let you down, but Scott felt sure that, if only he had a place of his own, he would never ever have to leave.

Eventually, Scott dropped out of school, aced the equivalency test and applied for financial aid to go to college. He left Amanda passed out on the sofa in that crummy apartment without saying goodbye and didn't hear from her until years later when she hit him with an embarrassing series of calls asking for money. He gave in the first two times out of guilt, but after that told his secretary not to take her calls anymore. He hadn't heard from her since.

Now Crane was a self-made millionaire several times over. He owned real estate all over California, New York and Florida as well as several holdings overseas, both in Europe and Asia. It was totally ridiculous that an irrelevant little tenement building in Los Angeles was the source of so much hassle. Originally, it had seemed so simple. Get all the trash out of that place, strip the worthless hovel to the foundations, and use the insurance money to fix it up. Turn it from a depressing rabbit warren for welfare cases and base-heads into hip, airy lofts for the young artists and trust-fund babies that were cautiously beginning to scout around the neighborhood like curious ants, leaving behind telltale spoor like open-mike coffee houses and body piercing salons. He had been thinking of starting at around fifteen hundred for the smaller units, and getting up to twenty-five hundred for the two storey spaces with a projected move-in date maybe three years down the road at the absolute latest. It was a flawless plan, or had been until that Russian slut and her cute little crippled kids had to go and spoil everything. Now it would be more like five years before he could rebuild without bringing down morbid media attention on the project.

For now, he would just have to sit on the property until the vultures moved on to a fresher carcass. It was not as if he was hurting for cash. Crane had devoted every waking minute of his adult life to making sure that he always had back-up funds, redundant hidden reserves in a hundred offshore bank accounts, but in his secret heart, he always feared it would not be enough. The idea that he might lose his house, his safe and comfortable stronghold where everything was just the way he liked it, was a theme of recurring nightmares for Crane. Now, with this colossal screw-up on the Heliotrope job, that patient demon of doubt had slipped a friendly arm around him again, whispering in his ear, counting out every dollar lost.

Crane mopped his brow with a silk handkerchief. It was awfully warm and stuffy in his office. He had just had the heater adjusted less than three weeks ago. It had been a horribly traumatic experience in which a man, a smug and arrogant man who smelled like a cologne factory and didn't even wipe his cheap, oily boots when he came tromping across Crane's lush white carpet, had needed to come inside for several hours, violating Crane's private space. The man scratched himself deeply and continuously, and insisted that Crane leave him alone to tinker with the heater. Crane sat in his office the entire time, watching the cretin on the security monitor and keeping one hand in the drawer that held his .44 Magnum revolver. If the man tried anything funny, Crane would shoot him without batting an eye. Lucky for him, he did nothing but fix the heater, though apparently not well enough because it was beginning to feel like Vegas in August inside Crane's office.

Crane mopped his brow again and when the pale silk passed over his eyes, he thought he saw a dark, fleeting shape on the monitor that showed the heater in the basement.

Without thinking, Crane had the revolver out of the drawer and in his hand, staring fixedly at the monitors. He muted the TV and waited. He heard nothing and none of the other screens showed anything unusual. He had been thinking about the repairman in the basement and his brain had played a little trick on him. He was under a lot of stress, what with the whole Heliotrope fiasco. He was about to put the gun away when he saw that same indistinct, dark shape undulate across the view of his hallway, right outside the office door.

Cold panic clutched at Crane as he gripped the gun tighter and listened. Nothing. No sound at all. He suddenly thought of Driscoll. Driscoll, who had threatened him, said he would burn his house down.

Could the arsonist have found a way past the security system and be somewhere in the house right now?

Shaking, sweat oily on his upper lip, Crane moved slowly towards the door of the office. It was locked, as usual. There were no sounds but the distant, idiot chatter of birds and the thick purr of a hedge trimmer as the gardener went about his routine outside the secure walls of Crane's fortress. Surely no one could have gotten inside without alerting Mr Tran, and it sounded as if the gardener was unperturbed, working steadily along the far eastern side of the fence. It might be a public holiday, but to Crane it was just another day and he'd never seen any reason why anyone he employed should have a holiday if he was working himself.

Still, Crane knew he would be unable to relax until he searched the house. Methodical as a detective, Crane walked cautiously from room to room, through the huge, sunken living room and bar area, through the spotless kitchen and the back bedrooms and the spa. He checked each closet, each cabinet and as he went, he found himself compulsively checking places far too small for a human to hide, like under the sink in the bathroom and inside old hat boxes at the back of closets. He knew the house was empty, but still continued to check every crevice of every room until there was nothing left but the basement.

The basement was clean and well lit, nothing like the spidery, dirt-floored cliché of horror fiction, but Crane still felt a thin thread of fear in the back of his throat as he slowly descended. The wide, low-ceilinged space was filled with well-organized storage bins and file boxes and in the center of it all, the troublesome heater. Everything looked normal. Crane examined the heater and found that it was set to his usual thrifty, but still comfortable seventy-two degrees. He would need to give the company a call again. After all, he'd had to put up with that awful man in his home and he expected results.

There was a faint sound behind him, a sliding whisper like small steps in sock feet. Crane jumped, whirling with revolver in hand, eyes desperate to look everywhere at once.

"Driscoll?" he called, appalled at the quavering, gutless sound of his voice. "There's a camera right there." He pointed to a tiny camera like an electronic spider clinging to the ceiling on his left. "My security team is monitoring everything it sees. Try anything and they will be here in under a minute. Do you hear me? Under a minute."

That was a bluff. At best it would take the team five to seven minutes to make it up the twisting mountain roads leading to Crane's house, and they would only come if he hit the panic button or the outside sensors detected an intruder. Those sensors were off now, because it was garden day, and they would stay off for at least another hour and a half. But Driscoll didn't know that.

"Show yourself!" Crane shouted. "Show yourself, you worthless little hustler, or so help me I'll shoot you dead."

Nothing. Just the gentle whisper of the heater and under it the barely audible drone of the hedge clipper.

Crane pulled the handkerchief from his pocket again and wiped his brow. After several more endless seconds, he started to feel truly stupid.

Shaking his head, Crane headed back up the stairs. It was the stress. He was letting the stress get to him.

He returned to his office and hit enough buttons to divert all his calls to his secretary's cell phone—she'd be at home, not in the Crane Property Management Inc offices, but she was paid to be available twenty-four seven. Then he lay down on the comfortable white sofa. After a minute, he decided on a Xanax after all, chasing it with fresh orange juice. He just needed to get a handle on this Heliotrope thing. There was no point in getting all jumpy. He rubbed his temples and switched on the vintage Atari video game he had recently bought for himself. You could get all those old games for your computer now, but it wasn't the same as the old, ugly box he'd had as a kid. Smiling, Crane lost himself in the simple pleasure of Missile Command. The coarse electronic sounds of the game covered the whispered sound of laughter that echoed down the long, empty hall outside Crane's office.

SEVEN

Sitting on the back bumper of her Blazer with one boot off, Kate Graham had to pause for a second and give her hands a few moments to stop shaking. She had sent the new pup back to the office with the evidence bags, telling him she would meet him there to fill out the incident report. She needed the private time to get her shit together.

Kate was forty-six years-old and in those forty-six years, she had made very few mistakes. From an early age, she knew exactly what she wanted and she thought through every single thing she ever did a hundred times, testing every possibility and exploring every scenario until the best course of action could be determined. So why on earth had she said yes to Jimmy Graham? There was no doubt in her mind that that moment was the point of origin, the smoldering cigarette bound to a matchbook that led inexorably to the out of control conflagration her life had become.

She had been Kate Kenlaw back then. Working in the 81st, the first company in Los Angeles to open its ranks to the fair sex, and taking on a crushing course-load of both Fire Science and LAPD crimescene investigation classes, Kate had little time for romantic interest. She was not exactly beautiful, with her then close-cropped, red hair and thick, athletic build, but her aloof demeanor and air of unknowable mystery was irre-sistible to the men around her. Firefighters love a challenge. Most of her fellow smoke-eaters had her pegged as a lesbian, but that didn't stop them from try-ing. It wasn't that she was uninterested in men in general, she just wasn't interested in them in particular. The last thing she wanted was to get involved with another firefighter. Still, in spite of her chilly demeanor, she held down the line like a champ, hauling fifty-pound hoses and vomiting, flailing civilians with equal unflappable confidence. In spite of her attitude, she was a highly respected member of the team because she could be counted on to stay cool when things got hot.

In grade school, a teacher once told Kate that only little boys could grow up to be firemen. From that moment on, a career with the LAFD was her only ambition in life. There was never any question in her mind that she would make the cut, and once she passed through her training as a probationary fire-fighter, all it took was one snide comment that there were "no dames in Arson" and she immediately set her sights on moving up to Arson Investigation.

When Jimmy Graham came up to her after a class in Scene Analysis Following Diffuse and Dense-Phase Explosions, she was fully prepared to blow him off.

"You're Kate Kenlaw from the 81st, right?"

She nodded dismissively, packing away her notes.

"I'm Jimmy Graham. I hear you're looking to move up to Arson," he said. "You want to come work for me, is that right?"

"Yeah," she said cautiously.

"I also hear you're a cast iron bitch."

She looked up at him sharply. He was a handsome Irishman with dark hair and arresting blue eyes and he always seemed to be barely repressing a smile. She would have wiped that smile off his face with her fist if he had not been the head of Arson Investigation in Los Angeles.

"We could use some iron in Arson," he said. "My current gang of chuckleheads hasn't got a decent pair of balls between them."

"I'm afraid I don't have any balls either, Mr Graham," Kate said, slinging her bag up onto her shoulder.

Jimmy grinned. "That's not what I heard."

When Kate made Arson Investigator a year and a half later, she was not assigned to work under Jimmy Graham. Instead she was sent out to the San Fernando Valley to work with a wiry, chain-smoking inspector named David Tobin, covering brush fires and torch-jobs in porno warehouses. Less than a month in, she ran into Jimmy again at a formal function for the retirement of one of the senior investigators. Kate was uncomfortable in a plain black dress and low heels, sitting alone by the door, when he came over to her.

"I'm really glad they didn't assign you to me," Jimmy said, putting a glass of champagne in her hand.

She frowned at him and put the drink on a nearby table, untouched.

"Because now that you belong to another department," he said, "it's not unethical for me to ask you on a date."

She said no that time, and the next ten times that he asked her out, but they kept running into each other everywhere she went. They were members of the same gym and Kate was embarrassed to find herself sneaking glances at Jimmy, shirtless and sweating on a nearby machine. He was in amazing shape for his age, and almost against her will, Kate found herself running scenarios and consequences of sleeping with him, trying to figure every angle and ferret out all possible downsides. Looking back, she could not pinpoint exactly what made her change her mind. One day, after a particularly hard workout, she went over and sat beside him in the juice bar.

"All right," she said.

He looked up at her, puzzled. His dark hair was tousled and still damp from the shower and his thick arms were sleek and pumped from his recent exertions. She hoped she was making the right choice.

"I'll sleep with you, but that's as far as it goes, understand?" She met his blue gaze without flinching. "I just can't do a relationship right now."

Jimmy's eyes widened and he laughed incredulously. "Jeez, quit beating around the bush and get to the point, willya?"

She had smiled a little then. She let him take her back to his place, and two years later, they were married.

In the years that followed, everything was close to perfect. They bought a beautiful, Craftsman-style house in Eagle Rock and Kate transferred down to Los Angeles proper, working Hollywood while Jimmy stayed down in Chinatown. She suspected Jimmy might be sleeping around—he often worked late and pulled all-nighters without calling to check in with her—but in truth she was not terribly worried about it. She was working compulsively, twelve and fifteen hour days, throwing herself utterly into every investigation. She had little time for domestic bliss. However, Kate did enjoy being married to one of the most popular and respected men in the LAFD. All of the ribbing and casual cruelty she had endured when she was single evaporated without a trace. It was as if being a woman no longer mattered, now that she was taken. Kate's life was exactly the way she wanted it to be.

She had just put down a very high profile case in which a disgruntled ex-lover had torched the famous restaurant of a well-known TV chef. The chef had insisted on cooking for Kate and her partner that night, and she came home bloated with truffles and department atta-boys. She found Jimmy in the driver's seat of his PT Cruiser, dead from a single shot to the head.

Kate did not cry, scream or throw up. Instead she called it in, calmly pulled latex gloves over her hands and began to work the scene.

There could be no question that this was a suicide: gun in his powder-burned hand, no sign of forced entry, pointblank entry wound in the roof of the mouth and big, showy exit in the upper rear of the skull. When the boys from the LAPD arrived, she gave her assessment of the scene and then went down to the station to fill out a report. It wasn't until several days later that emotion got the better of Kate when she discovered the true nature of the hell her life was about to become.

Jimmy was responsible for all the household finances. Kate had no interest in anything but her work, and she was more than happy to let him deal with distasteful tasks like filing taxes and balancing their checkbook. In the days after Jimmy's death, Kate discovered that not only were both their joint checking and savings accounts overdrawn, they were also deeply in debt. They owed several years worth of back taxes, and Jimmy had taken a second and third mortgage on the house without telling her, even going so far as to forge her signature on critical documents. Even if the life insurance had not been canceled due to nonpayment, there would be no money from Jimmy's death because it was self-inflicted.

Kate was sitting in the living room of her house that was about to be foreclosed, wishing desperately that she could cry, that she could let some of the vast, killing anguish inside her come out, like throwing up poison, but she couldn't. Instead her mind kept turning the facts over and over, struggling to piece them together into some kind of sense. Where had all the money gone? Was it a drug habit? Bad investments? Something so awful that the only way out was a bullet? How could Jimmy have let this happen? And more than that, how could she not have noticed? She just sat there, silently hugging herself until the sound of the doorbell startled her out of her bleak reverie.

On the porch outside was a slight, well-dressed Chinese man. He held an armful of beautiful white flowers and introduced himself as Mr Gong, an associate of Jimmy's.

"Please accept our heartfelt condolences towards you and your family," the man said, bowing slightly.

"We know how hard this must be for you right now, Mrs Graham. May I come in?"

Kate blinked and nodded, stepping aside to let the older man pass. He placed the flowers in her arms, went over to Jimmy's favorite chair and sat down.

"It is a terrible thing to lose a loved one. Please feel free to call on us for anything you may need in this, your time of grief."

"Thank you," Kate said, baffled.

"I understand that you are also an arson investigator, Mrs Graham."

Kate nodded again, shifting the flowers in her arms and feeling coldly uncomfortable.

"I see," Mr Gong said. "Interesting job."

"It is," Kate said, laying the flowers on the table beside her. "Look, I'm sorry, is there something I can help you with?"

Mr Gong smiled. "You Americans," he chided softly. "Always straight to business with you. It's like this, Mrs Graham. Your late husband still owes us over three hundred and seventy thousand dollars. These are..." he paused. "Gambling debts. While we cannot disregard such a substantial sum, we are also not without heart. We feel for you in this unfortunate situation and are prepared to offer you an option to eliminate this debt through... non-financial means."

"I'm afraid I don't follow you," Kate said, though in reality she was far more afraid that she did.

"You see, your late husband was very helpful to us. For example, the recent fire that devastated the Hop Ling Benevolent Society building, your husband ruled that fire to be accidental in nature, a verdict that was very beneficial for our organization. From time to

time, you may be called upon to provide similar ver-
dicts. Eventually, you will find your late husband's
debt erased and enough money in your pockets to
start your life anew."

Kate's mind was reeling. The Hop Ling fire had
been one of the most destructive in Chinatown's history. Sixty-seven people had died in that blaze,
including two firefighters, and Jimmy had covered for
the guys who did it. He let fellow firefighters die without avenging them because of his own gambling
habit. Kate felt sick with helpless fury.

"Of course, if you do have the three hundred and
seventy thousand dollars in cash," Mr Gong said,
"and you can get it to me by midnight tonight, then
our business together will be concluded."

"And if I refuse?" Kate asked, nails digging into the
palms of her hands.

"Mrs Graham," Mr Gong said. "I am very sympathetic to your situation. There are others who are not.
Surely you would prefer to avoid an encounter with
someone... less sympathetic."

Mr Gong smiled and left her with a gold foil business card that read "Gong Imports LTD" with both
Chinatown and Hong Kong addresses and several
phone numbers. She stared at that card with utter
loathing again and again over the next few hours,
running scenarios in her head. The cheerful Mr Gong
had said nothing explicit about what would happen if
she refused, but he didn't need to. Kate was widowed,
stone broke and utterly without options. She had
forty-one dollars and twenty-four cents to her name,
not including the pennies in the pickle jar or whatever change she could scrounge from the floor of her
Blazer. It was light-years away from three hundred

and seventy grand. There was no way to lay her hands on that kind of money in six hours, even if she called in every single favor she had ever been owed. On top of that, there was the ugly truth about Jimmy, a bitter secret hidden like a tumor inside her heart. She told no one. How could she? Instead, she called the Los Angeles number on the gold foil card, spoke the handful of words required and after she hung up, she was finally able to cry. She cried long and hard for over an hour, and when she was done, she didn't feel any better. Just cold, hopeless and utterly alone.

She went to stay with her parents. They were understanding and accommodating, but they had never been close and it was awkward for everyone. Kate had been adopted late in childhood and her parents, both university professors, were mystified by this large, athletic, redheaded cuckoo that grew up in their tidy little nest. They had been shocked and appalled by her choice to become a firefighter, but tried to be supportive. They dutifully attended her graduation and acceptance into the LAFD, but always seemed like they had accidentally wandered in from some other family. Even though they lived in nearby Rosemead, Kate would go for months without seeing them. They had become nothing more than hastily scrawled names on holiday greeting cards. When Kate called that night, her father did not recognize her voice at first.

The first time she was called on to doctor a report was the hardest. An obvious case of arson to conceal a murder, a body had been found in the back of a fabric store, burned beyond recognition. Kate sent her partner out to talk to the neighbors, and when he was gone, she carefully picked up the delay device hidden in a barrel of fabric remnants. It was a simple cigarette with two wooden matches bound to it with a rubber band. The oldest trick in the book. She removed the rubber band and the matches and slipped them into her pocket. Placing the cigarette butt into an evidence bag she walked stiffly out of the scene and promptly vomited into the gutter.

Her partner was solicitous and gentle with her. Everyone was after Jimmy's death. Her partner even wrote out the incident report for her, never questioning her scenario, explaining how the victim had been smoking when the improperly extinguished cigarette ignited some nearby fabric. When she went back to her parents' house that night, Kate stood under the cold shower for nearly an hour, hating herself and hating Jimmy for the vicious trap he had allowed her life to become.

After that first time, it just got easier and easier. Now Kate was close to breaking the stranglehold in which the Triad gangsters held her, but in truth, she found the corruption no longer really bothered her. The whole city was lousy with it, so what was the point of playing hero? She had a nice house now, her own place, and enough money stashed away to retire in less than three years. She kept to herself and refused to let anything get under her skin. Not until the Heliotrope fire, anyway.

It was supposed to be a simple insurance job in an empty building. Two kids were now dead and Kate was supposed to cover for this bastard, some sleazy American slumlord, who co-owned property in Hong Kong with Mr Gong. She fingered the rough lump of slag in her hip pocket, all that remained of the arsonist's incendiary device. There was just no way to feel good about this one.

EIGHT

Martin Tibbet hated people. Whenever he was forced to mingle with his fellow humans, he felt a crushing sense of suffocation and despair. He was thickset and soft-spoken with a deeply cynical worldview that he rarely, if ever, shared. Having just turned fifty, he found that the older he got, the less tolerance he had for the presence of other people.

They were everywhere: people, the lost and clueless hordes, bumbling thoughtlessly through life and getting on Tibbet's nerves, as inescapable as summer mosquitoes. They were on the freeway in front of him, talking to each other on their cell phones about golf and celebrity divorces and repeating lame jokes from sitcoms. They were in the supermarket, mindlessly filling their carts with low-carb candy and diet shampoo while their out-of-control offspring screamed for overpriced, blue sugar water in non-recyclable bottles shaped like the characters from whatever cinematic atrocity was currently being stuffed down their gaping throats by the media powers that be. They migrated like lemmings to and from soul-killing day jobs, and then made up for it by cutting loose on weekends and holidays, jamming en-masse into shopping malls, preposterously-named franchise restaurants or other pre-approved corporate-sponsored locations where they could participate in the sort of wholesome family fun the television told them they ought to have. Armies of nitwits, nattering on about their botox and their babies and breathing up all of Tibbet's air. Consumer zombies, every one of whom seemed to be in line ahead of Tibbet at the post office, wanting to pay with a check and trying to decide between the stamps picturing famous left-handed people, or the charity ones drawn by kids with no arms.

Tibbet hated people, but he loved his job. He was a security guard. In another, more genteel era he might have been called a night watchman. He didn't have a gun and had never been called on to do anything but be there. The way he saw it, he was basically paid to read. The warehouse over which he kept his nightly watch was filled with T-shirts featuring witless slogans like: "FBI: Female Booty Inspector" and lists of "Ten Reasons Why Beer is Better Than Women." Some kids had broken in a few years back and stolen a crate of shirts that said: "I'm not as think as you drunk I am" and since then, the owner of the company decided to employ a security guard at night. They hired Tibbet through his agency and when he got the offer, he was thrilled to leave the building downtown where he had been working at the time. The office building was too big for just one man and Tibbet was stuck with a brain-dead hipster kid who was working on a screenplay about security guards. He talked endlessly about his "pitch" and insisted on calling Tibbet either "Marty" (bad enough) or, inexplicably, "Martini," which made Tibbet envision various methods by which the kid could be done-in during the shift and the murder blamed on an intruder. In the T-shirt warehouse, Tibbet was mercifully alone from 10pm to 6am four days a week. Every Thursday, the beginning of his work week, he would stand at his kitchen table and ready a stack of books for the next four days, some fresh out of the mail from Amazon or ABE, some older titles that he suddenly had an urge to reread. Looking at that good solid pile of books and knowing there would be a paycheck at the end of them never failed to make him smile.

That night, Tibbet was getting ahead of himself. He had ripped through the two Shell Scott mysteries he had designated for that shift in record time and while he still had Barry Glassner's *Culture of Fear* as a back-up, it was only 2am and he was afraid he might finish it before the end of the shift. He decided to take an extra walk around the warehouse to kill a little time and see if that cat was around.

The cat in question was black and skinny with a rough, throaty yowl that made her sound like an old chain-smoking broad from Brooklyn. Tibbet did not presume to give her a name; since they'd only just met the week before, but he had given her some tuna salad out of his sandwich, and in return, she'd let him pet her sleek back for a few seconds before twitching her tail and disappearing into the shadows. After that, she kept showing up at odd moments and rubbing briefly against his leg while he was reading. She did not seem to mind that he was no Shell Scott, that he was bald and soft around the middle, with bad posture and a stucco complexion. She liked him, but unlike many of the women Tibbet had encountered in his checkered romantic career, she had her own life too. She would come around just long enough for a little affection, and then go about her own catty business, leaving him to his reading.

That night, however, she had not been around, even when he took his dinner break at one am. He had her favorite, tuna salad, but she never came. He supposed it didn't matter, but he found himself worrying about her in spite of himself. She might have been pinched by animal control or hit by a car. The city wasn't a safe place for cats. Tibbet even found himself toying briefly with a fantasy of buying one of those cat carrier things and taking her back to his house to live, but he thought she would probably be appalled by the idea of being a housecat. It would cramp her style.

Still, it would be nice to see her, just to make sure that she was okay. Tibbet toured the dim aisles of the dusty warehouse, making soft little sounds that seemed to him might attract the attention of a cat. He was standing in a cul-de-sac, surrounded by shrink-wrapped pallets, when he heard a very clear, very strange sound. It was definitely not a cat. It sounded almost like a child whispering.

Tibbet ran the beam from his mag-lite around the narrow cul-de-sac. He saw cobwebs and mouse turds and an old, torn skin magazine, stashed between two pallets by some furtive daytime employee. No cat and definitely no kid.

But there it was again, and it sounded closer this time, accompanied by a soft scurry of running feet. For some reason, Tibbet found the hair on his neck pricking as a sudden flush of heat swirled around him, as distinct from the rest of the cool winter air as urine in a cold pool. That was when he saw the cat.

She was crouched by the entrance to the cul-de-sac facing to the left. Every hair on her body stood as if electrified, her tail puffed and golden eyes wide. She was staring fixedly at something that Tibbet could not see, not hissing or yowling, just silently bristling.

Tibbet did not want to call for back-up because a cat was scared. A full minute had passed and he wasn't even sure of what he thought he heard anymore. Maybe it had been the cat after all. Or maybe a rat. Slowly, he walked up to the mouth of the cul-de-sac and shone his light in the direction that the cat was looking. It was a long straight way formed between rows and rows of shelving and the solid brick of the outside wall. There was nothing for as far as Tibbit's light would reach, but he just couldn't shake that creepy feeling that played over his scalp and down his neck. Plus it was hotter now, almost uncomfortably so. Tibbet was starting to sweat. The cat had not moved. Only her eyes seemed to follow something, as if someone were walking away from where they stood.

"Crazy cat," Tibbet said affectionately, mostly to calm himself.

He reached down to pet the cat and the cat nailed him with both sets of claws, screeching like an angry woman. He hissed and pulled back his bleeding hand and the cat bolted, terrified.

"Dammit," he said, holding his hand up to the light for inspection.

There were several long scratches across the back of his hand and wrist, the centermost of which was beaded with blood. Muttering to himself, he made his way to the bathroom.

He put his hand in the sink, flinching a little as the hot water ran down over the scratches. There was a first aid kit in the office where he could get a bandage and some sort of cream. Lord knew what germs could be on the claws of an alley cat. He was surprised by how hurt he was by the cat's unprovoked attack. What had he done wrong? He looked at himself in the mirror, feeling a weird kind of guilt and self-doubt. He cared next to nothing for the opinions of humans, but to be rejected by the cat hit him below the belt somehow. He was torn between wanting to find her to see if she was all right and hoping never to see her again. These were the thoughts running through his mind when he noticed he was not the only one in the mirror.

There were two dark-haired kids behind him, a boy and a girl, facing away from him, standing between him and the bathroom door. There was something wrong with them that he couldn't quite put his finger on. As if the corner of the mirror that held their reflection was dirty and warped. They moved slowly towards the door in a disturbingly smooth, tandem motion that made them seem suspended on wires.

Tibbet spun to look behind him, but there was no one there.

His mother, from whom he endured weekly phone calls, often told him it would make him crazy, working alone all the time. Now he was horrified to think she might actually be right.

In the highly unlikely event that there were kids in the building, it was up to Tibbet to locate them, give them a stern talking to and call their parents to come and take them home. But these were not teenagers like the ones who stole the shirts. These were children, nine or ten at most. The warehouse was located by the railroad tracks in a very desolate and industrial neighborhood, miles from any residential areas. It would be next to impossible for kids too young to drive to get anywhere near this place, especially not in the middle of the night.

The other option seemed far more disturbing. Was he losing his mind? Hallucinating? Suffering from early onset senior dementia? Cat scratch fever? Nothing to do but go back to the office in search of antibiotic and put all this nonsense out of his mind. He glanced at his watch and noticed that he had managed to kill nearly an hour with all this spook-house goofiness. At least he no longer needed to worry about finishing his book too soon.

Back in the stuffy little cubical that served as an office, Tibbet pulled out the first aid kit and laid it on the desk. Everything inside the rusty white metal box was old and yellowy, as if it had all been untouched for centuries. There was something called "First Aid Cream" in a stained foil envelope. Tibbet figured it was better than nothing. After he squeezed a dollop of the foul-smelling goo on his hand, he wasn't so sure. He slapped a square of gauze over the mess and fastened it in place with tape that seemed to have lost most of whatever had made it sticky. The whole sorry affair would undoubtedly fall off at some inopportune moment later in the night, but for now it was the best he could do.

Sighing, he settled back into the chair and reached for his third book. This one was a reread, but he had enjoyed it so much the first time that he had decided to give it a second go round. He had barely gotten through the first chapter when he heard the whispering again. This time it seemed so close it was as if it were mere inches from his ear. In spite of the closeness, he could not make out what was being said. Then he heard it again, and this time it sounded more like a stifled laugh. Annoyed now at whoever was playing tricks on him, Tibbet slammed the book down on the desk and stood.

"Who's there?" he demanded.

No answer. He looked over the list of emergency numbers pinned to the wall. A cell number for the owner of the company and the number of the landlord—Crane Management Inc. Tibbet did not want to wake the owner and figured Crane Management Inc was probably nothing but a machine for a nine-to-five office somewhere. He toyed with radioing the security company and having them send back-up, but he did not want to look like a scaredy cat, jumping at shadows and funny noises. Frustrated and wishing this losing his mind business could have waited until after his shift. Tibbet stood and poked his head out the office door.

He thought he saw something in the shadows at the far end of the building, by the emergency exit. Not a person, an object. Something small and dark and crooked. Again, he felt that flush of heat around him and the strange prickling feeling at the back of his neck, but he'd had it with funny feelings and was ready to put a stop to this game once and for all.

He strode purposefully down the length of the building but as he approached the strange object, it did not become clearer. Instead it became somehow harder to see, as if he were viewing it through dense, rippling smoke. When he finally got close enough to see what it really was, it was so odd that it still took several moments to register.

It was a wheelchair, a small, twisted wheelchair, which looked as if it had been smashed and set on fire. The emergency exit door behind it was ajar.

That, in and of itself, was strange. That door had an alarm that would have gone off if anyone had opened it. In fact, it should have been going off right then, but it wasn't. The big echoey space was utterly silent. No more teasing whispers now, just silence and heat and this weird, messed up wheelchair sitting like some kind of relic from another civilization. Without even being aware that he was doing it, Tibbet reached out and pushed the door wide.

Outside was the trash-strewn alley between the warehouse and its neighbor. Tibbet stepped out and looked up and down the alley, the beam from his mag-lite startling a rat in a pile of cardboard. When he heard the click of the door closing behind him, it was immediately followed by that stealthy giggle and he kicked the door, infuriated. There was no handle on this side of the door. He would have to go around to the front.

Grumbling and fishing the keys from his pocket, Tibbet decided he would need to call this in. Someone was playing a game with him and his sense of sportsmanship was starting to wear really thin.

When he came around the front of the building, he was still grumbling, but the words evaporated when huge, sudden eruptions of flame gushed simultaneously from every window of the building. Hot glass rained down all around Tibbet as he was thrown backward across the hood of a parked car.

He rolled off the hood, cowering behind the car with his hands over his head. When he dared to look, the warehouse was a blazing inferno. The heat from it seemed to be reaching invisible tongues across the parking lot to bake the skin on his face and cook his eyes in his head. His terror was immense and primal. In his entire life, he had never witnessed anything so beautiful and so awful. He turned away and staggered out of the parking lot, across to the other side of the street, and leaned against the Benelli Smoked Fish Company warehouse, sure he was about to pass out.

He rested his head against the brick for a few dizzy seconds, and when he turned back he saw the black cat standing unharmed and unruffled beside him. She looked up at him quizzically and then rubbed against his leg. He was so relieved that she was okay that he forgot about the scratches and reached out to pet her. She purred and pushed her butt up against his hand and the cheap bandage fell off. She sniffed at it where it lay and turned away, disdainfully washing herself. Shaking, Tibbet pulled out his walkie-talkie and radioed for help.

NINE

When Phillips arrived at the Arson office the next morning, the place was already hopping. There had been a massive warehouse blaze the night before and the office was humming with activity. It took him several minutes to find Kate Graham in the excitement, but eventually he discovered her in a back office. She was drinking coffee out of a plain white mug and talking on someone else's phone, looking soft and tired. Her red hair was coming loose from her braid and there were purple shadows like bruises under her eyes. When she saw Phillips, her face hardened and she held her palm up to him. Phillips waited like a naughty schoolboy on the other side of the desk while she finished the call and the coffee, nodding a lot and saying little. When she hung up, she grabbed her battered leather jacket off the back of the chair.

"Showtime, kid," she said.

Sitting in the shotgun seat of her big blazer, Phillips drank his own lousy take-out coffee while Graham filled him in on the day's assignment, rattling off a clipped list of facts.

"T-shirt warehouse downtown," Graham said. "Total destruction, burned to the foundation. Cops have a witness, security guard, but what he says doesn't make a lot of sense."

"Torch job?"

Graham shrugged.

"Could be, but the firefighters say there was no clear cause. No point of origin. Almost as if the whole place went up at once. I'm thinking they just can't see the origin because the damage is too extensive but it's weird. The guys are spooked."

Phillips frowned. "How do you mean spooked?"

Graham glanced over at Phillips. "You've been on the line," she said. "You know how sometimes fire can play with you. Make you think it's alive, sentient, even out to get you. Bullshit of course, but when you're in there, in the dark and smoke..." She paused, eyes back on the road. "It's a different story. You get spooked."

Phillips knew exactly what she meant. He remembered a high-rise fire down on Grand Avenue that put six guys in the hospital. He and Beto Velez had been cautiously scoping a long, smokey hallway when out of nowhere, a slender, twisting column of flame appeared in the middle of the carpet. It was human-sized, moving sinuously as a belly dancer with curious, undulating flashes of stunning turquoise blue flickering through the orange and yellow flames. They watched, mesmerized for several seconds, unable to look away as the column shivered liquidly and split suddenly into twins, seeming almost to mimic the positions of the two firefighters in the hall-way. If they had been looking elsewhere, they might have seen the blistering paint on the door to their left and the way that door was bulging ominously outward as the pressure behind it built up to lethal levels. Dewey had shouted a warning to them, telling them to hit the deck. Phillips went down, grabbing the back of Velez's coat and dragging his buddy down with him. Half a second later, the door beside them exploded outward in a violent burst of superheated gas and flaming wreckage. Phillips did not even realize he was on fire until he felt the icy slap of high-pressure water gushing over him where he lay. Had he and Velez been standing when that door blew, they both would have been pulverized, driven into the opposite wall with the force of the explosion. Instead, they were shaken and wet, but alive, with only second degree burns on their ears and the backs of their necks. It was hard not to think that the fire had been deliberately distracting them, setting them up for an ambush attack.

"The thing that's got the boys crossing themselves on this one," Graham said, dragging Phillips out of his reverie, "is the fact that they couldn't put it out."

"How do you mean?" Phillips asked, unconsciously fingering the thick ridge of scar across the back of his left ear.

"Here we are," Graham said suddenly, pulling into a parking lot adjacent to a large smoking hole in the ground.

Without another word, Graham got out, grabbed her tools and walked towards the taped-off border of the scene. Phillips dumped his coffee and scrambled to follow.

He caught up to her talking to a huge, burly firefighter so black with soot Phillips could not tell the origin of his race.

"There were no solvents, no chemicals," the guy was saying. "Nothing out of the ordinary on the premises. Just T-shirts." He wiped a big paw across his forehead, revealing a patch of clean brown skin. "But the fire just wouldn't give. It could not be extinguished. Not with water, not the fog nozzles, not foam, nothing could touch this fire. It just kept burning, even after there was nothing left for it to consume. It left the neighboring structures untouched while this empty lot burned like a dry Christmas tree for three hours. Then it just stopped."

"Stopped?" Graham was taking careful notes. "What do you mean, stopped?"

"It didn't die back or peter out," the firefighter said, looking anxiously over his shoulder at the smoldering hole. "It just... stopped. Just like turning off a burner on the stove."

Graham looked at what remained of the building and back at Phillips. "Phillips," she said. "Take down a field interview from Lieutenant Outerbridge. I'll meet you in the hole in fifteen."

Phillips watched her walk away, picking her way carefully down into the debris-filled pit. Then he turned his attention to the anxious lieutenant and the hateful stack of paperwork. All the usual dull, methodical questions he had hated answering when he was on the other side of the clipboard. On the twenty-sixth of December 2004, at 2:37am, did you have occasion to be at the scene of a fire/explosion incident at 321 S Commercial Way? On this date, what unit or apparatus were you assigned or detailed to? What were the exact location or locations where you performed your duties? All that carefully phrased bureaucratic ass-covering they needed to make a charge stick in court. It was the aspect of the job Phillips liked the least, but as the junior partner, it was clearly up to him to do the work. It didn't get interesting until he got to: did the fire resist the cooling effects of the water application?

Phillips really felt for Outerbridge. He knew what he was saying didn't make any sense, and in the few minutes that Phillips had been talking with him, it was obvious that Outerbridge was a practical, skeptical man who was highly respected by his team and not prone to flights of fancy. As the big man related his story yet again, Phillips could see in his body language that he was losing confidence in what he had seen. His phrasing went from solid, declarative statements to softer, half questions full of "I think" and "maybe." When the interview was over, Phillips put a friendly hand on the lieutenant's massive shoulder, thanked him for the information and told him to go get some sleep. The big man nodded, rubbing his sticky blackened eyes like a child.

"One more thing," Phillips said. "Has the property owner been contacted?"

Outerbridge gestured to a semi-hysterical Armenian man in his late sixties shouting at the police on the far side of the hole. "That's the T-shirt guy over there."

Phillips thanked him again and headed over to the shouting man. He showed his shield to the cops who laughed and shook their heads.

"He's all yours, inspector," a smirking female cop told him, throwing up her hands.

"Sir," Phillips said to the wild-eyed Armenian. "Are you the owner of this property?"

"I am renting this place," he said. "For my shirts. Now I have nothing." He went off on a roll in hysterical Armenian, waving his hands in the air.

"Sir, try and remain calm," Phillips said. "Can you tell me your name?"

"It's Bobby, Bobby Babaiyan."

Phillips noticed then that the man was wearing a T-shirt that read "Sexy Senior Citizen." He shook his head. "Mr Babaiyan..."

"Bobby, please," the man said. "I am ruined, there is no point in it Mr."

"Bobby," Phillips said. "Can you tell me the name of your landlord?"

"Crane Management," he said. "I call them, they say they are sending someone. Is anyone here?" He gestured across the blackened rubble and then spat on the ground. "No one here but Bobby."

The old man went off on another Armenian tangent, but Phillips barely heard him.

"Scotland Crane?" he asked.

The old man looked up at Phillips. "Yes, that's right."

Phillips frowned. "Will you excuse me, Bobby?"

Kate Graham stood alone in the center of a black, smoking pit that would not have looked out of place in post World War II Dresden. She was using a narrow metal tool to measure char depth on various pieces of debris and the results were so odd that she kept going back and rechecking to make sure she had not made some sort of mistake. What the firefighters had said seemed to be true. It was as if every single part of the building had burned at the exact same temperature for the exact same length of time, as even as a perfect piece of toast. For the first time in her career, Graham was genuinely baffled.

Sure there had been times when the cause of a conflagration was muddy or unclear. Situations in which the evidence needed to conclusively prove one way or another how a fire had started was close to impossible to find. But even in cases like that, Graham was able to conceive of possible scenarios that might have led to the situation in question.

This was different. There was literally no way that what happened could have happened. Barring the existence of a giant crematorium that the building had been placed inside, there was no known form of conflagration that could cause such an even, flawless burn.

Graham was staring at the reflection of the sky in an oily puddle at her feet when she thought she heard the shift of footsteps across the rubble. She looked up sharply but there was nothing. When she looked back down at her pale face reflected in the puddle, there were two small, dark silhouettes behind her, one on either side, reaching towards her with arms that seemed too thin and too long.

When a hand touched her shoulder, Graham spun, eyes wide, to face that grinning, dopey kid, Phillips.

"Try decaf," he said, dopey smile widening.

She was not armed but still found herself entertaining a pleasant fantasy of shooting him in his cheerful face. What the hell did he have to be so damn happy about, anyway? He looked like a teenager that couldn't wait to tell his buddies that Susie so-and-so had finally let him put his hand up her skirt.

"Listen," Phillips said. "Scotland Crane owned this property too."

Graham's heart stopped. "What?"

The kid nodded, shifting excitedly from foot to foot. "There's gotta be some kind of connection. Two properties owned by the same man burn one right after the other."

Kate felt a sudden wash of vertigo so powerful she had to bite down on the inside of her cheek to keep her reaction subterranean. What the hell was Crane thinking? It was beyond amateur hour, pulling a stupid stunt like this. Did he think she would throw this one in for free while she was at it?

Of course, in a horrible way he was almost right. She would have to cover for him on this in order to cover her own ass. If the pup started digging, her involvement in the Heliotrope fire would come out, and she could not allow that to happen. Not when she was so close to getting out from under Jimmy's shadow and leaving the game behind for good.

She couldn't figure out how the hell he'd done it, but there was no doubt in her mind that he was involved. She had to think fast and get the kid out of her hair. She had to talk to Crane.

"Tell you what," she said. "Get a statement from the security guard and I'll go have a talk with Mr Crane."

Phillips looked like she had just told him she was going to get ice cream and he couldn't come. He scuffed his foot and turned away, sullen as a child. As she watched him go, she wondered how long she was going to be able to misdirect him. He was like a puppy, but he was a pit bull puppy and once he really locked his jaws onto the idea that Crane was involved, there would be no stopping him. As she made her way back to her car, she found herself running scenarios, paths of action splitting off again and again and yet the outcome was always the same. Cuffs on her wrists and the end of everything she'd worked all her life to achieve. There had to be something, some way out, but first things first. She needed to have a heart to heart with Crane.

TEN

When someone rang the buzzer at Crane's door, he was flabbergasted. He wasn't expecting anyone and his was not the kind of house you came over to when you needed a cup of sugar. Crane was fresh out of the shower with a towel around his waist and had only one contact lens in. Annoyed, he put in the other lens, slipped into raw silk drawstring pants and a plain white T-shirt, and went into his office to see who on earth had taken it upon themselves to pay him a social call.

He was hoping that the time it took him to respond would make the person go away. No chance of that. Whoever was out there was buzzing away like it was the end of the world. Crane squinted at the monitor and saw the lady arson investigator Alexander Gong had turned him on to for the Heliotrope job. This couldn't possibly be anything but bad news.

"Inspector Graham," Crane said into the intercom. "I can't imagine why you would be paying me a visit. Any business between us is done."

"Mr Crane," Graham said, looking up into the camera. "I need to speak to you privately."

"I'm sorry, inspector," Crane replied. "I'm very busy at the moment."

"Look, Crane," she said, leaning closer to the camera and narrowing her eyes. "What I have to say is not something you want your neighbors to hear, but if you want me to I will be happy to tell you right here."

Crane cursed softly. No doubt she wanted more money.

"Fine, fine, come in, but I only have a few minutes." He clenched his fist and then opened it and buzzed her in.

"Please remove your shoes," Crane told her as she stood in the entryway, frowning at him. "I like to keep things clean here."

"I'll bet," Graham said, slipping off her chunky, mannish shoes. "Look, I'm not going to waste time and mince words. Burning another property was stupid. I don't know if I'm going to be able to keep a lid on this."

Crane blinked, unsure if he had heard correctly. "What are you talking about?"

"The warehouse on Commercial Way," she said, scanning his face as if trying to see through into his heart. "You telling me you didn't know about this?"

Horrified, Crane felt his legs weaken beneath him. Driscoll. It had to be Driscoll. He passed a hand over his eyes and quickly ushered Graham into his office.

Sitting at his desk, he saw several messages on his machine and his cell phone. From the office, no doubt, telling him that the Commercial Way property had burned to the ground. That son of a bitch.

"Inspector," Crane said. "I'll be frank. I believe this to be the work of the man I hired to burn the Heliotrope property. He was not pleased about the loss of life and tried to strong-arm more money out of me. He threatened to burn my house down."

Graham shook her head. "That puts us all in a tight spot, doesn't it?"

"If Driscoll is arrested in connection with this new fire," Crane said, "I have no doubt that he will rat us both out without thinking twice."

"Well then, you've got two choices," Graham said holding up two fingers. "One, make him happy. Give him more money, whatever he wants."

Crane frowned. "Failing that?"

Graham looked into Crane's eyes. "Kill him," she said.

Crane did not flinch from her dark gaze. This was a hard woman, not a bitchy yet powerless shrew like Risa, but a woman capable of doing anything to get what she wanted. In short, she was a lot like him. Under other circumstances he could easily fall for a woman like her.

"I appreciate your advice, inspector," Crane said, struggling to remain professional. "I assure you that I will handle this problem right away."

"See that you do," Graham said. "I'll let myself out."

Crane watched her walk away, distracted for a fleeting moment by the powerful set of her shoulders, eye drawn down to her long muscular legs and flawless ass beneath her tight jeans. When she was gone, he wiped one hand across his mouth, put on the headset for his phone, and speed dialed his secretary.

ELEVEN

Driscoll needed a little distraction. This Heliotrope thing was really starting to get to him. He had barely slept the night before, tossing and turning and hearing that soft, childish laughter echoing down the hallway of that crummy building over and over. When he did sleep, his dreams were dark and poisonous, filled with smoke and charred bones and teeth. He refused to turn on the television for fear of catching another glimpse of those two kids. He found himself showering too often, scrubbing his skin raw to wash off the stink of kerosene. Like his guilt, it never really seemed to go away.

So instead of staying in his hot, stuffy apartment and going slowly stir-crazy, he decided the thing to do was get out, have a few drinks and hit a few of his favorite strip clubs. There was nothing in the world that a nice set of legs in high heels couldn't cure.

Three bars and seven shots later, he sat in the back of the Wild Cherry Ferret, waiting on Kitty. She was his favorite, a saucy little rockabilly hottie with a line of tiny cherries tattooed down the back of each leg like stocking seams. She always wore ultra sheer nylons and open-toed heels to show off her perfect crimson toenails. Whenever she saw him, she would flash him a slow, lascivious smile and make a big show of adjusting the garters that held up those sleek black stockings. It made no difference to him that she was smiling because she knew he would drop several hundred dollars on her. At least in a strip club, the relationships between men and women were honest and open. With broads out in the so-called real world, you had to go through this stupid routine about love and commitment when in truth, they all wanted exactly the same thing the dancers want. Especially LA broads. Sure they'll say they want all that true love chick-flick crap, but only if you drive the right kind of car, take them to the right kind of clubs and buy them the right kind of jewelry. Here, in a place like this, Driscoll felt like there were no hidden land-mines, no mixed signals. Everything was simple, cut and dry. Give a woman twenty bucks and she'll rub her long, perfect legs all over you. Give her a hundred and she's your best girl till closing time, hanging on your every word, laughing at your dumb jokes. There was no way to screw up or say the wrong thing, so long as the green stuff kept coming.

"Hi, Rick," a strapping, black girl in a gold bikini called, waving at Driscoll and tossing her long braids over one shoulder. "Want me to tell Kitty you're here?"

"That'd be great, Mocha." Driscoll answered, smil-ing. He was feeling better already.

When Kitty appeared from behind the dusty, back-stage curtain, Driscoll's heart did a little shimmy inside his chest. She looked more beautiful than ever, lithe little body squeezed into a tight red minidress and heartbreaking legs sheathed in full fashioned stockings. Her black curls were piled up in a flawless nineteen-fifties style and she had on Driscoll's favorite shoes, glossy red open-toed sandals with six-inch heels. She gave him her famous smile and sashayed over to where he sat.

"Hiya handsome," she said, bending down to kiss his cheek and enfolding him in her smoky gardenia scent.

"Hi, Kitty," he replied, sliding one arm around her tiny waist. "You up next?"

"Yeah," she said. "But after that I'm all yours, baby."

Watching her walk away erased any other thought from Driscoll's mind. The rough, growling voice of Tom Waits came over the speakers as she climbed up on the stage and Driscoll watched her dance in a state of foggy, blissful contentment. After a series of acrobatic maneuvers on the pole, Kitty began to unfasten and peel down the top of her dress. Many of the other girls at the Ferret had those goofy fake boobs, but Kitty had the kind of sweet and perky little A-cups that made Driscoll crazy. He was breathlessly awaiting the reveal when he saw that beneath her dress, she wore a bikini decorated with flames.

Dress at her feet, she undulated her body and the flames danced with her. Watching, Driscoll started to feel inexplicably light-headed. The cartoon flames seemed to flicker and overlap the edges of the fabric, licking upward across Kitty's perfect white skin. Unbidden, an image rose in his mind of that dim, stinking hallway in the Heliotrope property, flames dancing across the ceiling. He shook his head to clear it and rubbed his eyes with the heels of his hands. His bladder felt heavy and there was a cold coil of nausea in the depths of his gut. Two strippers were laughing by the bar and Driscoll thought he heard that soft childish laughter woven under their voices. It was very hot inside the club.

Driscoll did not want to miss Kitty's dance, but he suddenly felt as if he had had far too much to drink. He needed to make his way back to the bathroom before this sudden powerful nausea got the better of him.

The bathroom at the Ferret was at the end of a long hallway and as Driscoll made his way back, the proportions seemed to trick his eye, getting longer and longer so that the bathroom got farther away instead of closer. The shadows on the wall looked like charred figures reaching long black arms towards him. He was sweating profusely when he finally made it to the bathroom door. It was locked. Occupied.

Driscoll cursed, leaning against the wall. He could still hear Tom Waits's "Heart Attack and Vine" filtering in from the stage under a wave of hooting and hollering that told him Kitty had stripped down to a tiny g-string and nothing else. His head was pounding at a discordant counter-tempo to the music. Just when he felt sure that he was gonna lose it right then and there, the bathroom door popped open and out came a sloppy-haired kid in an awful brown and orange polyester button-up shirt with a faded old Hooter's T-shirt on top of it. If Driscoll hadn't been feeling so shitty, that preposterous get-up would have earned the kid some sort of nasty comment. Idiot might as well be wearing his underwear on top of his pants, though if he had been, Driscoll would not have been even remotely surprised. Clenching his jaw,

Driscoll pushed silently past, ignoring the fashion victim's vague, stoned protest. With shaking hands, he swiftly locked himself into the bathroom.

The bathroom was small enough to touch both walls while you sat on the john. Rusty little sink, scuffed up hand dryer, and an old condom machine that had been out of order since he first came here three years ago. Everything like it ought to be and Driscoll was finally starting to feel in control again. The nausea faded as he pissed into the clogged urinal, idly chasing a drowning cigarette butt around with the stream of urine. He was just jumpy. The whole Heliotrope thing had him spooked. Best to put it out of his mind. After all, how was he supposed to know those brats would still be there when he torched the place? Was he supposed to go door to door? Put up a notice thirty days in advance? Pardon the interruption, but your building has been scheduled to burn to the ground at midnight on December twenty-fourth. Please be sure to collect all your belongings and rugrats and get the hell out by no later than eight pm on the designated date. Thank you for your cooperation. We apologize for any inconvenience. Yeah, right. Crane had said the tenants would be gone and Driscoll had no reason not to believe him. If anyone was to blame it was Crane. Anybody could see that.

Driscoll zipped back up and shook his head. He needed to put this all behind him and stop freaking himself out. The cops had nothing. Crane had that taken care of. Even the media had declared the fire a tragic accident. He had nothing to worry about.

He turned to wash his hands, banging on the cranky old soap dispenser until it disgorged a trickle of medicinal-smelling yellow goo. He lathered up and rinsed, then took a minute to smooth back his hair and check out his reflection, wanting to make sure he looked his best for Kitty.

When he was satisfied that he looked as good as he ever would, he punched the starter on the hand dryer and placed his hands beneath the nozzle.

Flames shot out of the dryer, engulfing both of Driscoll's hands. He leapt back shouting and plunged his burning hands into the stopped up sink. He watched, horrified, as puffy white blisters blossomed across his palms. Beside him the dryer burned furiously, thick smoke quickly filling the tiny, airless room.

Cursing, he shouldered open the door and ran to fetch the bartender. By the time they returned, a barefoot stripper in a pink sequined bra and camouflage army pants was spraying the little fire with a portable extinguisher.

The bartender laughed and slung an arm around Driscoll's shoulder. "You all right, buddy?"

Driscoll nodded, dry-mouthed and shaken.

"Come on then," the bartender said. "Let's ice those hands. Liquid painkillers are on the house."

Sitting at the bar with Kitty cooing over him, his mitts in a bucket of ice and two more shots in his belly, Driscoll started to see the humor in the situation. It would have been poetic justice in a way, after all the fires he'd started in his lifetime, to have died in an accidental fire, killed by a short in a girly-bar hand dryer. Kitty was caressing the back of his neck with her long red nails and he felt so good that he was actually considering asking for a date when his cell phone rang.

"'Scuze me, baby," he said, wincing as he dried his dripping hands on a bar rag and flipped open the phone. "Yeah?"

"Driscoll? Crane," said the crackly voice on the other end. "Where are you?"

"Hold on a second, willya?" Driscoll winked at Kitty. "It's the office."

Kitty nodded and Driscoll took his phone outside.

"That's better," Crane said, his voice clearer now. "Listen Driscoll, you win, okay?"

Driscoll frowned. Now that he could hear better, he could hear the anxiety in Crane's voice.

"Okay," he replied cautiously.

"I don't have one hundred grand handy at the moment, but I can make you a better offer. I own several condos in Malibu. Right off the beach. You can take any one you like. Just pick up the keys from my office first thing in the morning. The remaining money will be waiting for you there as well. Please, just give me your word that this settles everything between us. Don't burn any more of my properties."

At first Driscoll didn't know what to say. He had no plans to burn any more of Crane's properties. He had been pissed off, and more than a little freaked out when he'd called and threatened to burn Crane's house, but he hadn't really mean it. Well, something had changed Crane's mind and Driscoll wasn't about to argue with his good fortune.

"Scout's honor," Driscoll said. "No more fires."

"Fine," Crane said. "I don't expect to speak to you again." He hung up.

Driscoll shrugged and made his way back to Kitty. Things were looking up after all.

TWELVE

Justice Scofield thought he was going to have to quit his job when Liberdad got a bob haircut. He was tall and lanky, just turned seventeen and had been working part time at the Megaplex Seven for a year and a half. Now he was an assistant manager with keys and everything. The money was decent and hey, free movies.

Then they hired Liberdad Guererro, two weeks before Christmas. Liberdad was Mexican, from Mexico City and had a sly, streetwise sense of humor. She was sixteen, lushly built, curvy in all the right places, and she wore vintage nineteen-fifties librarian glasses. Every day she would come in fifteen minutes early wearing some floral-print, churchlady dress and no makeup. She'd duck into the john and emerge a few minutes later with Elizabeth Taylor eyes and black lips, clad in torn fishnet and vintage rags beneath her ugly green Megaplex vest. She had this kind of quirky, punk rock June Cleaver look going and Justice had flirted vigorously with her from the beginning, joking that they were meant to be together because of their names. Liberty and Justice just like

in the Pledge of Allegiance. She traded clever innuen-
does like a hardboiled femme fatale, but always
managed to change the subject if Justice got too serious. She kept him at arm's length and Justice was
fine with that. Until the haircut.

For as long as he could remember, Justice had a
fetish for women with black bobs. It all started with
silent movie star Louise Brooks and it had gotten to
the point where he had a collection of over fifteen
hundred vintage and modern photographs of women
with bobs. He had an extensive video collection too,
including a recently acquired how-to haircut video for
beauty school students that he had paid way too
much for on eBay. He frequently joked with his best
friend Cooper Lan that he needed a device like the
flying guillotine from old martial arts movies, that
basket-like thing that dropped down over someone's
head and cut it off. Justice wanted a "flying bob-
otine," a device he could throw at attractive long
haired girls that would drop down over their heads
and chop their hair into a bob.

He had even joked that Liberdad was a perfect can-
didate for the flying bob-otine, with her thick black
hair that she always pulled back from her face in a
thoughtless knot. So when she walked in one night
with a perfect, cheekbone length bob, Justice did a
triple take and accidentally squirted hot artificial but-
ter-flavored oil all down the front of his shirt.

It was unbelievable, sleek and flawless like liquid
vinyl on her head. The heavy swing of her glossy
hair against her cheek as she turned to laugh at him
was physically painful, a thousand times worse
than the hot oil. He could not take his eyes off the
back of her neck where the shorn hairline made a

perfect little V-shape beneath the mathematically precise edge of the bob.

"Smooth move, Ex-lax," Cooper had said, tossing Justice a damp rag to blot the front of his shirt. "Looks like you don't need the flying bob-otine after all."

After that it was impossible to do anything with her around. He would vacuum the same two feet of carpet for twenty minutes, watching her scoop popcorn and serve drinks. He suffered from persistent erections at the worst possible times and found himself ducking into the bathroom to placate the pesky thing two or three times per shift. He had even closed down the theater a few nights ago and, after walking Liberdad to her car, he had been engulfed in such a powerful hormonal monsoon that he had forgotten to lock up. He was more than halfway home when he realized and had to drive all the way back in a panic.

So it was Tuesday again, his night to lock up and everyone gone home except for him and the object of his obsession. He had done everything but outright ask if she had a boyfriend and had still found out next to nothing. If she did have a guy, she never mentioned him. Whenever he would ask her what she did over the weekend, she would always say something innocuous like "my uncle had a barbecue" or "I hung out with friends." Always with that sly smile that said she knew exactly what he was getting at and that she enjoyed making him suffer.

That night, she was counting out the registers, one thick, ebony curl of hair tucked back behind her ear as she scribbled down each amount. Justice was supposed to be wiping down the counters, but he was mostly just pushing the rag back and forth and watching Liberdad. He was trying to come up with something cool to say to her, something other than "I love you," "Marry me" or "Can I lick the back of your neck?," when she turned to him with that little smile, the curl of hair falling out from behind her ear.

"They're showing *Creature From the Black Lagoon* in 3D at the Egyptian Theater this weekend," she said.

Justice nodded. "Yeah, I know. I tried to get tickets but the *Creature* sells out every time in like two seconds. Me and Coop are going to *Revenge* on Sunday."

"I have tickets," she said, turning back to the register and closing it with a snap. "The Creature always was my favorite monster."

For what felt like a year Justice couldn't breathe. Tickets. With an S. That meant more than one. Was she implying she wanted him to go with her or finally admitting she had a boyfriend?

"That's cool," Justice said, waiting for her to elaborate and feeling like the world's biggest dope.

"Well, the show's at seven but I'm getting my hair cut at five." She smirked, running her chipped purple nails over the stubble on the back of her neck. "Why don't you pick me up at six fifteen?"

"Yeah, great, sure." Justice ran a hand nervously over his lips. "Just you and me, huh?"

"Just you and me," she said. "Liberty and Justice. What do you say?"

Then the lights went out.

Liberdad let out a little airless gasp and Justice quickly reached across the counter to take her hand, wanting to comfort her. He managed to get a handful instead of a hand and Liberdad laughed, pushing him away. Justice felt her crossing her arms protectively across her chest to block any further groping and he was glad of the dark because he was sure he was blushing.

"Oh fine," Liberdad teased. "Take advantage of me in the dark why don't you?"

"Sorry," Justice sputtered. "I meant..."

"You meant to do this, didn't you?"

She took his hand in the dark and put it on the back of her neck. The feel of her warm skin, and the soft triangle of stubble beneath the slick brush of her hair, was electrifying. No girl had ever done anything like that to him before. He needed to go find the fuse box and figure out what was up with the power and all that, but instead he leaned across the counter, cupped the back of Liberdad's neck and kissed her. It took a second to find his mark in the blackness, but when he did, it was amazing. She kissed him back enthusiastically, cooing as he stroked the back of her neck. He was seriously starting to worry that he was going to break through the glass he was leaning against and knock over all the Raisinettes and Jujubes inside the case if he kept this up, when Liberdad broke the kiss, gripping his arm.

"Do you hear something?" she asked.

Justice cocked his head in the dark. All he heard was his heart thudding like the bass on a jacked-up car stereo.

"Come around to this side of the counter," Liberdad said, clicking on the flashlight on her key chain and casting monster movie shadows up across her face. "Listen."

Justice did what she said, but now, standing right next to Liberdad and her bob and her soft, curvy body with her taste still in his mouth, he was even less interested in any funny sounds she might be hearing.

"I don't hear anything..."

Minutes passed and nothing happened. He rubbed his fingertips over the back of her neck, and slowly, waiting to see if she would let him get away with it, he lowered his mouth to the little V of stubble there. She didn't slug him so he ran his tongue up the deep groove in the back of her neck into her hairline and she made a soft little noise of approval.

"I can die now," he whispered into the curves of her ear.

She tilted her head back. "What?"

"I guess you know I wanted to kiss your neck since the day you cut your hair." He did it again. "I can die now."

"Well," she said, turning in his arms and sliding her hands up the sides of his body and across his back. "Not just yet, cowboy."

She kissed him and he lost track of everything until she broke the embrace again.

"Seriously," she said. "You don't hear that?"

He tried to bury his annoyance. "What is it?" he asked.

"It sounds like kids goofing around down on the escalators. Footsteps and laughing."

"Footsteps?" He grimaced. "Yeah, right, what are we in, a horror movie?"

He made his hands into claws next to his face and made spooky noises.

"Knock it off," she said, punching him in the arm. "Don't make me sorry I kissed you."

She played the beam of her flashlight around the head of the escalators. Nothing.

"Come on," she said, walking out from behind the counter, not seeming to care if he followed or not.

Of course he did. After that far too brief make-out session, he was pretty much willing to follow her to Antarctica if necessary. Anything to kiss the back of her neck again and maybe see what else she might be willing to let him do.

Justice clicked on his own little flashlight. It was weird walking down the frozen escalator and the lower level was dark and uncomfortably tomblike, but Liberdad did not seem scared so he did not want to look like a pussy.

"Shouldn't we find the fuse box first?" he asked.

"Later," she said. "Listen."

Justice actually did hear something. The soft heavy sound of a padded, soundproofed door to one of the theaters easing shut. The idea that someone else was down here with them effectively killed any amorous thoughts he might have been holding on to with cold, creeping chills.

"Maybe we should call someone."

He hated the way that came out, wimpy and tentative, but now she seemed scared too, clutching his arm and shining her light down the carpeted hall. The light hit the door to the last theater just in time to see it swing completely shut.

"Shit," she said. "I really think someone is in here."

"Hey, who's there?" Justice called in a sudden fit of bravado. "Show yourself."

The hallway swallowed his voice, giving back nothing.

"Let's check it out," Liberdad said, looking up at him with her eyes sparking in the dimness.

Justice realized that she was not clutching his arm because she was scared. She was clutching his arm because she was excited. He let her lead him down to the far end of the hallway.

"Don't worry," she said, palm flat on the door to the last theater. "As long as we don't split up or get undressed we'll be fine, right?"

Justice was not so sure, but her mention of getting undressed had him distracted again and staring at the back of her neck as she pushed the door open.

The theater was pitch black and coffin silent. The dark seemed filled with hidden things, skirting the edge of the flashlight beams like deep ocean dwellers avoiding a submarine. It was stuffy and unbearably hot. Standing there, sweating at the top of the center aisle, Justice felt five years old, waiting for the monster in the closet to spring out and eat him.

"Look, there," Liberdad whispered.

The beam of her light was jittering over the humped backs of the blue velvet seats and at first he could not tell what she was pointing to. Then she steadied the light, centering it on the last two seats on the far left of the first row, and Justice felt a thick, icy flush of fear through his veins.

There were two very small, dark-haired heads just barely visible above the backs of the seats, one slightly higher than the other. They were too small to belong to adults, but they sat far too still to be little kids.

"Hey, you," Liberdad called. "You can't be in here."

Not a sound. No reaction. The heads did not turn towards them, just stayed frozen still, facing the dark screen. Justice shivered.

"Where are your parents?" Liberdad asked.

Still no response. Liberdad started walking down the aisle towards the front. It was growing hotter and hotter inside the black theater.

"Wait," Justice said, gripping her arm. "This is weird. Why don't they answer? We should call someone."

Liberdad turned and gave him a withering look. "They're just kids," she whispered.

He took several shuffling steps after her, eyes never leaving those unmoving heads.

"Then why won't they answer?"

"It's okay," Liberdad said, approaching the first row. "You're not in trouble."

She directed the beam of her flashlight down to the end. There was no one in the last two chairs.

Justice shook his head. Impossible. He had not taken his eyes off the two heads for a second, yet somehow in the time it took him to look down the row of seats, they were gone. When he came to the last two chairs, he saw that the seat cushions were scorched and blackened. He reached out to touch the burned seats. They were still warm, almost too hot to touch. There was no way anyone could have been sitting there.

"What the hell is going on?" Justice asked, wiping sweat from his face.

Again the sound of a door swinging shut, only this time it was the emergency exit door, less than six feet away. Justice pointed his light in the direction of the sound and saw a swift blur of movement sliding through the door just before it clicked shut.

"There they go," Liberdad said, charging through the door. Justice had no choice but to follow her.

The emergency exit led to a set of concrete steps. Liberdad was tearing up the steps, and Justice was sure he heard more than just an echo up the steps ahead of them. He heard the sound of the outside door opening and Liberdad's voice calling, "Wait."

Justice caught up to her on the top landing, nearly crashing into her. Then he saw why she'd stopped.

There was a burning wheelchair at the top of the stairs. It was small, child-sized, and the pale flames dancing over its black and crooked surfaces generated no smoke whatsoever. The outside door behind it was ajar.

Liberdad skirted the flaming chair and ran to the door and Justice followed, pressing himself flat to the wall to get past the searing heat coming off the ethereal flames.

Outside, in the vast and empty parking lot, there was nothing. The big open space offered no hiding places and there was no way a little kid could run fast enough to get to the far end of the lot and climb over the fence before Liberdad and Justice made it out the door. Now that they were outside in the cool winter night, all the sweat on Justice's body chilled his skin, making him shiver.

"Damn," Justice said. "This is some freaky shit."

"Yeah." Liberdad was breathing hard, looking up at him with that same spark of excitement in her dark eyes. "Freaky."

She kissed him, pressing him back up against the rough wall of the theater. Her hands were all over him, erasing everything else and for a second of joyous disbelief, Justice thought she was going to do it to him right there in the parking lot. Then, like an angry chaperone, a massive explosion blew the emergency exit door off its hinges, knocking them both to the asphalt.

Justice threw his arm over Liberdad to protect her from the rain of flaming debris. Fire was shooting out of the stairwell, racing up the side of the building. Justice staggered to his feet, dragging the shaken Liberdad with him. Together they ran to the far end of the lot and Liberdad started crying, pressing her face into Justice's chest. Her bob was disheveled, bangs in disarray and black eyeliner running down her cheeks. She had lost her glasses. He put his arms around her and held her, trying to keep his fingers from straying up to the back of her neck.

THIRTEEN

Phillips stood in his kitchen with a white dish towel in his hand, waiting for Lucy to hand him another plate to dry. It was early still, and she was in pajamas, loose flannel bottoms with dinosaurs on them and one of his old T-shirts. Her dark hair was pulled up into a ragged ponytail, but uneven wisps kept escaping and tumbling down over her sleepy green eyes. Even though she worked from home and did not need to get up with him, she always did, always made him coffee and breakfast and made sure he did not forget his sunglasses or his cell phone. They had been together, on and off, for seventeen years. Watching her push the hair from her eyes with the back of a slender, sudsy hand, Phillips felt a rush of almost incredulous love for her. Sometimes he just couldn't believe that she was still there.

It hadn't always been easy between them. They'd met when Phillips was twenty and Lucy was nineteen and looking back, he still flinched at how badly he had treated her then. They were an unlikely pair, he a jock and a probie firefighter and she an artist going to college for graphic design. But they had a fierce sexual chemistry and a curious way of filling in each other's blanks. She was the calm, stable center of his chaotic, sleep-deprived and highly dangerous life. He would lay in her bed with his head on her belly and everything else would just drift away. Nothing existed except the feel of her fingers running through his hair. She was nurturing without smothering him, loyal but not clingy. She was there for him when he needed her, but busy with her own life when he was not around. It was ideal in so many ways. The problem was other women.

It wasn't that she did not give him enough sex. She was a skillful and voracious lover with an experimental open-mindedness that kept them from ever falling into a rut. It was just that Phillips was in his early twenties and as a young firefighter, he was surrounded by opportunity. Saving women's lives was a powerful aphrodisiac. Phillips even had one girl show her appreciation for being rescued right in the alley behind her burning building, egging him on while cold spray from the hoses rained down on them. The boys in the station were closer than brothers and it went without saying that if a man's wife or girlfriend phoned while he was off putting out a little bushfire, you covered for him. Lucy wasn't the suspicious type, so she never questioned the increasingly elaborate lies about where he had been or why he stood her up again and again.

After five years, guilt started to get the better of Phillips and he found himself wanting to get caught. He took more and more chances and made less of an effort to cover his trail, hoping that she would confront him and dump him like he deserved. He would come over to her little loft apartment, drunk and belligerent and trying to start a fight, and she would just gently help him to bed and be there in the morning with coffee and aspirin and her nonjudgmental, unconditional love. That more than anything made him feel lower than dirt.

When she finally found out about his infidelity, it got pretty ugly. She cried a lot and threw things. She was hurt and angry and totally in the right for telling him to get lost. Without Lucy, he found himself drinking too much, taking stupid chances on the job and sleeping with women he normally would not have looked twice at. It was a bleak couple of years.

Then he broke his leg on the job. The floor of a burning building gave out on him, dumping him through to the floor below. Lucy called him in the hospital and told him she had seen him being rushed into an ambulance on the news. She was nearly in tears, sick with worry. The TV had made it seem as if he was dying. When he told her it was just a busted leg, she laughed a little and asked if he needed a ride home from the hospital. Just hearing her voice again made him feel an overwhelming need to see her. He said yes.

When she walked in the door, she literally took his breath away. She had never been a knockout and there was nothing particularly sexy about the way she was dressed, but she looked heartbreakingly beautiful to him. She looked so small and pale and when she came and wrapped her arms around him, her familiar smell was so powerfully arousing it was almost painful. They made love in the hospital bed right there, laughing and awkward with the heavy cast on his leg.

She took him home and filled him in on her life since the breakup. She had gotten pregnant almost immediately after he left and the guy responsible agreed to marry her. Four months later, after she had a violent miscarriage that left her permanently scarred and unable to have children, the guy just sort of drifted away. They'd never really had all that much in common anyway. Since then, she had been mostly single, dating guys here and there, but concentrating primarily on her career. She was making good money as a web designer and had been able to save up enough for a down payment on a house.

Phillips asked her to marry him that night. She laughed and told him he was on crack for asking. They saw each other on and off for about a year and he kept on asking her to marry him again and again. She told him she couldn't, that she could never trust him again after the way he'd lied to her. She was scared of being hurt again and he didn't blame her, so he threw everything he had into proving to her that he had changed his ways and would do anything to make her happy. He was religiously faithful to her and spent all his free time helping her fix up her new house. He bought her a beautiful antique emerald ring to match her eyes and gave it to her at sunset on a wild deserted beach near Monterey. She finally said yes. He moved in with her a week later.

They were married on Saint Patrick's Day. They both wore blue jeans and green paper leprechaun hats and Lucy carried a bouquet of dyed green carnations. Her family was not thrilled, but Lucy seemed so happy that they had no choice but to grudgingly forgive him. Phillips's parents were both dead but his grandmother who raised him had been their witness at the tiny ceremony, along with her thirteen year-old French bulldog named Claude. Both she and the dog had also worn the silly paper hats. She'd loved Lucy from the beginning and was thrilled to see they had finally worked things out.

Now Lucy was his, every day and every night. Beside him in their bed, next to him on the sofa making fun of dumb blockbuster movies, across from him at the breakfast table playing footsie in her socked feet. She was everything to him and he never let himself take her for granted. Every morning that she was still there in her goofy pajamas was like some kind of miracle.

She handed him another plate and he grabbed her wrist and kissed her lips. She kissed him back, laughing into his mouth.

"I love you," he told her.

"I know," she said, green eyes crinkling around the edges.

The sound of Phillips's cell phone echoed through the house and he cocked his head, listening for where he'd left the damn thing. Smiling, Lucy wiped her hands and went to retrieve the phone. Not surprisingly, she knew exactly where it was.

"It's your new girlfriend," Lucy said, putting the phone in his hand and giving his ass an affectionate squeeze.

Phillips kissed her neck and flipped open the phone. "Graham," he said. "What's up?"

"17099 Lakewood Drive," Graham's tense voice answered. "Be there in fifteen."

She hung up.

Phillips blinked at the dead phone for a second before flipping it shut.

"Duty calls, huh?" Lucy asked, putting away the last of the dishes.

Phillips nodded, snaking an arm around Lucy's waist from behind and pulling her back against him.

"I'm afraid so," he said, kissing her cheek.

"But what about your husbandly duty?" she purred, grinding her firm little ass against him.

Phillips groaned. "Come on, baby, cut it out, I gotta go." He pulled away from her, adjusting himself. "Don't send me to work with Ice-Panties Graham like this."

She pulled him back to her, holding up five fingers. "Five minutes," she said.

Phillips looked at his watch and raised an eyebrow. "Five minutes, eh?"

She nodded and grinned, pulling the big T-shirt over her head and standing topless in the morning sun.

"Okay," he said, looking at his watch again. "Five minute sex drill starting... NOW!"

She let out a high musical giggle as he threw her over his shoulder and ran back into the bedroom like an eager probie carrying a length of hose up six flights of stairs.

FOURTEEN

Graham stood alone in yet another blackened pit that used to be one of Scotland Crane's properties. The edges of the pit seemed miles away, leaving her stranded in the center of a charred and dripping wasteland. She was standing over the twisted remains of a tiny wheelchair. It didn't make sense. The wheelchair had been found at the Heliotrope property, not in the theater, yet there it was. Graham was overwhelmed with a childish need to hide the chair, as if it could implicate her somehow, but when she bent to touch it, the metal frame was red hot and she yanked her hand back with a startled hiss.

She squeezed her hand into a fist, ignoring the pain throbbing like an angry heartbeat and sure that Phillips would show up any minute full of eager beaver questions she could not answer.

Stealthy rustles skittered through the wreckage all around her... Rats?

She saw something moving beneath the debris. Could someone be trapped? Buried alive beneath the charred and twisted beams and scattered metal bones of theater seats? Heart in her throat, she forgot the pain in her burned hand and began to dig.

Tossing bricks and sharp edged fragments of wood aside, her frantic search eventually uncovered an arm. The skin was peeling, flesh beneath barbecued red and black, burned to the bone in some places. A person could not possibly be alive, having sustained injuries that severe, yet the fingers clutched the air, stirring weakly.

Where the hell was Phillips? Where was anybody? There were a ton of LAPD squad cars blocking off the street and dealing with bystanders. Couldn't any of them hear her calling out for backup as she muscled heavy rubble out of the way?

Her digging soon revealed the back of a head. Patchy black hair remained in spots on the curve of the cracked and blistered scalp. Graham leapt back startled when the head began to tremble and twist from side to side, freeing itself from the debris until the exposed face turned up towards her.

It was the corpse from the fabric shop in China-town, empty eye sockets fixed in her direction as it struggled loose from the rubble. Its fleshless hand was reaching out to her, holding a cigarette with wooden matches bound to it with a rubber band.

All around her the wreckage was stirring with ani-mated corpses, clutching at her with scorched fingers. The stench of burnt flesh and hair was nau-seatingly intense as Graham's feet tangled in the debris and she went sprawling. She thought she saw Phillips walking away from her, but when his head turned, she saw that it was Jimmy. The gaping hole in his skull glistened in the pale sunlight and every step he took left behind footsteps of flame. The trail of fire was growing, flaming out of control and reaching for her as she crawled over piles of burned bodies, desperate to get away from the killing heat and the angry dead.

She was almost to the edge of the pit when the two kids from the Heliotrope fire appeared, looking down at her from the parking lot above.

"This is your fault," the boy said.

"Your fault," the girl repeated.

They began tossing handfuls of money into the pit. Bills fluttered down onto Graham's upturned face. On the way down, some began to catch fire, soaring on the hot updrafts like flaming butterflies. Then Graham was on fire, her hair and hands burning.

She woke with a start, unburned, unharmed but deeply shaken.

She made her way around the dark and silent bedroom to her immaculate bathroom, squinting fiercely against the harsh fluorescent light. Standing there, staring at her refection in the mirror, there was nothing out of the ordinary in her familiar features. She did not look insane.

Yet she was feeling more and more convinced that she was losing her mind. She had not slept more than ten minutes at a time since the Heliotrope fire and when she was able to drift off, she was haunted by nightmares like the one that woke her that night. First the strange vision at the scene of the warehouse fire and now the theater, yet another of Crane's properties, had gone up. Of course, Phillips wanted to bring Crane in for questioning. He was young, but he was not stupid and Graham was having a harder and harder time keeping him leashed. Earlier that day, at the scene of the theater fire, he had threatened to go over her head. She did not know how much longer his need to suck up to her was going to outweigh his heroic sense of right and wrong. She felt trapped, hemmed in with no way out. Crane was lying about the arsonist being responsible. She was sure that he had something against her personally and was trying to get her booted from the department, disgraced and thrown in jail.

Her mind struggled to follow every possible scenario and figure a way out of this situation, but she could not seem to focus. Possibilities overlapped inside her head and she felt more trapped than ever, tormented by howling frustration.

There was someone in her bedroom.

She spun, turning back to the open doorway, and saw a dark silhouette against the window, standing between her and the loaded .38 she kept in her bedside drawer. She could smell smoke and burnt flesh, and it suddenly felt intolerably hot in the bathroom. Reaching slowly across the wall for the bedroom light switch, she slid through the doorway, never taking her eyes from the inexplicably unclear shape. When she turned on the light, there was nothing there.

She searched every corner of her bedroom, but not a single thing was out of place. Everything was exactly the way she had left it. There was no excuse for this jittery, girlish behavior. Jumping at shadows, nightmares. Graham needed to pull herself together. She was only making matters worse by acting like some kind of frightened bimbo. There had to be a way out of this situation with Crane, it was just a matter of staying calm and thinking things through.

A distinct, stifled giggle sounded from the kitchen. Furious, Graham pulled the gun from her bedside drawer and barreled down the hall to the kitchen. Whoever was being cute and having some fun at her expense was going to be very, very sorry.

There was no one in the kitchen either, but all four burners on the stove were blazing. She turned them off, frowning. It was so hot in her apartment that she was pouring sweat, red hair plastered to her neck. Her thin, white, cotton camisole and underwear were soaked. She was starting to feel faint with heat exhaustion as she forced herself to check every door, every window. No sign of forced entry. There was no one. When she returned to the kitchen, the burners were on again and the wall above was smeared with soot in a dramatic V-shape leading up and across the ceiling. Letters were drawn in the soot with a tiny hand.

YOUR FAULT.

FIFTEEN

Crane was pacing back and forth in his office, forehead slick with sweat.

"Well, I don't care if the repairman said there was no problem," he said into his headset. "I'm telling you there's a goddamn problem. This heater has given me nothing but problems and I want it taken care of tonight. Not tomorrow, not in four to six business days, tonight. Look, put me through to your supervisor. No don't put me on hold... Damn it."

Cheerful music dribbled from the earpiece and Crane was about to fling the headset across the room when the tone indicating another call cut through the awful tune.

"Shit." He clicked over to the other call. "Crane."

It was his pal, the perky reporter. He placed his palms on the desk and sucked in a deep breath.

"No, there is absolutely no connection between the three fires." He pulled the silk handkerchief from his pocket and mopped his face. "I assure you the authorities are looking into it. I have every confidence in their ability to get to the bottom of this."

He pulled the revolver from his desk drawer and checked to be sure it was loaded.

"Of course," he said. "Every rich person has enemies."

He hung up, furious. It was time to take care of Driscoll once and for all. He had given the little rat too many chances already. Clearly he would not stop until Crane stopped him for good.

There was a business card on his desk, given to him by Alexander Gong several years ago. It was plain white, with a row of Chinese characters and a phone number. Beneath that, in handwritten red letters, the words "Mr Lo." It sat centered on the empty blotter where it had been sitting for two days while Crane tried every other way to deal with this Driscoll problem. The theater was the final straw. No more kid gloves. If that bastard wanted hardball, he'd get hardball.

Crane dialed the number on the card.

"Wei?" a Chinese female voice answered.

"Mr Lo, please," Crane said.

There was silence on the other end of the line, followed by a second voice, which was as perfect and accentless as a newscaster's.

"This is Mr Lo."

"Mr Lo, I apologize for the late hour. My name is Scotland Crane. I'm an associate of Mr Gong."

"Ah," Mr Lo said. "Are you also in the import/export business?"

"No," Crane said. "I'm in the real estate business."

"Is that right? My wife and I are hoping to purchase a new home this year. Perhaps you can give us some pointers."

"I would be happy to."

Crane knew from his dealings with the Chinese in Hong Kong that it was bad manners to come right out with a proposition, so he allowed the conversation to drift around the topics of real estate and investments and the weather in Los Angeles before Mr Lo finally asked if there was anything he could do for Crane.

"I have a problem with some trash removal in one of my properties. It would be very helpful to me if that trash could be cleared out tonight. I would like to be able to show the property in the morning and I will need it to be clean."

Mr Lo named a price. It was shockingly high, but Crane did not hesitate. He gave Mr Lo the address of the Malibu beach house where Driscoll was staying and spent another five minutes on casual, unrelated conversation before he finally hung up, feeling a thousand pounds lighter.

Then he heard footsteps in the hall outside the office door.

He stood so fast he almost swooned from the thick, suffocating heat. It was getting hotter and hotter in his office as he groped for his gun and wiped the sweat from his eyes with the back of his hand. The monitor that showed the hallway outside his door was inexplicably dead. Crane cursed silently, heart pounding in his throat. He punched the security panic button on his desk.

"Is there a problem, Mr Crane?" said a deep male voice over the speaker beneath the button.

"There's someone in my house," Crane said, struggling to keep his voice level. "Send an armed response team right away."

"But Mr Crane," the voice replied. "Our computers show that the outer perimeter is solid. There has been no breach in security."

"I don't care what your computers say, there's someone in my house. The hallway monitor is dead."

Crane heard the sound of tapping keys through the speaker.

"Sir, the feed from the hallway camera is fine on our end and we show no activity in that area." The voice paused. "Or anywhere else in the house. We can send a technician out to check your wiring first thing tomorrow morning."

There was another soft shuffle of feet in the hall, followed by a feeble scraping against the door. The hair on the back of Crane's neck bristled.

"Christ," he said. "You don't hear that?"

"Our monitors are silent, Mr Crane, but I assure you, there is no one in the hallway outside your office."

"What the hell do I pay you people for?" Crane took several wary steps towards the door, listening with his whole body. "Look, I've had threats on my life. Someone has been burning my properties. I want a team sent up here and I want it done five minutes ago."

There was another pause. Then: "Right away, sir."

The speaker went dead.

Crane put his hand on the doorknob and immediately yanked it back. The metal knob was too hot to hold. Cursing under his breath, he used his handkerchief to open the door and, leading with the pistol in his right hand, he slipped out into the hallway.

There was no one there, but the sound of stifled laughter remained, echoing down the length of the hall.

"Driscoll?" Crane called.

Nothing. Not relishing another anxiety-filled search through every corner of the house, Crane slipped back into his office and locked the door. The security team should arrive within five to seven minutes so there was no point in freaking himself out and exposing himself to danger. If Driscoll had broken in, he was not there to play hide and seek. Let the security team handle it. The office was safe, the safest room in the house. Locked down and secure. No one could get him in there.

The clock on his desk read 10:13pm. Five short minutes and the security team would be there to put an end to Rick Driscoll and his little games. If Crane was lucky, Driscoll would resist and the team would be forced to shoot the bastard. Even if he got away, he would find the patient Mr Lo waiting for him back at the condo. Now if only Crane could get this damn heater fixed.

It must have been a hundred and ten degrees in the office. Crane wanted desperately to open a window and let in the cool night air, but he was afraid to leave an unlocked passage, an easy opening for Driscoll to slip through the moment he let his guard down. It was 10:15. Only three more minutes. He went to mop the sweat from his face but his handkerchief was already so wet it just kind of spread the sweat around. The scuffling out in the hall increased to a frantic pitch as if little fingers were desperately scrabbling around the edges of the door. Crane felt as if little fingers were scraping away at the edges of his fraying nerves.

"What the hell do you want?" Crane yelled, training the gun on the door.

The sounds instantly stopped. A heartbeat ticked by, then two and three. The clock read 10:16.

Suddenly, the light in Crane's office clicked off. He could still see the glowing green numerals on the clock, still 10:16, and faint light spilled under the crack of the door, so he knew the power was not off in the whole house. Was Driscoll somehow able to cut the wire to his light? Did he also do something to the hallway camera? What about the rest of the security system? Could he be responsible for the heater malfunction too? Crane sat tense and sweating in the dark. He refused to be baited into leaving the safety of his office. He looked at the clock again. How could it still be 10:16? It felt like ages had passed.

The idea that some worthless maggot like Driscoll could violate the sanctity of Crane's home was intolerable. Burning his properties was reason enough to take him out, but to break into Crane's private sanctuary and play these kinds of games... Taunting him. Stomping around on Crane's carpet. Touching things. Utterly intolerable.

Crane's eyes did not seem to be adjusting to the darkness. He could still see the numbers on the clock, still inexplicably 10:16, but everything else in the room seemed inky and unclear, as if the room was filled with thick smoke. Wide-eyed in the blackness, Crane tried to focus, to distinguish the inert bulk of the couch, the rectangle of the television screen, the regular ordinary shapes that surrounded him every day, but somehow nothing seemed to be where he expected it and there seemed to be far too many things, all bunched up far too close to him. He reached out and his fingertips touched the soft arm of the sofa. Impossible. Even if the sofa had somehow moved magically across the room, there wasn't enough space for the sofa to fit behind his desk. And there was something wrong with it, too. It felt different. He could feel loose stuffing bulging out of a long tear in the fabric and the fabric itself felt too rough and scratchy. Not the familiar Italian silk he'd had specially ordered from overseas, but some kind of... well, almost like polyester.

He could still see the clock, still frozen at 10:16, but when he reached to touch the edge of the desk, it was not there. His fingers just groped into empty space. Struggling not to panic, he gripped the seat of the chair beneath him, sure that the room had somehow been rearranged in the dark. Where was his desk? Everything had been exactly the way he liked it for nearly ten years, yet now things were all wrong. He reached out again, trying to tell himself that he had just scooted back in his chair without realizing and that his desk had to be right there, when his questing fingers hit something totally unexpected.

It was small and round, hot to the touch and hard like unglazed porcelain. It felt gritty and greasy and seemed to leave flaky crumbs stuck to his hands. His fingers followed the curve of the mysterious new object and encountered a deep round pit above a smaller narrow hole and beneath that something that felt smooth like a row of little tiles. Or teeth.

When the object moved, turning and gliding closer to him, Crane yanked his hand away, his mind putting the tactile information together in a sudden awful picture of what he had just touched. What was now leaning towards him as if wanting to tell him a secret? It was a small, skeletal head.

A little hand closed around Crane's wrist and he screamed and stood, squeezing off three wild shots in the darkness. The large plate glass window shattered, a rush of cool night air chilling the sweat on his brow.

The familiar shape of the room became clear in the dimness. Everything in its place.

"Mr Crane?" an urgent voice called. "Mr Crane, don't shoot, it's Bulldog Security. Mr Crane, are you all right?"

Two men in matching navy uniforms appeared in the hole left by the broken window, guns drawn and pointed professionally downward. When they saw Crane they holstered their weapons and clicked on flashlights. One guy was black and model handsome, the other a blond surfer type. They both looked straight out of central casting, like Ken dolls molded from different colored plastic.

"Oh thank god," Crane said, letting his weak legs collapse as he more fell than sat back into his office chair. "There's someone in the house. He cut my wires and..."

He trailed off, unable to say more. The blond guy shone his light over the wall, searching for a light switch. When he found it, he walked over and flicked it. The light went on.

"Someone turned it off," Crane said, sounding like a petulant child but unable to stop himself.

"Okay." The blond motioned to his partner. "Don't worry, Mr Crane. Stay right here."

They returned less than five minutes later.

"The premises are clean," the black guy said.

"If there was someone here," the blond said, "he's gone now."

Crane was surprised the blond kid didn't say, "Dude." He shook his head, feeling wretched and humiliated. He poured himself a stiff shot of brandy with shaking hands.

"I'm sorry," Crane said. "I've had some death threats and I guess the stress is getting to me."

"That's okay, Mr Crane," the blond said with a big, toothy and agreeable grin that probably undid a whole lot of bikinis. "We get paid whether there's someone here or not."

"No need to apologize," the black kid said. "It's our job."

Crane nodded, staring into the bottom of his empty glass. Nothing felt real and the adrenaline that was screaming through his veins had leached away, leaving him exhausted and spent.

The pair took off and Crane called his secretary's cell phone. It was obvious that he had woken her up. He told her to contact a twenty-four hour glass replacement company and send someone up right away. He knew there would be no sleep for him that night, so he just poured himself another brandy, turned on a classic movie channel on the television and waited.

SIXTEEN

Anibal de la Paz was working late again in his tiny dry cleaning shop. It was nearly midnight and he still had two pairs of slacks to hem and a woman's jacket that needed its sleeves taken up. Anibal was seventy-one and his old arthritic fingers weren't as limber as they used to be. His eyes weren't what they used to be either, and even with his new glasses, he had to hunch down with his nose nearly touching the fabric as the machine's needle skated along the chalked hemline.

When he finished the pair of pants, he took the frumpy beige jacket off its hanger and examined it. It was really an ugly thing, plain and dull with no shape. Anibal did not understand what had happened to clothes in these modern times. In his day, women wore fine, structured suits and poured themselves into gorgeously fitted dresses that squeezed in their tiny waists and hugged their full hips. Men wore sharp hats and colorful ties and even the poorest man still wore a suit, no matter how threadbare. Nowadays, the kids slouched around in what looked like hugely oversized pajamas. Young mothers wore sneakers and sloppy sweatpants identical to those worn by their toddlers. Almost everyone walked around looking as if they had been driven from their beds in the middle of the night by a house fire.

When Anibal was younger, it was possible to make a decent living as a tailor. People appreciated fine, custom-made shirts and well-tailored suits. It made Anibal feel good to help people choose the right lapel to suit their body type, to create a perfect garment made solely for one individual. Now everything was off the rack. Identical T-shirts emblazoned with advertising logos, cut so loose and baggy that the shape of the body beneath hardly mattered at all. Anibal had been forced to turn his tailor shop into a dry cleaner's in order to make ends meet. Now, his fine tailoring skills were wasted on hemming slacks, a dull and mindless job a trained monkey could do.

Last year, on his seventieth birthday, Anibal had treated himself to a weekend in Vegas. He carefully selected his two best suits and packed several sets of matching ties and pocket squares. He had his shoes shined and his hair cut. He even splurged on a new tie tack that he could not really afford, a simple gold and onyx oval that complemented his favorite onyx cuff links and would go with almost any color tie. He knew that he was too old to hope for romance, but he still wanted to look his best.

When he arrived at Caesar's Palace, the casino hotel where he had booked his room, he was appalled by what he found. He was by far the most formally dressed person in the casino. Other than the cocktail waitresses, the majority of the people he saw parked before the jangling slot machines were in shorts, T-shirts and rubber flip-flop sandals. He actually saw one grossly obese woman wearing pink fuzzy slippers as she mindlessly fed bills into a *Creature from the Black Lagoon* slot machine. Were people not ashamed to walk around in public so unkempt? Did no one take the time to put together a nice ensemble before going out to a restaurant or a casino? Even the security guards wore T-shirts. It was soundly depressing and Anibal felt more lonely and alienated than ever.

He desperately missed Antonio, his lover, his life partner and best friend for forty-eight years. Antonio would have arched a scathing eyebrow and laughed with Anibal at all the fat, slovenly tourists and their ugly clothes. Antonio who had been so dapper, so well dressed, always with such an easy, effortless sense of style. Since the day they met in the spring of 1954, they had always felt as if they were both members of a separate species, two misplaced aliens who somehow found each other in a world of lesser beings. When Antonio died in 2002 of prostate cancer, Anibal's world fell apart. Now, on his first birthday alone, Anibal had wanted to do something to cheer himself up, to have some fun and remind himself that he was still alive. Instead, he wound up feeling worse, as if the world had gone and left him behind.

Anibal pulled the beige jacket out from under the needle and snipped the dangling thread. He was so tired, his eyes dry and scratchy beneath his glasses. He would have to come in early tomorrow and finish the two pairs of slacks. He just couldn't stay up late like he used to, though in truth, he knew he was forcing himself to stay up far beyond his usual bedtime so that he would be too tired to notice how empty Antonio's side of the bed still felt.

He was searching for his keys, cursing himself for misplacing them almost every night, when he thought he heard a strange sound: a kind of soft rustling amid the hanging, plastic-wrapped garments, followed by high, childish laughter. He turned down the little radio by his sewing machine and listened with his head cocked.

"Hello?" he called.

Could there be someone in the shop? A child? It didn't seem possible. Anibal checked the door. It was locked, just as it had been since he'd closed almost four hours ago.

"Is someone there?" he asked, peering fearfully between the slick silvery plastic forms of the clean garments.

There was nothing. Not a sound. He wondered if he was hearing things now. His eyes weren't all that great anymore but his hearing had remained solid and trustworthy. Up until now anyway. Anibal frowned and went back to searching for his keys.

But there it was again, clearer this time. A high-pitched, muffled giggle, like a child laughing behind her fingers. Wasn't it awfully late for a small child to be playing games? Anibal wiped his hands on the legs of his trousers and went into the back to find the little mischief-maker and return them to their worried parents.

Paungthip Wattanawanakul Underhill and her daughter, Star, were closing up their restaurant, Star of Siam, after a particularly busy night. The restaurant had always been a neighborhood favorite, but a recent write-up in the local independent newspaper had identified it as the best late night Thai food in the

area and consequently tripled the number of customers. Paungthip and Star were pleasantly
exhausted after the late rush of chowhounds and
trendy club kids and Hollywood hipsters. They had
been dishing out Paungthip's legendary green curry
until midnight and were still shaking their heads and
pointing at the "CLOSED" sign every few minutes as
hopeful pairs and trios would crowd up around the
door and tap on the glass.

Paungthip busied herself counting out the register
and waving goodbye to her kitchen staff. She was
plump and easy-going with a broad, open smile and
wore her hair in a long braid coiled at the nape of her
neck. More than anything in life, she had a passion
for food. She loved to cook and took pride in her ability to hunt down the freshest, most perfect
ingredients. Nothing made her happier than to see a
table of first-time customers oohing and ahhing over
her dishes, lost in pure gustatory bliss.

She had lived in the United States for twenty-six
years and had a great fondness for her adopted city of
Los Angeles. Her American husband Richard had
died in a plane crash before Star was born and
Paungthip never remarried. Star and the restaurant
named after her were Paungthip's whole world.

Star Underhill was an exceptionally attractive girl
with skin the color of raw almonds, warm hazel eyes,
and a reddish hue to her glossy dark hair. Petite and
slightly chubby from a life of Paungthip's culinary
indulgence, Star had a kind of childlike sweetness
that made men want to fall all over themselves to help
her with even the smallest task, but she disliked
being coddled and treated like a baby. She may have
looked sixteen but she was twenty and possessed a

fierce independent streak. She loved her mother, but often dreamed of running away to another city to start a whole new life, free of any strings or familial obligations.

Star had thrown together a few take-out containers of leftover vegetarian curry and rice as an excuse to go and visit their neighbor in the liquor store. Paungthip wanted to be the world's mom, especially when it came to food, and Star knew that if she mentioned Nuvraj was working alone until two am with nothing to eat but chips and candy bars, her mother would want to send him a little something. It had become a nightly ritual and Star was pretty sure that her mother was starting to suspect there was more to her visits to the Kwik-E-Stop convenience store than just a charitable sentiment.

Nuvraj was nineteen, handsome and intelligent with a very dry sense of humor. He was a little shy, but he never patronized Star, never treated her like a helpless little girl. The fat, red turban that he wore seemed odd to Star at first, but she could not deny there was a mysterious appeal to the unusual garb, like some romantic hero ready to battle animated skeletons and mutli-armed goddesses in an exotic fairy tale adventure. A lot of people in the neighborhood thought that he was some kind of Islamic terrorist because of his turban, which showed how much they knew. Star knew that Nuvraj was a Sikh, from India not the Middle East. People often thought Star was a foreigner, speaking to her in loud, simple words when she came to take their orders as if she could barely speak English, when in truth she had been born and raised in Hollywood just like them. Nuvraj and Star frequently commiserated with each

other about the false perceptions held by so many of
their Caucasian neighbors. They found that they had
a lot of other things in common as well. Both had lost
their fathers, Star's before she was born and Nuvraj's
in a recent event as yet still too painful for him to talk
about with her. Both had over-indulgent mothers and
both were independent and skeptical. Though she
would never admit it to her mother, she was develop-
ing a powerful crush on her mysterious neighbor and
she was pretty sure that he felt the same way about
her.

She kissed her mother on the cheek and gathered
up the take-out boxes.

"Be careful," her mother warned. "It's late, you
know."

"Don't worry, Mom," Star said, smiling. "It's just
next door."

Paungthip watched her daughter hurry across the
lot to the liquor store and shook her head indulgently.
It was just a harmless crush. Nothing to be worried
about, really. She knew the boy's mother, Sangeeta. A
quiet and slightly melancholy but perfectly nice
woman who was always courteous and also belonged
to the Asian Businesswomen's Association's Hollywood chapter. While she knew little about the Sikh
religion, Paungthip was fairly certain that, like others
from India, they preferred arranged marriages. It was
highly unlikely that anything would come of Star's
cross-cultural puppy love.

Paungthip remembered how furious her own
mother had been when she had announced her intention to marry the dashing American pilot who'd
stolen her heart and move away with him to California. She might as well have announced that she was

going to kill herself with all the weeping and rending of clothing that went on in her large, primarily female family. When Richard died, Paungthip's mother had been smug and satisfied, letting her pregnant and distraught daughter know that she would consider allowing Paungthip to come back to live with the family in Chiang Mai as long as she agreed to give the baby a Thai name. Paungthip named her tiny baby girl Star and never spoke to her mother again.

It was amazing to Paungthip that her tiny baby was a full-grown woman now. She still lived at home and still worked in the restaurant, but she was growing more independent every day. It would not be long before her daughter left the nest for good, though Paungthip sincerely hoped that Star would eventually take over the restaurant when she retired.

Provided, of course, that Paungthip was able to keep it going. The landlord had been jacking up the rent regularly because of the recent gentrification of the area and in spite of the busy nights brought about by the favorable article, Paungthip still struggled to make ends meet. She had been seriously considering looking into a new location some time early next year. Maybe something a little larger, close enough to keep her regulars happy, but with more space for all the newcomers. She had great affection for her little restaurant and she had been in the same location for almost fifteen years, but the landlord was really just impossible. Maybe it was high time she moved on.

Paungthip was dusting the altar above the register, removing some wilting flowers and adding a handful of jewel-colored candies when she thought she heard a strange sound, like children whispering. It sounded like it was coming from the kitchen. Her two cooks, a foul-mouthed, hot-dog and hamburger pair, who made up for their lack of social graces with smooth fluid chops in the busy kitchen, had left twenty minutes ago. The dishwasher and the bus boy were gone as soon as the sign turned to closed, along with the two chatty young waitresses. There was no one in the restaurant except for her. Yet she was sure that she heard whispering voices and stifled laughter. Frowning, she went back into the kitchen to find out what was going on.

Nuvraj Singh Kahlsa sat on a tall stool behind the register of the Kwik-E-Stop convenience store, thumbing through a hot rod magazine and pretending that he wasn't waiting for Star. She had been coming around every night just after midnight for the past week, and Nuvraj found himself eagerly awaiting her visits.

He had been deeply unhappy ever since he and his mother had moved to Los Angeles a year and a half ago. He grew up in New York City, coddled within a small but very close-knit Sikh community. He had lots of friends, excelled in school and spent his free time volunteering at the local Humane Society. He loved animals, especially cats, with which he felt a profound affinity. His life was happy. That was before the 9-11 terrorist attack.

He would never forget that horrible day as long as he lived. His father Charanjit was a cab driver for a company based in Tribeca, not far from the World Trade Center, and it was fourteen agonizing hours before they found out that he was all right, unharmed and stuck in Manhattan along with the thousands of others trapped by the bridge and tunnel closures. His mother, Sangeeta, was particularly affected by horrible, mesmerizing footage on the news and the senseless deaths of so many innocent people. She was unable to stop crying all morning and wandered hopelessly from room to room, holding one of their rescued cats in her arms. But while other families in the neighborhood hugged and supported each other as they waited desperately for news of missing loved ones, Nuvraj's fellow New Yorkers suddenly looked on him with naked hostility and suspicion.

He had been teased about his turban many times before and shrugged off witless and cruel comments on an almost daily basis, but suddenly the venom and anger increased a thousandfold. People threw things at Nuvraj and his mother and threatened to burn down their house. Someone tossed a brick through their window that night and an angry young man kicked in the headlights of his father's cab while he was waiting at a stop light. It was not enough that they had to live in fear of additional terrorist attacks. They also had to fear their fellow Americans. Nuvraj felt like he crossed some critical invisible border that day. His innocent faith in the goodness of his fellow man had been obliterated along with the twin towers.

But nothing could prepare them for the night three months later when a pair of plain-clothes cops arrived on the doorstep of their little house in Astoria, Queens. One was a large and soft-spoken black man and the other smaller, white and older who hung back and let his partner do the talking. The bigger man said that he and his partner were with the special hate crimes division and for a moment, Nuvraj thought they were there about the brick that had been thrown through their window. Sangeeta, on the other hand, instinctively knew the truth right away. As soon she saw the expressions on those cops' faces, she burst into inconsolable tears.

Apparently Charanjit had been found beaten to death, his turban unwound and tossed into a nearby trashcan. The big cop was embarassed and apologetic, trying to phrase the awful details in the safest, most neutral way possible, but when he told Nuvraj that the suspects had also "relieved themselves" on his father's body, a kind of white fury eclipsed Nuvraj's grief and he slammed his fist into the frame of the door, splitting open his knuckles. If he had not needed to keep control in order to comfort his mother, he did not know what he would have done.

When he went to court and had to look at the faces of the five teenagers who had murdered and defiled his father, he could barely control his rage. Five of them—five strapping youths to beat and kill a single defenseless fifty-one year-old man. All his life Nuvraj had been taught to love and respect others regardless of their beliefs, but in that moment, if he had a gun he gladly would have shot those smirking boys in their hateful faces. His mother had not been able to attend the trial. She had suffered a near total mental collapse after Charanjit's murder and stayed at home in the care of several older Sikh women, but Nuvraj felt compelled to be there. He wanted to see the perpetrators of this heinous crime receive the punishment they deserved.

None of them were old enough to receive the death penalty. Instead they were all given sentences that seemed far too lenient to Nuvraj. As the trial ended and his father's murderers were led away high fiving and unrepentant, the heat of Nuvraj's anguish and impotent rage boiled away, leaving him feeling hollow and dead inside.

Sangeeta could no longer stand to live in New York City. As much as she would miss her friends in the Sikh community, she could not stand to spend another day in their dark and quiet house, to sleep in the big, empty bed she had once shared with the only man she had ever loved. She had collected a decent sum of money from Charanjit's insurance and the day before Nuvraj's high school graduation, she sat him down and asked him how he felt about moving, maybe somewhere warm like California or Florida. Try to start a new life, far away from the gaping hole that used to be the World Trade Center.

How could he say no? His mother was all he had left. So they packed their three cats and their meager belongings into a truck and drove all the way to Los Angeles.

Nuvraj was lonely in Los Angeles. He didn't know any other Sikhs his own age and he was still continuously picked on because of his turban, called towel-head and Osama, and treated like an enemy everywhere he went. He still chatted with his old friends from New York online but he missed the warmth and comfort of their physical company. The long night shifts at the Kwik-E-Stop seemed to go on forever and he felt as if his life was foundering, trapped in a dead end. Instead of opening up a world of new opportunity, the move to Los Angeles just made him feel more isolated. He was planning to start applying to colleges, but in his heart he was afraid, afraid of harassment and rejection on the campus. Then he met Star, and he started to think that there might be hope for the human race after all.

When the sound of the door chime echoed through the little store at seven minutes after midnight, Nuvraj's heart leapt in his chest. Sure enough, it was her.

"Hey Raj," Star said, hefting the aromatic white boxes onto the counter. "How's tricks?"

"Tricky," he said. "Same as always."

She was so beautiful with her sweet, heart-shaped face and her intelligent, laughing eyes. Nuvraj didn't have much experience with women and often felt uncomfortable in their company, particularly if they were attractive. But Star had this goofy, self-deprecating sense of humor that put him instantly at ease. She made him laugh with her impressions of the trendy hipsters that frequented her restaurant and she touched his arm frequently while she talked, sending hot little shivers across the surface of his skin.

He found that he was simultaneously thrilled and intimidated by her worldliness. He had only ever dated shy Sikh girls who were even more sheltered than he was. Star was a year older than him and made no pretense of chastity. Her body language was saucy and confident and she looked right into his eyes when she talked to him. She behaved as though she were attracted to him, but he just couldn't be sure. Maybe she was just being friendly. He wanted more than anything to kiss her, touch her and other things as well, but he was afraid that his inexperience would be far too evident and she would surely laugh at him.

So instead, he made conversation and ate the delicious Thai curry she brought for him and asked after her mother. She told him about her customers and a visit from the health inspector. As she imitated the health inspector's high nasal voice, she laughed and put her tiny hand on his arm. Impulsively, he took her hand in his and squeezed it gently. She looked up at him and smiled, and he felt a rush of adrenaline racing in his veins.

The sound of the door chime startled him so badly that he yanked his hand back and accidentally knocked the plastic fork out of the take-out box, drops of pale green curry sauce splattering across the counter.

It was Star's mother. She looked terrified.

"Mom," Star said, running to take her mother's outstretched hand. "What's wrong?"

"There's a ghost in the restaurant," Paungthip said, flapping a hand in the direction of the door. "A tiny ghost, in the kitchen."

Nuvraj wiped the drops of sauce from the counter and frowned. A ghost? What on earth could she mean by that?

"Mom," Star said, an almost stern look on her pretty face. "You can't be serious."

"I swear," Paungthip said. "I saw it. Small and black, burned all over like a cooked pig."

Nuvraj brought his stool around to the front of the counter and helped Paungthip sit down. She was close to hyperventilating, shaking and wide-eyed with fear.

"Just relax, Mrs Underhill," Nuvraj said. "Let me get you some water."

He went to fetch a bottle of spring water from one of the coolers and cracked the cap, handing it to the older woman.

Paungthip drank deeply and wrapped her arms around herself, still shivering.

"Would you like me to go over and see if I can see anyone in the restaurant?" Nuvraj asked.

"We should go together," Star said.

"I won't stay here alone," Paungthip said, eyes wide and clutching at her daughter's arm.

"Fine," Nuvraj said, removing his Mossberg shotgun from its clips beneath the counter. "We will all go."

Nuvraj locked up the store and took the lead, the two women behind him. They were halfway to the restaurant when they spotted the tailor, old Mr de la Paz, coming out of his shop.

"Did you just see a small child run out here?" Mr de la Paz asked. "I thought I heard..."

Paungthip suddenly screamed and threw her arms around Nuvraj. "There," she whispered. "There it is."

At first Nuvraj couldn't see anything where she was pointing, over by the streetlight on the corner. Then he heard Star gasp softly.

"Oh my god," she said. "I see it."

"Where?" Nuvraj asked, frowning.

"There, by the paper machine," Star said.

Sure enough, there was a dark figure on the far side of one of the free newspaper dispensers on the sidewalk. It was small and inexplicably unclear, like a shadow or a smudge of dirt in the air. Mr de la Paz came forward and put protective arms around the two women as Nuvraj took a step towards the figure, the muzzle of the shotgun trained on the center of the strange apparition.

That was when a furious explosion ripped through the buildings of the mini-mall, tossing Nuvraj, de la Paz and the women like autumn leaves. He fell, shotgun clattering against the cement and sliding away under a parked car. His first thought was that this was another hate crime, an attack perpetrated by so-called patriots because of his choice of head coverings. His hands went unconsciously to his skewed turban as he pulled himself up to his knees.

Once he had his bearings, he instinctively reached for Star and Paungthip to make sure they were safe. Both were profoundly shaken, but unharmed. Paungthip helped Mr de la Paz to his feet and Star threw her arms around Nuvraj. The four of them watched with horrified fascination as raging flames engulfed their businesses along with the neighboring water purification store and beauty supply outlet. In spite of his fear and horror, Nuvraj could not help but be distracted by the feel of Star's shivering body next to his.

Paungthip clutched Nuvraj's arm and at first he thought she was crying, but when he looked down at her, he saw that she was laughing.

"I can't believe it," Paungthip said. "I was just thinking of moving, but didn't know how to get out of my lease. Guess I don't have to worry about that now."

Star looked at her mother and started to laugh too. "See, Mom," she said. "That ghost did us a favor."

"A favor," Paungthip repeated, shaking her head. "I just can't believe it."

"I guess I can finally afford to retire," Mr de la Paz said, wiping his mouth with a colorful silk handkerchief. "It's really quite extraordinary."

"Star," Nuvraj said.

"Yeah?" She looked up at him.

"Would you go out on a date with me?"

Star looked back at her mother and back at him. "You mean, like a *date* date?"

Nuvraj nodded. "A *date* date," he replied. "With Mrs Underhill's permission of course." He looked back at the burning inferno that used to be his store. "I suddenly find myself with quite a bit of free time."

Star laughed and her mother patted her hand, smiling.

"Sure," Star said.

He hugged her close as the mini-mall buildings began to collapse in on themselves, sirens wailing in the distance.

SEVENTEEN

Driscoll sat on a cream-colored, leather, sectional sofa that cost more than his car, staring out the picture window at the dark ocean while his nearly empty whiskey glass made a ring on the designer coffee table. He was surrounded by stylish luxury—Crane's beach front properties were all top notch—and yet every time Rick closed his eyes, he found himself back in that crummy, claustrophobic dump on Heliotrope Street. He just couldn't seem to let it go. He wasn't sleeping and when he did he was plagued by nightmares.

Nightmares in which flaming wheelchairs chased him down dark, smoky hallways, and black, twisted fingers forced themselves into his mouth and down his throat. Being awake wasn't any better. He kept hearing things, soft, stealthy shuffles around corners and a sound like quickly stifled giggles. He was constantly on edge and the whiskey he poured down his throat did nothing to dull his jagged paranoia. Being here alone in this high-class condo only seemed to make it worse. The unfamiliar angles of the rooms seemed weirdly flexible, as if they were subtly shifting while he wasn't looking. The heater was on the fritz and always seemed to turn itself on full blast while he was sleeping. He would wake up in a panic, acrid smoke in his nostrils and drenched in sweat, sure the place was burning, that he was burning. But there was nothing, nothing at all.

When he first got there, he called up a skirt he had been working on and asked her over to his new pad for a few drinks and a dip in the Jacuzzi. The girl was a bartender named Tanya, a slender brunette with killer legs. She had been giving Driscoll the hard-to-get routine for over a month, but she went all juicy the second she walked through the thick, expensive door, cooing over the opulent furniture and the luxurious carpet and all the fresh, exotic flowers. Driscoll had her on the leather sofa in record time, but just as he was undoing the second button on her blouse, the subtle, spicy scent of her skin was eclipsed by a powerful odor of burning flesh so rich and hideous it made him gag. He sat back and swallowed hard, wiping his hand across his mouth.

"What?" Tanya had said, propping herself up on an elbow, pouting elaborately and looking beautiful and disheveled.

"You smell something burning?" he asked, frowning.

She smiled. "Must be my panties," she said.

Driscoll laughed and tried to get back in the groove but that smell, that awful, yet somehow almost savory stench was still there, crawling deep into his sinuses. Like when his dad left the burgers on the grill too long because he was distracted by the game. Like when his first girlfriend burned her ear with the curling iron and wanted him to kiss it and make it better. Like when those kids burned to death in that lousy building on Heliotrope Street because of him.

That did it. He pulled away from Tanya and stood. He told her he needed to use the john and staggered down the hall. Shouldering open the door to the palatial bathroom, he barely made it to the toilet in time.

After vomiting over and over the stomach cramps started to die down and Driscoll hugged the cool porcelain lip of the toilet, shaking uncontrollably. It was unnaturally hot and stuffy in the bathroom. His shirt was completely soaked through with sweat as he struggled to his feet and staggered to the sink. He turned on the cold tap, intending to splash cool water on his face, but the gush from the faucet was scalding hot and he yanked his hand away from the stream, yelping in pain.

He heard Tanya's voice out in the hallway, asking if he was okay. When he turned towards the sound, he caught a glimpse of his reflection in the full-length mirror on the door and reeled back, a startled gasp rushing out between his clenched teeth.

In his reflection, he was horribly burned. His skin was streaked with lurid red and charcoal black, hair and clothes gone to ash, shoes melted to his twisted feet. His eyes and lips were gone too, burned away to yawning, empty pits and a frozen, skeleton smile.

Driscoll flailed his hand backward to catch himself on the sink and missed. A fancy soap dish went tumbling to the tile, smashing into a thousand pieces as he fell. Shards of pretty blue and green glass sliced into his palms, tearing through his clothes. He heard Tanya's voice saying his name, playful concern gone high-pitched and frantic. She came through the unlocked door and the hideous reflection tilted away, disappearing as the door swung back against the wall.

She fussed over him and helped him up, sitting him on the edge of the tub and wincing at his cuts. She wanted to bandage him up, but he just couldn't stand the feel of her hands on him. He did his best to reassure her that he was fine, but he could not hustle her out of the house fast enough.

When she was gone, he spent over an hour standing outside that bathroom door, working up the nerve to go inside and look in the mirror again. When he was finally able to push it open and peer around the edge of the mirror, his reflection was totally normal. He swore he heard that faint, musical giggle echoing down the hallway. That had been three days ago.

So now Driscoll sat, drinking and looking at the ocean, the cold, safe ocean, filling his vision like the opposite of burning. He had gotten a call an hour ago from an old buddy needing a partner for a fast insurance job downtown, but Driscoll had put him off, claiming to be sick. That wasn't far from the truth. He hadn't eaten since the mirror incident and had slept maybe three hours in as many days. He was terrified to leave the house. All he could think to do was get drunk and stay drunk.

He refilled his glass with the last of the whisky and knocked it back. As the liquor burned its way down his gullet, he was suddenly struck by the fact that alcohol was flammable. His belly and throat felt painfully hot and he was sure he was going to vomit again, but as he sat there with his palm on the coffee table, waiting to see if the nausea would pass, he heard the soft, breathy and utterly distinct sound of gas catching flame.

He stood and spun, heart in his throat. On the far side of the huge room, there was a large, gas fireplace. Driscoll had checked it out when he first arrived and was not at all sorry to discover that it wasn't connected. Yet now, inexplicably, it was on, cheery orange flames dancing across the surface of the artificial log.

Driscoll's cell phone rang, startling him. He fumbled to answer, eyes never leaving the flames. It was Crane.

"Driscoll, you bastard, you're a dead man, you hear me? A dead man."

Crane hung up and Driscoll just stood there with the phone in his hand. Two thin threads of dark and inexplicable smoke were pouring from the center of the fire. Driscoll knew better than anyone that there was never any smoke from a gas flame. Mesmerized, he took a step closer to the fireplace. The smoke seemed heavy with particulate matter and tiny flakes of black ash as it went swirling delicately through the air, coiling sinuously towards him.

Every nerve in Driscoll's body was screaming for him to run, but he couldn't seem to make his muscles obey as the serpentine licks of smoke thickened and the flames grew taller and brighter. He let the cell phone fall to the carpet, watching in horror as the smoke began to solidify, flakes of ash and char twining together to form crooked, reaching arms wreathed in flame. Delicate, child-sized arms that reached for him. Paralysis shattered, he turned and ran.

The room was choked with smoke and ash like black snow whirling around him as he instinctively bolted for the water, the chilly promise of the ocean.

In the second before he hit the plate glass window, he saw the reflection of two small, blackened figures with flaming hair and wide shrieking mouths, their burnt and shriveled legs hovering inches from the floor as they drifted towards him like smoke. He could feel their heat crisping his skin, flames licking his hair and clothing. Then the fire engulfed him as he threw himself with all his strength towards the cold, dark grace of the sea.

Mr Lo was rounding the corner of the beachfront condo when he saw Rick Driscoll smash through the window and go sailing out over the moonlit dunes like some mad, flaming angel. He watched, stunned, as the burning man fell to the sand, tumbling end over end down the beach and finally coming to a stop less than three feet from the water's edge.

Mr Lo didn't know as much about the nature of fire as Driscoll did, but he knew how hard it was to burn a human body and keep it burning. The flaming pile that had been his designated target was still burning merrily, as if he had been doused in gasoline. It looked almost cheerful on the dark deserted beach, flames reflecting across the dark waves. A guitar, some marshmallows and a couple of chicks in bikinis, and they'd be set. Mr Lo shook his head, pulled out his cell phone and called Crane.

EIGHTEEN

Phillips spent the entire drive out to Malibu practicing what he would say to Graham about Crane. With a forth and fifth property burned in the same night, there could no longer be any doubt that foul play was involved. Clearly she was feeling embarrassed because she had ruled the first one accidental, and now she was just being stubborn in trying to support her initial call. She did not strike Phillips as a person who could easily admit being wrong. However, at this point she was just going to have to face facts. The entire department was buzzing about the connection with Crane. Phillips just had to figure a way to bring up his theory that did not make it seem as though he was showing off or trying to make her look bad.

In his gut, he knew he was right. It seemed as clear as day to him, now more than ever. The Heliotrope fire was straight up arson for profit. No doubt about it. Everything about the scenario was by the numbers, like something out of one of his arson investigation textbooks. Crummy tenement building, supposedly empty of tenants. A fire in a rear top floor apartment and a big insurance payoff. Sure it could have been a lucky break for the landlord, but then you take the other four fires into account and you see the big picture.

Phillips figured that whoever had done the torch job for Crane had been stiffed on the Heliotrope gig and was now exacting revenge by burning viable, valuable properties, starting small with the warehouse and ending with this latest blaze in an expensive luxury condo. Whoever this guy was, he was clearly a genius. The method he had devised to incinerate the buildings with no damage to the surrounding structures and no detectable residue was unlike anything Phillips had ever seen or read about. In a way, Phillips actually felt a kind of awed respect for the guy. He couldn't wait to interrogate him, pick his brains and find out how he'd done it. Even Graham would have to be curious.

It was cold and foggy out in Malibu, ghostly scraps of mist clinging to the shoreline and swirling around the nose of Phillips's car. The property was easy to spot, like a missing tooth in the row of expensive beachfront condos. Phillips parked his car at the gate, flashing his shield at the silent, stone-faced sheriffs blocking the private road.

Of course Graham was already there. She was standing on the beach, staring off at the horizon. At her feet was a smooth blackened depression in the sand, slick in spots where the sand had melted into glass.

"Graham," Phillips called.

She did not turn or even acknowledge his voice. He took a few steps closer and called her again.

"What have you got there, Graham?"

She finally turned to him and he was appalled by how she looked. Her face was icy pale and haggard, lines around her eyes and mouth like deep charcoal slashes. Her hair was greasy and unwashed, falling loose from its braid, and her eyes seemed far away, glassed over and unreachable.

"Hey," Phillips said softly, forgetting everything he had planned to say. "Are you all right?"

She nodded slowly and looked down at the black depression at her feet. "This is where they found the remains of the occupant," she said, her voice almost lost under the whisper of the ocean. "Currently unidentified."

Phillips frowned and looked back up at the remains of the condo. It was a pretty far distance for a person on fire to jump, but people in dire situations were capable of some amazing things.

"This is the first fatality since the Heliotrope fire," Phillips said. "In the mini-mall, the theater and the warehouse, the people inside at the time of inception were tricked into leaving the building before the fire started by person or persons unknown. Almost as if the arsonist didn't want anyone to be hurt. What was different here?"

Graham said nothing.

"Graham," Phillips said. "We need to bring Scotland Crane in for questioning."

That wasn't how he planned to bring it up, but he didn't know what else to say. Graham was acting so strange that he was starting to feel uncomfortably sure that she holding something back from him. He braced himself for the storm of hostile attitude and when it didn't come, he just stood there, dumbfounded.

"Okay," she said, and turned away, looking back out to sea.

The two of them stood, about six feet apart and silent. Phillips was completely baffled by Graham's behavior. Her body language and the thousand-yard stare in her dark eyes reminded him of something he'd seen many times as a firefighter. The shell-shocked look of someone watching their home, their family and everything precious to them burn to the ground.

"Well, uh... Okay then," he said. "Do you want me to put in the request for a warrant? We can probably push it through and get the approval by tomorrow morning at the latest."

"Fine," she said. She pulled her battered leather jacket tighter around herself. "Finish up here and I'll see you then."

Phillips watched her walk away across the dunes. He had no idea what was wrong with Graham, but he would do whatever it took to get to the bottom of this.

Graham sat behind the wheel of her Blazer on the bluff above, looking out over the ocean. It was amazing to her how the world seemed to continue on as if it hadn't ended. The ocean still lapped against the beach, the gulls still surfed the breezes above and the world went on with its own business, not caring that the life of one insignificant little person was over.

The Blazer was filled with dirty clothes and fast food wrappers. Graham had not been back to her house since the incident with the stove and had not slept in more than twenty-four hours. She popped open the glove box and took out her .38, checking the cylinder for the hundredth time. It was still loaded. She found herself thinking of Jimmy, of how trapped he must have felt before he blew his brains out. She felt closer to him in that moment than she had since his death as she stared into the dead black eye of the gun barrel, wondering idly if it would hurt much. There was no other option now. She was tired of fighting.

When she heard a loud tapping on her window, she nearly leapt out of her skin. She was lucky she did not reflexively pull the trigger, but as she turned to face the window, stuffing the gun into the waistband of her jeans, she saw that there was nobody there. Slow and cautious, she opened her door and got out of the car, scanning the empty parking area. A few seagulls by the trash barrel, but other than that, nothing. When she turned back to her car, she jumped back in surprise, stifling a startled gasp.

Her car was in flames. She staggered backward and fell sprawling on her ass. She watched in horror as two skinny, burning figures climbed out of the car and started towards her, dripping fire and sizzling bits of themselves as they walked. Graham screamed as their flaming hands reached for her, clutching at her face and clothes and setting her ablaze.

Graham woke behind the wheel of her Blazer with the tail end of the scream clenched in her raw and aching throat. The gun was on her lap.

She wiped the back of her hand across her mouth and put the gun back in the glovebox, pushing aside several crushed boxes of cartridges to retrieve a bottle of Dexedrine. She thumbed off the cap and swallowed three of the jaunty yellow triangles, chasing them with the watery warm dregs of a Seven-Eleven Big Gulp.

As the drug sped through her system, she began to feel more focused. There had to be an answer, and eating a bullet was not it. She had been in tough situations before and she had always been able to think her way out. That's what she needed to do now. Think. There had to be options, she just wasn't thinking clearly. She was letting stress get the better of her and cloud her judgment. She needed to think things through and her course of action would be clear.

When it came to her, it was so simple and obvious that she could not believe it hadn't occured to her sooner.

The problem was Phillips. Everything had been fine until he came along with his eager, Cub Scout mentality and his ambitious desire to take over her job. Clearly none of this would have happened without his interference. She was probably too late to stop him from applying for a warrant for Crane's arrest, but if he did not follow through in the morning, it would be just a piece of paper, yet another bureaucratic dead end.

She had been intimate with fire and the myriad ways to start it for most of her adult life. She knew more about arson than most working arsonists. Just look at John Orr, the famous serial arsonist who had also been an arson investigator. Sure he got caught, but that was because he was compulsive. He could not stop setting fires. Graham could set a single, perfect, untraceable fire and never be caught. All it would take was one, then no more Phillips, no more problem with Crane.

Graham turned the ignition, feeling calmer and saner than she had in days.

NINETEEN

Graham watched Phillips pull into his driveway and get out of his car. He paused, rubbing his eyes with a thumb and forefinger, and then walked up to the door. A tiny, dark-haired woman let him in before he could get out his keys, throwing her arms around him like she had not seen him in weeks. The two of them went inside and Graham settled in to wait.

In the trunk of her car she had the simple but deadly device she had constructed that afternoon, together with the tools it would take to connect it to the gas main of Phillips's house. It was an ugly thing, thrown together too fast and lumpy with awkward solder, but she knew that it would work. All she had to do was wait until it was late enough for them to be in bed, sneak around the back, hook the thing up and get the hell out. The device would release enough gas into the house to make sure that Phillips was stupefied and unable to get away and then ignite the gas in a burst of killing flame that would finish him off.

Graham dry-swallowed another three Dexedrines and pushed the irritating hair back from her eyes. Time seemed to crawl as midnight came and went and Graham discovered that the Dexedrine bottle was empty, even though she was sure it had been more than half full the last time she checked. Well, no time like the present. She sucked in a deep breath, popped the trunk and went to open the door.

It wasn't locked, but the door would not budge. She reached across the passenger seat to try the other door, but no dice. Turning the key in the ignition had no effect. The engine wouldn't start, the car's electrics seemed dead and without them, the power windows could not operate.

"Come on, come on, come on... Shit!" Graham cursed, yanking futilely at the door handle. "God-dammit."

Even though the engine would not start, there was a sudden flow of hot air streaming through the vents and the temperature inside the vehicle was increasing by the second. Sweat was pouring off her and her hands were shaking as she struggled to grip her gun, not even knowing who she intended to shoot. She caught a glimpse of herself in the rearview mirror and was horrified. She looked like a madwoman—eyes wild, hair disheveled and thick beads of sweat running down her flushed cheeks. Then a flutter of movement caught her eye and she adjusted the mirror to see into the back seat.

The Heliotrope kids were in the back seat with their blazing skull faces and burning hands and then the hands were on her, around her throat and covering her mouth. Flames were shooting from the vents and Graham tried to scream, twisting furiously to get away from the inescapable heat and the clutching hands. Spiderweb cracks started forming on the windshield, joining to form letters: YOUR FAULT.

Through the smoke and flames, Graham saw that little woman, Phillips's wife, coming towards her car with a look of concern on her face. Graham wrenched herself loose and called out for help, slamming a fist into the window, twice and again then smashing her elbow into the glass, finally shattering it. She tried to throw her body through the broken window but a massive explosion rocked the car, killing heat and flame swallowing Graham, turning her inside out with searing agony. The last thing she saw were those leering skull faces in the rearview mirror and those damning words, "YOUR FAULT," burned forever into her soul.

Phillips woke with a start to find Lucy had not yet come to bed. She was working on a critical project and would probably be up all night. He missed her warm, dozy body next to his. He had been dreaming something. He couldn't remember exactly what, but it filled him with anxiety and an irrational need to make sure she was okay. He thought he heard her voice calling out on the street below the bedroom window and staggered sleepily to his feet to see what the hell was going on. Yanking on sweatpants, he made his way to the window and pushed the curtain aside.

Lucy was crossing to the other side of the street. Was that Graham's Blazer? He watched her approach the car and then shock and horror drenched him as an explosion ripped through the vehicle, tossing Lucy backward like a rag doll. His eyes did not believe what he was seeing. It looked almost as if the flames bent around Lucy, pushing her without touching her. But he could not just stand there and watch. He was down the stairs and out the front door before he even knew what he was doing, yelling her name.

He found her sprawled out in the neighbor's lavender, terrified but unharmed. Her clothes were burnt to rags, but the skin beneath was pristine, save for a few minor scratches from her backward tumble. He took her face between his hands.

"Baby," he said. "Oh my god, baby are you all right?"

She nodded, brushing crushed, sweet-smelling sprigs of lavender off her blackened jeans. "I think so," she said. "Tommy, what happened?" She looked back at the flaming car. "Graham... is she?"

Phillips turned her face away from the fire, cradling her against his bare chest. "I think so, baby," he said. "Look, I need to call this in. You sure you're okay?"

"Yeah," she said, letting him help her to her feet. "But how did this happen?"

"I don't know yet," Phillips said. "But you better believe I'm gonna find out."

TWENTY

When Mr Lo phoned to tell Crane about Driscoll, Crane had to restrain himself from cheering out loud until after he hung up. He was ready for the cops when they arrived at his doorstep with a warrant two days later. It was Graham's rookie partner Phillips, along with a pair of grizzled older detectives from the LAPD. He offered them coffee and asked them to take their shoes off, playing the gracious host to the hilt. He was appalled to find that he would actually have to go downtown, to the dirty, claustrophobic police station like a common criminal. Battling the choke-hold of anxiety that gripped him the second he left his safe and comfortable home, he managed to remain calm and deliver the story he had been practicing since Driscoll's fortunate demise.

"Rick Driscoll was a scammer and lowlife scum-bag," Crane told the detectives, shifting uncomfortably in the ancient, rickety interrogation room chair. "He found out about my problems at the Heliotrope property and offered to burn it down for a substantial sum. Of course, I refused. Driscoll went ahead and torched the building anyway, then tried to force me to give him the money he felt he was owed."

Crane moved the dented paper cup of pale, awful coffee he had been given farther away on the graffiti-covered table and pulled out a sanitizing wipe from his pocket and cleaned his hands. His skin was cringing from the filth and unsanitary conditions all around him. His gaze kept returning to a belly-up cockroach on the hideous green tile about six inches away from his left foot. How long were they planning to just leave it there? Didn't they have a janitor or something? Maybe that was part of their scheme to upset him, to fluster him so that he would make a mistake. He closed his eyes and imagined himself in his clean comfortable office, alone, until he was able to go on.

"When I wouldn't play ball," he continued, "Driscoll went on a mad arson spree, burning several of my Los Angeles properties as retaliation against me."

"Why didn't you go to the police sooner?" Phillips asked. "Have Driscoll arrested?"

Crane shook his head. "How could I? Driscoll had made several explicit threats. He said he would burn my house down and burn me alive." Crane paused dramatically. "Obviously, I was in fear for my life."

Phillips didn't seem to be buying it, but the LAPD guys were sold. The older and more talkative of the two detectives asked Crane to go on.

"Well, that's all really," Crane said. "Clearly karma caught up with Rick Driscoll when he died trying to burn one of my beachfront properties. Obviously no one deserves to die like that, but I must say I will sleep better knowing that crazy firebug is no longer on the loose."

"And what about the death of Arson Investigator Katharine Graham?" Phillips asked. "That took place after the death of Rick Driscoll."

Crane looked into Phillips's angry face. Was he telling the truth? Crane hadn't heard anything on the news.

"This is the first I've heard," he said.

"What did Inspector Graham ask you about when she came to talk to you after the warehouse fire?"

Crane frowned. "She wanted to know where I was at the times of the fires."

"What did you tell her?"

"The truth," Crane said. "I was home, in my house."

"What else did you talk about?" Phillips asked.

"She asked if I had any enemies."

"Did you tell her about Driscoll?"

Crane shook his head. "I told you already. I was afraid he would kill me if I went to the police."

"So you're telling me you don't know anything about what happened to Inspector Graham?"

"Why should I?" Crane pointed at the dead bug. "I don't know what happened to that cockroach either."

The two detectives swapped grins, but Phillips kept at him.

"Can you verify your whereabouts last night between midnight and one am?"

Christ, this kid was really on a tear. Still, Crane wasn't worried. He really didn't have anything to do with the lady arson investigator's death, and besides, he had an ironclad alibi.

"My home is wired with security cameras. An independent company called Bulldog Security monitors the cameras. Whoever was on shift last night can confirm that I did not leave my home. In fact, inspector, I rarely leave my home for any reason. This little excursion is my first outing in over a year. I do everything I can to arrange my life in such a way as to avoid ever having to leave my home. And if you gentlemen are through with me, I'd like to return there as soon as possible."

His three keepers left him then, and Crane could hear the muffled sound of a heated argument on the other side of the one-way glass. Several minutes later, the two detectives returned without the young arson investigator.

"Mr Crane," the older detective said. "Thank you for your cooperation. You are free to go."

On the way out, Crane passed Phillips in the hallway. He was fuming, giving Crane a look of barely restrained hostility. Crane ignored him, using his cell phone to call his secretary and arrange for a car to pick him up ASAP.

"And make sure it's clean," he said, using a tissue to open the front door of the precinct. "I'll be out front."

When the limousine arrived to take him home, it was obviously recently scrubbed, but Crane couldn't help imagining drunken prom queens vomiting on the seats and giving sloppy blow jobs to their sweaty jock boyfriends, dressed in unclean, rented tuxedos. The ride home felt like it took an eternity, and when the car pulled up to the gate of his house, the wash of relief that hit him was so strong he could barely make his fingers move over the security keypad. Once inside, he got down on his knees and kissed the clean white carpet.

He stripped naked in the entry hall and stuffed the clothes he had been wearing, including his shoes, into the trash. Naked, he made his way back to the master bathroom and spent a luxurious hour stripping every trace of the horrible experience from his psyche. He used a mint and rosemary sea-salt scrub and a rough loofah to scour his skin and washed his thinning hair twice with a clarifying shampoo. Clean and pink from scrubbing, he dried himself with a clean white towel and slipped into a brand new white terrycloth bathrobe. He brushed his teeth vigorously and rinsed his mouth with Listerine. Slowly but surely, he began to feel like himself again. This whole disaster with Driscoll was finally behind him. Of course, he would have some major financial repercussions to handle in the wake of all these fires. His insurance would go through the roof, if he could still get insurance. He would have to sell more than half of his holdings to stay afloat, but he was a careful man and had prepared for disaster several times over. While he would be taking a substantial loss, at least he knew his house was safe and taken care of until he could get back on his feet.

When he opened the bathroom door, there were greasy black tracks on the hallway carpet.

They were about two feet apart and an inch wide each, running parallel down the hall and into the living room. Black grit was scattered in the wake of the tracks, as if someone had been pushing an overflowing wheelbarrow filled with coal and ashes.

Baffled and furious, Crane followed the tracks into the living room. They appeared to go meandering through the room, around behind the bar and out into the kitchen.

In the kitchen, in the center of the neat white tiles, stood a small twisted wheelchair. Its frame was warped and blackened and from one of the handles dangled a tiny plastic charm shaped like a little girl with a giant head and huge round eyes.

It had to be some kind of sick joke. Maybe the guys from the security company were making fun of him for his panicked call the other night. Whatever it was, it was not even remotely funny. He reached down to push the disgusting thing outside and yelped in pain. The metal frame was sizzling hot. Crane could smell the stink of burned flesh on his hand as he shook it. Long, slender blisters were forming on his palm, joining together until they almost seemed to take the shape of letters. An M, an R and a D and then Crane realized that a word was forming in the palm of his hand, clear as a brand: MURDERER.

Crane gripped the wrist of his burned hand and staggered back in horror as the little wheelchair shuddered and began to turn towards him, rolling crookedly and impossibly forward. The kitchen floor seemed suddenly filthy, black tracks spreading until the entire floor was covered with soot and grime. More than that, the smooth, expensive tiles were cracked and misaligned, as if they had been neglected for years. In fact, the entire kitchen was grungy and disused, covered in dust and scraps of old food. Cabinet doors hung skewed, and bugs skittered across the greasy countertops. There was someone standing by the fridge, someone small and dirty with no hair or clothes, but they were difficult to look at, as if obscured by filthy glass.

Crane turned to run, but there was another person blocking the doorway. Why couldn't he see them clearly? This one was less than six feet away, yet the dark figure seemed to flicker, like an image projected on smoke.

Bracing himself to touch the dirty figure, Crane pushed past the person in the doorway and ran into the living room. His fingers encountered nothing but heat.

He was planning to run to his office and hit the panic button again, but what he saw in the living room drew him up short.

Like the kitchen, the living room was dirty and violated. The entire room had somehow been vandalized. The furniture was smashed and shredded, artwork destroyed and the walls sullied with filth and graffiti. In huge red letters across the far wall: MURDERER.

Those two dark and unclear figures were there too, silent, accusatory. Crane ran for the office, refusing to see the stains on the carpet, the sooty handprints on the walls, the degeneration of his clean, perfect sanctuary into a squalid crack house. None of this could be real. He was having some kind of breakdown. That was the only possible answer. If he could just make it to his office, he would be alright.

When he came around the corner to his office, there was no door in the doorframe. He proceeded cautiously but other than the lack of a door, everything seemed okay. Furniture where it should be, everything clean and normal. Flooded with gratitude, Crane staggered towards his desk.

But before he could reach the desk, he saw two dark-haired kids, a boy and a girl, standing there, holding hands and blocking his path. It took a second for him to place them and when he did, sudden realization drenched him like ice water. It was the two little brats from the Heliotrope fire, looking just as nauseatingly cute as they did in the sappy photos they kept showing on CNN. But the girl, the cripple, was inexplicably standing. Their dark eyes were like holes in their pale faces.

"What the hell do you want from me?" Crane asked. "Why are you doing this?"

"You are a bad person, Mr Crane," the boy said.

"You killed us," the girl said.

"Look," Crane said. "It wasn't me. It was Driscoll."

"Liar, liar, pants on fire," the girl said in a soft singsong voice. Her smile was more awful than anything Crane had ever seen.

"I have money," Crane said.

"So?" the boy replied. "We don't want your stupid money."

"What about your mom?" Crane asked. "I could make sure she never had to worry about money again."

"It's too late for bargains," the boy said.

"Too late," the girl said.

Suddenly the wheelchair was there in the doorway. Crane tried to run, but he felt frozen to the spot, unable to move a muscle as the chair slowly wobbled across the room towards him. The places where the wheels touched the carpet blossomed with mildew and dirt, spreading like a disease across the floor and up the walls. The chair nudged against the backs of his legs and he collapsed back into it. The little chair was barely wide enough for him and the frame was red hot, searing his skin. Crane screamed as twisted fingers of metal reached up from the chair and hooked through his flesh, holding him down and winding around his throat. He struggled furiously, but he was utterly immobilized and watched with a kind of bleak horror as the room around him seemed to shimmer and melt until it was half the size. There was a crummy thrift store bed against one dirty stucco wall and a peeling white dresser beside it. Nauseous disbelief washed over Crane as he realized he was in his old, awful bedroom, the one he had worked so hard to get away from.

The two kids were laughing silently, ethereal flames dancing on their lips. The chair beneath Crane lunged forward, smashing him headlong into plate glass and then he was outside, out in the immaculate garden of his own precious house. He was bleeding from a thousand cuts as he fought and struggled against the chair's iron grip, but he could not get free. The chair spun him back to face his house and flames gushed simultaneously from every window. A howl of despair burst out of him as he watched his beloved house burn, unforgiving fire devouring everything.

In a matter of minutes, his home was reduced to ashes before his eyes. He could hear the sound of sirens as fire engines wound up and around the narrow twisting roads through the hills, but he knew they were too late to save him. He screamed and screamed, but there was no escape as the fires of vengeance consumed him.

EPILOGUE

Dimitri and Sonia stood silent in Tom Phillips's bedroom. He and his wife were sleeping, but his slumber was restless. He tossed and turned, twisting the sheets around him.

"He deserves to know," Sonia said.

"He won't believe it," Dimitri replied.

Sonia stepped forward and straightened the sheets around Phillips. "He may not, but he still deserves to know."

She leaned over the sleeping man and whispered in his ear. As she spoke, his body stilled and the troubled lines in his brow smoothed away.

"It's time to go, Sonia," Dimitri said.

Sonia nodded and smiled. Phillips's wife rolled over in her sleep and Phillips pulled her to him, snuggling against her.

"Okay," Sonia said.

Together, the two children walked down that long smoky hallway to the door marked EXIT. The firefighter was there with a big grin on his sooty face and he laid a hand on each of their shoulders. "Good job, kids," he said.

Dimitri took Sonia's hand and she smiled.

"Let's go," she said.

Together, they went through the exit.

An old saying that bears repeating, "Play with fire and you'll get burned." A lesson well taught... in The Twilight Zone.

ONE NIGHT AT MERCY

Based on the Teleplay written by
Christopher Mack

ONE

Remember the last time you stopped and smelled a rose? For Dr Jay Ferguson it's been a long time. But tonight, this first-year resident will meet a patient who will make him stop and smell this rose in The Twilight Zone.

"Scoop and run arriving in ten minutes."

The dispatcher's disembodied voice echoed down the over-lit, white hallway where Dr Jay Ferguson hastily finished suturing a young man with a nasty facial laceration. There were four other victims from the same nearby automobile accident. All of them had glass embedded in their faces, hands and arms. One pretty teenage girl had bits of glass strewn in her hair like frozen raindrops. Her eyes were distant, dull with shock. She and her friends had been escorted by the police, as undoubtedly there was nothing left of their vehicle. Their clothing gaped in places where the teeth of the wreckage had chewed them up and they were too dazed to cover themselves. One of the attending physicians was working with the trauma team to help the driver who had flown head first

through the windshield. Dr Ferguson heard over his
shoulder that the patient had so many fractures in his
face that his skull had essentially collapsed, like a
gory game of Jenga.

Nurse Gina Scavone helped another one of the
stunned victims, fighting to staunch the bleeding as
Dr Ferguson received one patient after another, triag-
ing them to whatever surgeon, nurse, or clinic they
needed to visit after he did what he could to stabilize
them. Since Midway, in the next county had closed its
doors last month due to lack of funding, Mercy was
now the one and only trauma center in the tri-county
area, serving a little more than twenty-five million
people. The hospital's traffic had increased at least
six-fold, yet staffing had barely doubled to absorb the
new patient flow, putting a greater strain on the new
residents than usual.

Dr Ferguson was still new at Mercy, so didn't see it
so much as an increase in stress, but viewed it more
like learning to swim in a volcano. He had begun his
residency less than a week ago, having moved from
Chapel Hill, North Carolina, where he had studied
medicine at UNC. He had been born and raised in
charming, progressive Asheville—the "little San Fran-
cisco" nestled in the misty Carolina hills—which
colored his liberal political palette, yet coddled him
enough to shield him from the brutal realities of an
urban trauma center like Mercy. In just a few days,
he'd treated myriad types of exotic trauma that he'd
only read about at UNC-CH, but never thought he
would ever actually see. Chemical and radiation
burns. High powered automatic weapon wounds that
would not seem out of place in a military MASH unit.
Sexual assaults with bizarre and inexplicable objects.

The matching program seemed to have sent him as far afield as he could possibly want—perhaps even a little too far—but there was never a dull moment and he was learning to think on his feet, to improvise and multitask and most of all, to get the job done. It was fascinating but exhausting, challenging but terrifying. In truth, it was precisely what he wanted.

Once he had graduated, he had sworn to push himself harder than ever. He had been in the top of his class, a major distinction at UNC's widely respected school of medicine. The importance of medicine as a profession saturated almost every community within a three hundred mile radius. Dr Ferguson remembered as a child hearing adults talk proudly about this or that older child going off to Chapel Hill. The school was established in 1879, although some historical records indicated that medicine had been taught there even before the Civil War.

"You know," Gina told him as they buckled a groggy suicide attempt to a gurney. "I don't think I believe you're really a southern boy."

The suicide was a bony scrap of a woman with long brown hair and splatters of black vomit and liquid charcoal decorating the front of her oversized hospital gown. Although she had lapsed into semiconsciousness again, upon wakening she could easily try to hurt herself in some other way, once she realized that she wasn't dead from all the pills and whiskey they had pumped from her stomach. Gina had told Dr Ferguson that she recognized the woman from an earlier admittance. Apparently, the suicide was a famous poet who insisted the voices had told her to put double-edged razor blades in her whole milk yogurt and eat it. The ensuing operations were ghastly. Now it seemed the voices had a new plan, one that involved far less metal and a lot more barbiturates. And if the voices told her to take the pills and whiskey, then they might also tell her to chew open her wrists or bang her head against the wall until her cranial juices stained the white latex paint.

"You have no accent," Gina said as they pushed the woman's stretcher close—but not too close—to the wall. "What gives? Last southern boy we had through here sounded like that cartoon rooster. He only lasted two weeks. I think we rubbed the bloom off him."

The older nurse had more than a little Brooklyn in her quick, clipped voice and made no attempt to hide it.

"Not everyone from the south has what could be classified as a southern accent," Dr Ferguson replied.

That wasn't precisely true. He had done everything he could to burn every last trace of the south from his voice, but there were still certain words or phrases that gave him away. He usually just avoided them altogether.

Dr Ferguson had all sorts of prejudices assigned to every shade of southern accent. Of course, down in Alabama just about everyone drawled like Uncle Jeb from the Beverly Hillbillies. But while the Carolinas bred a lot of the same prejudices as the rest of the south, they often did not breed the same voices. Regardless, Dr Ferguson always strove for clear, clinical enunciation and preferred to inject as little of his personal background into his voice as possible.

Gina shrugged, yanking the restraining straps tighter on the scrawny limbs of the suicidal poet.

"Nobody's ever gonna mistake me for Scarlet O'Hara," she said. "I'm a Noo Yawka through and through."

Swarmed on both sides by nurses in blue scrubs with clipboards, Dr Ferguson briefly glanced back into the waiting room and discovered that it had already received at least another twenty patients, every age, race and creed. They crammed into the seats, the aisles, leaned in doorways and slumped against the walls with arms folded over nauseous stomachs and aching chests. In addition to the genuinely sick and injured were the usual dozen or so homeless people who showed up almost nightly in emergency rooms throughout the city, most with vague phantom complaints that could be solved only by prescription pain medication and a warm bed.

Half the wailing and vociferous protests came from potential patients who were being denied immediate service. Overworked nurses were performing triage in the waiting room to route patients to other hospitals, explaining patiently in various languages that they were not sick enough to be there or that there was another hospital that could see them sooner. Not everyone understood. It didn't help that most of the nurses were condescending towards the masses of desperate patients. Dr Ferguson couldn't help but notice the way so many of them talked to everyone as if they were mentally challenged children. It was as if the nurses expected everyone to understand the routine as well as they did. Just because they could sleepwalk through every procedure in the book, they expected everyone else to be the same, when in truth very few people really knew what to expect in the hospital. So many forms, rooms, procedures, tests, and insurance numbers, all just disappearing in the billowing haze of anxiety and fear.

Dr Ferguson remembered all too well escorting his mother to the hospital when she went in for her first biopsy. His mother had been a college professor, intelligent and independent, yet she turned into a waffling, squinting numbskull when confronted with the numerous medical releases, arbitration papers, and questionnaires. Dr Ferguson now realized that her fear and exhaustion probably hadn't helped matters. She wanted desperately to make the right choices, but she had always hated to ask anyone for help. The medical staff even then was at times incredibly condescending. As if everyone should know instinctively that, if the woman at the desk tells you to sit in a lobby in another room, you should expect a nurse to pop out of a room in an adjacent hallway to call your name. This happened so often that he began to anticipate it as a rule rather than an exception when he was helping his mother. What she really needed was a native guide, a navigator, someone to help her through the confusing legalese. She was too busy trying to be brave as every successive test uncovered more despair...

"Heads up, kid!" Gina called sharply.

Dr Ferguson turned to her immediately as yet another patient was wheeled in—this one a hit and run accident, involving a young Filipina female with a TBI. An older woman shrieking with anguish in the waiting room shouted something in Tagalog over and over. The girl's skull sagged slightly above her right ear. A patch of her slick black hair was soaked with what looked like dark cherry syrup, dribbling down her cheek and staining a pink T-shirt that read "Princess" in flowing gold script. Dr Ferguson rattled off a series of terse commands as the trauma team burst into the room and rushed the young woman straight into the operating theater. As they flew by, Dr Ferguson grabbed the receiver on the wall to notify the neurosurgeon on call. When that whirl passed, Dr Ferguson slumped slightly against the wall, his head dimming a notch as he calculated that this was his thirtieth hour straight. No, thirty-first.

He had taken the critical incident stress management classes at UNC. In theory, he could cope with all kinds of disasters or merely an unusual influx of patients. He could even deal appropriately with the cumulative impact of losing several patients in a row, again in theory. The classes were supposed to help them learn how to cope, but he wondered now if all his training—not just the medical studies—could possibly pull him through this endless deluge of pain, suffering, and death. Gina told him that the entire ER staff at Mercy had taken similar classes shortly before he arrived, when they first learned that Midway was going to be closing.

"What did you think of the program?" he'd asked her.

Gina had looked up at him as she worked, saying simply, "When you've been in the pit as many years as I have, you don't need those kind of classes."

"And how long would that be?"

"Fifteen years," she said.

He sincerely believed that she didn't need to be taught a thing. She certainly commanded the trauma center like it was an extension of herself. She knew every inch of that space, every piece of equipment, and could probably tell you what was in every drawer in every room, including the dispatch. Her hands moved with a flawless and economic grace that only came from years and years of experience. There was never a single wasted movement. She could smoothly insert a Foley catheter into the genitals of a flailing, coked-out gangbanger, or slip a butterfly IV needle into the hair-thin vein of a newborn baby with equal ease and finesse. Some of the staff appreciated it, while others resented her attitude of indispensability. She was a fixture whose presence permeated the trauma center every minute of every shift. Despite rumors that she was as insensitive as a clam, Dr Ferguson occasionally noticed small glimpses of compassion escaping the clamped edges of her chitin in the way she helped a patient sit up or even gave an injection. On the outside, she was sharp as a sterile scalpel blade, cool, calm, and utterly focused, but Dr Ferguson suspected there really was a deeply caring soul buried under all that cynical armor.

Gina also kept very close tabs on Dr Ferguson. She would raise her eyebrow at him, surveying his every action like a mother predator, watching as her off-spring toyed with an injured mouse. He could never tell if he was cutting the mustard or failing to measure up. She always kept her own council.

Tonight would be a true test of everything Dr Ferguson had learned. He had never operated under so much pressure before. This was his first Saturday night at Mercy and it was as if the streets themselves crumbled to admit the surging legions of hell into the trauma center.

In his quest to master the art of medicine, Dr Ferguson had spent many painful years learning to wad layer after layer of insensitivity around his core to keep the one thing that was once hurt from ever being hurt again. The agony of losing his mother to breast cancer when he was still in high school stayed fresh because he kept resurrecting his grief, allowing it to stumble-chase after him with arms outstretched. Someone should have been able to prevent it. Someone. No matter how slowly it lumbered, the only way to outrun it was to try to prevent history from repeating itself in any way, shape, or form. This way, even the cases where he merely healed, rather than saved, chipped away at his enormous emotional need to change the past. While he tried not to personalize every patient—every night he wiped their faces fresh of his mother's features—subconsciously he imprinted his own savior complex on each and every case he attended. That and the white surge of adrenaline drove him hard enough to go thirty-one hours straight without even realizing it. He had colleagues who went longer. He could surpass them as long as he kept caffeinated and focused. Frosty.

That was when the double glass panes slid open and three EMTs rushed through with a young Asian man on a rickety gurney that buckled when it hit the slightest rise in the floor. The EMTs slid the gurney straight towards Dr Ferguson, who jogged alongside them as he in turn called to Gina to page the trauma surgeon.

Scoop and run. A gunshot wound to the thoracic with possible trauma to the spinal cord. It was always best to grab the patient, slide him onto a gurney, and get him to the trauma center as fast as possible. Any time the EMTs spent performing any kind of intervention—including intravenous fluid resuscitation and routine arteriography—had proven useless over the years. As little as ten minutes made a tremendous difference whether the patient lived, died, or remained a paraplegic for the rest of his or her life. This one clearly had no friends or anyone else who was willing to drive him to the trauma center. He would have gotten to the center faster if they had. Such was the irony of emergency medical responses in the US, ambulances were better for cardiac arrest and overdoses. Not so great for gunshot wounds.

While this man looked so young and helpless, Dr Ferguson was relieved that at least the patient was not a child. Those cases were the hardest and as yet he had been spared that particular horror. If anything could shatter his newly molded, university-bred optimism, it would be to see an innocent little kid with a gunshot wound. He heard of things like that so often when they talked about this city—the gangs and the violent crime. Children jumping rope on the sidewalk just a little too close to the roar of a gangbanger's car as it slowed to make a hit... Nearly all of his colleagues had those kind of small tragedies arrive on their shifts. They were almost always DOA, shipped straight off to the county coroner. How could the paramedics stand to zip up one of those clear plastic body bags over the face of a child? A face that probably still bore faded traces of painted cat whiskers from an afternoon birthday party.

The trauma team was still working with the TBI that had just arrived, so Dr Ferguson took the vitals on the patient before him: a twenty-seven year-old Asian male, blood pressure eighty over sixty and dropping. The white gauzy layers of the pressure pad had been applied to his left pectoral to stop the bleeding, but his entire torso was slick with blood. Surely the internal bleeding was much, much worse. From the trajectory, it didn't seem as though he had been hit in the spine, but gunshot wounds by their nature usually involved multiple organs. On the Abbreviated Injury Scale, this one was definitely a four, as the bullet would have surely shredded the chest wall and possibly a lung. The patient's breathing was extremely shallow—significant respiratory distress. They had applied oxygen, but that wasn't enough.

"There's hypotension, but we think that's the only wound," the EMT said. He looked to be in his late twenties and he hunched his shoulders when he spoke. "Witnesses said he was attacked by several assailants and left for dead."

"Open cut down IV access kit," Dr Ferguson said to Gina. "Intubate him with a size nine orthotracheal and start crystalloid infusions."

He quickly stabilized the patient's cervical spine and then placed a thorascostomy needle between the patient's ribs just below the bullet wound to release trapped air inside the chest cavity that was preventing his lungs from expanding. There was a thin hiss of escaping air and the patient's breathing immediately improved. While Dr Ferguson assessed that it was unlikely the bullet had hit the patient's spine, something still felt profoundly wrong. There was no reason to think that he wasn't doing exactly what he was supposed to be doing. Still, the niggling doubt in his gut developed into a full-blown quarrel with his perceptions. As he examined and reexamined every inch of the young man's prone body, Gina swiftly began the tracheal intubation while another nurse miraculously appeared to assist and quickly retrieved the access kit from a nearby supply. A beat later, Dr Ferguson realized what was bothering him.

"Wait, where's his shirt?"

The retreating EMTs looked at one another with puzzled frowns and after some comedic shuffling, one of them finally produced the shirt in a sealed plastic bag. It had already been prepared as evidence for the police. They tossed it to Dr Ferguson, who ripped open the bag without a second thought and meticulously examined the large black T-shirt emblazoned with the Chemical Brothers logo. It had been sliced up the middle to remove it from his chest, carefully cut to avoid disturbing the gunshot area. Located right at the pectoral and singed with gunpowder, the entrance hole was sizable. Whoever shot him was using a .38, or better, and standing at close proximity. Dr Ferguson found a hole on the other side, confirming that it was a clean shot. It might have cleared the ribcage, but he couldn't believe it also cleared the scapula. Maybe it had. Still, something didn't sit right. He held the the badly bloodied shirt up to the greenish fluorescent light and turned it over to look for another bullet hole.

Sure enough, towards the bottom edge he found another hole where a bullet had passed through—a somewhat smaller hole than the one that had pierced his shoulder—but no second hole to indicate an exit wound. The wound was tiny and it could have evaded detection if it was clean enough. It was very possible that there was no external bleeding. He'd seen a similar case just the night before when a homeless junkie named Lindy showed up claiming to have been shot. At first the triage nurse did not believe her, since she was a regular visitor and well known to the staff as a compulsive liar, but on closer examination, she did in fact have a tiny, nearly bloodless hole in her left thigh. It was entirely possible that with a patient as bloody as this young man, there could be another, less obvious wound. In the load-and-go they could have easily missed it. They would have been entirely focused on providing oxygen and putting pressure on the showier wound with all the external bleeding. Dr Ferguson loosened the patient's black parachute pants waist and discovered a clean little part in his skin, which was yellowing and swelling. Soon it would be badly distended. The bleeding was minimal, but surely the internal hemorrhaging was considerable. The bullet had probably blown out his kidney and colon. If so, there was probably fecal matter everywhere inside the abdominal cavity.

"OR's backed up," another nurse interjected.

Dr Ferguson nodded, wadded up the shirt and stuffed it back in the evidence bag.

"Cut off his pants and X-ray him. We need a trajectory on this second wound in the lower abdomen."

There were two X-ray rooms on this side of the trauma center, and one next to the operating theater. Patients moved in and out fairly quickly, but the diagnostics of the film took some time. In this case, it seemed the patient was stable enough until the trauma team could take over and operate. The hypotension was responding to the pressure. He was taking the fluids well. As Dr Ferguson rattled off the list of pictures that would be required, Gina and the other nurse grabbed the gurney bars and IV stand to roll the patient into X-ray. Just before the gurney started to move, Gina raised a dark eyebrow at Dr Ferguson. It wasn't her usual cut of skepticism, but rather an almost appreciative look. Almost. Dr Ferguson knew she was tight with compliments, not just from rumors but also from experience. This was about as close as she got to admitting surprise that he'd not only made a good call, but brought a little something extra to the table. Then she lowered her eyes to help the radiologist prep the patient for the pictures, and Dr Ferguson wondered if he might not have imagined it after all.

TWO

Rhonda Seed first noticed the dead man at 2:27am on Friday night. The Roaches had been giving Rhonda a particularly hard time that day and it took her over three hours to find a safe path back to the abandoned warehouse that she had been using as a temporary sanctuary. Rhonda was thirty-two and looked easily twice that. She had been homeless for more than fifteen years, bounced from various underfunded mental health facilities to living on the street and back again. She was very dark-skinned and tiny with only seven teeth left in her head, all molars. The ones in the front had been smashed out with a pipe when she was attacked and nearly beaten to death at age sixteen. After that, the mind control devices implanted in everyone's front teeth at birth were gone and Rhonda was able to see what was really going on with the Roaches and that radio disk jockey, and all the franchise restaurants.

If she were shaved and stripped naked, she would have weighed only ninety-five pounds, as thin and fragile as a baby bird. But the seven layers of purple clothing (purple being the only color the Roaches couldn't see), each layer meticulously lined with scavenged bits of foil, combined with her nearly floor length, wrist thick and foil wrapped dreadlocks, added another twenty-five or thirty pounds and gave her a bulky, Eskimo silhouette.

Rhonda crouched below the broken window that served as an entrance to her safe house. She checked the seven bottles of urine she had left to protect the window and looked at the seven watches on her left arm. They were all set to different times in order to confuse the Roaches, but she knew the system and saw that it was actually 2:18am. That upset her, because she could only enter the safe house on times that ended in a seven and that meant she would have to wait out in the open for a full nine minutes.

It had been a bad luck day from the start. There was a new guy working at the soup kitchen and he had turned the radio to the station with that disk jockey while Rhonda was sitting there gumming her day-old muffin. Laura, the nice familiar soup kitchen lady who wore a purple scarf and was safe to talk to, was in the bathroom and was too late to stop him. The thick, roachy sound of the disk jockey's voice had caused Rhonda to projectile vomit almost instantly and she had run screaming out into the street, leaving a whole bag of foil behind. With the poison of the disk jockey's voice eating its way through the foil beneath her clothing and into her vulnerable body, the Roaches immediately started hounding her, chasing her through the streets and brushing their quivering antennae against her eyelids everywhere she turned. She hid in the park, laying very still beneath a bench with protective foil gum wrappers over her eyes. The horrible voices hissed and screamed and raged around her like a hurricane. Rhonda just lay there, concentrating on staying hidden and keeping very still, just like she used to do when she was a little girl. Her mother's wrath would fill their tiny apartment and Rhonda, and her little sister Kimmie would hide under the bed. Rhonda missed her sister. She was not allowed to see Kimmie anymore, after she had broken in to Kimmie's foster parents' house and tried to pull Kimmie's front teeth out with pliers so that she would be able to see the Truth. Now Kimmie was lost, just like everyone else who ate the franchise hamburgers and listened to that disk jockey.

Rhonda took a few minutes to replenish the bottles that were getting low and by the time they were all topped off, it was 2:27 and she was able to enter the safe house.

Once inside, the first thing she saw was the dead man. There was nothing roachy about him at all. He was just dead. He hung there, thick, creaking rope around his skinny neck and scruffy boots dangling six inches above the concrete floor. She only knew it was a man because he wore no shirt, scrawny concave chest conspicuously free of feminine curves. He had no body hair and his face was bland and genderless. His dark hair was cropped down to almost nothing and his skin, grayish pallor notwithstanding, was an utterly unremarkable medium beige tone that could be white or black or Latino, or maybe a mix of any or all of the above. His brown eyes were wide and staring, their surface filmed with a fine layer of dust.

Rhonda approached the dead man slowly, circling warily and checking him out from every angle to make sure he was completely free of roachy influence. Nothing about him posed any kind of threat whatsoever. He just swung gently back and forth, silent and unchanging, and so she left him like she found him and concentrated on shoring up the protective barrier around her inner sanctum.

Rhonda's inner sanctum was a child's fort of blankets and foil covered cardboard, protected from the Roaches by seven key objects arranged in a careful circle with the most sacred and critical item, a purple plastic number seven that used to be part of a video store sign, positioned right at the threshold. Some of the objects, like the jar full of slain enemies or the cracked picture frame holding a magazine photo of the disk jockey with his mouth torn out, were warnings. Others, like the doll head stuffed with foil or the cut crystal doorknob had significance so profound and so secret that even Rhonda was not allowed to know their true meaning. Each object had to be carefully marked with her urine every day to keep them safe from roachy influence. When each object was marked and safe, she crawled inside the inner sanctum and lay down on her nest of blankets. She never really slept, but she was able to stop thinking for a few precious hours, which helped to wash away the memories of that awful day and the lingering sound of the disk jockey's voice.

The next day, when she crawled out into the dusty warehouse, the dead man was still there, twisting in the weak morning sun as motes of dust drifted around him. He looked unchanged from the night before. Rhonda whispered good morning to him as she inspected and mended the foil layers inside her clothing and carefully pressed down any peeling foil in her hair. She waved goodbye at 6:07am and ventured down to the soup kitchen to see if it was safe.

Laura had saved Rhonda's bag of foil for her and the guy who put on the bad radio station was not there. On her way down to the park, a fat lady gave her five dollars and Rhonda was able to buy a whole roll of brand new foil, a grape soda and two safe, foil-wrapped candy bars. As she sat in the park on her favorite bench, sucking chocolate off her fingers and wrapping fresh foil around her feet, Rhonda decided that the dead man was a good omen. She wondered how long it would take him to fall apart and slide off the rope. Maybe she ought to keep his skull as a lucky talisman, once all the flesh came off. She used to have a lucky dog skull, but the Roaches stole it while she was locked up for visiting Kimmie.

The rest of the day was quiet and uneventful and she was able to return to her sanctuary earlier than usual, slipping through the window at 10:57pm. She stood at the feet of the dead man, looking up into his serene, unchanging face, when it occurred to her that he might have some important objects for her tucked away in the pockets of his threadbare and faded blue jeans. Change, matches or maybe some foil. She reached up and slid a tiny hand into the left pocket. Empty. She checked the two back pockets and then the right front pocket. In the right front pocket she felt a little book like the kind that men use to keep women's names and numbers in. She started to pull it out when the man's hand shot up and locked around her wrist.

She screamed at the top of her lungs, struggling fiercely against his iron grip.

"Rhonda Seed?" he said softly, sounding slightly befuddled, like someone who had just been awakened by the telephone. "It's not your time."

He let her go and she fled shrieking from the building.

Officers Daniel Pitchner and Alphonso Lopez were driving down Division Avenue when Lopez spotted Rhonda tearing out into the street like she was on fire. He hit the brakes, narrowly avoiding running her down. Pitchner squeezed his paper go-cup of Diet Coke in surprise and the lid popped off, dumping icy soda down his leg.

"Shit," Pitchner said, mopping his trouser leg with a handful of Seven-Eleven napkins. "What the hell is her problem?"

Pitchner was young and blond, good looking and worked out to within an inch of his life, barely able to contain all the bulging and superfluous muscle beneath his bulletproof vest. Lopez was older, tall and slender with a standard issue cop mustache and a mildly amused expression. He had been breaking Pitchner in for almost a month, and the kid was all right, though still a little cocky. Pitchner had yet to see any real "action" as he put it and often complained about that fact to Lopez during the long, uneventful nights. Lopez had seen far too much "action." He was glad to get a break.

Lopez pulled the car over and got out. "Rhonda," he called. "What's wrong, Rhonda?"

Rhonda sidled up to the car, eyes darting wildly up and down the street. "The dead man," she whispered. "The dead man grabbed me."

Pitchner got out of the car, rolling his eyes dramatically. "What dead man?" Pitchner asked, voice heavy with sarcasm. "Napoleon?"

"Knock it off," Lopez said out of the corner of his mouth. "What dead man, Rhonda?"

"The dead man hanging." She pointed back towards the warehouse. "I saw him last night at 2:27am and he was dead. That was last night. This morning at 6.07am he was still dead. But at 10:57pm, I tried to take his book and he grabbed me. That was 10:57. He grabbed me."

"You saw a dead man hanging in the old warehouse?" Lopez looked back at Pitchner. "A suicide?"

"He grabbed me," Rhonda said, holding up her skinny wrist as proof. "Right here. He grabbed me at 10:57."

"Damned fruit loop," Pitchner said.

Rhonda blinked and ducked her head as if Pitchner had slapped her.

"Hey, come on," Lopez snapped. He lowered his voice. "Rhonda's okay, aren't you honey?"

Rhonda nodded, still blinking rapidly. There were several Roaches on the other side of the street, but they were hanging back because of the cops so she pretended she didn't see them.

"Look, Rhonda, I got something for you." Lopez reached in the car and pulled out the piece of foil that used to contain his chicken salad sandwich. Her eyes lit up. "You want to show us where the dead man is?"

Rhonda took the foil, smoothed it out and folded it carefully before sticking it in her pocket.

"Okay," she said. "But I didn't do nothing wrong, right?"

"Right," Lopez said.

"Right," Pitchner said, rolling his eyes.

"Call it in," Lopez said. "Investigating possible suicide at 7117 Division Avenue."

Pitchner did as he was told and the two of them followed Rhonda around to the broken window, patiently waiting for it to be 11:07, and climbed in after her. Pitchner's massive shoulders could barely fit through the window and Lopez had to stifle a laugh, watching his young partner wriggle through and tumble awkwardly to the floor inside the warehouse.

As Pitchner stood and brushed off dust, Lopez spotted the dead man, just as Rhonda had described him.

"That him?" Lopez asked.

Rhonda nodded but refused to go anywhere near the corpse. Lopez stepped up to take a closer look. Even though Rhonda claimed he had been there nearly twenty-four hours, the corpse still looked very fresh, face smooth and perfect. None of the classic signs of death by hanging, the bulging eyes, the swollen tongue. Lopez was no detective, but he did not think this man had died by hanging. He wondered if someone might have killed the victim elsewhere and hung him here to make it look like a suicide. There were several crates nearby that could have been used to stand on, or might have been planted to shore up the phony suicide setup.

"Well," Lopez said. "Guess we better call in the dicks."

That was when the dead man's dusty eyes slowly blinked, fingers flexing cautiously and reaching out to brush Lopez's sleeve. Lopez was so startled that he stumbled back.

"Holy shit," he said. "He's alive."

"I told you," Rhonda said, pressing back against the wall. "I told you he grabbed me."

"Pitchner, help me get him down," Lopez said, pulling a Leatherman tool from his belt and sawing through the rope.

Pitchner came forward and lifted the man's slight body to give Lopez slack on the rope. When the rope was cut through and pulled off the man's neck, Pitchner laid him down on the cement floor while Lopez radioed for an ambulance.

"Daniel Pitchner," the man whispered, his voice raspy and barely audible. "The rookie cop. Right?"

Pitchner frowned. "You know me?" he asked.

"Don't worry," the man said. "You'll get plenty of action, Daniel. I promise."

"What are you talking about?" Pitchner backed away, wary and uncertain.

"Sir," Lopez said. "Just try to relax. Ambulance is on the way."

A wailing siren sounded in the distance, getting louder and louder.

"You'll get your wish in twenty-four days, Daniel," the man said. "But you won't see me again until next February when you finally decide you would rather take your own life than live the rest of your days severely disabled, incapable of lifting a weight or making love to a woman."

"Great, just what we need," Pitchner said, eyes wide and voice tight with forced humor. "Another damned fruit loop."

"Please, sir," Lopez said. "Don't talk. Just relax. Ambulance is almost here."

The paramedics arrived, swarming over the man like a race car pit crew. Lopez stood back with Pitchner. He could see the younger man was deeply disturbed by what the guy had said. That's when Lopez noticed that Rhonda had disappeared.

"Can you tell us what happened to you, sir?" a burly paramedic asked, shining a light into the man's eyes.

"I'm just tired," he replied.

"Sir, did someone do this to you or did you try to kill yourself?"

He did not reply, just quietly submitted to the poking and prodding of the paramedics.

"Can you tell me your name, pal?" the other paramedic asked.

The man wiped the back of his hand across his mouth. He shrugged.

"I'm Death," he said.

THREE

Dr Ferguson was stitching up an ugly, triangular scalp wound on a tiny Chinese woman so drunk that he was sure he was catching a contact high just from her breath. The cops had brought her in wearing a police windbreaker and nothing else. She was in her late fifties with a deep, raspy voice and she hollered in Chinese at the top of her lungs at anyone and everyone who came near her. She tried to grab Dr Ferguson's private parts more than once as he examined her, and he was eventually forced to restrain her. When Thu, the Vietnamese X-ray tech who spoke some Chinese, came in to assist with translation, she turned beet red and at first refused to translate the woman's vehement exclamations. Finally, when Dr Ferguson insisted, Thu ducked her head and looked away.

"She wants a man," Thu whispered.

Dr Ferguson frowned. "Excuse me?"

"She says her husband is cheating and now she wants revenge. She wants..." Thu turned even redder. "A big American doctor man."

Gina appeared in the doorway at that moment. "Excuse me, big American doctor man," she said, face smooth and deadpan. "I need to speak with you for a moment."

Dr Ferguson finished the last of the sutures, tossed his gloves and came out into the hall.

"We've got an attempted suicide," Gina said. "Probable psych admission, but get this, he asked for you by name. He won't talk to anyone else."

"That's odd," Dr Ferguson said.

"I can finish up here," she said, gloving up with fluid grace. "Go talk to the suicide."

Dr Ferguson bit his lip. Psych evaluation was completely alien to him. He was a medical doctor, interested only in human hardware, not the complex and tricky software.

"What should I say?" Dr Ferguson asked. "I can't just... ask him where it hurts."

Gina turned back to Dr Ferguson, her hard eyes warmed slightly by a spark of empathy for her younger colleague.

"Well," she said. "Put it like this: on a scale of one-to-ten, with one being slightly at odds with reality and ten being barking mad and ready to tear out into the street wearing women's underwear on your head and singing the theme song from *Cheers*, how would you rate your psychosis tonight?"

For a second, Dr Ferguson just looked at her cool, emotionless face and thought she might be serious. Then she smiled, just a little, and he burst out laughing. He and Gina both used the one-to-ten pain scale a hundred times per shift.

"Look," Gina continued. "All you need to do is establish whether or not he intends to try and do himself in again and if so, does he have the means to carry out that intention. If he answers yes to both questions, then he gets sent upstairs for three hots and a cot until the psych staff can legally evaluate him." She tipped her head down the hall. "He's in the pelvic room."

Dr Ferguson nodded and turned away. He wondered briefly why a psych patient was in the pelvic room, but as he walked the gauntlet of the jam-packed ward, every room filled and patients on stretchers pushed against the hallway walls, the answer was obvious. No room at the inn.

It made Dr Ferguson angry, people pulling this "cry for help" bullshit, taking up valuable space and staff time when there were so many patients in legitimate need. Dads with chest pain and sick babies, car accidents and gunshot wounds, innocent victims who were forced to lay out in the hallway while some guy whose girlfriend dumped him sits moping in the pelvic room.

These thoughts did not put Dr Ferguson into the most objective frame of mind as he entered the room where the psych patient was waiting. The man was thin and spare, with a smooth androgynous face and nasty, but superficial lacerations around his skinny neck. It was impossible to tell his age or race as he looked up at Dr Ferguson with bleak and weary dark eyes. He sat hunched over with his large, bare feet dangling between the stirrups on the gyno table.

"There you are," the patient said softly.

"Hello," Dr Ferguson replied. He picked up the patient's chart. John Doe, attempted suicide by hanging. Vitals slightly low, but still within normal range. No drugs or alcohol. "I don't think we've met. I'm..."

"Dr Jay Ferguson," the patient said. "And we have met, more than once. Only you don't remember me.

The ones left behind never do." The patient turned to absently study a chart demonstrating the various stages of development in the fetus. "Gina, she knows me very well. We're old adversaries, Gina and I. But she doesn't fight me like she used to. She knows how to let go when someone's time has come."

"Well," Dr Ferguson said testily. "Why wouldn't you talk to her then?"

"Because I want to talk to you, Jay." The patient turned back to him. "I've had it with all this dying."

"I'm sorry?" Dr Ferguson had no idea where this was going or how to bring the conversation back to the task at hand.

"I mean sure, there are some who are glad to see me." The patient looked back at the chart. "But even then, there are the loved ones who don't want them to go. It wears on me, all that hostility and anguish."

"Is that why you tried to kill yourself?" Dr Ferguson asked. "Because you are tired of death?"

The patient laughed, a small bitter chuckle. "I couldn't kill myself any more than you could crack your own chest, Jay," the patient said.

"So if you can't kill yourself, why did you put a rope around your neck?"

The patient shook his head. "I don't know. Some kind of foolish, masochistic self-punishment, I guess." He rubbed the palm of his hand over the deep purple groove in his throat. "I am... prone to fits of melancholy. I feel guilty. The other day, there was a car accident. I had to take a woman's unborn baby, her husband and her dog. All at the same time. Then while she was in the hospital, I had to take her fish and all her treasured African violets too. It's just not fair."

Dr Ferguson frowned. "What do you mean by 'take' her baby and her husband?"

"Take their souls," the patient replied. "Their life essence."

Dr Ferguson was becoming increasingly uneasy. Was the man talking about murder? Should he call the cops? Dr Ferguson felt utterly out of his league.

"You mean you killed them?"

"No," the patient said, shaking his head as if explaining something to a child. "The head-on impact with the drunk teenager's Mustang killed them. I just took their souls."

"But not the woman's?"

"It wasn't her time," the patient replied. "Believe me, I wish I had control over who I take. I know you understand what I mean. Remember, on your first shift, when that cop came in along with the guy who shot him? You got the shooter and you had to save him, just like any other patient. You had no choice. Just like I had no choice about taking the cop. It was his time, not the shooter's. You and I, we're just doing our jobs."

Dr Ferguson remembered it all too well. The shooter had been conscious and belligerent, shouting and cursing and demanding a lawyer. He was high on every controlled substance known to man, covered in bad prison tattoos and already sporting more than one healed bullet wound on his muscular chest. Not a nice man. The guy was holding steady and then suddenly started crashing. His heart went V-fib and Dr Ferguson stood over him, holding the paddles and thinking: what if I just... don't?

Of course he did and the guy's heart got right back into the groove on the first try, just like kicking a skipping jukebox. The guy was fine. Dr Ferguson was not and had to go stand outside the sliding glass doors alone for a few minutes before he could face the furious cops waiting to hear how the son of a bitch who shot their brother was doing.

"Well, then who is it who decides who will live and who will die?" Dr Ferguson asked the strange patient. "Who chooses? God?"

"Don't ask me," the patient said. "I have no idea whose hand is on the crank of the big lotto machine in the sky. I just read off the numbers."

Dr Ferguson could not believe he was allowing himself to get sucked into this conversation with a patient that was clearly profoundly disturbed.

"I remember the very first patient to die here at Mercy," the patient said. "Heart attack. His name was Bill Breem. He didn't want to go and cursed me eight ways to Sunday. He fought like a bear, but in the end he came along quietly, just like they all do."

"Dr Ferguson!" It was Annie, the triage nurse, poking her head in from the hallway.

Dr Ferguson went to the door. "What's up?" he asked.

"We got another incoming trauma," Annie said quietly. "Seventeen year-old black male with a sucking chest wound."

"Okay." Dr Ferguson nodded and turned back to the psych patient. "I'm afraid I have another patient to attend to. If you'll excuse me, Mr..."

"Death," the patient said. "But don't worry, I'm not taking that kid yet."

FOUR

It was a hairy and furious battle, but eventually the black kid was stabilized and ready for the OR, and a brief lull like the eye of a storm found Dr Ferguson standing dazed and silent in the hallway near the nurse's station. Gina strode past the young resident with a pair of urine samples and Dr Ferguson called out to her.

"That suicide in the pelvic room," Dr Ferguson said. "He says he's Death. He's tired of taking souls and wants to take a break."

"Great, guess that means we can retire," she said, bagging the urine to be sent down to the lab.

"He said the kid with the sucking chest wound would make it." Dr Ferguson rubbed his eyes. "He said, 'I'm not taking that kid yet.'" Weird, huh?"

"I oughta talk to him about my stock portfolio," Gina said, turning to walk away.

"Gina?" he asked. "Just out of curiosity, do you know the name of the first patient to die here at Mercy?"

Gina turned back and shook her head. "No, but I could look it up," she replied. "Why?"

"No reason," Dr Ferguson said.

Another nurse named Irene arrived at the station, stretching up on her tiptoes and twisting at the waist.

"My back's killing me tonight," she said. "Dr Ferguson, there's a severe laceration on the buttock in three. Don't ask how it happened, just stitch the poor guy back up, will you?"

Dr Ferguson nodded, turned and headed down the hall. Gina watched him go, wondering for the hundredth time if he was going to be able to cut it. He was blond and handsome, body fit and lean beneath his bloody scrubs. He looked more like some soap opera doctor than a real ER grunt, but he had been consistently levelheaded and reliable in the midst of the firestorm of trauma, multitasking like a pro and staying frosty when things got hot. The only time she saw him crack was when they lost, when all the multitasking and quick thinking in the world couldn't put Humpty Dumpty back together again, and Dr Ferguson had to make the call. There had been several times when Gina had to put her hand on Dr Ferguson's arm as he was elbow deep in a cracked chest, furiously squeezing a dying patient's heart as if he could bully it into beating again with the sheer strength of his will. She had to look into his eyes and shake her head, and she could see that it killed a little piece of him each time he had to let go and admit defeat.

Gina had learned that lesson years ago. When she'd first started at Mercy she'd seen death as an enemy to be thwarted at all cost. Not so much to make the family happy or to save a life, but just to win, to achieve victory every time. Like a video game. If the patient died thirty seconds after they left

the ER, it didn't matter to Gina. If they were paralyzed for life or succeeded in their next attempt at
suicide, it didn't matter. All that mattered was that
they came in to her ER dying and left alive. When a
patient came in with a self-inflicted shotgun wound
to the face, the front third of his head churned into a
ghastly stew of red nothingness, but still horribly
conscious and aware, she worked right alongside the
trauma team to save the life the young man had tried
so hard to take. Even with years and years of agonizingly painful reconstructive surgery, he would never
be anything close to normal. The only blessing, if
you could even call it that, was that his eyes had
been destroyed so he would never be able to see the
monster that he had become. Yet when they rolled
what was left of that boy out of the ER and into
surgery, Gina and the cocky Indian resident working
with her at the time had high-fived with blood-
gloved hands, congratulating themselves for yet
another victory over death.

Fifteen years later, Gina saw things differently.
Sometimes letting someone die was infinitely more
compassionate than dragging them kicking and
screaming back from the brink. No one would ever
accuse Gina of being softhearted. She was a hardened
combat veteran with armor a foot thick, but she
understood that a patient was more than just the sum
of their injuries. Sometimes the best thing for them
was to simply let them go. It was not an easy lesson
to learn and in learning it, she knew that she had lost
her optimism, her youth and the thick coating of
polite ignorance so many people use to protect themselves from the ugly truth that waits for every last one
of us.

When Gina had first started working at Mercy, she was thirty years old, married with a three year-old daughter and an active social life filled with other young professional couples and their children. Her husband, Matteo Ciavarella, was a handsome, northern Italian architect who loved her dearly and worshipped their daughter, Danica. Her marriage was passionate and solid and they had a lovely home in a respectable, upscale neighborhood. Everything was storybook perfect for the little girl who'd grown up as the forgotten eighth child of a huge extended Catholic family living in a tiny row house in Sunset Park, Brooklyn—the girl who went to nursing school because she wanted to help people.

Her first shift in the horrific gore-drenched war zone of Mercy's ER had been a true trial by fire. The twelve-hour shift brought in one critical trauma case after another. Gina struggled to keep her hands and nerves steady, imitating the older, more jaded nurses she idolized. But when a little three year-old girl came in with a gunshot wound to the head, a girl in pink footie pajamas with curly, dark hair just like Danica's, Gina started to crack. The child had been playing happily on the floor in front of the television when a stray bullet smashed through the window and slammed into her temple. Her anguished father had carried her into the ER in his arms, blood soaking the shirt of his brown UPS uniform. She died while Gina was struggling to get an IV line started, and Gina was still trying to find a vein when the doctor took her hand away from the tiny arm and squeezed it gently.

"She's gone," he said softly, and Gina dropped the unused butterfly needle to the ground, her whole body numb and cold.

She watched the doctor walk out into the waiting room to give the father the bad news and saw the man's face slowly cave in with incomprehensible grief. The man, a big strapping fellow with broad biceps and the face of a roguish hero in a Spanish soap opera, sat down in one of the plastic waiting room chairs and began to cry silently. There was no one else there with him, no other family, no one to comfort him—not that there was any kind of comfort that could be offered in such profound depths of sorrow—and Gina could not stop her own tears from coming. She called Matteo and made him wake Danica up so that Gina could tell her own daughter that she loved her.

After that, something changed inside Gina. She stopped thinking of the patients as people. She referred to them only by their injuries; sexual assault with head trauma in room two, chest pain in four, gunshot in five. They became nameless puzzles to solve; theoretical decision trees with a simple binary outcome of win or lose, life or death. She found herself totally unable to relate to her friends and acquaintances in the outside world. People who lived in happy bubbles, where the worst thing that could happen to their child would be a scraped knee or a failed test—people who believed that God looked after drunks and little children. Gina saw plenty of both in the trauma center and they died right alongside nice old grandmas and stone cold gang bangers. There were no such things as miracles, only sweat and steady nerves, and the occasional totally baffling and utterly random coincidence. Bad people lived and good people died. A guy with a six-foot long piece of rebar through his skull healed up with nothing but a pair of quarter-sized scars and a great story to tell his grandchildren while a woman who slipped in the shower would never walk again. There was no guiding hand, no benevolent, heavenly Father in the sky watching over us all. Any dregs of childhood Catholicism that might have clung to Gina were sandblasted away in that first year at Mercy, leaving her empty and cynical, totally incapable of carrying on a "normal" conversation with her vapid and shallow friends.

She would find herself cornered at one of the parties thrown by Matteo's firm, surrounded by earnest blond yuppies who would go on and on about how they "just love that ER show" and wanted her to tell them all about her cool exciting job. What could she possibly say to them? How could she take the daily litany of misery, cruelty and ugliness, and turn it into witty, PG-rated anecdotes to entertain these clueless, button-eyed muppets who skipped happily through life without ever seeing a person with no lower jaw, projectile vomiting through the hole in their face or having to clean the last earthly shit off the legs of a corpse?

In the ER, social niceties were a hindrance to getting the job done. The time it took to add the word "please" to a sentence could mean the difference between life and death. Everyone spoke in stripped down, staccato commands and replies. Gina found it increasingly impossible to function in the world of "Would you be so kind," "Thank you very much" and "Have a nice day." Worse, she found herself withdrawing from her family.

Weekends and holidays were the busiest times at Mercy, and Gina was rarely, if ever, able to get a weekend off. She worked three Christmases in a row, showing up at home battered and exhausted the next day and trying to seem interested in presents, and candy canes and Santa Claus, all the while able to think of nothing but the families who would not be celebrating, children whose shiny wrapped presents sat unopened beneath the Christmas tree because they had chased a ball into the street or played with matches or daddy's gun or because they just didn't wake up on Christmas morning.

Gina saw that her marriage was crashing, the vitals weaker and weaker every time she crawled into bed beside her sleeping husband. Her sex life was comatose, unresponsive. She could no longer stand Matteo's cheerful and frivolous romantic nature, all the roses and kisses and lovey-dovey words that had first won her heart now seemed so empty and foolish, soft and sugary lies that meant nothing in a world where you could lose everything in the blink of an eye. She was not even remotely surprised when he filed for divorce, asking for sole custody of Danica. Of course there was someone else, a pretty young photographer who specialized in sappy portraits of babies and pets. Gina did not fight, did not ask for a cent. She quietly moved into a studio apartment closer to the hospital and changed her name back to Scavone.

She had occasional affairs, short but fierce sexual collisions with men as cynical and armored as she was. Police. EMTs. The closest thing she had to a relationship was with a combat photographer named David Lind who had done tours of Bosnia, Rwanda and Iraq. They saw each other several times over the course of two years, sharing cigarettes and a blistering, black sense of humor. She saw a profound humanity in his horrifying images of violence, grief and death. She also saw a kindred soul. He taught her how to walk the line between compassion and detachment, how to tolerate the intolerable with humor and grace, and how to see the humanity beneath the bloodshed—that faint shimmer of hope in a sea of hate and fear. David was killed by friendly fire in Afghanistan, but Gina never forgot him. It was because of him that she was able to rekindle her relationship with Danica.

Gina realized that she had kept her own daughter at arm's length because of the possibility that something could happen to her. She never could have admitted that before she lost David, but she understood that if her daughter died as a stranger, that would be a thousand times worse than loving her and losing her. It was not easy at first. Dani was bitter and hostile, angry at having been emotionally abandoned, but she was older now and more able to understand her mother as a fellow human being. Gina took two weeks' vacation to spend time getting to know her then fifteen year-old daughter. The girl was smart, creative and witty, swiftly growing up to be a real heartbreaker. She had Gina's thick, dark hair and determined chin, combined with Matteo's clear blue eyes and winning smile. She wanted to be an actress and had already done several commercials along with some print modeling. Gina had no doubt that Dani could do anything she set her mind to.

Together, Gina and Dani drove up the coast, along with Dani's dog Cody, a sweet natured mutt with only one eye that Dani had rescued from the pound. They spent a lot of time on deserted beaches and walking through silent primordial forest, just enjoying being together. There were tears, but there was also a new understanding forged during that time. Gina went back to Mercy with a renewed determination to make things better for the people under her care.

Fifteen years after that first shift, Gina was still there, still at Mercy. There was no doubt that she was a lifer, addicted to the adrenaline rush of saving lives. It was grueling and awful, but it could also be wondrous and amazing. She could not conceive of doing anything else.

Gina went to assist the new kid with the laceration on the buttock. She normally had very little respect for doctors and even less for callow interns who were just doing time in the ER until they could get a "real" job in some cushy suburban practice. Rich med school mamma's boys who turned green at the first sight of the less romantic bodily fluids. Then there were the doctors who were too high and mighty to empty a bedpan, or hold a dying child's hand. Doctors who were irritated to be dragged out of bed for some hostile felon with no insurance, who treated the nurses like servants whose job was to wipe their asses and hang on their every word. But this new kid, this Ferguson, he seemed like he could have potential. This was his third consecutive shift and he was still holding steady. His clever call on the abdominal gunshot showed a meticulous and quick-thinking nature. Only time would tell if he would be able to survive this bloody and chaotic madness and find a way to make it his own.

Gina found Dr Ferguson stitching up a long, deep vertical slice in the firm and perfectly muscular buttock of a very chagrined-looking young man. The tableaux of a handsome, blond doctor hunkered down and serious over the ass of a young man on his belly with his hospital gown bunched up around his waist struck Gina as preposterously funny. They both had such painfully straight expressions on their faces, as if to make sure every one in the world could see that this was perfectly normal and not what it looked like at all.

Dr Ferguson was done and stepped back to allow Gina to give the kid his meds and follow-up info. When she was done, she walked over to the young resident and looked up at his tired face.

"How are you holding up, Jay?" she asked.

"Fine," he said, pinching the bridge of his nose between his thumb and forefinger.

"If you want to grab a few minutes in the call room..." Gina said.

"Sleep is for pussies," Dr Ferguson said, grinning. "I'll just get some more coffee."

Gina nodded and watched him walk away. He was going to be fine.

FIVE

Dr Ferguson was sitting alone in the staff room, yet another sludgy cup of awful coffee in his hand, staring out into nothing. Every detail of the shabby room seemed over-bright and unreal. He was so far beyond tiredness that he was feeling close to hallucination when Gina strode purposefully into the lounge, poured a cupful of the vile brew and tossed it back like a shot of whiskey.

"NT in room five," she said, then turned on her soundless rubber heels and left.

Dr Ferguson's veins flushed with ice and he was suddenly very awake. NT. Nonaccidental Trauma. That was obtuse medicalese for abuse, usually to a child. The last NT that came in had been an infant, scalded from the chest down. The sullen teenage mother had casually admitted to Dr Ferguson that she had in fact dunked the baby into scalding water on purpose because, "He cries." It took every ounce of willpower not to take the scissors he was using to cut the dead and dying skin away from the screaming baby's hideous burns and plunge them into the uncaring mother's carotid artery.

Dr Ferguson stood for a moment outside room five, struggling to smooth down his cool professional exterior. When he pushed the door open, he found a pretty, light-skinned black woman in her mid-thirties and a very thin, very small six year-old girl with frizzy blonde hair in four stubby braids. The child was white as a sheet and shined with sweat, two bright blotches of red on her cheeks. She had splashes of vomit on her hospital gown and there was a very full basin at the foot of the examination table. Her green eyes were dull and half-shut. She sucked her thumb in silence.

"Doctor," the woman said. It was obvious that she had been crying. "You gotta help my grandbaby."

Dr Ferguson frowned. Grandbaby? This woman was far too young to be a grandmother.

"That's what I'm here for," Dr Ferguson said. "What's your name, sweetheart?"

The little girl said nothing, just stared at Dr Ferguson as if she did not speak English.

"Her name's Diamond," the grandmother said. "She been hurt."

"I see," Dr Ferguson said. "Can you tell me what happened to her?"

That was when Dr Ferguson noticed the burns. The little girl had six perfectly round burns on her left arm. Clearly made with cigarettes. Dr Ferguson swallowed hard.

"My daughter Celia, she's on the pipe," the woman said, tears starting again. "I tried and tried to help her, but she can't stop. I beg her every day to let me take Diamond and then tonight, she must have left her outside my building because my neighbor, Mrs Peña, saw Diamond just sitting by herself on the stoop."

The woman pulled a crumpled tissue from her purse and dabbed her eyes. "She's got marks. And a fever. She won't stop throwing up."

As if to demonstrate this condition, the kid let loose another volley of clear yellow bile into the basin and then put her thumb back in her mouth.

"Okay, Mrs..." Dr Ferguson checked the chart. Diamond Day. Jeez what a name. "Mrs Day. I'm going to examine Diamond's body now. I may need to take some photographs as well in order to file a report of child abuse. Do you understand?"

"Ms," she said.

"Huh?"

"It's Ms Day," the woman said. "But you can call me Lita."

She dissolved into loud, braying sobs. "I'm sorry, doctor," she said. "It's just... well... CeCe's not a bad person. She just fell in with a bad crowd and got caught up in the drugs."

Dr Ferguson nodded, silent. It was not his place to judge, only to diagnose. He removed the child's hospital gown and was appalled by what he saw. Her pale, bony body was covered in a rainbow of bruises. There were long thin U-shaped marks that looked like they might have been left by an electrical cord doubled in half, and more burns, some old and healed, some oozing and fresh. The child submitted to Dr Ferguson's examination with absolutely no reaction whatsoever.

Dr Ferguson carefully noted all the apparent injuries and their locations on the chart, burying his emotions in technical jargon.

"Okay, Diamond, Lita," Dr Ferguson said, clearing his throat. "I'm going to get a lady nurse to help me take some photographs and then I will need to examine..." He struggled not to stutter. "The vaginal and rectal area."

"Is that really necessary?" Lita asked, hand pressed to her mouth. Diamond said nothing, just sucked her thumb.

"I'm afraid so," Dr Ferguson said. "I'll be right back."

Dr Ferguson found Gina assisting with the insertion of an IV into a shrieking, cursing eighty-five year-old woman. When she had succeeded she turned to Dr Ferguson with an arched brow.

"Rape kit for five?" she asked.

Dr Ferguson nodded wordlessly, amazed by the older woman's near telepathy. "Who's on call for Pediatrics?" Dr Ferguson asked as he struggled to keep up with Gina's brisk stride.

"Cohen," Gina replied. "I'll have him paged."

He grabbed the digital camera from the cabinet in the nurses' station while Gina made the call and then together they headed back to room five. Dr Ferguson could not shake a sick kind of dread that had taken up residence in the pit of his belly.

Gina swiftly cleared out the full basin and replaced it just in time for another bout of vomiting. Then they shot meticulous photos of the bruises and burns and finally, Gina broke open the rape kit while Dr Ferguson helped Diamond lay down on her back and gently removed her pink Barbie underpants.

Dr Ferguson exhaled sharply through his nose, struggling to keep his reaction subterranean.

"Trich," Gina said, handing Dr Ferguson a sterile swab without missing a beat.

Trichomonas vaginalis: a virulent bacterial infection, a venereal disease common in women with poor hygiene and multiple sexual partners. There could be no doubt that sexual abuse had occurred. Dr Ferguson was sickened and infuriated. Who could do something like this to an innocent child? It was one thing to read about it in a textbook, but something all together different to witness the ravages of sexual abuse first-hand. He clenched his teeth and swabbed the area carefully, returning the swab to Gina to bag and send down to the lab.

"What's wrong with her?" Lita asked, her voice tightening into a prelude to hysterics. "What's wrong with my grandbaby?"

Dr Ferguson struggled to put the facts into the most delicate terms possible, but when comprehension started to dawn on the woman, her face went scarlet with rage.

"You saying somebody did sex to my grandbaby?" she asked.

"I'm afraid so," Dr Ferguson said.

The woman exploded into a volley of curses more vehement and colorful than a gut-shot gangbanger. Dr Ferguson just stepped back, unable to respond. Diamond continued to suck her thumb in silence.

Dr Cohen arrived then, looking exhausted and rumpled and sporting a jaunty SpongeBob Squarepants tie. Gina tried to calm the grandmother while Dr Ferguson filled Cohen in on what had transpired. Cohen ordered intravenous antibiotics started right away and talked softly to Diamond about SpongeBob while Dr Ferguson filled out the rest of the forms and left to contact the child abuse councilor on duty, a chubby Hispanic woman, also coincidentally named Lita. On his way out, he found he had to pause and lean back against the wall.

There was something about that little girl that disturbed him deeply. It was not just the fact that she had been abused, though of course that was part of it. It was her total lack of reaction to anything that was happening around her. Dr Ferguson had seen dying patients with more light in their eyes than that little girl. The scalded baby had screamed in pain and fury, fighting to live with every breath in his tiny body, but the little girl was like a walking corpse. It was as if something inside her had died along with her innocence. Yet again, Dr Ferguson found himself thinking of the human software, the patient inside the flesh and bone. They could cure her infection and heal her injuries, but would the girl inside every really be better? Would she laugh and play, grow up and pick a dress for her prom, find healing love and maybe have a child of her own? Issues like these were too vast, too complex to even consider. Dr Ferguson knew instinctively that the only way to keep his sanity in check was to stay focused on the task at hand; to black out the big picture and concentrate only on the here and now, the forms, the medications, notification of correct agencies and authorities. He needed to do his job and do it well. No more and no less.

SIX

It was 4:00am. Hour forty. Dr Ferguson had just finished giving his report to the police for the NT case and was seriously considering going to lie down for a few minutes in the call room when Gina pulled him aside.

"The suicide in the pelvic room's pulled a Houdini," she said. "Annie didn't see him leave so my guess is he's still somewhere in the hospital. Any idea where he might have gone?"

Dr Ferguson shook his head. Everything around him now seemed dull and muffled, and his limbs and eyelids were leaden. He was having trouble tracking Gina's words.

"Oh, and one other thing," Gina said. "Bill Breem."

Dr Ferguson's head snapped up at the mention of the familiar name but at first he could not remember where he'd heard it before.

"Who?" he asked.

"Bill Breem," Gina repeated. "First man to die here at Mercy. There were a couple of DOAs before him, but he was the first to go here in the hospital. Heart attack. May third, 1968."

Bill Breem. The patient who thought he was Death had mentioned the man's name. Dr Ferguson thanked Gina and walked away, slowly shaking his head. Well, it was no secret. Hospital records weren't exactly public but it was not impossible to gain access. The patient must have looked the man's name up. No surprise there.

That brought Dr Ferguson to the question of where the patient could have gone. As exhausted as he was, it did not take long for him to deduce where the wannabe Angel of Death might have gone.

The Mercy Hospital's morgue was in the basement of the building, far removed from the bright, cheery public areas of the hospital. There were no cute and educational posters, no artificial plants, no soda machines or chairs, just a dull green hallway ending in double doors. A blunt dead-end, the ultimate dead end, Dr Ferguson supposed. He pushed through the doors and found a chipper redheaded pathologist busily rifling through the wide-open abdomen of a black male cadaver. It had not been one of Dr Ferguson's patients.

The pathologist turned and gave Dr Ferguson a warm, flirtatious smile that seemed totally at odds with her current task. "Hey there," she said. "What can I do for you, doctor?"

Dr Ferguson pressed the back of his hand to his lips. He felt inexplicably nervous talking to an attractive woman and he realized two things almost simultaneously—the fact that he had not showered for almost two days running, and the fact that he had not been on a date in over a year.

"This may sound odd," Dr Ferguson said. "But I've got a missing psych patient and I have reason to believe he might have come down here. I believe he has an unhealthy fixation on death."

The pathologist nodded thoughtfully. "Funny," she said, gently removing the stomach from the cadaver and emptying its contents into a steel basin. "My mom said the same thing about me."

For a moment, Dr Ferguson just stood there, feeling like an awkward teenager at a school dance. He wrinkled his nose at the appalling odor as the pathologist sifted through the stomach contents, trying not to show his distaste in front of a colleague, especially not one so attractive.

"Well," she said softly. "What do you know?"

She held up a wrinkled, knotted condom.

"That was inside his stomach?" Dr Ferguson asked, curious in spite of himself.

"Tell me, doctor," she said. "Why would a young man want to swallow a condom?"

"Drugs?" Dr Ferguson suggested.

"Bingo," the pathologist said. "COD was a massive heroin overdose. Clearly he meant to pass the condom full of dope at a later time. Unfortunately for him, the condom burst and... that's all she wrote."

Dr Ferguson nodded, unsure of how to respond.

"So you haven't seen anyone down here?" he asked instead. "A slender, dark-haired guy in a hospital gown with ligature marks around his neck?"

"Haven't seen a soul," she said. "Well, nobody alive anyway, but you're welcome to check in the meat locker if you like. I sometimes get caught up in my work and don't pay much attention to the world around me. Somebody could have slipped past."

"Thanks..." He realized that he didn't know her name.

She looked up at his pause and smiled. She really was very pretty, with milky pale skin and a scatter of freckles across her upturned nose. Wide green eyes and slender gold hoops in her delicate earlobes. Her body was thin and boyish beneath her white coat and her curly red hair was caught away from her face with a toothy, clear plastic clip.

"My name is Megan McDermott," she said, eyes sparkling with mirth. "My quiet friend here is the late Reginald 'Lil Ace' Lindo."

"Jay Ferguson," Dr Ferguson replied, smiling back.

"Resident?" she asked.

He nodded.

"Well," she said. "Welcome aboard, Dr Ferguson."

"Thanks," he replied.

He stood there smiling like a dope for several seconds before he remembered the reason that he'd come down in the first place.

"So you think my AWOL patient might be in the..." Dr Ferguson paused. "Meat locker?"

"Oh yeah," Megan said, indicating a heavy steel door at the far end of the room with her chin. "Back there. Though if the guy you're looking for is wearing one of those skimpy, backless hospital gowns, I doubt he would want to spend more than a minute in the meat locker."

"Thanks again," Dr Ferguson said, heading for the indicated door.

Sure enough, he found his patient inside, standing quietly over a sheet-covered body, one of many on stretchers. All around him were row after row of vaguely human forms, nothing visible but pale waxy feet sporting colorful toe tags. Behind him there was a wall of human-sized steel drawers. It was cold, deathly cold, and Dr Ferguson could see his own breath in the still, chilly air. The patient looked up at Dr Ferguson but said nothing.

"I thought I might find you here," Dr Ferguson said.

"Why is that?" the patient asked, eyes narrow and suspicious.

"You know, being Death and all."

"Don't patronize me," the patient said sharply. "I don't come down here any more than you do. By the time a person arrives in this place, both your work and mine are already done. I'm here now because I find it... peaceful. There's nothing for me to do here. Everything is already taken care of. Loose ends all sewn up." The patient placed a hand on the sheeted body before him. "Look at Rachel Silverberg here. She fought me tooth and nail all the way. She was dying for years. AIDS. She was an artist and an activist, a passionate woman who was a great inspiration to others. She fought and fought, tried every medical poison and voodoo cure, vitamins and visualization, herbs and acupressure, and in the end, she spit in my face and cursed me. Told me to go fuck myself, can you believe that?"

Dr Ferguson couldn't imagine what to say to that so he just shook his head.

"It wasn't my fault that she was sick, that it was her time. I didn't plan her demise, I was just taking care of business." The patient shook his head. "Everyone wants to shoot the messenger."

He walked away from the body of Rachel Silverberg and laid a hand on her neighbor.

"Lucinda Carmichael, on the other hand," he said. "She was a piece of cake. The kind of death everyone wants. Ninety-one years old and still walking to the park every day. Surrounded by beloved grand and great grandchildren, she just looked up and me and said, 'Well, okay then.' I wish everyone could be so calm."

He walked across the room to another sheet-covered cadaver.

"Even the ones who think they want to see me often change their minds when the time comes. Like Jesse Bailer here. Tormented by voices, haunted by childhood abuse, Jesse ripped his wrists open with a jagged piece of plastic from a smashed videocassette, begging me to come and take away his pain. Then when I show up at the appointed time, was he grateful? Did he shake my hand and smile and say how glad he was to see me? No. He looked into my eyes and he started to cry. He said he was afraid. He wanted to know what was on the other side, if the voices would be there too. What was I supposed to tell him? I've never been to the other side. I have no idea what's over there. Heaven? Hell? A fresh start or empty black oblivion? How should I know? What am I, a tour guide for the afterlife? I'm just the conductor. Watch the closing doors and have a nice day. But I'll tell you, Jay, I'm sick of this one-way train. For once, I just want to look into someone's face and watch them breathe and blink then watch them walk away, whole and unharmed. I want people to say hello to me then go do something else. I need a vacation."

Dr Ferguson arched an eyebrow. "So what you are saying is that you are going to stop taking people's souls?"

"Yeah," the patient said. "Not just people, everything. And not forever, just for a few weeks. Even trauma junkies like Gina take a vacation every now and then. I haven't had a vacation in over two billion years. That's billion with a B. You think Saturday nights at Mercy are busy, try working through one of the great extinctions."

"Two billion, huh?" Dr Ferguson said. "You don't look a day over five hundred million."

"Laugh it up, wise ass," the patient said. "This..." He pinched the flesh of his cheek between a forefinger and thumb. "This is just the standard uniform I wear so you humans won't be any more scared than you have to be."

Dr Ferguson nodded, trying to look thoughtful and understanding while attempting to figure out how to talk the patient into coming back up to the ER and allowing himself to be admitted. He really had a fascinating delusion, quite baroque and well thought out. He was going to make a very interesting case study for someone in the psych division.

"Well," Dr Ferguson said, trying to humor the patient. "Sounds reasonable to me. Everyone deserves a break. Besides, I'd love it if no one had to die for the rest of my shift."

"Really?" The patient eyed Dr Ferguson warily, trying to determine if he was getting his leg pulled or not.

"Absolutely," Dr Ferguson replied. "Who wouldn't want their sick and injured loved ones to live instead of die? Any doctor would agree. What is the point of my job if not to save lives?"

"Man," the patient said. "I can't believe someone finally sees things my way."

"So can I get you to come back upstairs and fill out some paperwork for me?"

The patient smiled. "Sure thing, doc."

On the way out they passed the pretty red-haired pathologist stapling closed the Y-shaped cut on the black teenager's torso.

"Found him," Dr Ferguson said.

She looked up, thin red eyebrows pulling together in a puzzled frown.

"That's your guy?" she asked. "I swear I never saw him come in."

"Don't worry, Megan," the patient said. "You won't see me again for quite some time."

In the hallway outside the morgue, Dr Ferguson turned to the strange patient. "How did you know her name?"

The patient shrugged. "You like her, huh?" he asked.

Dr Ferguson blushed. "Well..."

"I know, with a life like yours it's hard to meet women and harder still to maintain a relationship." The patient looked up into Dr Ferguson's eyes. "But take it from me, you better seize the goddamn day. You may never have another chance."

Together they stepped into the elevator and Dr Ferguson pushed the button for the ground floor.

"You said she wouldn't see you for some time." Dr Ferguson looked back at the double doors to the morgue as the elevator doors slid shut. "Does that mean you know when and how she will die?"

"You really want to know, Jay?" the patient asked. "I don't think so."

"Why not?"

"Would you have wanted to know about your mother?"

Dr Ferguson turned sharply towards the patient as the doors to the ground floor opened. "What do you know about my mother?"

The patient shrugged again. "Look," he said. "I'm on vacation now. Let's not talk about death anymore. Let's talk about the weather. Or how about sports? What's your favorite team, Jay? Do you like the Lakers? The Knicks? Or are you a Bobcat man?"

Dr Ferguson rolled his eyes in frustration. He could not believe he'd allowed himself to be sucked in yet again by the strange patient and his curious delusions.

"If you'll just wait here," Dr Ferguson ushered the patient into an empty exam room, "I'll have a nurse come in and help you fill out the paperwork that will allow you to be admitted."

"Admitted?" The patient ran his fingers through his short hair. "You mean to the loony bin?"

"Our psychiatric facility is state of the art."

"I don't know if I really want to spend my vacation at the loony bin. I was thinking maybe..." The patient looked off into space. "The beach or something, I don't know."

"Look," Dr Ferguson said. "I have some other patients to attend to right now. Just sit here and think about it for a little while and then the nurse will be in to help you decide, okay?"

"What's your hurry, Jay?" the patient asked. "I told you no one is going to die."

Dr Ferguson smiled, suddenly feeling very, very tired. "Right," he said. "Guess I'll see you later."

"You bet," the patient said. "Oh hey, that reminds me."

Dr Ferguson turned back and frowned as the patient dug in his pocket.

"I meant to give you this," he said, handing Dr Ferguson a small black address book. "I won't be needing it."

"Thanks," Dr Ferguson said and turned to go.

The little book was packed with neat block letter names. Dr Ferguson flipped casually through the gilt-edged pages. There were names of every ethnicity and nationality including many written in cyrillic, arabic and kanji. He shrugged and slipped the little book into the pocket of his scrubs. After several minutes of standing pointlessly in the hall staring at the cracks in the linoleum, Dr Ferguson decided he needed to go sack out in the call room for a few minutes before he fell over or amputated the wrong foot.

SEVEN

Laying in the dim, quiet call room, sprawled across one of four narrow hospital beds no different than the ones in the patients rooms, Dr Ferguson could not seem to make his exhausted mind stop racing. One of the attending physicians, a fast-talking New Yorker like Gina with a long white braid and a thick, stocky body, lay curled on her side on one of the other beds, catnapping with her glasses skewed on her face and snoring softly. Dr Ferguson could not get that strange patient out of his mind. It was odd that he seemed to know so much, even going so far as to mention Dr Ferguson's mother. There was no way he could have known about her and what she had been through. Must have been a lucky guess. As Dr Ferguson lay there not quite asleep and not quite awake, drifting in a loose net of tangled memories, he found himself remembering his mother and the terrible, inevitable nightmare of her death.

Karen Ferguson had had a chance at one point, but she hadn't realized it soon enough. The mammogram found several small lumps, two in the left breast and three in the right. When the oncologist performed the biopsy, his mother still would not admit the possibility that she was in the advanced stages of a life-threatening illness. He would lie awake at night in his bed, listening to his mother talking on the phone with relatives when she thought he was asleep. He knew she had gone back to the doctor, that she had had some more tests, but she would not tell him anything more. When he asked, she would always answer: "Well, now the doctors don't exactly know yet. Just wait until they finish all their poking and prodding. I'm sure by then they will know."

But his mother began to deteriorate rapidly during the poking and prodding. Soon, even he could see something was very wrong with her. What had started as a casual cough turned into an uncontrollable hacking that doubled her over. She sometimes had to sit down when an attack came on. His mother had never smoked in her life, and was rarely sick at all. She didn't even have any allergies that he knew of. When he found the wastebaskets filling with bloodied Kleenexes, he confronted her. He was fifteen, not a little baby. He was part of this family too and demanded that he be included. That was when he started coming to the hospital with her again.

The last test indicated that his mother had lung cancer that had metastasized to her breasts... and her lymph nodes. It was only a matter of making her comfortable enough until the time came.

She fought it at first. She secured approval from the insurance company for a second opinion and found another oncologist—one a little older, more experienced, a Lutheran like his mother's family.

But after several more tests, he said the same thing: go home, make preparations, and rest until the end.

His mother refused to lay down and die. She was a tough woman who had weathered many personal tragedies. A childhood car accident that destroyed her left leg from the knee down and put her through years of painful physical therapy and recovery as she became accustomed to the new prosthetic limb. The death of her beloved husband three months after Jay was born. She struggled financially to make ends meet, wanting the best for her only son. Jay had overheard her telling her brother that she simply could not die until after her precious Jaybird graduated from college.

She had been contracted to write a textbook about teaching special needs children and instead of lying around, she worked every day on the book, talking frequently with her editor about the details of each chapter. She provided him with a thorough outline and a full list of references. In her own way, Jay supposed, she admitted what was coming.

When the relatives began visiting shortly thereafter, she welcomed them. Her brother, who was a struggling comedian and playwright from New York; her sister in Austin to whom she had not spoken since The Incident at Christmas in 1982; aunts and uncles, nieces and nephews. He didn't realize there were quite so many relatives and wished that they had been there all along, like his mother's cousin Holly, who lived in Orlando for several years before moving to an adjacent county for a paralegal job with a major firm that specialized in workers' compensation. Karen and Holly were very close friends. However, she didn't tell cousin Holly the

truth about her condition right away, and Jay was
certain that Holly's feelings were hurt by this omis-
sion, just as his had been. In spite of that, Holly did
not hesitate to move in with Karen and Jay to help
manage things around the house, make sure Jay
still did his homework and ate something other
than Snickers and Poptarts for dinner. It did not
help Jay's tumultuous state of mind that Holly was
ten years younger than his mother and stunningly
beautiful with sleek, waist-length dark hair and a
flawless hourglass figure. In the depths of his sorrow and fear for his mother, he would catch a
glimpse of Holly dashing from the bathroom clad
in only a towel, damp skin pink and fresh from a
shower, and he would suddenly be drenched in
thick, swampy desire so powerful it was almost
nauseating, followed swiftly by tidal waves of con-
fusion and guilt.

Meanwhile, the parade of relatives continued. They
whisked his mother away to the movies, the park, the
Grand Canyon. To high-class and trendy restaurants
she could never have afforded to eat at. When she
wasn't in obvious pain, she seemed to enjoy herself
much more than he would have dreamed possible.
Still, he and Holly were the ones who watched her
fade into the bed sheets. Soon, she was unable to get
out of bed at all.

They eventually hired hospice care, turning the
master bedroom into a sickroom. The pretty, antique
brass bed was taken apart and put into storage, and a
hospital bed was installed. Relatives still came, but
now they stood silent vigils by her bed as she slowly
lost consciousness with a steady morphine drip
lodged in her arm. She did not seem to be in pain at

all, although at times she reached for people, half-lidded and semiconscious, opening her mouth wide to make shapeless, breathless sounds.

Jay almost could not bear to be at home, but he could not bear to be away, either. He fantasized endlessly about some confident, Marcus Welby-looking doctor in a clean white coat who would stride through the door and say in a deep, clear voice: "Don't worry, son. I'll take care of everything."

The doctor would have some test, some obvious but overlooked procedure and he would give Jay's mother a pill or injection then she would smile and hug Jay and everything would be okay. Needless to say, that never happened.

It made Jay angry that his mother would not go back to the hospital. He did not understand how she could just give up. While she could still speak, she had said that she did not want to die in a hospital. She hated hospitals, ironic considering her only son would wind up endeavoring to spend all of his adult life in hospitals and it was his mother's death that would inspire him to do so. Because of her, he would strive to become that confident, lifesaving doctor that he had wished would show up and save her. Without a doubt, those torturous four weeks of watching his mother deteriorate changed the course of Jay's life forever.

Before her illness, he had vague thoughts of joining a band—he was a passable guitar player with a love for rowdy punk rock—or maybe becoming a writer and hitchhiking across the country in some neo-beat literary adventure. But afterwards, he knew there was nothing else that he could do, but dedicate his life to saving lives, to making sure that no one else had to feel the pain he felt that day, the day his mother died.

She died in the late afternoon, a picture perfect autumn day, crisp as a fresh apple and warmed by the scent of burning leaves. Jay was home, sitting at the kitchen table and staring blankly at a sheaf of pointless homework, when Holly entered the kitchen and placed her hands against her cheeks, staring at the counter, and he knew. He just knew. Jay stood slowly and walked with the horrible inevitability of a nightmare down the long dim hall to the master bedroom.

The door was ajar. Inside his mother's room it was dim and stuffy. In one of her last spells of coherence, she had asked Holly to draw the curtains and that was how they'd stayed. It was as if she could not stand to watch the outside world go on without her. There was music playing, a soulful Cuban jazz CD that was one of her favorites, and she lay there on her bed, just as she had when he had come in to check on her twenty minutes earlier. She was nothing but skin and bones beneath her red flannel pajamas and colorful Peruvian shawl, curled on her side with her knees drawn to her chest like one of those mummies found in the Andes mountains on National Geographic. Her blonde hair had gone totally silver in the past few months and it lay spread across her pillow in a thin greasy tangle. Her mouth hung slack and gaping, her eyes were slanted, not quite closed but not quite open. He could see the blurry hemispheres of her unseeing blue irises beneath the wrinkled lids. There could be no doubt that she was dead. In the space of a single breath, she had gone from being his living mother to a lifeless object: a cool, solid lump of matter as meaningless as the bed beneath her. The woman who raised him and made his favorite curried tuna salad, who tucked him into bed at night and taught him that whatever didn't kill you made you stronger, that person was gone forever. The complex dance of electricity and mysterious chemicals inside her brain that added up to Karen Ferguson was over, the stage on which they had performed rapidly deteriorating into organic slush right before his eyes.

The hot, brutal anguish that hit him at that moment literally doubled him over and he collapsed backward into the chair Holly had placed beside the bed. He wanted to scream and howl and cry, but the huge and searing grief had cauterized all other emotions. Jay was paralyzed, unable to move or speak. In his darkest heart, he had wished for this day to end her suffering, and more selfishly his own, but now that it was here, he felt as if a part of him had also died.

Holly must have come in and taken him out of the room, but he had no memory of that or anything else that followed. He simply found himself lying on the couch alone in a dark house. His mother was gone, her empty room somehow worse without her. Windows were wide open, the stale dying smell washed clean by the cold night wind. It hit Jay then that she really was gone, gone forever, and the decision to go to medical school came complete and fully formed in his mind precisely at that moment. Standing in his mother's empty room, surrounded by things she would no longer need, he knew that he would become a doctor.

From that day on, nothing else mattered to Jay. Dating, social life, all those things went by the wayside in his almost obsessive quest to be accepted at UNC-CH and graduate at the top of his class. The occasional woman that he became sexually entangled with never lasted more than a few weeks. He simply didn't have time to invest in anything like a relationship, and few women could tolerate his single-minded ambition. He had sex with the same preoccupied and careless speed as he ate, showered or brushed his teeth, just another nagging physical need to be handled as succinctly as possible so that he could get back to his studies.

He stayed in touch with Holly, who was there at his graduation with tears in her eyes. She hugged him tight and told him his mother would be proud.

Then he took the residency at Mercy and he began to realize the true nature of death, to look into the eyes of the dying over and over again as he battled to save them, to make up for not being able to save his mother.

It was becoming clear to Dr Ferguson that no matter how tired he was, there would be no sleep that morning. It was now 5:30am. There was always a slight lull in the very early morning. The time when the drunk drivers and knife fights, the partying and full throttle fury of the night before, started trickling away to the last and most determined, but before the road rage of the morning commute got going and people started having chest pains over their Wheaties or realizing that something was very wrong with the baby. It didn't matter. That strange patient had really gotten under Dr Ferguson's skin. In spite of his profound exhaustion, he could not sleep. He slowly stood and pressed his thumb and forefinger into the inner corners of his eyes, shook his head, and went in search of more coffee.

As he downed a lukewarm cup of the awful staffroom coffee, immediately pouring himself another, he found himself thinking again of the strange patient and his claim that he would not be taking any more souls. It had surely been a quiet hour since he'd made that preposterous claim. Dr Ferguson imagined what it would be like never to lose another patient. To never have to see the desperate hope extinguished in the eyes of anxious family members. To know that never again would he or anyone else feel the way he had felt that afternoon when he lost his mother. It would be wonderful. A miracle.

As he left the staff room, he found himself laughing out loud, shaking his head. He could not believe he was seriously considering such a ridiculous concept.

"Don't worry," Gina said. "Laughing out loud for no reason is perfectly normal during the final hours of four back-to-back shifts."

Dr Ferguson turned to face the nurse. She was calm and alert, dark hair flawlessly coiled at the nape of her neck and a faint ghost of a smile on her lips. He did not know how she did it. He felt like he had been chased by stampeding bulls for forty-one hours and undoubtedly looked like it. She was composed and unchanging, no sign of weariness or fatigue in her dark eyes.

"You know," Dr Ferguson said. "That crazy suicide, the one who thinks he's Death and says he is going to stop taking souls, I swear he almost had me believing him for a minute."

Gina smirked. "Keep laughing," she said, putting a tightly rolled copy of the morning paper in his hand.

Dr Ferguson glanced at the paper. There was ordinary mundane news, nothing to catch the eye. He frowned. "What?"

"Check the obituaries," Gina said.

It took a minute for Dr Ferguson to find them. The reason they were so difficult to find was that there were none. Just a short note from the editor beneath the standard obituary heading that stated that for the first time in the history of the newspaper, not a single obituary had been received that morning.

"Well, not everyone who dies gets an obituary in the paper," Dr Ferguson said. "Poor people, homeless people, all the John Does and unidentified remains, they are never listed."

"I know this is your first weekend at Mercy," Gina said. "But this was the first Saturday night that I can remember where we didn't lose a single patient. No DOAs, nothing." She raised her hands near her face and made a spooky noise. "Weird, huh?"

"You don't seriously believe this guy?"

"I don't believe anything, kid," Gina said.

Annie came striding over to where they stood. "Well, can you believe this?" she asked. "We've got a thirteen year-old with severe abdominal pain. Parents brought her in. She's five two and three-hundred and ten pounds."

Gina whistled. "Let me guess," she said. "Pregnant?"

"Give that woman a cigar." Annie shook her head. "The kid's waters broke in the waiting room."

"Jesus," Dr Ferguson said. "She had no idea?"

"She says she only had her period the one time." Annie said. "She thought she was too young to get pregnant."

Gina laughed. "Well," she said to Dr Ferguson, "shall we?"

The pregnant girl was so grossly obese that she could barely walk. Her shoulder length hair was lank and blonde and her tiny features were nearly lost in the center of her vast face. Dr Ferguson found himself thinking unkindly that he could not conceive of anyone willing to engage in the act that got her into her current state of advanced pregnancy in the first place. But as she lay there gasping and sobbing on the pelvic table, she grabbed one of Dr Ferguson's hands in her chubby fist and looked up at him with tears rolling down her massive cheeks.

"I'm awfully scared, doctor," she said, and he felt like a heel for being so judgmental.

"You're going to be fine, Jennifer," Dr Ferguson said. "Women do this every day, all around the world. Just keep breathing."

Dr Ferguson sat on a tiny rolling stool between her elephantine thighs and caught the slick red infant as it came barreling out into the world as if shot from a cannon. It was a girl, healthy and squalling with a full head of thick black hair.

When the young mother saw it her eyes went wide. "Is that real?" she asked. "Is that my baby?"

Dr Ferguson laid the infant on her enormous belly and she put her thick arms around it. "It's real," Dr Ferguson said.

He stepped back and Gina swiftly took over, speaking quietly to the tearful girl and her anxious mother.

As Dr Ferguson stood over the sink, washing his hands, he thought again about the lack of obituaries. Drying his hands swiftly beneath the dryer, he was struck with an idea.

Megan McDermott picked up on the first ring. "Morgue," she said. "You kill 'em, we chill 'em."

Dr Ferguson laughed. "Morning, Dr McDermott," he said. "Jay Ferguson here."

"Jay," she said, sounding pleasantly surprised. "How goes the good fight?"

"Astonishingly well, actually," he replied. "Listen, this may sound odd, but have you had many bodies come down last night?"

"Funny you should ask," she said. "There've been none since the OD. I was starting to feel unloved."

"Don't you think that's peculiar?" Dr Ferguson asked.

"Stranger things have happened," she replied. "But yeah, it's a little odd, especially for a Saturday night. Why?"

"Oh, no reason," he said. He thought again of the strange patient and the things he'd said. "One other thing."

"Shoot," she replied.

"I hope you won't think this is presumptuous," Dr Ferguson said. "But I was wondering if you might want to, well, go out some time. With me."

"What," she said. "On a date?"

"I mean," he stuttered. "I understand if you're busy or have a boyfriend or something, I just..."

"I'd love to," she said. "You off at noon?"

"Yeah," he replied.

"How about a little breakfast before you crash?"

"Sure," he said, a big goofy smile spreading across his face.

"Okay then," she said. "I'll let you get back to keeping people out of my morgue."

"Great," he said. "See you later."

He found himself holding the phone long after she had hung up, staring off into space. All the thoughts of death and dying were eclipsed by visions of the red-haired pathologist and the thin gold hoops in her pale earlobes.

EIGHT

The execution of Robert Vine was to be Lucius Cosper's first. Lucius was fifty-one, tall and rangy with steel gray, slicked-back hair and a thoughtful, quiet nature. He was not a grandstanding macho bad-ass like so many of his fellow correctional officers, yet something in his eyes and the way he carried himself told those around him that he was not to be taken lightly. He rarely had to ask the inmates to do something more than once.

He had been working death row at the Nebraska State Penitentiary for just over seven years when Warden William Enquist approached him to see if he would consider taking on the difficult job of executioner after the retirement of the current man, a solemn and deeply religious Native American named Frank Water. Lucius said that he would have to think it over. He was not an impulsive man, and he wanted time to weigh the pros and cons, to talk it over with his wife and be sure it was the right thing to do.

His wife Inez had listened thoughtfully to his concerns as she always did. She had been raped as a teenager, an event that rendered her unable to have children. Her boyfriend at the time had been murdered after being forced to witness her rape. Her assailant received only life in prison. Inez was a passionate supporter of the death penalty.

They had been married for twenty-four years. Lucius loved her fiercely and trusted her judgment. She put her arms around him, brushed back a stray lock of hair from his forehead and told him she thought it was a good idea.

The special training course required to take on his new duty was fairly simple and straightforward, treating the taking of human lives as a no-nonsense, cut and dried task just like any other. The warden personally congratulated Lucius on his completion of the course and said that he was very pleased to have Lucius as part of the team.

Lucius and the execution team had run through the "mock" execution the night before, making sure Lucius was ready and knew exactly what to expect. Nebraska was the last state in which the electric chair was the sole means of executing death row inmates, and the procedure required a complex series of maneuvers to make sure that everything went smoothly and according to the book. Phone lines were tested and tested again and they ran power leads from Ol' Sparky into a large plastic barrel of water, hitting the juice for a full minute and testing the charge to be sure it remained within the expected range of three to ten amperes. Everything was perfect and went off without a hitch, but Lucius knew it would be different when it came time to put the juice to a living, breathing human being.

It would not be the first time that Lucius had taken the life of another man. He had shot and killed two inmates during the riots back in Tecumseh, but both of those men had been actively trying to kill Lucius and his fellow guards and would have succeeded if Lucius hadn't put bullets in their brains. While Robert Vine was unquestionably a bad man and a convicted murderer, his crimes had been committed long ago, perpetrated against people Lucius had never met. It was one thing to protect yourself and the ones you love. It was a whole different story to kill a man in cold blood who had never done a thing to you.

Lucius had reviewed Vine's file, just to remind himself of why he was doing what had to be done. In 1992, Robert Vine had murdered a young waitress with the unlikely name of Silky Fassbinder. There was a photo of Silky. She was blonde and sweet-faced with a gap in her front teeth, big plastic earrings and the sort of frizzy, teased-up perm that had been popular back then. She was nineteen and worked at a burger joint with a 1950s theme. She had dated Vine for several months, and then for reasons known only to the deceased, she decided she did not want to continue the relationship. According to witnesses, he had been harassing her for about a week, calling endlessly and following her around, begging for another chance. Then, on July thirteenth at 9:45pm, he had followed her to her car after work and confronted her in the parking lot of the burger joint. When she refused to speak to him, he had pulled out a gun and shot her in the face. She clung to life for three horrible, agonizing days before she finally died.

Vine had been a quiet prisoner in the seven years Lucius had known him. He was heavyset and morose with thinning, mousy brown hair and thick glasses

that magnified his large blue eyes. He read compulsively and his cell was filled with books on every kind
of subject. He had several pen pals and contributed
regularly to various prison literary projects. He was
an atheist and always refused visits from the chaplain. His last meal had been some weird French thing
called foie gras. Lucius thought maybe it was some
kind of liver, but he'd never heard of it. He did have
to admit that it smelled pretty good.

Vine had no family to speak of and his only visitor
the night before had been one of his pen pals, a
chubby little thing with a purple streak in her curly
brown hair and far too much eye-make up. She came
all the way from Scottsbluff to see Vine for the first
and last time and she had dressed up in a flowing,
black velvet dress and high-heeled boots. She cried a
lot when she left and Lucius had given her his handkerchief. She returned it covered in gooey black
mascara and asked if Lucius had ever read any of
Vine's poetry. He told her he hadn't. She told him he
should, that it was really beautiful. Lucius didn't think
it was a good idea to read the poems of a man he was
about to execute but he told her he would just to make
her feel better. She had no idea that it would be Lucius
who would put the juice to her doomed poet.

When the time came to fetch Vine from his cell, to
shave the crown of his head and his right leg from
knee to ankle and escort him to the shower, Lucius
was beginning to feel a bit uneasy. He told himself it
was natural to feel anxious the first time. He had gone
to lunch with Frank Water the day before and the
older man had given Lucius some pointers, patting
him warmly on the shoulder and assuring him that he
would be just fine. He said that it was only human to

feel anxious, but that he should take comfort in the fact that the true outcome for Robert Vine was not up to Lucius, but in the hands of the Almighty.

Lucius watched Vine slowly dress in the prison issue clothing for his execution—underwear, socks, trousers and a shirt. He was not given shoes. He did not seem overly frightened, just tense and silent. The chaplain made one last attempt to talk to Vine and the prisoner thanked him politely, but told him he required no spiritual council.

Lucius left Vine then and went into the execution chamber. The electric chair was just as it had been the day before, just as it had been every day since 1923 when it was introduced as a humane alternative to hanging. It was constructed of thick, sturdy oak and bolted to the concrete floor through a black rubber mat. It was really just a piece of equipment, built by human hands to perform a distasteful task, but there was something about Ol' Sparky that made it seem ominous and sinister in the brightly lit execution chamber. Almost as if it understood its killing nature and was looking forward to its date with Robert Vine.

Lucius looked away, concentrating instead on watching fellow guards Ed Schoen and Lamont Teaberry mix the thick salty brine and dunk the two sea sponges that would help conduct the current into the body of the offender. Lucius remembered reading about this and other details of the execution process while studying for his test. The man about to die was always referred to as "the offender," never by name. Not the man, the person, the poet, the lover, the son, the brother. Just "the offender." As if a man's crimes wipe away everything else he had ever been, everything he might become. Within minutes, Lucius would be pumping 2,450 volts of killing electricity, not into lovesick poet Robert Vine, but simply into "the offender." Vine would be masked, faceless, just another piece of the execution puzzle, like the sponges and the conductant gel. Lucius struggled to put the chubby girl and the poems and the foie gras out of his mind and concentrate on doing his job.

The offender was escorted into the chamber. He paused for a moment and his eyes found Lucius. He was squinting a little, since his glasses had been taken away, and there was a glint of raw fear beneath the thin veneer of nonchalance. Lucius was horrified by how young he looked.

Warden Enquist read off the death warrant and asked the offender if he cared to give a last statement. The offender shook his head, a quick, terse shake and dropped his gaze to the ground.

The escorting guards quickly left while Schoen and Teaberry sat the offender down in the chair, removed his wrist restraints and strapped him in, cinching the brown leather straps around his chest, lap, forearms and wrists. Then the leg restraints were removed and his ankles strapped down tight. His right pant leg was rolled up to the knee and Teaberry applied the elecro-conductant gel and then attached the leg piece to the offender's right calf, the smaller of the two brine-soaked sponges placed between his pale shaven skin and the metal face of the electrode.

As Teaberry worked on the leg, Schoen placed a dollop of gel and the larger sponge on the offender's shaved scalp, strapping down the headpiece and securing a snug fit, then wiping the dripping brine from the offender's face with a pristine white towel.

Again, the offender's eyes found Lucius and this time
the fear was hotter, sloshing over the edges of the
tough guy routine. Lucius figured right about now the
truth of the situation was really sinking in for that
kid. He knew this was it and he was terrified. Lucius
was deeply relieved when the black leather mask was
pulled down over those scared blue eyes.

Schoen and Teaberry hustled quickly from the
room, leaving Warden Enquist, his deputy warden, a
fat, sullen man named Kenneth Orr, and his adminis-
trative assistant Stanford Nest, a short and grizzly old
bird three weeks shy of retirement. Also present was
the prison physician, Dr Paul Fine. He was a deeply
cynical and jaded bastard whose other duties con-
sisted primarily of stitching up shiv wounds, treating
VD and filling out paperwork explaining how the
bruises and contusions found on the body of an
inmate could have easily been caused by struggling in
restraints, rather than by contact with the gun butts
and billy clubs of the blameless guards. And there
was Lucius of course.

Warden Enquist picked up the phone and made the
obligatory call. There were no stays of execution. He
put the phone back in its cradle and nodded to Lucius.
Lucius nodded in return, closing the safety switch and
engaging the circuit breaker. He put his hand on the
execution switch, taking in a deep, shaky breath.

The offender sat completely still and silent, like
some display in a wax museum. Faceless and inhu-
man beneath the black leather mask. The warden
raised his hand, eyes on the clock. When the second
hand hit twelve, the warden brought his hand down
and a cold spike of adrenaline shot through Lucius's
chest. He pulled the switch.

Lucius had read plenty about what happened next. An automatic four-part cycle is initiated, starting first with a high jolt, then a longer period of lower voltage and a pause, followed by a second round of higher voltage, then low. Altogether, the cycle lasts a grand total of precisely sixty seconds. One single minute. Of course, nowhere in the book did it mention how horribly long that one single minute would seem as Lucius stood there watching the offender twitch and shudder in the chair. There was a sound not unlike the sound of frying eggs on a short order grill as the tiny room began to fill with thin smoke and the stink of burning flesh. Blood drooled from beneath the mask, staining the offender's clean white shirt. He defecated noisily, his desperate, dying body ridding itself of last night's foie gras and adding to the stomach-churning stench. The horror show continued as the second hand made its lazy trip around the face of the clock. When it hit the half-way point there was a pause, during which the offender slumped forward, gasping, chest heaving. Then the current hit again and his body clenched, spasming and twisting in his bonds.

Lucius had planned to look away during this minute and think about something else. A trip he was planning to Acapulco as a surprise for Inez on their twenty-fifth wedding anniversary; a spy novel that he had just purchased and was looking forward to reading; that old primer gray '63 Mustang that he'd been tinkering with on his days off and what color he would eventually want it to be. Simple things that occupied his mind on long boring shifts, but standing there in the execution chamber, he couldn't think of a single thing. He couldn't take his eyes off the jittering, swollen and smoking form of the offender. The dying man: Robert Vine.

The seconds stretched into centuries and Lucius just stood there, transfixed and horrified. He kept on reminding himself of what Water had said about the judgment of the Almighty. This dying man before Lucius had felt no remorse or regret when he had taken the young and blameless life of Silky Fassbinder. It had taken her far longer than sixty seconds to die and her family continued to suffer to this day with grief and loss and the painful reminders of what might have been. When Vine's sixty seconds were up, he would have the Lord to answer to. Lucius's hands were clean. He was doing the right thing. It had been out of Lucius's hands since the day Vine pulled the trigger. This was justice. No more. No less. Lucius banished the man's name and history from his mind again and concentrated on doing his job.

Lucius swallowed hard and saw the second hand make its final crawl back up to twelve. The juice died back and the offender's body slumped forward again. Lucius closed the safety switch and disengaged the circuit.

The offender's fingers twitched. He sucked in a wet, shuddering breath and then began to pant like a dog, more blood dribbling from beneath the mask.

Lucius had been prepared for this eventuality. Offenders often required more than one cycle of juice to meet their maker. Water had told him that it was fairly common with some of these tough old boys and that he shouldn't let that get to him. Really they were as good as dead already, only their black little murdering hearts didn't quite seem to know it yet. Just stay calm, stick to protocol and give the SOB another round. Water had told Lucius about a huge, muscle-bound rapist and murderer named Don Solano who had survived three rounds in Ol' Sparky before finally submitting to the current. It was really nothing to worry about, just part of the job. What Lucius was not prepared for was the wait.

There was a mandatory wait of two minutes for the body to cool enough for Dr Fine to examine and pronounce it dead. If the offender was still alive, they could not hit the juice again until the doctor could officially confirm this fact. If Lucius thought the sixty seconds were long, the ensuing two-minute wait for the cool-down was close to intolerable. The offender was gasping and choking, gurgling blood beneath the mask. No one spoke. They all just stood there, not meeting each other's eyes, waiting. The offender's arms and legs had swollen to the point of bursting, ripping the seams of his sleeves and trousers. His broken fingernails clawed at the wooden arms of the chair. They waited.

When it was finally time, Dr Fine strode in and made a cursory examination, pulling on rubber gloves and using his stethoscope to listen for the pulse still defiantly beating in the offender's chest. He nodded to the warden and skittered back, putting as much space as possible between himself and the smoking offender in the space of the small room.

Warden Enquist in turn nodded to Lucius. Lucius took in another deep breath and reinitiated the procedure, shutting the safety and reengaging the breaker. On the warden's signal, he hit the execution switch a second time.

A horrible, muffled yowl like a cat in a pillowcase echoed through the room as the offender's head burst into flames. There was nothing they could do until the cycle was complete so they had to just watch him burn, pressing themselves back against the walls and exchanging nervous glances. The smoke was thicker now, the stench unbearable.

The moment the cycle ended and the safety was opened, Lucius grabbed the nearby fire extinguisher and drenched the offender with flame suppressant foam. They all stood there, enduring the two endless cool-down minutes in stunned silence. Then the warden put a hand on Lucius's shoulder.

"Good job, Cosper," he said. "Doc?"

Dr Fine stepped up to the blood and foam splattered form in the chair and first listened, then felt for a pulse in the lobster-red wrist.

"No pulse," the doctor said. "Call it 5:24am."

"5:24am," Nest repeated, scribbling on his clipboard and then handing the death certificate over to Fine for his signature.

Teaberry and Schoen returned to remove the body from the chair. They had removed the chest strap and one wrist strap when the offender gave a huge, whooping gasp and flailed out with his now free hand, nailing Schoen squarely in the crotch. Schoen doubled over and staggered back while Teaberry cursed and grabbed the flopping arm, buckling it back into the strap.

"He's not dead, you asshole!" Teaberry shouted at Fine, wrestling to fasten the chest strap again. "What are you, deaf?"

Fine spluttered and swore and the deputy warden turned and walked chalk-faced from the room. Loud retching sounds were clearly heard in the hallway before the door could click shut behind him. Warden Enquist struggled to keep the situation under control.

"Cosper," he said, his voice still deep and authoritative but with an edge of tight-laced panic. "Prepare for another cycle."

Lucius nodded grimly and forced his hands to move across the board, performing the required tasks. He found himself thinking of Don Solano. Next to Solano, Vine was a marshmallow, a bookworm. It was unthinkable that he would duke it out for three rounds with Ol' Sparky. But Water had assured him that it could happen, and Lucius took his word for it. Lucius had never lost his cool in the fifteen years he'd worked as a Nebraska State correctional officer and didn't plan to start now.

The warden signaled Lucius a third time, and for the third time, Lucius hit the juice.

There was no sound from the offender this time, just that cheerful frying sound, a happy morning sound like bacon and eggs that was so utterly out of place in this room full of smoke, stench and tightly contained madness. They all watched as the offender bucked and shuddered in the grip of the current and they waited breathlessly for the cool-down minutes to pass.

"Jesus," Teaberry said softly.

Schoen said nothing, just stood, back against the wall, eyes huge and ringed in white.

"That had to do it," Warden Enquist said.

He was wrong. Before the doctor could get close enough to the body to check for a pulse, the offender began struggling in his restraints again, screaming breathlessly beneath the mask.

"Do something for Christ's sake," Teaberry said.

"Again," the warden said.

Lucius gave the offender two more rounds with the current. As he danced, spit and suffered, every man in the room was slowly becoming unraveled. Warden Enquist developed a tic beneath his right eye, clenching and unclenching his fists. Nest was pale as ice, bending his pen back and forth until it abruptly snapped in half, blue ink gushing like the offender's blood. Teaberry was cursing louder and more violently. Schoen just stood there cupping his wounded testicles, eyes dull and shell-shocked. Only Lucius stayed cool, hands doing their jobs as if they belonged to someone else.

After the fifth cool-down, the offender's skin was as black as coal with wet red bone showing through in several places. His clothing was burned to rags. The doctor approached warily, stethoscope in his shaking hand. He placed it on the offender's black and crispy chest.

"Nothing," the doctor said.

"Not a minute too soon," the warden said, wiping sweat from his wide pale brow.

The doctor leapt back with a surprised grunt as the offender shuddered and began to struggle feebly again.

"Oh, you have got to be kidding!" Teaberry said.

"There's no pulse," the doctor said, backing away from the offender as if he were contagious. "I swear it."

The warden yanked the stethoscope from around the doctor's neck and listened to the offender's chest. When he heard nothing he threw the stethoscope to the ground and tried to feel the offender's wrist. The warden yanked his hand away, hissing as if he had just touched a hot iron.

"Goddamn it," the warden said, his face going a deep, angry red. "Well, now what the hell are we supposed to do?"

"With all due respect, sir," Lucius said. "May I suggest that we remove the offender from the execution chamber at this time and run some tests on the equipment. Clearly equipment malfunction is the only possible answer for what has occurred here today."

The warden looked at Lucius like he was an alien who had just stepped out of a flying saucer. Then he blinked and rubbed the back of his hand across his mouth.

"Right," he said. "Right, equipment malfunction. Nest, get the electrician down here right away. Teaberry, Schoen, will you please remove the offender."

"But sir," Teaberry said, eyeing the twitching black mess strapped into the chair. "He ain't dead."

"I am well aware of that fact, Mr Teaberry," the warden said. "Just do as I say. Put him on the stretcher and move him into the hallway while we get to the bottom of this equipment malfunction."

"But sir..."

"Just do it!" the warden snapped.

Teaberry tentatively stepped up to the chair and the offender gave a fierce shriek, slamming his skull back against the chair and skewing the electrode strapped to his head. Teaberry flinched and staggered back.

Up until that point, Schoen had been motionless and silent. When he heard that shriek, it was as if he had been hit with the juice himself. He stiffened, eyes huge in his head and, to the amazement of everyone in the room, he drew his sidearm and emptied it into the smoking wreck of the offender's body.

The gunshots were deafening in the tiny room. Lucius's ears sang and all other sounds were buried in thick cotton wool. He watched as Teaberry wrestled his coworker to the ground, tearing the gun from Schoen's white-knuckled grip. There was excited yelling and cursing as Nest turned blue-white, clutching his chest, gasping as he fell to the floor, with the doctor beside him. Lucius heard nothing. He just dropped his hands to his sides, turned, and walked out of the room.

There were crowds rushing towards the chamber door. People threw questions at Lucius, but he still heard nothing. He did not stop as he slowly made his way through the checkpoints and out of the building, into the staff parking lot and behind the wheel of his car. He drove home in ringing silence and when he got there he dropped to his knees and wrapped his arms around Inez's thick waist.

It took several hours for him to be able to speak and many more after that before he was able to tell her what had happened. What he could not tell her, what would haunt his nightmares for the rest of his days, was what he had seen just before he left the execution chamber.

One of Schoen's bullets blew off the offender's mask before plowing into the face beneath. The face beneath, the face of Robert Vine, would stay with Lucius until the day he died. Vine's eyes had popped out and cooked on his barbecued cheeks. Smoke poured from his eye sockets and from the bullet hole in his forehead. His swollen tongue had been nearly severed by his cracked and blackened teeth. All those things were horrible, but the most horrible thing about that face, the thing that Lucius would never

forget, was that it was still impossibly alive, still
screaming in intolerable agony.

Lucius Cosper never set foot in Nebraska State Penitentiary again.

NINE

Melodie Welles had decided to kill her husband.

She had been sitting in the women's bathroom at the McDonalds in the same lot as the Safeway, staring dumfounded at the little pregnancy test stick. It was blue. No ifs, ands, or buts about it. She had buried the pregnancy test box and the receipt from its purchase deep beneath the other garbage in the built-in trashcan beneath the paper towel dispenser. She planned to do the same with the stick when she was done, but at that moment, she just held it in one hand, staring at the result. The decision to kill Brian had popped into her head as a simple, matter of fact kind of answer to the problem of the blue stick.

Abortion would not be an option. Brian would never allow it and there would be no way to do it without him finding out. He watched her every move like a hungry predator, a big deceptively lazy predator who only looked like he was sleeping until you made a mistake and then BAM! Just stealing these precious minutes to take the pregnancy test while out picking up groceries would arouse a vigorous interrogation. She had already carefully sculpted her alibi.

She had forgotten they were nearly out of mouth-wash, she would tell him. She'd had to go back in after she had already loaded the other groceries into the car and wait in line a second time. He was very particular about oral hygiene and could not stand to go more than a few hours without rinsing his mouth with Listerine, the good old-fashioned plain yellow kind, not that new minty stuff. She planned to go back to the Safeway and buy the mouthwash as soon as the test was finished so that he would see the extra receipt with a slightly later time and hopefully believe her.

Brian was a police detective. When they'd first met, this had seemed cool and exciting. He was always surprising her with little gifts on her car windshield or tucked into her in-box at work. He always seemed to know exactly where she would be and his ability to discover all her favorite things without even asking bordered on psychic. It was sweet and charming and for Melodie, a middle child who was mostly ignored by her large Scandinavian family, it made her feel special. He asked her to marry him after they had been dating exactly one year.

In typical Brian fashion, he orchestrated a complex surprise for her that involved pretending to forget their anniversary and getting all the employees of her favorite Chinese restaurant to go along with the scheme. Whenever Brian worked late, Melodie would get a quick dinner at the Golden Butterfly Pavilion. After she was done with her usual mu shu pork and her egg drop soup, the waitress brought out the check, along with a single fortune cookie, just like always. Only the cookie looked a little different than usual. It was bigger, slightly darker in color and the plastic wrapper was clear, devoid of the usual cookie company logo. She also couldn't help but notice that the entire staff of the restaurant was staring at her, including a totem pole of hairnet-clad heads poking around the corner from the kitchen. She could smell that this had something to do with Brian, but nothing could have prepared her for what actually happened.

When she broke the cookie open, a stunning white gold diamond ring tumbled out onto the black plastic tray that held the check. The little paper strip inside read: My beloved Melodie, Will you marry me? Love forever, Brian.

Melodie burst into tears as a gaggle of cooing Chinese women crowded around her.

"You very lucky lady," the owner of the restaurant told her.

The men in the kitchen were talking excitedly as they pushed a blushing Brian out into the main dining room. He was holding a single red rose and he got down on one knee and slipped the ring on her finger. Needless to say it was a perfect fit. How could she say no?

They were married six months later. Brian seemed to enjoy planning the wedding even more than she did. To Melodie, it all seemed like a hugely intimidating hassle consisting of one complicated task after another, but Brian took care of everything with calm confidence. He really seemed to enjoy picking out the designs for the invitations and planning the menu with the caterers and even helping her pick out her dress. Looking back on it now, she might have taken that as a sign of things to come. He didn't really just help her pick out a dress. He picked one for her. True, it was exactly the one she would have picked, but there was never any doubt who had the final say in everything.

So where did it really start to go wrong? Could she pinpoint some single event? Some Rubicon between the ring in the cookie and deciding to murder him? Was it when he had her old cat Ducati put to sleep without consulting her?

"He was suffering," Brian told her, not looking up from his newspaper. "It was the best thing for him."

And it was true that Ducati was getting on in years and had begun to have some thyroid issues, but he still seemed to get around fine and enjoy his catty life, laying in puddles of sun and watching birds through the window. Brian had said he was taking Ducati in to get his teeth cleaned. When he came back alone, Melodie had an awful, sinking feeling in her heart. Brian had never liked Ducati and the feeling was mutual. She always felt like she had betrayed her faithful feline friend by marrying a man he didn't like. Now Brian's rival for her affection was gone and that was that. No point arguing. It was the best thing for Ducati.

Or was it the first time he hit her? The shock of the slap, followed by disbelief, shame, and ultimately, fear. She had been back home for her younger brother's wedding, a grim and depressing visit with a family she seemed to have less and less to say to every time she saw them. When she got off the plane, she ran into an old friend from high school. His name was Tim van Zwoll, and he was not an old boyfriend, although he was male. He was just a guy that had dated her best friend Lena during senior year. He was waiting for a plane to Chicago and they wasted a good half hour chatting and catching up. He was a guitar player and had been in a band back in the old days. To her surprise, the band had actually done rather well after graduation, making two mildly successful albums and touring around for several years. Now he was working regularly as a studio musician. He was married, not to her old best friend, but to a fairly well known female singer. They had two kids, girls aged two and four. He showed Melodie photos of the two girls, flashing big gap-toothed smiles in the arms of their beautiful and famous mom.

On the way home, Melodie thought about telling Brian about the encounter with Tim, but decided against it. For one thing, Brian was intensely jealous and did not like her talking to other men, especially when he wasn't around. Also, the famous singer was black and Tim was white, and Melodie knew that Brian did not approve of mixed-race couples, especially if kids were involved. All in all, it would not be worth the hour-long lecture she would receive. So when she got home, she told Brian that her flight had been delayed.

The second the words came out of her mouth, she knew she had made a horrible mistake. His eyes went cold and hard and he tilted his head, squinting slightly. Then, out shot the hand, cracking her across her face, knocking off her glasses.

It shocked her more than it really hurt. She had never been hit by anyone in her life. Her parents could barely pick her out of a line-up, let alone take the time to scold, spank or strike her. She put her hand to her burning cheek.

"Don't ever lie to me again," Brian said.

Of course, when she had not come home precisely on time, he had called the airline. They confirmed that her flight had arrived right on schedule. He immediately phoned a friend of his who worked security at the airport. The friend reported back that he had seen Melodie talking to a handsome young man with a guitar case.

"Now why on earth would my wife want to hide something like that from me?" he asked.

She shook her head and started to try to explain about Tim.

He cut her off. "Melodie," he said. "You ought to know by now that you can't hide things from me. If we don't have trust in this marriage, than we have nothing. Now go unpack your things and have a shower. I'll be there in a minute."

When she got out of the shower, he was waiting for her in bed. He was very rough with her, and she couldn't help but feel that he was marking her somehow, like a wild animal. She had trouble sleeping that night, lying there wondering what was happening to her life.

After that first slap, Brian began hitting her more and more regularly. Not just slaps either, he also started using his belt on her as a form of punishment for various intolerable infractions, such as flirting with the guy behind the counter at the gas station or leaving an empty cup on the coffee table. Folding his shirts wrong or forgetting to return a rented videotape or turn all the lights off when she went out. Her primary emotional reaction was embarrassment and shame. She was a smart girl, a modern girl who never let anyone push her around. So why didn't she just leave him? She was embarrassed. She didn't want anyone to find out that her marriage was anything less than perfect. When she didn't leave after the first slap, she began to imagine friends asking why she had put up with it for so long. She didn't have an answer. So she just kept smiling, kept telling her family that everything was fine. She bought new, larger sunglasses and became adept at the casual shrug and laugh when confronted about her bruises. "I'm so clumsy," she said again and again.

If she thought things were bad then, they got much worse after Brian was shot.

He had gone to take a teenage suspect into custody for the rape and fatal stabbing of a seventy-three year-old neighbor. The suspect's mother had shot Brian in the back and leg while he was putting the cuffs on her beloved firstborn.

Brian spent several months in the hospital and had been home on disability for nearly a year. He had made her quit her job teaching elementary school when they got married, because he didn't want people thinking he couldn't support his wife. Now that he was on disability, she begged him to let her go back to work to help with the mounting medical bills. He would have none of it. He needed her at home and that was that.

With him home all the time, any shred of freedom she might have had went right out the window. He had to know where she was and what she was doing every minute of every day. He only tolerated her brief absences for approved tasks like grocery shopping or picking up his medication from the pharmacy. Since being discharged from the hospital, Brian had developed a gorilla-sized addiction to pain killers, which he supplemented liberally with Jack Daniels and beer. Under the influence of this toxic cocktail, he became more vicious, more violent than ever. All his frustration and anger at his invalid state came out as hostile aggression towards her. He was constantly accusing her of having an affair and of wanting to dump him. He would wrap his arms around her and sob uncontrollably into her hair, begging her not to leave him. She did her best to reassure him, feeling more and more trapped every day. Where could she go? He controlled all the finances. She had no money of her own and was not authorized to make any withdrawals from the bank or own a credit card. And what would happen to him without her? He needed her, that much was obvious. So she stayed.

Things had gone swiftly downhill since then. He broke three of her ribs when he found a franchise coffee cup in her car. They didn't have the money for her to waste on expensive lattes. Did she think their coffee at home wasn't good enough? Of course, primarily young, attractive men staffed the coffee bar in question and she was obviously sleeping with every one of them. Melodie knew the doctor didn't believe that she fell, but she stuck resolutely to her story and when she got home Brian was tearful and apologetic. Didn't she see how much he loved her? She did, and it terrified her.

He blacked her eyes on a regular basis and the entire inside of her mouth was becoming a mess of scar tissue. She "fell" several more times, breaking a wrist, dislocating a shoulder, and knocking out a front tooth. Just last week, she had awakened in the middle of the night to find Brian hunched over her in the dark like some fairytale troll, his breath a vile mix of Listerine and alcohol. He was holding his Colt automatic pistol, the barrel a vast and gaping maw less than six inches from her face.

"If you ever leave me," he whispered, "I'll kill you."

He passed out beside her a few minutes later with the gun still clutched in his hand like a child's teddy bear, but Melodie did not sleep again that night. She lay there, stiff and terrified, listening to his soft drunken snores and wondering how long it would be before that promise came true.

Of course, now there was a whole new life at stake. A tiny little knot of flesh growing inside her, which soon would be a living, breathing person. A vulnerable person whose soft little body would not be as tough as hers. The thought of explaining to a pediatrician that her son or daughter "fell" made her feel physically sick. She could never allow that to happen.

That was why she knew the only way out would be to kill him.

Their home was full of firearms. There was one in every room, within easy reach anywhere in the house. Brian was convinced that there were legions of lowlife scumbags, specifically black men, who were lurking behind every bush, waiting for Brian to let his guard down long enough so they could come swarming into the house and "do things" to Melodie. Brian had forced Melodie to take a gun safety class and tested her randomly almost daily on her readiness to handle these phantom rapists. So as much as she hated the heavy, menacing and ugly guns hidden in every drawer and clipped under every table, she knew how to handle them. How to load and check them and how to put neat little holes right in the middle of the man-shaped paper targets at the shooting range.

Could she put a hole like that in Brian?

She knew she didn't have much time. She knew he would only buy her story about going back to get the mouthwash if less than ten minutes elapsed between the times on the two receipts. She wrapped the positive pregnancy test stick in toilet paper and stuffed it into the trash, along with the box and the separate receipt for its purchase. It took only three minutes to get back to the Safeway, grab two economy sized bottles of Listerine and make her way through the express checkout line. The fat black girl at the register raised her eyebrow at Melodie's healing bruises, and Melodie clutched the paper bag to her chest, flushed with shame.

"I'm so clumsy," she said, a thin little breathless laugh escaping through her clenched teeth.

The checkout girl narrowed her eyes. "I used to be clumsy too," the girl said. "You don't have to be, you know."

Melodie could not respond. She just took her change and receipt, ducked her head and hustled out the door.

When she got home, Brian was on the couch, watching those Nazi shows on the History Channel that he loved. He snatched the two receipts from Melodie's shaking hand and examined them like they were critical evidence in a murder case. Eventually, he grudgingly accepted Melodie's tale of the forgotten mouthwash and sent her to put the receipts into the dated receipt file in his office.

The rest of that day was the longest day of Melodie's life. Brian was remarkably laid back and although he would not let her get up off her place beside him on the couch for any reason other than to visit the washroom or get him dinner or another beer, he seemed almost back to his old self. He held her hand while he watched TV and she could not bear to look at him. He seemed almost childlike with his disheveled hair and oversized sweat pants. How could she possibly do it—put a gun to his head and pull the trigger? She put her hands against her belly, imagining that she could feel the life growing inside her. She waited.

Brian noticed her touching her stomach and asked her what was wrong. She said she thought maybe she was going to be getting her period soon. He nodded dismissively. He hated even knowing about that kind of female stuff and forced her to keep her tampons in a plain plastic box under the sink so he wouldn't have to look at them. Any talk of that time of the month was a sure way to get him to change the subject.

The evening continued in excruciating slow motion. He graduated from beer to Jack Daniels and started slurring his words and going for longer and longer periods of time with his eyes closed, head tipped back on the couch. The blathering pointlessness of the television droned on and on like the irritatingly perky salesman it was and Melodie ignored it, staring with nauseous intensity at her passed out-husband. Nearly an hour went by and he didn't move.

A commercial came on the television, some kind of shampoo or soap. A beautiful young woman held a perfect, rosy naked baby in her arms, gently washing its laughing face. The breathy, female voiceover asked Melodie if her baby's health and safety was her number one priority.

Melodie nodded and reached for the compact Sig Sauer P230 clipped to the underside of the coffee table.

The tiny sound of the gun coming free from its clip seemed huge in the dim living room and Melodie's heart stopped and then revved loudly in her chest. Brian did not move.

All the guns in the Welles' house were loaded, and Brian made sure that Melodie could load each and every gun in the house with her eyes closed. Now all Melodie had to do was thumb off the safety and pull the trigger.

Brian slept, oblivious. His hair needed to be cut rather badly, and Melodie wondered with jittery hilarity if the mortician would cut it for him. He looked so sweet, so innocent, like a kid who had tried to wait up to watch the late night monster movie and had fallen asleep half way through. She remembered the look on his face when he came out of the Chinese restaurant's kitchen with that one red rose. How could she do this? Kill her husband in cold blood?

She thought of the narrow suspicious look in his eyes before he would order her to go get the belt. She thought of the black muzzle of the bedside Colt an inch from her face.

If you ever leave me, I'll kill you.

She had no choice. She put the gun to her sleeping husband's head and thought of her baby, her tiny, vulnerable baby. She pulled the trigger.

The sound of the gunshot ripped through the dozy quiet of their little house. Blood drenched the back of the couch behind him as Brian's eyes flew open and he let out a startled grunt, hands flying up off his lap. He turned to her, dark blood trickling from a neat hole just above his left eye. His eyes were rapidly swelling shut, the hole ringed with black powder burns. His fists clenched and he opened his mouth, a thick gagging noise coming out. Melodie sat frozen in horror.

"You..." he whispered. "You... bitch."

"I..." she said. She had no idea what she was going to say. She wanted to throw the gun away but it felt welded to her hand.

"...You shot me!" Brian gasped.

He reached out and grabbed the front of her shirt, easily ripping the SIG from her shaking hand. He cracked her across the mouth with the gun's butt and she felt her new artificial front tooth shatter. She fell off the couch, head bouncing painfully off the corner of the coffee table. Stars blazed across her vision.

"Shot me," he said again, fingers traveling across the wet mess the back of his head had become.

Melodie looked up at Brian standing over her. How could he not be dead? It was impossible. The bullet went right through his brain, blowing an exit hole the size of a compact disk out of the back of his skull. Yet there he was, standing over her like some kind of horror movie monster, undead and invincible: like a zombie from *Dawn of the Dead*. He kicked the coffee table out of his way and pressed one knee down into the center of her chest. She gasped, dizzy and struggling to breathe.

"Bitch," he said.

He proceeded to erase her face with the butt of the gun. The pain was huge and horrible as she writhed and struggled beneath him. When he pulled the SIG back and shot her three times in the stomach she screamed and screamed, imagining the safe dark sanctuary of her baby's world torn open by bullets. She imagined the tiny knot of soft tissue blown to pieces inside her. The emotional agony and loss at that moment far outweighed her physical pain as he

continued to kick and beat her. She prayed for uncon-
sciousness, for death. Her prayers were not
answered.

TEN

Former Thai boxing champion, Randy "The Hammer" Mallinger, was smoking a joint of low-grade Thai weed and surveying his handiwork. He was tall and lean with a shaved head, chilly blue eyes and a hard, angular face. He had been in Battambang, Cambodia, for just shy of one week and he was already convinced that this lawless land of Khmer Rouge gangsters, unexploded land mines, inexpensive heroin and underage prostitutes was the ideal place for him.

Randy grew up dirt-poor in Birmingham, Alabama, son of an alcoholic mother and an unknown father. He was brawling almost before he could walk and suffered from a killing temper so vicious that he often felt like a helpless observer trapped inside his own hot, enraged flesh. Eventually he began to channel that rage and hostility, first into traditional boxing, then the more violent and complex Thai boxing. He was very good. He traveled throughout Southeast Asia, making buckets of money and blowing it all on his other newfound anger management aid, prescription pain medication: Vicodin, OxyContin and eventually, heroin. He had left the United States for good a little more than five years ago while under investigation for the statutory rape and "accidental" death of a young Vietnamese exchange student. He never looked back.

Since the exchange student, Randy had killed nineteen girls. In the urban slums of Southeast Asia it was ridiculously easy to get away with murder. The kind of girls Randy craved, tiny, slender, brown-skinned nymphets with gutter mouths and jaded eyes, they were a dime a dozen on the back streets of Bangkok, Saigon and Phnom Penh. They were disposable, easily replaced. They were never missed.

Randy found transcendence in the bloody undoing of these perfect little girls. He drew strength from their tortured deaths and as they screamed and suffered beneath him, he felt calm and centered, the red demon of rage banished and replaced by a kind of crystal clear focus he never felt any other way. And when he was done, he tore through the sultry nighttime streets on his battered motorbike, flying on Tiger Beer and fresh cobra's blood, Thai weed and black tar heroin. At times like that, Randy began to feel as if the secrets of immortality were nearly within his grasp.

That was before this latest girl, this latest gracile, tawny-skinned sacrifice to the ravening monster inside Randy. What the hell was her name again? Chanlina? Chantrea? Chan something anyway. When he picked her up outside the Karaoke brothel down the street from his hotel, he had arbitrarily decided to call her Tiffany. She had laughed and told him in her broken English that he could call her whatever he wanted, so long as he paid in advance. The price for the unrestricted use of her young body was twenty-seven thousand riel, which was about seven American dollars. She was four-feet eleven inches tall and could not have been more than thirteen or four-teen. Her slick black hair was held back from her narrow brown face with a pink plastic hair band. She wore a man's military fatigue shirt knotted up high above her navel and a loose fitting red miniskirt that just barely stayed up on her tiny, childish hips. She had a thin, silent baby wrapped in a knock-off Poke-mon blanket that she handed off to an even younger friend in order to go and conduct business with Randy. That had been just over twenty-four hours ago.

"How are you feeling now, Tiffany?" Randy asked, taking a last deep drag off what remained of the joint.

The only response was a faint, liquid wheezing from the mess on the bed that had once been a young prostitute named Chan something. Just looking at her made Randy feel a loose, hot excitement coiling in his belly. It was nothing short of incredible that the girl was still breathing. He spit in his palm, extinguished the joint in the gob of saliva, and went to lie back down beside her.

As he stroked her blood-slicked hair, he finally understood what was really happening. In absorbing all the rich and vital life essence from all the girls he had murdered, Randy had become like a god. He had the power to keep his perfect little girls suspended in a state between life and death. The hardest part of killing for Randy had always been the letdown when he realized that his playmates had left him and that he was alone again with yet another pile of lifeless meat. This time it was different. This one wanted to stay with him, almost as if she loved him. Randy felt tears of gratitude welling up in his eyes as he pulled the battered and broken girl close to him, kissing her soft, lumpy forehead. He felt unworthy of her boundless love.

He found himself suddenly remembering his recent visit to Angkor Wat, the crown jewel of the ancient Khmer Empire. He had left the stunningly beautiful temple complex after only five minutes, convinced that the massive stone idols and the mystical faces in the intricate bas relief carvings were hissing and whispering to him. Now he wished he had stayed and listened. They had obviously been trying to tell him something of critical importance, old dead spirits welcoming him home to the land where he would reign as the new immortal god king.

The girl made a new kind of sound against his neck, a sort of low breathless moan.

"I know, baby," he said, kissing her wet, swollen lips. "I love you too. I just need to go out for a little while. I promise I'll bring back a surprise for you, okay?"

Randy tied her skinny ankle to the rickety bed frame with a torn strip of fabric from her red miniskirt. She probably wouldn't be going anywhere in her current condition, but Randy figured it would be best not to take a chance.

He showered in the dingy bathroom, holding the cheesy little shower nozzle over his head and scrubbing at the clotted blood that had worked its way into every wrinkle and crevice of his body. There was no shower stall to speak of, just this rusty nozzle, two cracked faucets sticking out of the no-longer-white tile wall and a large, hair-clogged drain in the center of the floor, so it took several minutes of rinsing and wiping to clean the spattered blood from his body and the tile around him. There were many other, older stains on the bathroom walls that led Randy to believe he was not the first person to engage in this messy kind of romance here at this less than delightful establishment. He did not clean too carefully.

When he was relatively blood-free and dressed in his usual black fatigue pants, black tank top and jump boots, Randy left the gurgling Tiffany in search of breakfast, more dope and a pretty new playmate to join his happy little family.

ELEVEN

Dr Ferguson stood outside the room where little Diamond Day lay waiting for a bed to open up in the pediatric ward. She looked so tiny in the center of that hospital bed, barely even making a shape under the white blanket. Her fever was still high and she was not responding to the antibiotics. Dr Cohen had gone home and Dr Ferguson was debating calling him back or just ordering another stronger antibiotic, but he was feeling thick and stupid, fatally tired and was second-guessing himself. He found himself wishing selfishly that a bed would hurry and open, taking this pesky problem out of his hands and into the hands of someone who had slept at some point during the past twenty-four hours.

Lita Day came out into the hallway where Dr Ferguson stood. Her eyes were wet and red and she had that look, that desperate, needy and helpless look Dr Ferguson recognized all too well as the face of the next of kin watching a loved one struggle to survive.

"Doctor?" she said softly.

"Yes?" Dr Ferguson replied.

"Will my grandbaby be okay?"

Dr Ferguson looked into her drawn and worried face and then down the hall at the closed door of the room where the strange patient waited to be admitted. Dr Ferguson had been taught how to handle the families of the fatally ill and mortally injured as part of his preparation for ER duty. Never lie. Don't give false hope or try to sugarcoat the facts. But he was so tired, the past forty-two hours weighed on him like concrete blocks, and he just didn't know what to say.

"Well, Lita," he began. "Diamond is suffering from several different competing bacterial infections, none of which are normally life threatening. However, because of her young age and poor health, the combination of these simultaneous infections can be quite dangerous."

Dr Ferguson heard his own voice as if over a bad PA system. It sounded reasonable, but he felt like he really had no idea what he was saying.

Lita's brown eyes were wide and liquid, lower lip quivering. "She ain't gonna die, is she?"

Dr Ferguson's gaze drifted back to the closed door of the exam room that housed the patient who thought he was Death. "Death said he won't be taking any souls this morning," Dr Ferguson said. "So there's really nothing to worry about."

"Doctor." Gina gripped Dr Ferguson's arm. Nurses had a certain way of making the title "doctor" sound like the vilest insult and Dr Ferguson cringed at the hostile fury in Gina's voice.

"I need a word with you," she said, hauling Dr Ferguson away from the baffled grandmother like a naughty schoolboy.

"Are you out of your mind?" she spat when they were out of earshot.

"Sorry," Dr Ferguson said, hanging his head, "I guess I'm just a little punchy."

"There is absolutely no excuse for that kind of behavior," Gina said. "We are professionals and must act accordingly, regardless of the way we feel."

"I know," Dr Ferguson said. "I know."

"Now go pull yourself together," Gina said. "Splash cold water on your face and have some more coffee. I'll go and clean up your mess."

She turned on her heel and walked back over to Lita Day, putting a hand on her shoulder and speaking softly to her. Dr Ferguson turned away, feeling ashamed of himself. It was so important to him to prove his chops, to hang with the big boys and tough out the long and grueling shifts without breaking a sweat, yet he could feel that he was cracking. He was in the home stretch, the last six hours of the final shift, and he couldn't afford to lose it now. It was that strange patient. He had really gotten under Dr Ferguson's skin. All that talk of death and dying. He needed to stay focused and make it until noon. Just make it until noon.

He remembered the date that he had made with the pathologist, Megan. Maybe it wasn't such a hot idea. He would hardly be at his best, unwashed and punch drunk, but on the other hand, when Death tells you to seize the day, you know you really ought to listen.

Dr Ferguson laughed out loud as he pushed open the door to the restroom. He really needed to put that strange patient out of his mind. As he splashed icy water on his face he found himself wishing for an influx of trauma, something complex and difficult to occupy his mind for the rest of the shift. As soon as that thought had formed in his mind, it was followed by a swift flush of guilt. That was a terrible thing to wish for. To wish that someone would be fatally injured just so he would have something to do.

Then, as Dr Ferguson was staring at his own pale and dripping wet reflection, he abruptly got his wish.

The voice over the PA announced incoming trauma. Gang-related shootout. Several members of both sides were coming in with a variety of injuries. Dr Ferguson readied himself along with all the rest of the trauma team and the eager attending physicians. Everyone was bored and a kind of pre-game excitement was crackling through the team. Dr Ferguson was not the only one wishing for something to do.

When the injured gang members started to arrive, Dr Ferguson was shocked to discover that they were all female. There were ten of them, six from one gang, four from another. Still heavily made up and dressed to the nines from the night before, the young women were Latina and tough as nails, many still drunk, high or both. There were gunshot wounds, stab wounds and some horrifying blunt trauma. Those who were not rendered unconscious by their injuries still struggled to get at each other in the hallways and their police escort was forced to separate a sudden furious fist fight that erupted in the waiting room between two girls so bloody they were as slippery as greased pigs and nearly impossible to catch. One girl in particular was extremely belligerent and hostile. She was sixteen and quite attractive under her thick make-up, but the words coming out of her mouth would have made some of her male competitors blush. She was also hugely pregnant. Amazingly, she was not the only one. Another pregnant girl had been shot in the head and was rushed immediately into the OR.

As the gang members were triaged and transferred to other facilities where possible, Dr Ferguson, being the low man on the Mercy totem pole, drew the short straw of caring for the belligerent pregnant girl. She had been suffering the contractions of labor since she had been shot and was undoubtedly ready to drop at any moment.

In spite of her obvious pain, she immediately began speculating aloud about Dr Ferguson's sexual orientation and the possibility that his parents had not been married at the time of his birth. As she continued to berate him between contractions in both Spanish and English, Dr Ferguson attempted to discover the nature of her injuries. She was dressed in a preposterously sexy outfit, black hose and spike heels and a tight black dress stretched over her massive belly and cut low to display her milk-swollen cleavage. She told Dr Ferguson that he better not "try anything" or she would "sue his ass" and then her bad-ass boyfriend would find him and kill him. In fact, she would kill him herself if she were not unfairly restrained. If she wasn't pregnant, Dr Ferguson would seriously consider the unethical but very appealing idea of sedating her, just to shut her up.

She had two gunshot wounds, one in her right shoulder and one in her right hand. The bullet that had struck her hand had blown off three fingers. The pinkie and ring finger were gone and the middle finger was hanging by a thin strip of skin. The EMS team had done a very good job stabilizing and wrapping the hand and preserving the severed ring finger in ice, awaiting reattachment. The pinkie, apparently, was never found. There was nothing more that Dr Ferguson could do for the hand, other than alert the surgeon on call and prep the patient for the OR. The shoulder wound was a nice clean shot. All that was really needed there was to staunch the bleeding, treat her for shock, and if necessary, deliver the baby.

The patient cursed and flailed in her restraints, but eventually Dr Ferguson was able to get an IV line in. He cut off her pantyhose and lacy little underwear, but when he attempted to insert the catheter into her urethra, she went completely ballistic, shrieking as if he were murdering her. Gina came to his aid, but just as he managed to get the tip of the Foley catheter in, the girl's water broke in a sudden gush, drenching Dr Ferguson's shoes.

"You're killing my baby!" the girl screamed.

Dr Ferguson had to bite back on his response. No, he wanted to say. You're killing your baby by drinking and snorting cocaine and getting shot up in some stupid gang war.

But he said nothing. Instead, he simply continued to work, ignoring her cursing and shouting as if it were something on television in another room. The ORs were full with more urgent cases, so he was stuck with Miss Congeniality until they could TRF her away to some other hospital or one of her fellow women warriors either stabilized or died, freeing up one of the ORs. The contractions were coming faster and faster and lasting longer and longer and Dr Ferguson started to fear something might not be right with this pregnancy. At the climax of a particularly long contraction, the patient screamed at the top of her lungs, "It's stuck!"

"Okay..." he checked her chart again. "Miss Alverez. I need you to help me here."

"Damn you," she replied.

Dr Ferguson ignored her. "I need you to breathe deeply and only push when I say so."

"Damn you," she said again and then let out another howl of anguish, followed by a string of Spanish curses.

Dr Ferguson took a deep breath and reached a gloved hand inside the girl's vagina. Unsurprisingly, this action precipitated a new volley of inventive profanity. He struggled to tune the patient out and concentrate only on what he could feel with his right hand. He was questing for the smooth curve of the baby's head when his fingers instead encountered something that felt very odd, something small and soft with a peculiar, nubbly texture. Could she have some sort of object stuck inside her? It was a fairly common complaint in the ER and both men and women came in with an amazing variety of items stuck fast where the sun don't shine. On Dr Ferguson's last shift alone they had a potato, an air freshener and a jar of Vaseline. The gentleman in the last case must not have realized that you are supposed to take it out of the jar first. But why would a pregnant girl have what felt like a little rubber finger puppet inside her vagina? It took several seconds of blind groping to realize what he held in his gloved hand. It was a foot—the baby's foot.

"Gina," he called, a flush of adrenaline in his belly. "We've got a breech birth here."

Gina nodded and wordlessly left to page the OB/GYN on call. The neonatal crash team was tied up with the headshot, struggling to save the premature baby whose mother had been reduced to little more than a vegetative incubator with a single bullet. Dr Ferguson was alone.

"Miss Alverez," Dr Ferguson said. "I need you to listen very carefully to me now."

Something in the tone of his voice cut through the girl's mad cocaine-fueled fury and she just looked at him, eyes wide like a trapped animal's, sweat pouring down her face.

"Your baby is positioned the wrong way inside the birth canal," Dr Ferguson said. "Instead of head first, your baby is coming out feet first."

"Yeah, so?" she said.

"So this is a very dangerous situation for you and your baby," Dr Ferguson said. "It is imperative that you listen very carefully and do exactly as I tell you or your baby could die. Do you understand?"

The girl looked at Dr Ferguson and all the toughness and venom seemed to drain out of her. She suddenly seemed like a child herself. Apparently all the warnings not to do things like take drugs and get shot while pregnant meant nothing to her, but confronted with the reality that her baby could actually die right here, she finally seemed to fully understand that there was a little living person inside her. She was suddenly terrified.

Gina returned then with the neonatal crash cart. "Tones?" She asked.

"No fetal heart tones yet," Dr Ferguson said. "Trying the Doppler."

Dr Ferguson used the Doppler to scan the girl's massive belly. He and Gina both stood clenched and silent, listening with their entire bodies for the sound of the baby's heart. Instead of the normal, rapid pulse, there was nothing but a slow, barely audible sound like the swish of wet tires on a rainy street. Dr Ferguson counted the beats: seventy-nine, far below normal.

Dr Ferguson began to sweat. The baby was obviously in trouble. His instinct was to wait for the OB/GYN guy, but with fetal distress, every second was critical. The baby might not survive the wait.

The girl was quiet now except for breathless gasps that ratcheted up to stifled, clenched-teeth screams with each contraction. Dr Ferguson could feel two feet now and the legs beyond. The baby was coming, like it or not. He was terrified that the baby's head could get caught up at the cervix and it could suffocate. The surgery to remove a trapped baby like that would require splitting the pelvis and opening up the girl's entire lower abdomen, cutting through the cervix and uterus. It was a gory, difficult procedure that rarely delivered a live baby.

"Sixty-one," Gina said.

The baby was crashing. It would not make the forty-five minutes it would take the OB/GYN guy to get there. Dr Ferguson had no choice but to attempt delivery.

He struggled to remember everything he had read about breech births. OB/GYN was his least favorite subject and he had spent far more time on chest and head trauma than the obscure mysteries of "down there." He remembered reading that a breech baby must be delivered in a sort of rotating, corkscrew fashion, allowing the hips and shoulders to come out one at a time. It was one thing to read about it and quite another to do it, knowing that one wrong move meant lawsuit city. This girl was not exactly the poster child for prenatal care, but you better believe that if Dr Ferguson made a single mistake, one tiny error in judgment, this foul-mouthed, coked-up gang banger would instantly become the Blessed Virgin, an innocent girl whose beloved baby was killed by the thoughtless incompetence of a lowly intern. Lawyers would be lining up around the block, licking their chops. It would be a blood bath for him and the hospital, but what else could he do? The baby clearly would not wait, and with a heart-beat so low, it did not stand a chance without immediate intervention. Could Dr Ferguson allow an infant to die to protect his own ass? Obviously, there was no choice.

"Okay," Dr Ferguson said to no one in particular. "Here we go."

He could feel the baby's tiny buttocks and back as he struggled to grip the slippery little thing and start rotating its body clockwise inside the vaginal vault. First one foot then the other appeared. They were dark, inky blue.

"Prep a two point five endotrach," Dr Ferguson said. "And the smallest laryngoscope blade we've got. We're gonna have to intubate."

Sweat was pouring off Dr Ferguson as he continued to rotate the little body. One hip popped out, followed swiftly by the other. It was a boy. The patient was bearing down furiously, screaming out loud and for a horrible moment, Dr Ferguson was sure the baby was stuck, its tiny neck clenched in the muscular grip of the cervix. This was only his second delivery ever, and the first one had practically delivered itself. This was impossible, impossible. The baby would die. His career would be over.

Once again, Dr Ferguson thought of that strange patient, his dark, weary eyes, his wintry smile. No more death, he had said. Dr Ferguson shook his head, banishing the vision of that odd little man and forcing his mind back to the task at hand.

For an eternity nothing happened. The patient panted like a dog, and Gina stood at his side, bright eyes fixed on the little blue legs, her fists clenching and unclenching at a slow, even pace. Then all of a sudden, another ear-shattering scream and a tiny arm and shoulder squeezed free, followed almost immediately by the other arm and shoulder then the neck and chin and Dr Ferguson saw that the umbilical cord was snagged tight around the baby's throat.

"Shit," he said, before he could stop himself.

Gina scowled at him and grabbed scissors and clamps from the drawers in the neonatal cart. She handed Dr Ferguson a sterile towel and the second the head was free and the baby slipped down into the waiting towel. Dr Ferguson turned and set it in the Isolette, clamping and cutting the strangling cord with shaking hands. The baby did not breathe.

"Come on, kiddo," Dr Ferguson said, stimulating the baby with the towel. "Breathe."

It looked like a tiny, wizened blue gnome from a children's fairy tale. It was still not breathing, pulse sluggish and dropping. There was no way Dr Ferguson could work on a tiny thing like that. It was impossible. Wordlessly, Gina placed the slender, delicate laryngoscope blade in Dr Ferguson's hand.

"Heart rate forty-nine and dropping," Gina said. "No pressure, though."

Dr Ferguson looked up at Gina and she was smiling, just a little. At first he was confused. No pressure? No blood pressure? Then she realized that she meant no pressure on him and he let himself smile back, a tiny breath that was almost a laugh stealing out between his teeth. In the heat of panic and madness, Gina's bone-dry sense of humor pulled Dr Ferguson firmly back to reality. He could do this. There was no other choice.

The intubation process is never easy, even in full-sized adults. It is often difficult to see well enough to slide the blade over the tongue, under the epiglottis and past the vocal cords, into the trachea. In an infant it is even harder to find that tiny opening. That little blue fairytale creature laying there, close to lifeless in the Isolette was by far the smallest baby Dr Ferguson had ever seen. He took a deep breath and steadied himself, then opened the baby's mouth, pressing down on its jaw and inserting the blade.

After an endless moment of awkward fumbling, he felt the blade slip down inside the trachea. He let out his breath slowly and squeezed the Ambu bag. The baby's little potbelly puffed up and deflated and Dr Ferguson swore under his breath. The tube was in the esophagus, not the trachea. The bag was pushing air into the baby's stomach.

"Where's my baby?" the girl cried. "I want my baby."

He forced himself to remain calm, withdrew the tube and started again. Gina leaned forward and placed her hand on the baby's scrawny neck in an attempt to make the vocal cords more visible. The blade kept on bumping against soft tissue, going nowhere and Dr Ferguson struggled to hang on to his calm while his inner voice was screaming: You incompetent fake! You're not a doctor, you're just an overeager wannabe with more academic credentials than common sense. Who ever told you that you could practice medicine? You shouldn't be allowed to carve a goddamn Thanksgiving turkey.

But then the blade suddenly slid home, the tiny chest rising and falling and the heart rate climbing. Gina inserted an IV line into a bulging blue vein in the baby's paper thin scalp and to their amazement, the tiny fingers began to twitch. The deep blue color of the baby's skin gave way to warm, oxygenated pink like the night sky surrendering to the rosy flush of dawn. The skinny legs begin to kick and a shaky gush of laughter escaped Dr Ferguson before he could stop it. Gina touched her elbow to his, the post-HIV, universal precaution equivalent of a high five.

"Good job, kid," she said.

"Is my baby gonna be okay?" the girl asked in a tentative, broken voice.

Gina turned back on the girl with withering scorn. "Your baby will live," she said.

The girl frowned. She could not quite comprehend why what should be a positive statement sounded so hostile. Dr Ferguson understood far too well.

Here was a little life begun inauspiciously in the midst of violence and hate. With no prenatal care of any kind and with a drug-addicted gang banger for a mother, not much hope for postnatal care either. Yes, Dr Ferguson had saved the baby's life, but what kind of life would he have? Would Dr Ferguson see him again in six years with burns and bruises like Diamond Day? Or maybe in sixteen years with gunshot wounds of his own? By doing his job and saving this small, innocent life, had Dr Ferguson made the world a better place or merely assisted in the continuation of the vicious cycle of poverty, drugs and violence? The high of his success began to sour and curdle inside him. He removed his gloves and silently left the room.

In the hallway, he saw the strange patient standing in the doorway of his room.

"You look like shit, doc," he said.

"Thanks," Dr Ferguson said, running his fingers through his hair.

"I don't know why you're knocking yourself out like this," the patient said. "I told you, I'm not taking any more souls."

"Are you saying that baby lived because you didn't take his soul?" Dr Ferguson was feeling prickly and hostile. The last thing he wanted was to get into another one of these conversations.

"That baby should have been born dead," the patient said, cocking his ear to the sound of a high-pitch cry from the newborn. "I love being on vacation."

Dr Ferguson said nothing. He just turned and walked away.

TWELVE

Arthur Sternberg woke from a dim and awful nightmare to find his Boston terrier, Cricket, licking his face. He fumbled around on the table for his glasses, focusing slowly on Cricket's flat, gray-streaked face. She looked at him intensely, as if she were deeply concerned about his nightmare.

At first, Artie hadn't even wanted a dog. Once their kids were grown and he and his wife Jo were retired, Artie was really enjoying the freedom and lack of responsibility. He didn't even like houseplants because it meant having to make sure someone watered them if you went out of town. But Jo was on the Internet one evening and she found a website for New York Boston Terrier Rescue. Her family had had Boston terriers growing up and she kept on showing Artie pictures of these smush-faced little black and white dogs, each one with some sob story about how they had been badly treated and needed a good home. Artie had argued halfheartedly, but he knew Jo. They had been married for forty-one years and he knew perfectly well that once she set her mind on something, there would be no stopping her.

First they'd had to fill out this long form and then the lady from the rescue group came to visit their little house on Tibbett Avenue in the Bronx. She looked at the fence in their back yard and all around the house to make sure that it was safe. She explained that Boston terriers are indoor dogs and can never be left outside in the cold or heat. She asked a ton of questions and then showed them a photo of Cricket. Jo was in love from the second she saw that picture of skinny little Cricket looking up into the camera with big sad eyes. She weighed a mere twelve pounds and had only the thinnest white line between her eyes instead of the usual thick Boston blaze. Her ears were huge on her tiny apple head and her tail was just a twisted little nubbin. Even Artie had to admit that she was cute, though to be honest, he would have preferred a "real" dog, like a German shepherd or a lab or something.

The lady explained that Cricket had been used as a puppy mill breeder, kept in a filthy cage every day of her young life and forced to have litter after litter. She was only three years old, but some reproductive infection had rendered her unable to continue breeding, so the owner brought her to the vet to be put to sleep. The vet contacted the rescue group and they agreed to take Cricket. The rescue lady explained that Cricket had never been socialized or house trained and that she was terrified of other dogs. The person currently fostering Cricket was working on the house training, but felt that Cricket would need to be an only dog in a family with no small children. Jo agreed that they only wanted one dog, while Artie silently fumed at the prospect of taking care of a dog that was not house trained. The rescue lady thanked them and said she would be in touch.

There was just no arguing with Jo on the subject. She ordered a special dog bed online with the name CRICKET spelled out across the front and bought tons of toys and treats, a shiny red collar and a whole bunch of little sweaters. You'd think she was having another baby with the way she was acting.

When the rescue lady called and said they were approved to adopt Cricket, Jo burst into tears. Artie held her, baffled by her reaction, but glad that she had gotten what she wanted.

It wasn't easy at first. Cricket was very fearful of everything and when Artie scolded her for peeing on the floor, she would tremble and shake and act as if she were awaiting a deathblow. She would flinch any time Artie moved his hands too quickly, as if she expected to be hit. Sometimes if Artie raised his voice, Cricket would let out a little trickle of pee because she was so scared. She did not seem to know what to do with all the toys Jo had bought and was afraid of the squeakers. She clung to Jo like glue, but as the days went by, she would creep slowly across the couch and snuggle up next to Artie while he was reading. If he didn't pet her she would gently place a paw on his leg, staring up into his face with those big brown eyes.

There were little milestones as the first year went by. The first time she picked up a stuffed plush snake and shook it fiercely, then carried it to her bed to chew on. The first time she made it through a whole day and night without a single accident. She learned to sit and to shake and while she was still terrified outside the house, Artie could see that she was gaining confidence every day. She was learning the routine. Every time she peed outside she would run over to the counter that held the treat jar and sit, expectantly licking her chops. She would jump into the bed every night at precisely 10:30, tapping her paw on the edge of the bedspread and waiting for Jo to lift the covers so she could burrow down under to her usual spot between their feet. She knew when it was time for breakfast and time for dinner, and if Jo and Artie got busy with other tasks, she would remind them by scooting her empty bowl across the floor with her nose and bumping it against their shoes. Every morning when they woke up, she would roll on her back and wiggle and squirm, kicking her legs and snorting until Artie couldn't help but laugh. Her eyes were so thoughtful and intelligent. Artie could swear sometimes that she was almost human. She had an incredible ability to sense her human companions' moods. When either of them was down, Cricket would come over and sit beside them, concerned little face looking up into theirs. When they were happy, she would do a funny little pirouette and then stand up on her hind legs, paws in the air. As the years went by, she became the center of their world, more precious than a child.

Then, one morning three years ago while they were at the breakfast table, Cricket seemed strangely agitated. She kept running from Artie to Jo and staring up at Jo with a worried look on her face. Jo bent down to reassure Cricket and her face went white, eyes wide with surprise. She clutched at her chest and collapsed to the floor. Artie dialed 911 while Cricket stood anxiously over Jo where she had fallen. By the time the paramedics arrived, Jo was dead. She'd had a massive heart attack. There was nothing they could do but reassure Artie with shallow platitudes that at least it had been quick.

Cricket would not leave Jo's side. When they bagged Jo's body and took her away, Cricket followed them to the door and waited there for nearly a week. Artie had to move her food and water dish over near the door because she would not leave her vigil. He knew how she felt.

Those strange, sludgy days following Jo's death were a blur to Artie. His two grown sons came to help with the arrangements. His older son Stephen was a lawyer, a micromanaging control freak who treated Artie like a child, not allowing him to do anything. Artie was too tired to fight about it. His younger son Josh was an actor, or more precisely a waiter, skipping from job to job while chasing auditions, bit parts and outside chances. He was handsome and easygoing, easily hurt. Artie always thought he was too thin-skinned to make it as an actor, but never told him so. It was important to Artie to be supportive no matter what. When Josh had sat Artie and Jo down, just two days shy of his twenty-first birthday, and explained in an agonizingly roundabout way that he was gay, it had come as no surprise to either of them. Of course, Artie had been supportive. He didn't get it, but he wanted Josh to know they were behind him one hundred percent, no matter what. Now, when it was Artie who needed the support, he still found himself holding Josh up. Jo's death hit Josh particularly hard.

It still seemed impossible for Artie to accept that she was dead. Jo had always been so much stronger than him. She was never sick, while Artie always seemed to be fighting some cold or another. Then, with no warning, she was gone, and he and Cricket were alone.

For nearly six months after Jo's death, Cricket reverted to her old scared self. She peed on the floor. She flinched when Artie touched her. She would spend hours waiting by the door before she would give up and go lie down in Jo's favorite chair. Artie knew how she felt. Everywhere he looked, the house was full of memory traps: Jo's latest mystery novel, unfinished on the nightstand. He probably owed a ton of back fees to the library for that book, but he could not bring himself to return it only half-read. Her clothes, her slippers, her favorite cup—what was he supposed to do with these things? Give them to the Goodwill? Throw them away? Make them into a shrine? Every night he forgot she was gone and would reach for her in the morning. Cricket would be there, looking into his face with her worried brown eyes, almost as if she understood.

Josh and his partner moved to Los Angeles and Stephen and his new wife moved up to Scarsdale. They called occasionally, Josh more than Stephen, but mostly, Artie and Cricket were alone.

The years went by and Artie and Cricket settled into their Jo-less routine. They walked down to Van Cortland Park every Saturday in the summer to watch the white-clad East Indian men play Cricket's namesake game. They went together to the same pet shop down on Broadway at the end of every month to buy Cricket's food, which Artie would push home in his shopping basket with Cricket sitting like a princess on a folded sweater on top of the bag. People in the neighborhood knew them both and would say hi to Cricket, giving her a little pat on the head. The butcher, an amiable Irishman named Malloy, would always have a little tidbit for her whenever they came by. She was no longer afraid of strangers and accepted worship from her subjects like the canine royalty she was. It seemed like Cricket had always been a part of his life. It was unbelievable that there had been a time when he had not wanted a dog.

Then, one morning Artie noticed Cricket was limping on a hind leg. It was the eighth anniversary of her adoption and every year, they had celebrated that day with special yellow cupcakes. Cricket was given a single cupcake topped with strawberry yogurt on a cheerful paper birthday plate. The year Jo had died was very hard for Artie in a million ways, but he remembered vividly struggling to figure out the instructions on the back of the yellow cake mix box, wanting Cricket to have her anniversary cupcake no matter what. He had cried into the batter, leaning against the counter and wishing for the thousandth time for Jo to come over and say in her exasperated voice: "Here, let me do that."

But, of course, she didn't and the cupcakes still turned out okay, even though he overcooked them a little.

That day the cupcakes came out perfect, but Cricket didn't eat hers. She just licked at the yogurt topping and then went to lie down in Jo's chair.

Cricket was getting older. There was no doubt about that. Her muzzle was all gray now and Artie could see that her old bones ached just like his in the wintertime. He didn't think much of the limping that day or the next. He limped a little too. They were both old.

When she started to seem short of breath and remained uninterested in food, Artie began to panic. He took her in to see the vet, Dr Tavish. He sat in the waiting room with his heart in his throat.

Dr Tavish was a heavy-set older woman with brisk, mannish body language and a "straight shooter" personality that made Artie feel very comfortable. There would be no BS from Dr Tavish. He felt that he could count on her to give it to him straight no matter what.

The news was not good. In fact, Dr Tavish showed the X-rays to her partner in the practice just to confirm the diagnosis: Osteosarcoma. Bone cancer. It was extremely rare in small dogs and far more likely to be found in the giant breeds. Great Danes. Wolfhounds. Saint Bernards. That was why Dr Tavish had wanted a second opinion. Unfortunately there could be no doubt of the culprit responsible for Cricket's pain. The cancer had begun at the site of an old healed fracture in her rear left leg and was beginning to metastasize into her lungs. She could not be cured and treatment would mean radical amputation and chemotherapy. It would buy her three to six months at best.

Artie struggled not to let his feelings show in the vet's office. He looked down at Cricket, stroking her ears gently, and told Dr Tavish to do whatever it took to help his best and only friend. Jo hadn't even had a chance. Cricket would get the best medical care money could buy.

Artie went deeply into debt, jacking his credit card to the limit to pay for Cricket's surgery and subsequent chemotherapy. At first she was miserable every day and Artie wondered if he had made a mistake, if he was being selfish by keep Cricket alive and suffering. Then, she seemed to rally, making it around on three legs just fine, and Artie wondered if maybe the doctor was wrong, if Cricket might be the one who would beat the odds and live another year or two or more. All through her recovery and the slow poison of chemotherapy, she seemed more concerned with Artie than herself, struggling to follow him everywhere and always looking up into his face to be sure he was okay.

Then, that morning, when Artie awoke from that half-remembered nightmare, he put his arm around Cricket's neck and she yelped in pain. He drew back, startled by her reaction. "What's the matter, kiddo?" he asked.

She looked at him intensely, as if frustrated by her inability to speak. Then she looked away and lay down.

For the next hour, she would not get up. Not to eat, not to go outside. She started to whine softly, panting rapidly. Artie went to get the mail and when he retuned to check on her, she had wet the bed, but would not get up and move out of the puddle. She was still whining, her eyes unfocused. Artie wrapped her in a clean towel and rushed her to Dr Tavish.

As soon as Dr Tavish came back from the X-ray, Artie could tell by her face that the news was not good. The cancer had spread to the bones in her neck, just below where the spine joined the skull. The voracious tumors were growing rapidly and would soon start putting pressure on Cricket's brain. There was nothing they could do. She could not survive more than a few days and each day that passed, she would be suffering, losing control of her functions and herself as her brain was slowly crushed by the blossoming tumors around it. The kindest thing to do was to let her go, to put her to sleep.

Artie could not stop the tears from coming. Dr Tavish, who was experienced with the pain that this kind of decision brings, left Artie and Cricket alone for a few minutes.

Artie hugged Cricket close, his tears falling onto the soft fur of her neck. He stroked her ears, her big bat-like ears that had always been so expressive. Now they were pinned back flat to her head with pain and fear. She looked up at him and licked his hand, as if to say that she trusted him to make her better. How could he agree to have her killed, murdered essentially, when she was counting on him to take care of her? He wished that Jo were there. She was so much stronger than him. She would know the right thing to do.

But Jo was dead and soon Cricket would be, too, and then Artie would be alone. It wasn't fair. He didn't have all the answers. He didn't know what to do. He didn't want Cricket to suffer, but he didn't want her to die either. How could anyone make a decision like that? It was impossible, cruel and unusual. It would help if he could delude himself into believing that Jo would be waiting for Cricket and eventually for him on the other side of the rainbow bridge, but as he got older, he found that charming fairy tale harder and harder to buy. And if this was all there is, how could he make the decision to take that away from another living being, especially one he loved like a flesh and blood child?

But how selfish that was. Artie was hemming and hawing and worrying about his feelings when it was Cricket who was suffering. She had always been so brave, but he knew she was hurting. If it had been a choice for him, there would be no question. He would much rather die with his faculties about him, clear-headed with loving arms around him, than to perish in slow lingering agony, feeling his mind slipping away piece by piece. So why was it so hard to make that decision for Cricket? As difficult as it was to admit, Artie knew there was only one choice.

When Dr Tavish returned, Artie reluctantly agreed to allow her to put Cricket to sleep. What a ridiculous expression that was. Put her to sleep. She was going to kill Cricket. It was that simple. The doctor asked Artie if he wanted to hold Cricket while she administered the fatal shot. He said that he did. As much as he might like to run and cover his eyes, he knew that Cricket took comfort in his presence and that she would be scared if he left. He owed it to her to be there.

He did not watch as Dr Tavish prepared the injection. Instead he concentrated on Cricket, petting her gently, telling her that he loved her, that she would not be hurting much longer. She looked up at him with a quizzical look as if to ask why he seemed so sad. She was not whining and she seemed to be able to breathe normally for a moment and Artie panicked. Was she getting better? Was he making a terrible mistake? Then the doctor gave Cricket the shot.

Cricket jumped a little at the pinch of the hypodermic needle. Her body shuddered in Artie's arms and she began to pant again.

Dr Tavish frowned. Artie could see a flash of anxiety in her eyes.

"What's wrong?" Artie asked.

Dr Tavish shook her head. She picked up the vial from which she'd drawn the fatal shot and looked at the label, then back at Cricket. Cricket licked Artie's hand and whimpered softly.

"That's odd," Dr Tavish said.

"What's odd?" Artie asked. He was starting to feel intensely uneasy.

Dr Tavish fumbled in one of her drawers and pulled out a fresh vial, still in the box. Using a fresh needle, she drew another dose and injected Cricket a second time. This time Cricket yelped and her body went into helpless seizures.

"What the hell is happening?" Artie asked.

A tech came in to assist Dr Tavish. They both looked terrified and their fear did not help Artie. Blood and foam flew from Cricket's mouth and her little body bowed and flexed on the table. Urine squirted from her, drenching Dr Tavish's cheerful cartoon scrubs.

"I'll need you to wait outside," Dr Tavish said.

Her voice was so authoritative that Artie did not hesitate to obey. When he was out in the hallway alone, he burst into tears.

It was nearly half an hour before Dr Tavish came out. Her right hand was torn and bloody where Cricket must have bitten her in her seizure. She looked like she had been through a war.

"Mr Sternberg," she said, "I have been a veterinarian for thirty years. I have euthanized thousands of animals during that time, but I have never in my life seen anything like this."

"Is Cricket..." Artie struggled to spit out the dreaded word. "Dead?"

"Well," Dr Tavish said, "not exactly."

"Not exactly?" Artie frowned. "What the hell is that supposed to mean?"

"I won't mince words, Mr Sternberg," Dr Tavish said. "Cricket has no heartbeat and does not appear to be breathing. However, she was still seizing vigorously as of two minutes ago. The seizure has calmed and she appears to respond to light and tactile stimulus. That is not clinically possible, because she is, for all intents and purposes, dead."

Artie didn't even know what to say. He wanted to knock the doctor's lights out. He wanted to shake her and demand to know what she had done to his beloved Cricket. But he was also terrified. He could not seem to wrap his brain around the things the doctor was saying. Cricket was dead but still moving? Still responding to the world around her? How could that be possible?

"Can I see her?" Artie asked.

"Normally, I would say it wouldn't be a good idea," Dr Tavish said. "But we are so far off the script right now I have no idea what to tell you. If you want to see her, I guess you can go on in. I need to make some calls."

The doctor turned and walked away. Artie paused with his hand on the doorknob. Did he really want to do this? Then he heard the soft sound of Cricket whining in pain and his eyes filled with tears. He opened the door.

Cricket lay on the table in a puddle of blood and urine. The tech was trying to soothe her and looking completely terrified. The girl was Puerto Rican and a little overweight, wearing too much make up and looking like she couldn't have been older than twenty.

Artie stepped up to the table and put his hand on Cricket's head. She rolled her eyes towards him, looking up as if begging him to do something. She licked his hand and he lowered his face to her wet, stinking fur and cried.

THIRTEEN

Jerry Paderewski had worked the bolt gun in the kill shed at the Cook and Sons Custom Meat Processing Plant in Oklahoma City for just over four months. It really wasn't such a bad gig, despite what all those animal rights nutjobs might have to say about it. He did have to get up real early and often worked weekends to keep up with the never-ending demand for burgers and steaks from a ravenous American public, but his five fellow butchers in the kill shed were a cheerful and talkative lot. Even the USDA inspector who was there to be sure they dotted all their Is and crossed all their Ts wasn't really a bad guy, in spite of his chilly, businesslike exterior.

Jerry himself came from a long line of butchers. His dad, also named Jerry, had been a butcher before the cancer got him and so had his grandpa Pawel. His mother's four brothers worked in the plant and so had her father. Jerry had worked various jobs all around the plant before he got the offer to work over in the kill shed. He would probably be rotated out pretty soon. The company didn't like to have one guy work the bolt gun for too long. They said it wore on a man, all that killing. Jerry didn't really know what they meant by that. For the most part, he enjoyed his work.

Jerry was not a mean guy. He did not hate animals. In fact, his wife Lizzie would often tell her friends that he was really just a big old pussycat. He and Lizzie had two big rangy bloodhounds that were like children to them. Their names were Boomer and Betsy and he brought them bones and other delicacies from work every single day. Lizzie said that he spoiled those hounds rotten, but he couldn't help it. He loved them. When he came home exhausted from a long day at work, he would still take the time to play with the hounds out in the yard, rough housing and rolling in the grass while Lizzie looked on indulgently from the back door. It made Jerry angry when the animal rights people picketed their plant. There were people starving every day in cities right here in the United States. Why didn't those jokers go hand out tofu to the hungry and homeless instead of trying to stop Jerry from making burgers?

That morning, Jerry was feeling extra slow. In spite of four cups of strong coffee, he was finding it harder than usual to get started. Lizzie had been feeling frisky the night before and they had recently decided to start trying to have a baby. Needless to say, Jerry hadn't gotten much sleep. Not that he was complaining, mind you. Lizzie was an amazing woman, fierce, strong and passionate, and Jerry figured he'd do just about anything to make her happy. He wondered if there might be a tiny little spirit growing inside her. The thought made him smile as he parked his cranky old Suburban in the lot and headed into the plant.

Jerry was so used to the smell that he hardly noticed it anymore. The morning group of butchers was there already, hosing blood off the concrete and smiling, exchanging pleasantries as Jerry passed, wiping the sleepy seeds from his eyes. He ducked into the locker room to don his white uniform, his thick rubber boots and apron, his hard hat and his goggles then headed out back to the kill shed for the morning shift.

The cows were already backed up in the chute. Jerry slapped hands with his buddy Roland, the butcher manning the second station. As he passed, Jerry endured some lewd comments about his tired condition and some humorous speculation about his sperm count. He laughed good-naturedly and went to prod the first cow into the killing stall.

She was having none of it, so Jerry had to zap her three more times before she finally staggered into the stall. He was thinking about baby names, girls' names since he really wanted a little girl, when he raised the bolt gun and let Bessie have it between the eyes.

The cow fell flopping and shuddering to the floor. She seemed to be fighting more than usual as Jerry looped the chain around her right hind leg and hit the hydraulic button to hoist her up until she dangled about three feet off the floor. Roland slit the hanging cow's throat and stepped aside to avoid being drenched in the downpour of blood.

Michelle? Miranda? Jerry liked M names but wasn't sure if they would go well with Paderewski. He prodded the next cow into the stall and fired the bolt gun into her head. How about a nice Polish name? Marta? Monika? Magdalena? His maternal grandmother had been named Magdalena. She would have been pleased at the prospect of a namesake great grand-daughter. Magdalena, Maggie for short. Perfect. As he was hooking the chain around the second cow's leg, Roland called out to him.

"Yo Jer," he said.

Jerry turned to his friend. Roland was standing there with the cow's severed head at his feet and the skin about a third of the way removed.

"Is it me," Roland asked, "or is this one still ticking?"

Jerry squinted at the headless upside-down cow. Roland was right. It was still kicking, still struggling. Jerry had heard of chickens running around with their heads cut off, but never cows. In the months that he had been working the bolt gun, he'd never seen anything like that. He looked down at the other cow at his feet. She lay on her side, eyes rolling wide and terrified. She was panting, pale tongue lolling. The smooth, almost bloodless hole between her eyes was just like it always was. Yet, she was inexplicably still alive. Jerry checked the bolt gun by firing the bolt out and retracting it back in again. Totally normal.

But even if the bolt gun were somehow malfunctioning, that would not explain how the headless cow could be hanging there drained of blood and still alive. The cow head at Roland's feet was moving as the jaw opened and closed, air sucking through the severed neck.

"I don't know about this..." Jerry said, frowning.

The USDA inspector, an older man named Bob Gower, came over with the air of a high school principal about to bust kids for smoking. "What seems to be the problem here?"

He looked down at the cow head, white eyebrows knitted with consternation.

"Well, sir..." Roland began, but could not seem to think of how to continue.

"Paderewski?" Gower asked.

Jerry shrugged, toeing the prone bovine at his feet. She mooed pitifully, blood and drool gurgling from her mouth. In the chute, the other cows were panicking, bucking against the metal walls with increasing desperation. The three of them stood there, all trying very hard not to look at the horribly animated head at Roland's feet.

"Okay," the inspector said, seemingly to himself. "I'm gonna call for a halt in production while we get to the bottom of this issue."

Roland looked down. "Okay, sir," he said. "But what should we do about these two?"

The men looked at each other. The head rocked back and forth as the jaw worked ceaselessly against the concrete. The cow at Jerry's feet panted and gasped, twitching and rattling the chain around her leg. The cacophony of panic from the cows in the chute became louder.

"I have absolutely no idea," the inspector said.

Jerry wiped his mouth on the back of his hand. He wondered if it might not be time to look for a different job.

FOURTEEN

It was a bleak and chilly desert night, the kind of night that sucks all the heat out of your marrow and leaves you feeling like a mummified Neanderthal man inside the meager warmth of your uniform.

Some of the soldiers had started a sad little bonfire, but no one stood around it that night. There was something far more interesting going on down on the other side of the encampment.

Several jeeps and trucks had been pulled into a rough circle. In the center of the circle stood two prisoners of war. One was taller and broader, but more sickly looking, his face still a colorful palate of healing bruises. The other was small and wiry, tough as a desert reptile, eyes bright with terror. They were scrawny, unshaven and shivering, shirtless in the night chill. Their eyes were huge in their gaunt faces as the soldiers laughed and poked them with the muzzles of their automatic weapons. The physique and condition of each man was discussed and odds were drawn. Money changed hands as bets were taken.

The two prisoners had developed a cautious kind of friendship over the weeks since their capture. To fill the endless days, they whispered to each other, telling of wives and children and the details of each man's life before the war, before this. That tentative friendship made their current situation a thousand times more difficult. Although neither man spoke the language of their captors, they were made to understand through rough gestures and prodding with high-powered weapons that they must fight each other.

The shorter prisoner made a wild attempt to bolt. He was easily caught and shoved roughly back into the makeshift arena. The two prisoners looked at each other with dawning horror. It was becoming clear that one of them would not leave this circle alive. If they did not fight, they would both die. It was an agonizing choice. No choice at all really.

One of the soldiers helpfully placed a rock in the taller man's hand. The man looked down at the rock like it was an alien artifact. The helpful solider made a throwing gesture and indicated the other prisoner with his chin. The taller man looked at his friend. The other man's eyes were ringed with white. He thought of the man's young wife alone and struggling to care for his twin sons. He thought of his own wife and daughter. He threw the rock.

The rock hit the other prisoner, bouncing off his shoulder. He grunted and raised his hand to rub the spot, brows knitted above disbelieving eyes. The helpful soldier made sounds of approval and pressed a second rock into the taller man's hand.

The man looked down at the new rock. It was slightly larger than the first, almost the size of his fist. It was heavy and cold, gritty with sand. He shut his eyes and threw it.

The rock hit the shorter man in the side of the head. He cursed and collapsed to his knees, blood coursing over his neck and down his dirty chest.

The soldiers cheered. The taller man was appalled. He wanted to rush to his friend's side and comfort him, to apologize a thousand times. He took an unconscious step towards his fallen friend. He was startled and shocked when the shorter man looked up at him through a mask of blood, eyes filled with anger and hate. His hand skittered across the dirt for the bloody rock and before the taller man could react, he flung the rock as hard as he could. It slammed into the taller man's face, smashing his nose with a wet crunch. The sound of excited cheers was washed away beneath a massive wave of pain.

The taller man struggled to regain his bearings as he heard a furious howl tear up and out of the shorter man. His friend, his fellow prisoner, whose family he had promised to take a message to if the shorter man did not make it, this man he thought he knew was charging at him like an enraged bull. The taller man met the charge with equal fury, but the shorter man ducked low and slammed a shoulder into the taller man's stomach, lifting him and driving him backwards, into the curved metal flank of a battered truck. The taller man collapsed, winded and dazed, to the ground.

The shorter man was still screaming at the top of his lungs. He tried to kick his fallen friend, but the taller man threw himself to one side, narrowly avoiding the blow. The shorter man's foot slammed into the dented side of the truck, inches from his friend's head.

Infuriated and terrified, the taller man struggled to his feet and punched his friend. The blow was wild, but still managed to connect with the side of the shorter man's head that had been struck by the rock. The mushy feel of the shorter man's head beneath his knuckles and the hot spray of blood that flew from the shorter man's nose and mouth as he stumbled backwards and collapsed to the ground horrified the tall man.

Without allowing himself the luxury of consideration, the taller man kicked his fallen friend in the ribs as hard as he could. The shorter man grunted and rolled over. The taller man attempted to push his advantage by kicking the shorter man again, but the shorter man grabbed his foot.

The taller man fought to keep his balance, swinging and missing as the shorter man stood, still clutching the taller man's foot. Teetering on the verge of falling, the taller man watched in slow motion horror as the shorter man kicked him with all his strength, squarely between his splayed legs.

The pain and nausea that rocketed through the taller man obliterated all thought. He collapsed, dry heaving on the stony ground. He was on the verge of losing consciousness when an explosion of blinding agony smashed through his skull. The shorter man had kicked him in the face, jarring the shattered cartilage of his broken nose and setting off red and black fireworks inside his head.

Through his tunnel vision, the taller man spotted the rock he had thrown a thousand years ago. Barely aware of what he was doing, he grabbed it and swung out at the shorter man, smashing the rock into his temple. The shorter man spun away, blood jetting across the uniforms of the cheering soldiers.

The taller man squinted at the crowd of soldiers. They were slapping each other on the backs and money and packs of cigarettes were swiftly changing hands. The shorter man lay on the ground, not moving. The taller man felt stinging liquid in his eyes, but he did not know if it was blood or tears. He suddenly realized that he had forgotten the message, the message for his friend's family. He pressed his forehead into the dust.

He jerked his head up when a flurry of surprised exclamations traveled through the crowd. The taller man followed the pointing fingers of the soldiers and saw what they were so excited about. His friend was not dead.

The shorter man shuddered, fingers gripping the bloody ground, forming into fists. All around them money was changing hands again and one of the soldiers poked the taller man with his rifle. The taller man heard a scuffling sound behind him and turned just in time to meet the shorter man's fist.

The huge cheer from the crowd got all mixed up in the taller man's mind with the pain and blood as he staggered back, dazed. He did not see the shorter man pick up the rock, but he felt it when it crashed into his mouth, teeth shattering and flying everywhere. That tiny patter of teeth hitting the stony ground around him seemed huge to the taller man as he stumbled to one knee. He tried to get up again, but the shorter man hit him again and this time blackness wiped across his vision and he was out before he hit the dirt.

Consciousness came back slowly. The pain was beyond anything the taller man had ever felt. There was nothing he could even compare it to. It was like the ocean, or the sky, unlimited and indefinable. Through that enormous pain, the taller man was able to see his friend holding the rock and looking terrified. The soldiers were silent with anticipation. The taller man's eyes rolled up to the vast night sky, strewn with glittering stars. For several seconds he lost himself in mindless anguish, but then he suddenly noticed the sky was marred by fog. A thin curling mist was obscuring his crystal clear view of the distant, uncaring stars. When he realized that the steam was his own breath, he could not help but wonder how it had not been there just moments ago.

He pushed the pain and fear down inside himself and struggled to his feet amid the riotous cheers of the soldiers. The shorter man rushed him, swinging with the rock. The taller man more staggered than dodged, escaping the blow and kicking out, hitting the shorter man in the lower back. The shorter man slipped and fell, his face connecting with the fender of a parked jeep. The sound of that connection was something the taller man would never forget. The juicy snap of bone and the dull thud of his limp body hitting the ground. The shorter man had broken his neck. As he lay in the blood soaked dirt, his head was skewed at a nauseatingly wrong angle. But that was not all. He was also trying to get up.

A medic came rushing into the circle, trying to still the flailing prisoner. The tall man backed away, unable to watch as the man's head flopped backwards on his wobbly neck until the back of his head touched down between his shoulder blades. He struggled not to vomit and feared that he might lose when something happened that short-circuited any other thought.

There were several small explosions, one after another, and the soldiers grabbed weapons, their little game forgotten. The taller man heard gunfire and the helpful soldier who had handed him the rock went down at the taller man's feet, shot in the neck and drowning in his own blood. Another explosion rocked the camp and there were loud agitated cries as the soldiers around him hit the dirt. The taller man followed suit as a massive blast shattered the ring of vehicles. The taller man felt flying shards of metal slice into him as the hair burned from his face and head. All around him, soldiers were screaming. The medic lay on his side, gasping in a pool of his own blood and entrails. Men were on fire, running in mad panicked circles, and the taller man was appalled to feel his stomach rumble at the smell of cooking meat. He had not eaten in six days. He put his head down in the crook of one elbow and began to cry.

FIFTEEN

Dr Ferguson was not cheered by the succession of miracles in the ER that morning. Every time he overheard another impossible success story, it made him feel nauseous. The gang girl who had been shot in the head was holding steady, vegetative and non-responsive, but breathing without assistance. Her tiny premature baby, a girl, was also breathing without assistance and had set a new hospital record for the smallest baby delivered alive. That baby was a fighter, the head of the neonatal team told his breathless audience of cooing nurses. That baby wanted to live.

The girl with a bullet hole in her aorta apparently also wanted to live. Against all odds, she had survived the desperate race to mend the tear and bring her back from the very brink of death.

The worst was the blunt trauma case, the girl who had been beaten with bats, pipes and anything else the rival gang could get their hands on. Apparently it was her savage beating that precipitated this entire battle. Members of one gang had isolated this single member of the rival gang and beaten her into unrecognizable jelly. Her sister gang members found out and rushed to her aid with guns blazing. They should have been too late, but somehow the smashed and swollen thing was still horribly alive. Her head was completely pulped. Her ribs were shattered, collarbones snapped. The trauma team had her in the OR in seconds, fighting to reconstruct the girl who by all rights should have been dead and gone. They were proud of themselves. Dr Ferguson was horrified.

He stood for a moment in the doorway of the room where the strange patient lay catnapping on the hospital bed. He had to breathe deeply for several seconds to suppress an urge to grip the sleeping man by his shoulders and shake him, demanding that he tell Dr Ferguson what the hell was going on here.

"Hey doc," the patient said, face still turned to the wall. "How's it going?"

Dr Ferguson stepped into the room. "Prove it," he said.

The patient sat up, brows knitted. "Whatever do you mean?"

"If you're really Death," Dr Ferguson said, "prove it."

The patient shook his head. "What you see with your own eyes isn't enough?" the patient said. "The babies, those young women, no obituaries? Those things aren't proof enough for the skeptical young Dr Ferguson, is that right?"

"Those things are all unusual, but possible." Dr Ferguson said. "I want solid proof."

"Proof," the patient said thoughtfully. "He wants proof." He nodded. "Well, I guess I can do that for you, doc. We're friends, right?"

"Right," Dr Ferguson said.

"Then why don't you come here and sit beside me," the patient said.

Dr Ferguson felt a sudden spike of irrational fear.

"Oh come on, doc," the patient said. "I'm not going to hurt you. I'm on vacation, remember?"

Dr Ferguson reluctantly came forward and sat down on the bed beside the strange patient. The patient gripped his wrist with cold, strong fingers and Dr Ferguson gasped as the bland beige wall of the hospital exam room crumbled and fell away in a vertiginous whirl.

Then suddenly he heard the soulful muted trumpet notes of Cuban jazz and he found himself standing in his mother's bedroom back in Asheville. Holly stood beside his mother's bed, beautiful as ever in spite of the puffy red eyes and pale, drawn brow. And on the bed, curled on her side in her red flannel pajamas and striped Peruvian shawl, was his mother.

Dr Ferguson watched with a kind of sticky, nightmare horror as the strange patient walked across the room and put a hand on his mother's head. He wanted to scream at the patient to get away from her, but he could neither move nor speak. He watched in helpless anguish as his mother's body twitched and shuddered and then a single long breath slipped between her chapped lips and she was still.

Holly stood for a moment, looking down at his mother's body, then slowly turned and left the room. To Dr Ferguson's amazement, he saw his mother stand up and stretch up to her tiptoes, pushing her hair back from her face. This did not seem possible because he could still see her body lying just like he remembered it behind her on the bed.

"Am I dead?" she asked, pressing a hand to her skinny chest.

The strange patient nodded silently and reached out to her. She looked down at his offered hand, then back at the door of the bedroom. To Dr Ferguson's amazement, he saw his younger self enter the room and walk slowly over to the bed.

"Jay-bird," his mother said. "Kiddo, I'm so sorry."

She reached towards the younger Jay and her hands went right through him like water.

"He's gonna be fine, Karen," the patient said, curling the fingers of his offered hand. "It's time for us to go now."

"But..."

She looked back over her shoulder. The younger Jay collapsed into the bedside chair, sobbing. She turned back to the patient, anxious wrinkles across her forehead. The patient took her hand. Together they turned to leave.

"I love you, Jaybird," she said over her shoulder as she went. "Don't you ever forget that."

Then, abruptly Dr Ferguson was back in the exam room. He was horrified to find that he was holding the patient's chilly hand. He yanked his hand away.

"Now do you believe me, Jay?" the patient asked.

Dr Ferguson rubbed his eyes. Had he been dreaming? Was that some kind of sleep-deprived hallucination? He wanted to turn and run screaming out into the street. Instead he just stared, slack-jawed, at the patient.

"She really loved you, Jay," the patient said. "More than anything."

"How can you know that?" Dr Ferguson said.

"Do you still refuse to believe?" the patient asked.

More than ever, Dr Ferguson felt sure that it was a good idea that no one should have to die. No one should ever feel the way that he had felt that autumn afternoon. But how could it possibly be true?

"I just don't know what to believe," Dr Ferguson said.

"Well," the patient said, "believe what you like. You've got more incoming trauma to deal with right now."

Dr Ferguson frowned at the patient as the dispatcher's voice came over the PA system. Incoming trauma: a bus crash. He looked at the patient with wide eyes. How could he have known that?

"Go on, doc," the patient said.

As Dr Ferguson left to meet the new wave of pain and suffering, he heard the patient whistling softly to himself. It was the slow, mellow Cuban song that had been playing the day Dr Ferguson's mother died. The sound of it sent deep, creeping chills through his body as he walked swiftly down the hall.

SIXTEEN

Joey "The Cannibal" Canalucci and Louisville Lou Pigozzi stood over a shuddering, bloody pile named Frankie Carr. Well-dressed and sporting a trendy goatee, Frankie Carr was really not such a bad kid. He was just a little misguided. He thought he was in love. Poor bastard.

"One more time, Frankie," Lou said quietly, nudging the kid with his foot and holding the pipe cutter up so Frankie could see it. "Where is she?"

Lou was not from Kentucky. He'd gained the moniker "Louisville Lou" from his predilection for baseball bats. That had been in his younger days, of course. Now he left most of the heavy lifting to guys like Joey.

"I told you, I don't know nothing," Frankie spat, rolling over and curling in on himself. "You can kill me if you want."

"I can?" Lou asked. "Oh thank you very much, I really appreciate your permission."

Lou nodded and Joey "The Cannibal" kicked Frankie in the stomach. The kid gasped and spat blood on the concrete warehouse floor. Lou really enjoyed working with Joey "The Cannibal." A lot of guys thought Joey was a psycho, and there were plenty of wild rumors regarding his acquisition of the nickname "The Cannibal," but Lou genuinely appreciated Joey's enthusiasm for the work. Joey was a stand up guy. He could be counted on when things got messy, not like so many of these softhearted pansies working in the Outfit today.

"Frankie," Lou said, hunkering down beside the groaning, writhing kid. "Listen to me. I know how she is. She gives you a little lovey-dovey, a little pussy, eh?" The kid tried to roll away and Lou smacked his face and rolled him back. "Oh yeah, believe me, I know how it is. That girl really knows how to work it. Makes you feel like you're the only man in the universe. I oughta know, being her husband and all."

Lou nodded to Joey again. Joey gave the kid another nice solid kick in the gut. Frankie started sobbing softly.

"You think getting killed protecting that piece of Long Island trash is romantic or something?" Lou poked the kid with the pipe cutter. "You think she hasn't already got some other kid lined up to take your place? Someone even younger, harder and dumber than you?"

Frankie was shaking his head and snuffling through his broken nose.

"Oh no, she wouldn't do that, right?" Lou rolled his eyes. "She loves you." He nodded. "Of course she does."

Lou lit a cigarette and Joey arched a disapproving eyebrow at him.

"What?" Lou said to Joey.

"You said you was gonna quit," Joey said softly.

"I will, I will. Christ." Lou waved the smoke away from Joey. "What are you, my mother?"

"Those things'll kill you," Joey said.

"Look," Lou said. "I can't quit smoking right now with this whole Veronica thing happening."

"Suit yourself," Joey said, shrugging.

"Thank you." Lou turned back to Frankie. "Where the hell was I?"

"I don't know nothing, I swear," Frankie blubbered.

"No, no," Lou replied. "We did that part already." He parked the cigarette in the corner of his mouth and hefted the pipe cutter. "Oh yeah, now I remember."

Lou nodded and Joey stepped on Frankie's right arm, trapping his hand against the concrete floor.

"Now, some guys are into fingers," Lou said. "But I don't go for the whole 'this little piggy' routine. It's a waste of time if you ask me. Me, I like to cut right to the chase."

He placed the jaws of the pipe cutter around Frankie's wrist and Frankie began to scream and flail. Joey pulled out his gat and pointed the muzzle at Frankie's forehead. The kid went still and white as a sheet, trembling, staring as if hypnotized into the bore of the gun.

"So what I'm gonna do, Frankie," Lou said, "is I'm gonna ask you one more time where that no good tramp ran off to. And you, you're gonna tell me. Because if you don't, I'm gonna cut off your right hand. And believe me, now that Ronnie's ditched you for some other sucker, you're gonna be needing it."

Frankie said nothing, his eyes huge in his pale face.

"Where is she, Romeo?" Lou asked, closing the jaws of the pipe cutter so that they dug into the skin of Frankie's wrist.

"Please," Frankie begged. "Please I swear I don't know..."

"Wrong answer, kid."

Lou cut off Frankie's hand.

Frankie screamed, high and shrill, as blood sprayed across the concrete.

"That hurts, don't it?" Lou took a last drag from his cigarette and flicked it away where it died hissing in a puddle of blood. "Now are you gonna open up to me, tough guy, or am I gonna take the other hand?"

Frankie blubbered and gasped, not making anything like sense, but still whipping his head back and forth in a wordless negative.

"Look, kid," Lou said. "This is stupid. I'm gonna find that bitch whether you give her up or not. You're only making it worse on yourself." He nodded to Joey, who stepped firmly on Frankie's other hand. "So one more time. Where is she?"

Frankie said nothing, just moaned and writhed on the floor.

"Can you believe this guy?" Lou asked.

Joey shook his head.

"Unbelievable." Lou said. "You want me to cut off your other hand too? Is that it?"

Frankie continued to shake his head, shuddering and bleeding, eyes rolled up and teeth clenched.

"Okay," Lou said, clamping the pipe cutter around Frankie's other wrist. "You asked for it."

Frankie screamed in terror. "Please..." he begged. "Please I told you..."

Lou cut Frankie's other hand off.

The amount of blood was starting to get out of control. Lou had not worn one of his favorite suits because he knew how things would be, but seriously, this was starting to get ridiculous already.

"How about now, tough guy?" Lou asked. "Feel like talking yet?"

Frankie just shuddered and panted between his teeth. Joey shot Lou a frown. This was not going well. The kid would be blacking out soon and all this blood would be for nothing. Lou had to give him credit. The kid had some balls—there was no doubt about that.

"Fine," Lou said. "Have it your way." He turned to Joey. "Kill him."

Joey smiled and put a bullet in the kid's head.

The kid didn't die. Instead he flopped around like a fish, slamming his head against the concrete again and again. When the twitching stilled, he looked up, one pupil all blown wide and black, the other tiny as a pinprick. He reached a bloody stump towards Lou.

"Hurts..." he whispered.

Lou looked at Joey and back down at Frankie.

"Man this kid is tough," Lou said. "You got something to say to me now, tough guy? Some illuminating last words?"

"Daytona," the kid said.

Lou arched an eyebrow at Joey. "What did you say?"

"Daytona... Beach," Frankie said.

"Atta boy," Lou said, smiling. "Daytona Beach, eh? I might have known." He nodded to Joey. "Do the kid a favor, would you?"

Joey but three more bullets into Frankie's head. To Lou's amazement, Frankie continued to twitch and shudder, writhing in a lake of his own blood.

"Unreal, this guy," Lou said. "Well, I guess we better go ahead and put him in the river."

Together they wrapped the impossibly shuddering body of Frankie Carr in chains, weighted him with cement blocks and dumped him off the end of the pier.

Lou stared thoughtfully at the slow trickle of bubbles in the brown sludgy water. "Joey, you hungry?"

Joey nodded. "I could eat," he replied.

"I could go for a little antipasto," Lou said. "A nice linguine pomodoro. Something light, y'know." Lou turned back to Joey. "You?"

"I'm on that low carb thing," Joey said.

"What, that Atkins thing?"

"Yeah."

Lou shook his head. "Are you out of your mind? Your mother, God rest her soul, would smack you good if she heard that kind of nonsense coming out of your mouth. Atkins." Lou spat into the water. "Let me tell you something, life without pasta is like a life without pussy."

"I gotta drop ten pounds," Joey said.

Lou shook his head and squinted at Joey. "So you eat all that steak and bacon and you think you're gonna lose ten pounds? What's wrong with a nice light pomodoro?"

"The carbs, you know," Joey said. "They're just like sugar."

"Just like sugar," Lou said, flapping his hands. "Give me a break." He patted his waistline. "Look at me. Am I fat?"

"No," Joey said.

"You think I could have kept up with a Ferrari like Veronica if I was some fat slob?"

"No," Joey said.

"Thank you," Lou said. "And I been eating pasta every day of my goddamn life. I'm sixty-one years-old. Atkins, my ass."

Lou fished around in his pocket for another cigarette, stuck it in his mouth and lit it.

"Lou," Joey said. "Come on."

"What, what?" He made an exasperated sound and tossed the cigarette into the water. "There, you satisfied?"

Joey nodded.

"I swear to Christ, Joey, you're like my mother sometimes." He turned and walked down the length of the pier. "Look, let's go get a decent dinner into you. Some nice osso buco, how about that? That's low carb ain't it?"

"No risotto, though, okay?" Joey said.

"You got it," Lou said, cracking a broad grin. "That airline food is the worst and it's gonna be a long flight to Daytona."

Lou's extinguished cigarette floated in lazy circles on the surface, tossed by the little spiral currents created as the bound man beneath the water continued to struggle fiercely.

SEVENTEEN

Denny McKay had been working for Armadillo Armored Transport for five days. In spite of all the dire warnings and training he had undergone to handle "violent interpersonal encounters" of every conceivable stripe, it was turning out to be one of the most boring jobs he'd ever had. Denny was twenty-three, six foot six with a lean, well-proportioned build, affable blue eyes and a boyish grin. He'd worked as a bouncer and done all sorts of private security gigs. In spite of his deceptively laid-back exterior, he held a black belt in Brazilian JuJitsu and had grown up around firearms, taking the junior sharpshooter championship at age twelve. Generally speaking, Denny was someone you didn't want to mess with.

His two partners were both older and more experienced. The driver was a sawed-off little bastard named Rob Decker. He was five foot seven and had a massively overmuscled, unnatural and troll-like physique, his already thick simian features made even more prominent by the excessive abuse of steroids and human growth hormone. His lats were so over-developed that he could not put his arms down flat at his sides, and as a result he moved kind of like a little kid in a thick padded snowsuit. He was always making the most horrendous comments about women, and would frequently indicate his interest in a passing female by commenting on her "hot little pooper." He was forever dispensing helpful romantic tips to his younger colleague in order to assist Denny in his dealings with the fairer sex.

"Don't waste your time on good lookin' broads," Rob would say as they grabbed a quick lunch at the local Tastee Burger. "Good looking broads don't know how to have sex. They think being pretty means they can get an A just for showing up to class. Ugly girls have to earn it. Say you meet three girls together in a bar. Go for the chubby one, the one that's not as cute as her two friends. She's used to being left out while guys are all over her cuter pals. Trust me, she'll be so thrilled that you picked her that she'll put out right away. She'll do anything you want and be grateful."

Denny, who was married to his high school sweetheart and still deeply in love, often tried to derail these pearls of wisdom by pointing to his wedding ring.

"I'm covered in that department," he'd say. "But thanks anyway."

Rob invariably scoffed at Denny's fidelity. "Nobody's that married."

Rob had been divorced three times and was currently embroiled in a legal battle to bring the new future ex-Mrs Decker into the United States from Malaysia.

"I love Asian broads," Rob said, showing an appalled Denny a very revealing photo of his new bride to be. "They don't talk back."

"That's because she doesn't speak English, Rob," Denny had replied.

"She don't have to," Rob said, winking and tucking the photograph back into his uniform pocket. "If you know what I mean."

Denny's other companion on the endless, boring shifts was the taciturn and buddha-like Samoan who rode in the back with the dough. His name was something with an apostrophe in it—Toa'ale or Toa'ake or something like that—but everyone just called him Tiny. Tiny Afato. Tiny was Denny's height but nearly one hundred pounds heavier, able to sling the heavy bags of cash around like they were down pillows. He had been working for the company since Denny was in diapers and had personally foiled three armed robberies over the course of his twenty-year career. Tiny had said a grand total of seven words to Denny in the past five days. Most of the time, Denny basically forgot Tiny was there.

Denny sipped his lukewarm Seven-Eleven coffee and tried to tune out Rob's latest rant, something preposterous about being able to tell if a woman had VD by smelling her breath. Denny didn't know how Rob was able to start that kind of talk this early in the morning. The man did not seem to have an off switch. Denny looked out the window as they turned onto Broadway. It was still fairly deserted this time of day but there were a few scattered people, homeless mostly and sleepy shopkeepers and various other early birds walking quickly with their hands stuffed deep into their pockets.

Denny's eye caught a clumsy-looking young girl on skates a little bit ahead of them. She was skating in the street, both hands out as she struggled to keep her balance on expensive, in-line roller blades that seemed far too big on the ends of her skinny little legs. She was maybe twelve or thirteen with long blonde pigtails and a backpack shaped like a furry panda. She had a pink helmet on her head, but the strap beneath her chin was unbuckled, hanging loose on either side of her face. It didn't seem like such a good idea for her to be in the street like that. Clearly she was just learning how to skate. Denny figured she probably resented the pink helmet, thinking that it was uncool and just wearing it so her mom wouldn't worry. She had on knee and elbow pads too, but they were black and sleek, far more businesslike than the goofy helmet. She looked up at Denny and waved, big sunny grin on her face and coltish legs wobbling beneath her. There was a stop sign coming up and Rob was starting to slow down for it. Denny was afraid his lewd partner would see the girl and make some horrible sexual remark about her. That was when Denny noticed the pothole.

It was broad and deep, about the size of a watermelon. The girl was headed right for it.

"Hey, kid, look out," he said through the rolled up window.

The girl frowned at him, a puzzled expression on her face as she tried to make out his words through the bulletproof glass. He pointed emphatically towards the pothole and she turned to look. When she saw what he was pointing at, her eyes went wide and she awkwardly swerved to avoid it. To Denny's horror, she stumbled and fell directly into the path of the armored car.

There was a sickening thump and the pink helmet flew into the air, smacking against the windshield and flipping up over the roof. Rob slammed on the brakes.

"Holy shit," he said. "Tell me we didn't just hit a kid."

Denny didn't bother to answer. He flung the door open and ran around the back of the armored car. Rob jumped out after him.

"You see anything?" Rob asked.

Denny shook his head and realized that the girl must still be down under the wheels. A sick kind of dread filled his belly as he crouched down to look beneath the vehicle.

The girl lay prone and groaning beneath the rear axle, her blonde hair wet with blood. Amazingly, it looked like she'd fallen directly between the wheels, narrowly avoiding being run over by the car's fat, puncture-proof radials. She held a bloody, shaking hand out towards Denny.

"Help me," she whispered.

"Tell Tiny to call an ambulance!" Denny told Rob as he reached out to help the girl.

She clasped his hand and began to crawl out from under the car.

"I don't think you oughta move, kid," Denny said. "You could have broken something."

"I think I'm all right," the girl said. Her voice was high and breathless. "I'm all right."

"You might be hurt worse than you think," Denny said, helping her over to the curb and sitting down beside her. Blood was dribbling down along her jaw-line and splattering onto her Hello Kitty T-shirt. "Just sit here and wait for the ambulance, okay?"

"Okay," she said, carefully pulling her panda back-pack off her back and unzipping it. "Let me just..."

"What do you need, kid?" Denny asked as she rummaged groggily through the bag.

"All your money," she replied sweetly, pushing the muzzle of a cute little Baby Eagle 9mm pistol into the soft hollow beneath Denny's chin. "Motherfucker."

"Aw, shit," Denny said.

The heist had been Courtney's idea. Courtney Aimes was a former stuntwoman who made a career of doubling child actors. She was five feet even and ninety-eight pounds soaking wet, though she was certainly no weakling. She had retired at the age of twenty-three, coincidentally the same age as Denny, forsaking the movie biz for a far more lucrative life of crime. A former gymnast and martial artist with an expensive taste in clothes, cars and cocaine, Courtney found the outlaw lifestyle suited her perfectly. She was a good actor and could run brilliant scams, wriggle through tight spaces and shoot the ace out of the ace of spades from fifty yards.

Courtney had planned every aspect of this score down to the millisecond. It was not her first criminal endeavor, but this one was her baby, the first heist she'd planned herself from start to finish.

The first phase of the operation had gone like clockwork. The bump, the fake blood and most importantly, the military issue concussive limpet mine she'd secretly attached to the belly of the armored car as soon as she went under. Everything went perfectly according to plan. That mine was built to blow holes in the hulls of ships, but the way it was shaped, the fire went down and the bang went up. Theoretically, it should send up a concussive blast strong enough to tear a hole out of the bottom of the truck, blow off the back doors and pulverize the guard sitting in the back before he had a chance to call it in.

Courtney smiled at the big goofy guard that had helped her up, pressing her pistol harder against his neck. Less than a heartbeat later, the cavalry arrived, right on schedule. Her boyfriend Sykes, his buddy Kyle and a cheerful psychopath named Lenny all zipped up on roller blades, black clad and armed to the teeth. They all wore plastic Hello Kitty masks. The resulting look was really quite disturbing.

"Just stay cool and nobody gets hurt," Sykes said, escorting the short guard around the side of the truck to join his tall buddy at the business end of a Glock 31 while Kyle backed it up with a sawn-off shotgun and Lenny handled the crowd and kept everyone polite from a distance with his new Kel-Tec SU-16.

That SU-16 rifle was Lenny's new favorite toy. A gas operated semi auto, built to fold up like a beach chair and fit inside a briefcase, he referred to it as his "go anywhere" gun. Lenny fancied himself a survivalist of sorts and was really into things that folded up. He was dying to use his new toy on a live target, but Courtney hoped it wouldn't come to that.

Sykes had vouched for Lenny a million times, but Courtney still wasn't completely sure. He was an odd duck with one eye that tended to wander away while you were talking to him, but Sykes swore Lenny was solid and Courtney trusted Sykes's judgment. They had been dating for nearly eight months and Courtney was starting to fear that she might be falling in love with him. They met on a dangerous daylight bank job and the chemistry between them was immediate and incendiary. He was thirty-nine, a demolitions man with a military background and had the kind of hard, blue-eyed good looks that could have gotten him work in action films if he weren't wanted in eleven states for a list of felonies so long his rap sheet read like a legal textbook. He liked Courtney to wear school uniforms, saddle shoes and white cotton panties. She called him Daddy, but there was no question who wore the pants in their relationship.

Courtney only looked sweet and helpless. Beneath that candy coating, she was a supreme and expert manipulator, as amoral as a rattlesnake. She had learned how to crack men like safes long ago and did whatever it took to get exactly what she wanted. But Sykes, he was different. He had backbone. He indulged her in everything she wanted, but she got the feeling that he was allowing her to manipulate him, like a grown lion indulgently tolerating the play attacks of a rambunctious cub. He was starting to earn her respect. Not to mention the fact that sex with Sykes was the best she'd ever had. She found herself lost in rosy, Bonnie and Clyde daydreams of them living happily ever after, until they went down side by side in a hail of bullets. She had never told him that she loved him, but she found there were more and more breathless, pregnant pauses in their lovemaking where they would look into each other's eyes and it was almost as if she could hear those unspoken words resonating between them.

"You okay, baby?" Sykes asked Courtney from beneath his weird, mouthless, cutsie kitty face as he skated up beside her.

"Peachy," Courtney said. "Where's our ride?"

"On her way," Sykes said. "No worries."

The fifth wheel of the operation was Courtney's good friend Mickie, a saucy stunt driver with natural double-D breasts and a sailor's mouth. She would be pulling up in the florist's van as soon as the mine detonated, which, Courtney thought, should be right about...

Now.

The sound of the explosion was a deep, weighty slap that pressed in viciously on the air inside Courtney's ears. The armored car jumped up as if startled by the blossom of flame beneath it then fell over on its side like an injured rhino. The back doors flew off just as predicted. From there, Courtney's neat little plan went to hell in a handbasket.

Courtney and her entourage watched in utter jaw dropping disbelief as approximately two point three million dollars went violently airborne, enveloping them in a flapping green cloud of hundred dollar bills. All around them, people were squealing ecstatically and running into the street, snatching at the money and stuffing handfuls down their shirts. Kyle hollered for the civilians to stay the fuck back, punctuating this request with a throaty blast from the shottie. The basso profundo roar of the sawn-off Remington 870 made Courtney jump but seemed to have no effect whatsoever on the greedy bystanders.

Mickie pulled up in the florist's van, flying money swirling in her wake. She got out, staring up at the cash fallout with hands on her hips.

"You have got to be kidding me," she said.

That was when the third guard, the back guard who by all rights should have been as dead as Dillinger, fired several wild shots, hitting Mickie in both the gut and the throat.

Mickie fell to the ground in a spectacular fountain of blood as the third guard slowly crawled from the back of the armored car. His entire body looked flattened and crushed as if he had leapt from a skyscraper. He was hemorrhaging freely from every orifice and it was just not possible that he could still be alive, yet there he was, blindly dragging himself along the street and leaving a thick trail of dark blood.

Upon seeing the pitiful state of his fallen colleague, the short guard went ballistic, hollering like a baboon on crank and grabbing Sykes's pistol. Lenny whooped and put a slug in the back of the guy's shaved head, but that did not stop the guard from turning the Glock on Sykes and ventilating his chest several times at close range. Kyle let the short guy have it with the shottie, vaporizing everything above his navy blue collar into a fine red mist and showering them all in hot sticky gore. Courtney screamed Sykes's name and the tall guard took that opportunity to neatly break her right arm, sending the Baby Eagle skittering across the bloody pavement. Her scream ratcheted up an octave and she fell to the ground cocooned in hot red agony.

Lenny saw what was going down and quickly grabbed himself a handy civilian, a terrified Korean shopkeeper. He slung the SU-16 back over his shoulder and pressed his compact Para Warthog .45 into the depression beneath her left ear. She dropped the plastic bag she had been filling with flying bills and screamed. Lenny scooped up her bag and headed for the still idling van, figuring now would be a swell time to cut and run.

A sudden burst of heat and pain blossomed in his right thigh and Lenny went down on one knee, pulling the shopkeeper down with him. He turned towards the sound of a second shot and fired out of instinct, narrowly missing the shopkeeper's armed and furious husband.

"What the hell is happening?" Courtney screamed, cradling her broken arm and watching helplessly as her perfect score rapidly collapsed into a lunatic free for all.

The headless guard was wandering around like a bad actor, arms waving like someone imitating a zombie. Sykes lay on the street, eyes wide and teeth clenched as his blood ran down the gutter. Mickie was trying to pull herself up into the driver's seat of the van, but kept slipping in her own blood. Kyle and the tall guard were grappling furiously. Lenny was engaged in a wild shootout with an angry Korean shopkeeper. The pulverized rear guard crawled in slow, blind circles while all around him, people danced and chased the flying bills.

Sykes was dying. There was no way he was going survive those chest shots. She crawled across the asphalt and took him in her arms, pulling off the bloody mask. She caressed his sweaty brow and bent to kiss his lips.

"I love you, Daddy," she said, taking his hand and reaching for her fallen Baby Eagle.

"I love you too, baby," Sykes replied.

She squeezed his fingers and he squeezed back as she pressed the muzzle of the gun to her temple. She pulled the trigger.

She did not die. Neither did he.

Every time Rhonda was in the hospital, the doctors that she talked to would always try to convince her that she was seeing things that were not real. They patiently explained over and over again that there was this problem with the chemicals inside Rhonda's head and those wrong chemicals made her see things that were not there. Rhonda nodded and acted like she understood what they were talking about in order to get free, but in truth, she always suspected them of trying to trick her. Until now.

Now, for the first time in her life, Rhonda was starting to wonder if what she was seeing could possibly be real. As she stood at the corner of Broadway and Lincoln, surrounded by a whirlwind of flying hundred dollar bills, she simply could not believe her eyes.

There was an amazing riot going on amid the spiraling storm of cash. Roachy-looking SWAT cops were battling a futuristic Sanrio roller derby team. Regular people were shot a whole bunch of times and crawling through drifts of bloody money. No matter how many times the police snipers shot the Kitty-faced roller derby guys, they just kept on fighting. One guy had a lady hostage and was shouting out incoherent demands. Authoritative voices told him to remain calm, but he didn't listen. Fascinated Roaches clustered around the edges of the action, watching silently with feelers quivering in disbelief. Even they were too shocked and enthralled by the grisly spectacle to notice Rhonda. News vans arrived one after the other, daredevil camera crews competing to capture the most horrifying footage. Helicopters circled overhead like huge noisy flies. Sirens screamed and so did the injured. Chaos and madness seemed to have completely swallowed the familiar intersection. No one was paying any attention whatsoever to Rhonda.

Rhonda fished inside her roomy pockets for the brand new, folded up, extra thick Hefty trash bag the nice lady at the soup kitchen had given her. It had never been used before, and Rhonda had been planning to either wear it as an extra shirt or use it to shore up her little fort. Instead she shook it open and started filling it with hundred dollar bills. Ever since she'd found that dead guy who wasn't dead, things had been strange and wondrous for Rhonda. At first she was terrified, but now, she saw the true nature of her good fortune. With all these hundred dollar bills, she could buy all the fresh foil she wanted. She could have new foil every day for the rest of her life. Sure, it was too bad for all those shot people who couldn't die, but they were all controlled by the Roaches anyway so it wasn't like their lives were ever going to amount to anything.

When her bag was full, Rhonda slung it over her shoulder and quietly slipped away.

EIGHTEEN

Every year since she was nine, Danica Ciavarella had been traveling to Bologna to spend the summer with her father's mother, Nonna Ermelinda. Now she was seventeen, about to celebrate her eighteenth birthday that August, and this year things were a little different. This year, she was in love.

Ermelinda's husband Giancarlo had been a professor at the venerable and ancient University of Bologna before he died, and she'd never moved out of the bustling college neighborhood that was still the center of her social life. She rented rooms in her beautiful old house to students during the school year in order to make ends meet. In the summers, she had Danica.

Danica spent most of her time hanging around the the edges of the campus the locals referred to as UniBo and the little cafes and trendy shops that cropped up all around it. She was fluent in Italian and considered herself nearly a native, but as she grew older, she began to realize the exotic allure of her foreign accent and tended to play it up when flirting with the handsome young students. Nonna

Ermelinda worried and fretted endlessly about Danica's virginity and tended to watch her alluring American granddaughter like a hawk, never knowing that Danica's precious virginity was already long gone. In spite of this, Danica had to admit that she liked being fussed and fretted over. Her mother never seemed to care what she did and her stepmother was too enthralled with her father to bother advising Danica about the birds and the bees. It was nice to have Nonna Ermelinda worrying about her virtue and telling her that she was too skinny.

Danica always gained five or ten pounds in Italy. It was impossible to avoid all the tempting sausages, pastas and pastries. Nonna Ermelinda was always chasing Danica around with spoonfuls of sauce and slices of cheese. Plus Italian men were so much more appreciative of her budding curves and she always got more whistles and catcalls towards the end of August than when she first arrived. No worries though, she would spend a few weeks on the treadmill when she got back to the States and would be ready to start auditioning again by the beginning of October.

Of course, having Nonna Ermelinda watching her every move made the temptation to sneak out all the more powerful. The nightlife in the student quarter was always jumping, even during the lazy summer, and Danica could not resist slipping out at night to clandestine meetings with eager young men. Summer was a time of flux and change in Bologna. Students coming and going, moving in and moving out, and it was easy to enjoy frivolous flings with boys she knew she would probably never see again. None of them had really made much of an impression on Danica. Not until Alessandro.

He was a local boy, a guitar player with fierce dark eyes and a charismatic smile. The only son of a notorious local chef, he grew up in the kitchen of one of Bologna's most famous restaurants. His father fully expected his son to follow in his footsteps, but Alessandro had other ideas. He wanted to travel to America and study American blues guitar. Obsessed with Robert Johnson and Stevie Ray Vaughn, he had a fetish for all things American. He loved the sound of Danica's voice and wanted to speak only English when they were together. Danica had a warm, husky singing voice, too, and he would always beg her to sing with him. He played three nights a week at a local bar and every time she came to see him, he would drag her up on stage to do a few numbers. She didn't put up much of a fight. Danica was an actress at heart and loved showing off. The chemistry between then was intense and undeniable.

They were together for less than two weeks before they began talking of finding an apartment together back in the States and embarking on an epic road trip down through the American south, from Memphis to New Orleans. Danica had considered applying to UniBo, but lately she was starting to think that going out and living life was far more important to her development as an actor than a university education.

That night, Danica snuck out to meet Alessandro, and he picked her up on his vintage '53 Motto Guzzi Falcone Sport, looking handsome and roguish as always. They made out for several breathless minutes before she climbed on the back of the motorcycle and rode off into the hot summer night, arms wound around his narrow waist and hair flying behind her, belly full of luscious anticipation. They sped all the way back to Alessandro's tiny garret apartment and spent the next few hours lost in each other's arms, making love and making plans for their exciting new life together. They drank expensive wine pilfered from the cellars of his father's restaurant and promised to love each other until the end of time. It was perfect, and as they rode back to Nonna Ermelinda's, Danica felt happier than she had ever been.

As they sped down Via Zamboni, Alessandro was briefly distracted by the caress of Danica's hand on his denim thigh. That was all it took.

A cured meat truck was backing out of an alley and did not see the motorcycle coming. Alessandro spotted the truck too late and tried to swerve out of the way. The bike skewed sideways, slamming into the side of the truck at eighty kilometers per hour.

Danica felt a thunderclap of pain, followed by a deluge of black, drowning dizziness. She did not remember hitting the truck, but the image of the happy little calf with a crown on its head, the meat company's logo, was burned into her mind. How morbid, she thought, that the cute little calf is encouraging people to eat his brothers. That was the last thing she remembered before waking up in the hospital to the most unspeakable pain she had ever experienced.

Gina was filing some backed-up paperwork when she heard her name over the PA. A phone call. In an instant, her blood went to ice. There was only one reason why she would be receiving a phone call at Mercy. Her work, home and cell numbers were all listed as emergency contact information inside Danica's passport.

The overseas connection was bad, faint and crackly, and the doctor on the other end was close to hysterical. His English was not good and Gina could not make sense of what he was telling her.

"Your daughter Danica, she has a moto crash," he was saying. "She is hurt very much in the neck and the head."

There were a thousand medical questions flooding into her mind, but the Italian doctor did not seem to understand anything she was saying. He kept on repeating that Danica was "not alive," but when Gina asked if Dani was dead he would say no, she was not dead, but not alive. Frustrated and furious, she took the number of the hospital and called Matteo.

"Hello?" asked a sleepy female voice. The new wife. Great.

"Cynthia," Gina said, her own voice calm and steady. "I need to speak to Matteo."

"What time is it?" Cynthia asked vaguely.

Gina took a deep breath. "It's an emergency," she said.

There was a muffled shuffling and Gina could hear Cynthia's syrupy, lovey-dovey voice talking to Matteo. She wanted to reach through the phone and strangle the woman. Finally Matteo's familiar voice came on the line.

"What's wrong, Gina?"

"Dani has been in a motorcycle accident," Gina said. "She's in critical condition. I need you to call the hospital in Bologna and get some solid information right away. Get a pen."

She gave Matteo a list of specific medical questions to ask the doctor.

"Call now and call me back," she said, hanging up without saying goodbye.

As she stood, one palm on the desk, nauseous chills racing through her body, she felt as if her hand on the desk was the only thing stopping her from flying into a thousand pieces.

She grabbed the receiver of the phone the second she heard the crackle of the PA system, but it was not her phone call. It was incoming trauma.

NINETEEN

Dr Ferguson put his knuckles to his mouth and cocked his head. Even listening to the truncated and simplified announcement over the PA system sent waves of anxiety and anticipation through his churning guts: a city bus crash involving a gasoline tanker truck. Over fifty individuals were severely injured, and of those fifty, nineteen of the injuries were critical and life threatening. All nineteen were en route to Mercy. There was nowhere else for them to go.

The ambulances started to hit the loading area three minutes later, EMS personnel swarming the ER like soldiers storming the beach at Normandy. The injuries were all hideous beyond belief and triage was next to impossible. Every single patient that came through the door was burned over more than fifty percent of their bodies. Pages were sent out to every physician within a hundred mile radius as Dr Ferguson and the ER staff struggled to stabilize screaming, agonized patients, all with catastrophic inhalation injuries from breathing superheated smoke and flame, panicking as their airways were sealed by creeping edema. Dr Ferguson did tracheotomy after tracheotomy until he was starting to feel more like a butcher than a doctor. Gina was close behind him, struggling desperately to find any good veins to draw blood for ABG and carboxyhemoglobin levels and to start the critical IV fluid replacement, but Dr Ferguson could see there was something wrong with his normally rock-solid coworker. Her hands were shaking worse than his. But the patients just kept coming and there was no time to ask if she was okay.

Hispanic male: seventeen, sixty-one percent burned. Hispanic female: eleven, seventy-eight percent. Hispanic female: fifty-three, sixty-seven percent. Asian male: sixty-nine, fifty-two percent. Black male: twenty-one, eighty percent. White female: eighteen, fifty-nine percent. White male: forty-seven, an unbelievably gruesome ninety-eight percent of his body burned. And they just kept on coming, an endless parade of numbers and percentages that started to mean less and less to Dr Ferguson, as a kind of shell-shocked war zone mentality took over, moving his hands on autopilot, hustling any emotions out of his mind. He felt nothing. He could not see people, only tasks, one after the other.

Together, he and Gina concentrated on their current task, an overweight black woman, apparently the driver of the bus. Her eyes were huge and terrified in her barbecued face and her artificial braids had melted into the charred skin of her scalp and neck. Her name was Linda and Dr Ferguson could hear Gina trying to say the woman's name again and again to keep her focused.

"Can you hear me, Linda?" she asked. "I need you to hang in there, Linda. Hang in there, okay? We're here to help you, Linda. Can you hear me?"

The woman's massive limbs were burned completely away below the knees and elbows. There was no unburned skin anywhere on her arms or legs so Dr Ferguson was forced to start a subclavian IV. As he did so, the woman twitched and twisted, hissing like an angry snake through her tracheotomy. It took him three tries to finally sink the needle in. She had thick, leathery and inflexible eschar around what remained of all four limbs and banding her wide thorax, restricting her breathing and trapping the rapidly swelling tissue beneath. Dr Ferguson knew he was going to have to perform an emergency bedside escharatomy, a procedure he had only ever read about and never even seen, let alone performed. It was not complicated in theory, he merely had to make a careful incision along the stiffened area, penetrating to the depth of the superficial fascia. On this woman, that would entail long cuts down both legs and arms, and also an H shaped cut on her chest with the bar of the H falling just below her sternum. Of course, in real life, it was not quite so simple. The woman had massive breasts that he would have to cut into and she was flailing and shuddering, air still hissing violently through the hole in her throat.

Dr Ferguson struggled to calm himself and took the scalpel Gina placed in his waiting hand. He forced himself to focus and slowly, deliberately began to cut.

Once the pressure was relieved, he and Gina began the daunting task of debriding her burns. There was so much charred and dead tissue that they hardly knew where to begin. Dr Ferguson ordered Gina to hit the patient with a heavy morphine drip and then they went to work. The only blessing with burns this deep was that many of the nerve endings are destroyed in the process, killing the ability to feel pain in that area. However, that did not stop the agony of her swollen lungs and the rampaging terror inside her all too conscious brain.

Not a minute later, in spite of their ongoing efforts to prevent burn shock, their patient started crashing fast, going abruptly V-fib. Before Dr Ferguson could put down the scissors, she had gone apneic, pulseless. Yet to Dr Ferguson's utter amazement and disbelief, the patient was still fully conscious, still looking up at him with pleading eyes that seemed to beg him to do something, anything to help her. He struggled to restart her heart, to no avail, but he could not bring himself to stop trying, to give up and declare her dead, because she somehow wasn't. She kept looking right into his eyes, still impossibly conscious, still suffering. How could he declare someone dead while they were still conscious, watching him?

Suddenly, he realized what was happening. It was that strange patient. The man who said he was Death. He said that he would not be taking any more souls and in a sudden awful burst of understanding, Dr Ferguson knew exactly what that really meant. The lack of obituaries, the gang girls, the patient in front of him, it all added up and he saw with a horrible clarity what was really going on.

"It's Death," he said. "I have to find him."

Gina looked up at him as if he had lost his mind. Then, he saw a kind of horrified realization dawning in her eyes. She pressed her lips together and nodded slowly.

TWENTY

The exam room, where the man who called himself Death had been waiting to be admitted, was now occupied by a small child, burned beyond any recognizable gender. A team of doctors was fighting to resuscitate their technically lifeless, yet horribly conscious patient while the child cried and cried, a hoarse, breathless and miserable sound that hurt to listen to.

Determination renewed, Dr Ferguson frantically searched through the maze of Mercy Hospital. As he passed a small knot of nurses, he overheard their gossipy tones discussing Gina's daughter. The girl had been in a motorcycle crash and was brain dead. Yet another victim, frozen in agonizing limbo. He had to find the strange patient. Dr Ferguson checked the morgue and found no one but Megan. She asked what was wrong, but there was no time to explain. The hospital complex was vast and he was beginning to lose hope when he saw the mysterious patient standing alone on an observation deck overlooking the city, holding a single perfect white rose plucked from one of the nearby bushes.

"Hi Jay," the patient said, smiling beatifically. "Isn't it a beautiful morning?"

"You have to stop this," Dr Ferguson said.

"What?" The patient frowned.

"You have to let people die."

"But Jay," the patient said, "I thought we agreed that it would be a good idea if no one had to die. I thought we were on the same page."

"When you said you weren't going to take any more souls," Dr Ferguson said, "that no one would die, I thought you meant no one would be hurt."

The patient looked at Dr Ferguson, incredulous. "What, do you think I'm some kind of god?" he asked. "That I have the power to stop bullets and car crashes and disease?" He made a soft, dismissive noise. "Give me a break. I'm just a civil servant."

"You have to start taking souls again," Dr Ferguson said. "There are people in there, people in horrible, unnatural agony. You are the only one that can help them."

The patient didn't seem to hear him. He simply held up the pale, flawless blossom, contemplating its full-blown perfection.

"You want me to start taking the plants again too, huh?" The patient brought the rose to his face and inhaled its fragrance. "Plants, animals, even all those pesky little microscopic critters you and your lot are always fighting against."

Dr Ferguson's eyes went wide and he realized that the current pain and suffering was only the tip of the iceberg. He thought of that little abused girl, wasting away from ravenous bacterial infections that would not respond to antibiotics. He thought of every virus and germ that would not die inside the autoclave, spreading unchecked through every patient and staff member in the hospital on permanently contaminated instruments and surfaces. The implications were unspeakable. He shook his head.

"Yes," Dr Ferguson said, more determined than ever. "Yes, you have to start again. You can't just turn your back on all this suffering."

"Can't I?" The patient turned away, looking out over the hazy morning cityscape. "It's not my problem. I feel fine. Better than ever, actually."

"Please," Dr Ferguson said. "I'm begging you."

"You are begging me?" The patient smirked. "Dr Jay Ferguson, saver of lives, is begging me to start taking his patients again?"

"Yes," Dr Ferguson said. "You've made me understand that death is not always the enemy. That you are a critical part of life and without you, the world would be a hellish nightmare of unending suffering."

The patient cocked his head, curious. "You really mean that?"

Dr Ferguson nodded. "Please," he said. "You have to help those people. That little girl. They need you. Please."

"Do you still have my book?" the patient asked.

Dr Ferguson frowned. For a second he did not know what the patient meant. Then he remembered: the address book. It was still in the breast pocket of his bloody scrubs right where he'd left it.

"Here," he said, pulling the little book out and offering it to the patient. "Take it, it's yours."

"Why don't you have a look inside, Jay?"

Dr Ferguson flipped through the pages. They were the same as before, a variety of names. He was beginning to feel sharp hooks of frustration sinking into his belly, but he sensed there would be no rushing the strange patient.

"It's full of names," Dr Ferguson said. "The names of people meant to die?"

"That's right, Jay," the patient said. "Why don't you read the first page?"

Dr Ferguson clenched his teeth, biting down on his growing frustration. He opened the little book to the first page.

The first entry in the book read Dr Jay Ferguson.

"Is this for real?" Dr Ferguson asked, eyes wide.

The strange patient nodded. "I'm afraid so, Jay," he said. "Are you still so eager for the dying to start again?"

Dr Ferguson thought of lovely Megan and the date he'd made with her. He thought of his future, children he wanted to have someday and a whole lifetime of experience that would never be. He thought of cousin Holly, clutching the telephone and sobbing, broken-hearted to have lost yet another beloved family member. Then he thought of the bus driver, her terrified eyes begging for him to stop her pain, and the little girl, the burned child, his friends and colleagues who would be infected and sickened by plagues of undying viruses. He knew there was no choice. No choice at all.

"Yes," Dr Ferguson said. "I'm sure."

The strange patient looked at Dr Ferguson, searching his face and looking deep into his eyes. Dr Ferguson met that ancient dark gaze without flinching. He knew he was doing the right thing. The only thing.

"I am very impressed, Jay," the patient said. "Your noble sacrifice makes me think that there might be hope for the human race after all."

The patient held out his hand.

Dr Ferguson looked down at the patient's slender hand. A cold lick of fear coiled inside his heart. Could this really be the end? The end of everything?

At the far side of the observation deck, a scrawny young woman appeared through the wide glass doors. She was black, but very pale skinned, with short frizzy reddish blonde hair that had been scraped back into a small, uneven pony tail, but was fighting to escape its bonds, sticking up in uneven licks all over her head. She wore dirty red sweatpants and a stained, oversized white T-shirt. She had heavy dark circles under her wide, manic eyes, and moved like some kind of jittering animated scarecrow.

"You Diamond's doctor?" the woman asked.

"Yes," Dr Ferguson said, looking at the strange patient then to the skinny woman.

"You think I hurt my baby?" the woman asked, her voice grating and full of nails. "Is that what you think?"

"It's time, Jay," the strange patient said.

Fear was huge and running free inside of Dr Ferguson now. His guts felt loose and sick and he suddenly had to pee rather badly. He looked down at the patient's offered hand and took a deep, shaky breath.

Just as Dr Ferguson's fingers closed around the patient's cool, outstretched hand, an enormous sound shattered the morning stillness. Dr Ferguson was amazed and appalled by what he saw.

While he remained standing, holding the strange patient's hand, Dr Ferguson saw his own body fall away from him, spinning and spraying blood as it collapsed to the ground. There was no pain. He saw the madwoman step forward and empty the clip of a cheap pistol into his twitching body. Security guards poured though the doors, wrestling the screeching, flailing woman to the ground. In spite of her scrawny frame it still took more than one man to hold her down and disarm her. Gina appeared, running to the aid of his swiftly dying body. Her face was calm and collected as always as she smoothly administered hopeless CPR, but Dr Ferguson was shocked to see a single tear sliding down her right cheek.

"Well, Jay," the strange patient said, "I've got quite a bit of catching up to do."

When Dr Ferguson turned back to the strange patient, there was a small crowd of people around him. The bus driver and a dozen others from the bus crash. Two petite Asian girls, arms wrapped fearfully around each other; a surly, overweight man with glasses; a young, well-dressed man with a goatee; a knot of frightened soldiers and a pair of thin, ragged men. A beautiful teenage girl with dark hair who looked painfully like Gina; a black-clad cluster of skaters and some SWAT cops; the gang girls and their babies. Two docile cows and an exuberant little black and white dog that jumped up and licked the strange patient's fingers. And there were more and more every second, forming a large, amorphous crowd that stretched back farther than Dr Ferguson could see.

The perfect white rose in the strange patient's hand began to wilt, delicate, ruffled petals browning around the edges. He let it fall to the ground, where it landed in a puddle of Dr Ferguson's blood.

"Sorry for the delay, everyone," the strange patient said. "We now return to your regularly scheduled deaths. Right this way please."

The strange patient led his growing crowd through the hospital corridors, towards a large red door marked EXIT. As they went, Dr Ferguson spotted little Diamond Day on a stretcher in the ER hallway. She was sleeping peacefully, her fever finally broken. Lita was at her side, stroking her sweat damp hair. Dr Ferguson knew without a doubt that he had done the right thing.

Say goodbye to Dr Jay Ferguson. Those who knew the good doctor will say his death was untimely, that it came out of nowhere. But after one night at Mercy, we know that is not true. His death came from somewhere—in The Twilight Zone.

ABOUT THE AUTHOR

Born in New York City on June 21st 1969. Divorced parents. Ran away a lot. Wrote a lot. Sold her first story in 1994. First novel in 1998. Doesn't plan on stopping any time soon. Loves vintage high heels and Mexican wrestling. She owns two dogs: Boston Terriers named Butch and Emma. Previous novels include *Control Freak*, *Triads* (with Poppy Z Brite) and *Hoodtown*. Faust previously wrote for Black Flame with *A Nightmare on Elm Street: Dreamspawn*. The rest is none of your business.

"Christa Faust is a Veronica in a World of Betties."
— Quentin Tarantino

Also from Black Flame
The Twilight Zone

MEMPHIS · THE POOL GUY

by Jay Russell

After what seemed like an eternity, Ritchie's name was finally called over the crackly loudspeaker and he was directed to an examination room. Once inside, he was told to remove his shirt and wait for the doctor. He started to do so as the attendant left the room then decided that he would prefer to leave his shirt on for the moment. Much as he couldn't resist scratching at the itchy wound, Ritchie realized that he didn't want to sit there and have to look at it the whole time. He would wait until Dr Rosoff arrived and take his shirt off only when he really had to.

Another long wait ensued in the examination room. Ritchie sat on the exam table for a while, but his impatience grew. He got up and paced around the perimeter of the room, reading the dull charts and posters on the walls about measles vaccines and sexually transmitted diseases and the amazing advantages of breast feeding. That one made Ritchie snigger as he read it twice: he was all in favor of breast feeding whenever possible. Heh heh.

Ritchie was re-reading the detailed instructions over the sink on the proper way for medical professionals to wash their hands, when the exam room door flew open and Rosoff came in. She didn't look up, but continued to read a chart in her hand as she walked. She was carrying a whole stack of them under her arm. Her stethoscope was draped around her neck like a boa and she wore black denim jeans and a plain, pale yellow blouse under her stained white lab coat.

Rosoff wasn't an unattractive woman, though with her dark brown hair pulled back tightly in a bun she looked more than a little severe. Probably on purpose, Ritchie guessed, to keep the patients at a distance. He tried to imagine how she might look after hours and he suspected that with her hair down, a little make-up on and a blouse with two buttons undone, Rosoff wouldn't look half-bad. She could certainly breast feed Ritchie from that ample chest of hers any old day. Ritchie reckoned that Rosoff was about his age, thirty-seven, which for some reason always made him a little bit angry. He knew it was foolish and irrational, but the fact that a contemporary of his could be so much better off than he was—so much smarter, richer, capable, professional—just plain cheesed him off. Deep down he knew that the feeling was all about him and had nothing to do with the doctor herself, but it still bristled at something inside of him.

Even so, Ritchie had come to sort-of like Dr Rosoff. The first time she'd come through the door to examine him he had demanded to see a different doctor because he didn't like the idea of being examined by a woman. But that complaint had fallen on deaf ears. He was told, in no uncertain terms, that he could see the doctor assigned to him or he could walk out the door. Ritchie had been so sick with the flu that day that he couldn't say no and so Dr Rosoff it was. As it turned out, he decided that women doctors were okay; after all, they were a little easier to talk to than men about some things. That was why, today, he'd been so insistent that he could only be examined by Dr Rosoff.

"Ritchie," Dr Rosoff said, still reading the chart. "Long time no see. Always a good thing in a patient."

"Heya, Doc," Ritchie replied.

Doctor Rosoff offered him the briefest of smiles then flipped through the pages on the chart. She tossed the rest of her paperwork down on a stool and gestured for Ritchie to take a seat on the examination table. Surprised by his own high level of anxiety he climbed aboard, dangling his legs over the edge.

"So, how have you been, Ritchie? I knew it had been a while and I see from your records that you never showed up for your last appointment."

"I've been okay, Doc. I mean until today. I... I didn't think I needed that other appointment. At the time, you know?" Ritchie nervously licked his lips and drummed his fingers on the hard padding of the table.

"Uh-huh," Rosoff said. "So what happened today then? What brings you here?"

Ritchie realized that he didn't know where even to begin. The entire experience was so crazy, so weird. How could he explain what had happened in his dream, how terrifying it was, to this stern looking doctor standing in front of him with a million other patients—old ladies and kids, for Chrissake—demanding her more immediate attention?

"Ritchie?" Rosoff said, a hint of annoyance in her tone.

"It's..."

"I haven't got all day, Ritchie. You know what it's like here."

Ritchie nodded in reply, then shook his head and finally, in exasperation, lifted up his T-shirt.

"Here," he said. He pointed a finger at the scar above his heart.

Doctor Rosoff leaned in to take a closer look. She gently prodded the skin around the scar, then turned and pulled a pair of rubber surgical gloves out of a box hanging on the wall. She carefully slipped them on and walked back over to Ritchie who was still sitting there holding his shirt up.

"Why don't you take that shirt right off?" the doctor said.

Ritchie slipped the T-shirt off over his head.

Doctor Rosoff ran a gloved finger along the inside edge of the scar. It wasn't itching so badly now, but it still felt slightly raw as she poked at the loose flaps of skin. In Ritchie's mind's eye he saw the dark-haired man with the beady eyes standing in front of him. As Rosoff pressed a little bit harder against the center of the scar, Ritchie could have sworn he felt the bullet once more penetrating his chest. He flinched and let out a little grunt.

"Is that very sore?" the doctor asked.

"It's a little sensitive, yeah," Ritchie told her. "It's crazy, huh?"

Doctor Rosoff stepped back and looked Ritchie in the eye.

"How did you get the scar, Ritchie?" she asked.

"That's what I mean," Ritchie said. "It's totally crazy."

"I'm afraid I don't understand."

"I just woke up this morning and it was there."

Rosoff did a double-take.

"I'm sorry?" she said.

"It was worse this morning, though. First thing, I mean. It was kind of... weepy I guess you'd call it. And it was a lot redder too. Kind of wet, you know? Like it was fresher or something."

"What happened to you in the night, Ritchie?" the doctor asked.

"Nothing! Well, I mean nothing really. I had this dream, see?"

Doctor Rosoff picked her papers up off the stool and tossed them onto the counter by the sink. She dragged the wheeled stool over and sat down on it, taking a good measure of her patient.

"You had a dream," she said.

"It's crazy, I know. I can hardly believe it myself."

"I'm just not following you here, Ritchie. You're going to have to make a little bit more sense."

Ritchie shook his head. "That's just it, don't you see? It doesn't make no sense at all. I mean it was just a dream, right? And they don't always make sense, I know that. But I dreamed that someone shot me, you know? Right here." He pointed to the scar on his chest. "And in the dream it was so real, it was just like it was really happening. It hurt like a sonofa... It really hurt. And I could feel myself dying, you know? I could feel that my heart stopped beating. And I started to scream and my roommate, Leonard, he... Well, it don't matter about Leonard. But he had to come and wake me up out of it I was screaming so loud, and when I woke up in my bed, I had this."

Ritchie ran his finger along the scar again.

Doctor Rosoff slid the stool back and slipped the gloves off her hands with a pop. "Look, Ritchie, if you don't want to tell me where you got this injury that's up to you, but—"

"I just did tell you!" Ritchie shouted. The doctor eased her stool back another foot. "I dreamed that someone shot me, right? A man with dark hair and nasty, tiny black eyes. He had a big gun and he pointed it at my chest and he pulled the trigger and when I woke up..."

"You had this," Rosoff said.

She sounded doubtful. Who could blame her? Ritchie knew how loco it sounded.

"I knew it," Ritchie exclaimed. He slapped his hand against the table with considerable force. The tissue paper sanitary sheet tore and fluttered to the floor. Doctor Rosoff watched it fall then flicked her eyes back to Ritchie. He was staring down at the floor and said: "I knew you wouldn't believe me."

Ritchie started fiddling with the scar again. It was itching like crazy now, starting to feel sore again.

"Calm down, Ritchie," Doctor Rosoff said. She pulled her stool back closer to Ritchie and rested a calming hand on his knee. "Do you remember the last time you were here? Before the appointment that you skipped?"

Ritchie nodded his head. He felt a nervousness in his stomach, though, suddenly as distressing as the itching of the scar on his chest. He started to sweat again, too.

"Do you remember what we talked about then?" Rosoff asked him.

"That was when I hurt my hand."

"Yes," the doctor said. "You put your hand through a plate glass window, remember? You cut yourself quite badly."

Ritchie involuntarily shuddered. He was feeling very cold now without his shirt, but he made no move to put it back on. He wrapped his arms around his chest, covering up the scar there but displaying for the doctor the vestiges of the scars on the back of his right hand and wrist.

"And you were experiencing a number of other difficulties at the time as well. Insomnia, loss of appetite, you reported some depression..."

"It was at the Eumenide place," Ritchie said, staring off into nothing. "They had that pool house out in back. I was reaching back with the skimmer and I busted right through the window of the little house. Mrs Eumenide was inside changing at the time. She said I gave her a real scare. Cut my hand up bad, but she didn't even notice that. I finished the job off, though, and then I came over here."

"Ritchie?" Doctor Rosoff said. He gave a little shake of the head and came back to the present moment. "You complained of feeling depressed. I just looked over my notes from that appointment and you told me you were in some despair at the time."

"I remember that," Ritchie said. "Just some rough times. It's been a tough couple of years. You know, the economy and all. Even rich people been cutting back."

"I understand that. At the time, we talked about the possibility of you going to see a therapist. A psychiatrist maybe. You were supposed to come back for an evaluation appointment with our counselor here. But that was the appointment that you never showed up for. That was six months ago."

Ritchie was shaking his head. "I don't need a shrink. What would be the point, anyway? I know exactly what a shrink would say to me."

"And what would that be?" Doctor Rosoff asked.

Ritchie snorted in reply.

"Ritchie?"

"I'll tell you what he'd say. He'd say: 'Ritchie, you are a thirty-seven year-old pool guy with no home, no wife, no kids and no life worth mentioning. You live in a ratty little apartment with a dickhead of a roommate you can't stand because you can't even afford your own goddamn apartment. You are depressed, my friend, and you have got every right to be depressed. Because you, Ritchie Almares, are a big time loser.' That's exactly what he would say."

"That is definitely not how it works, Ritchie. Therapy is not like that at all. It can be an extremely useful tool to—"

"Not be a loser?" Ritchie asked.

"Do you think you maybe have some self-esteem issues, Ritchie?" Doctor Rosoff asked.

"I got plenty of self-esteem," Ritchie told her. "For a loser."

A silence ensued between them. Ritchie began idly playing with the scar on his chest again. It was suddenly itching like mad.

"Are you telling me the truth, Ritchie?" the doctor asked.

"What? About being a loser? You bet your ass. You look in the dictionary under loser, you see my picture."

"No, Ritchie," Rosoff intoned. "I'm referring to the scar. Are you telling me the truth about that? How did you really get that injury? It looks at least two months old to me and if not for the location, I'd swear it was a bullet wound."

Ritchie leaned forward. "What do you mean there about the location? Why couldn't it be a bullet wound in that location?"

"Because no one could receive a bullet wound in that spot and live to tell about it. If that was a scar from a gunshot wound, the bullet would have blown your heart to little wet bits. And while I haven't actually listened to your chest today, since you're sitting here talking to me, I have to assume that your heart is still beating in there."

Ritchie reached up and covered over the scar with the palm of his hand. He rubbed it up and down then took his hand away. He looked down.

"Still there," he said softly. He looked back up at the doctor. "But I promise you that this scar was not there when I went to bed last night. I swear to you, Doctor Rosoff. It wasn't there last night. Not before I had that dream."

Doctor Rosoff shook her head, scratched it then threw her hands in the air. She leaned forward and took another look at the scar. Ritchie felt a burning sensation in his chest every time she touched him and had to work hard not to let the pain show. Rosoff sat back once again and let out a long breath.

"I have read of instances where extreme stress can cause certain... psychosomatic reactions."

"What does that mean?" Ritchie asked.

"Psychosomatic. From the mind. Rare occurrences such as... Oh, stigmata is an extreme example. I'm talking about physiological manifestations of psychological disturbances. Things in the mind made real. I've never seen such a thing in my entire career, though. And I thought I'd seen it all at this clinic."

Ritchie felt deflated. He scratched at the scar yet again and visibly shuddered. The doctor didn't miss it.

"So you're telling me that I am nuts," Ritchie said. "What do I need a psychiatrist for when I got you, Doc? Diagnosis complete. Rubber room this way."

Doctor Rosoff dropped her weary head into her hands. She pulled at her cheeks with her fingertips. Then she looked up at Ritchie and said, "Let's tackle this from another angle. You say you had a dream last night in which you were shot and when you woke up you had this scar."

"That's exactly what happened," Ritchie affirmed.

"Then let's see if we can't analyze this more carefully and systematically. Let's try and take it apart a little bit. The man in your dream, the one who you say shot you. How was it that you described him?"

Ritchie shuddered again. "Cold. He had really dark hair, black like the night, and wavy. And eyes just the same: black, I mean. They were the tiniest, death-like eyes you've ever seen. They weren't human eyes."

"Okay," Rosoff said. "This dark-haired man. Did you recognize him? Was it someone that you know or have met before?"

Ritchie thought about it. He had been so terrified by the dream, and its aftermath, that he realized he hadn't much thought about who the man was until now. His face had been so awful, but...

"You know," Ritchie said, closing his eyes, "I'm not sure. I don't think I know him, exactly, but now that I think about it, there was something familiar about him. Distorted like, but familiar."

"Dreams always distort the familiar, don't they?" Rosoff asked.

"I guess so. But I can't think for sure who he might be. It's like on the tip of my tongue now, you know, like the answer to a sports trivia question. I know it, but I don't." Ritchie opened his eyes and shook his head. "No, I can't figure it out. Anyway, who would want to kill me? I'm just a pool guy, you know? What have I ever done? Put too much chlorine in the water?"

Doctor Rosoff studied him, but couldn't provide any answer to his question. She glanced at her watch. Ritchie realized she'd been in with him for a very long time on this busy day.

"Ritchie," she finally said. "Would it be all right with you if I asked one of my colleagues to help out with this? Get some additional input on what might be going on here?"

Ritchie shrugged. "I don't mind. I need all the help I can get about now. Bring 'em on."

"I'll just be a minute then," Rosoff told him. "He's just down the hall and if he's not in with a patient, I'll have him come in. Just wait here."

Rosoff pushed the stool back into the corner and walked out of the examination room. Ritchie took advantage of the moment to slip his shirt back on. He still felt a chill, but having his chest covered left him feeling less exposed and vulnerable. He sat back down.

He waited.

Doctor Rosoff didn't return.

So he waited some more.

Ritchie started to grow impatient. He began pacing around the edges of the room again. He was about to take yet another lesson on hand washing techniques when he noticed his file still sitting on top of the counter where Doctor Rosoff had left it. He glanced at the door, then at the clock on the wall. Feeling only slightly guilty, he flipped open the file and started to read.

The doctor's handwriting was typically hard to make out and he had a difficult time negotiating his way through her tiny italic scrawl. The notes on the top page were from his previous appointment six months earlier. Some of it was the standard recording of his complaints and the various data which had been collected about his height, weight, urine, blood pressure and so on. But there was a section for the doctor's comments at the bottom of the page and though this was even harder to decipher, the notes made Ritchie's heart start to race. Ritchie began to read:

Patient is at extreme risk for clinical depression. Possible bi-polar? Family history! Definite risk to self, possibly to others? Severe anger management issues related to stress and yet origin to be ascertained. Recommended for...

The door to the exam room opened behind him and Ritchie quickly closed the file and tossed it back on the pile where he had found it. He'd only managed to take one step back in the direction of the exam table when Doctor Rosoff came through the door. She was speaking to someone Ritchie couldn't see behind her.

"Ah, sorry to be so long. The doctor was in with a patient and then I got called away to answer the phone. In any event, I want to introduce you to an associate of mine from the clinic. I've given him a brief rundown of the situation, Ritchie, and I believe that he can help you out with some of your problems. I think he knows exactly what it is you are going through."

She stuck her head back out the door and said: "Come on in, now, he's ready for you."

Ritchie took a step forward and started to raise his arm to shake hands with the new doctor.

He threw himself backwards, staggering against the examination table and sending it flying over with a loud, metallic clatter.

The dark-haired man with the tiny black eyes entered the room. He was wearing a white lab coat like Doctor Rosoff, but his face was as cold and hard as the last time Ritchie had seen him in the dream. The dark-haired man drew his thin lips back in that death's head mockery of a smile. Ritchie knew that it was time to die.

"That's him!" he screeched.

He scrambled back to his feet, looking for some place to run. He was trapped in the corner of the examination room.

"Doctor Rosoff!" Ritchie pleaded. "That's him! That's the guy who shot me!"

Rosoff leaned over and whispered something in the ear of the dark-haired man. The man nodded and his awful smile grew broader across his pale, white face. He reached inside one of the big pockets of his white coat.

He drew out a gun; a hand-cannon. The same gun he had used to shoot Ritchie with next to the Hunts' pool.

He aimed the broad black barrel at a point in the middle of Ritchie's stomach.

"Wake up," the dark-haired man said.

He fired the gun, which exploded with the noise of a howitzer.

The bullet ripped apart Ritchie's guts. As he fell, he saw a ragged strand of intestine spill out from the gaping wound in his belly. He could smell his own feces bursting out through the newly-blown hole in his middle.

Ritchie screamed.

**Read two more awesome stories
with a sting in the tale in
The Twilight Zone: Memphis / Pool Guy
out now from Black Flame!**

FINAL DESTINATION

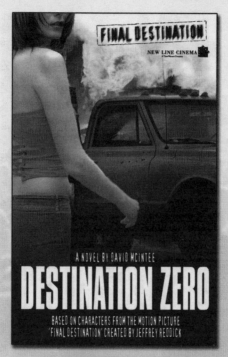

DESTINATION ZERO

1-84416-171-4   £6.99/$7.99

WWW.BLACKFLAME.COM

TOUGH FICTION FOR A TOUGH PLANET

FINAL DESTINATION™

DEAD RECKONING

1-84416-170-6   £6.99/$7.99

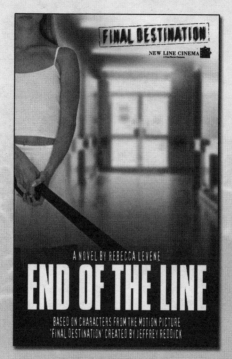

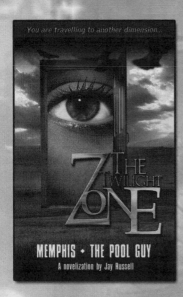

THE TWILIGHT ZONE

THE TWILIGHT ZONE
INTO THE LIGHT / SUNRISE
1-84416-151-X
£6.99/$7.99

THE TWILIGHT ZONE
CHOSEN / THE PLACEBO EFFECT
1-84416-150-1
£6.99/$7.99

TOUGH FICTION FOR

CHECK OUT THESE FANTASTIC TITLES AVAILABLE FROM BLACK FLAME!

JUDGE DREDD

Dredd vs Death
1-84416-061-0 • £5.99 • $6.99

Bad Moon Rising
1-84416-107-2 • £5.99 • $6.99

Black Atlantic
1-84416-108-0 • £5.99 • $6.99

Eclipse
1-84416-122-6 • £5.99 • $6.99

Kingdom of the Blind
1-84416-133-1 • £5.99 • $6.99

The Final Cut
1-84416-135-6 • £5.99 • $6.99

Swine Fever
1-84416-174-9 • £5.99 • $6.99

STRONTIUM DOG

Bad Timing
1-84416-110-2 • £5.99 • $6.99

Prophet Margin
1-84416-134-X • £5.99 • $6.99

Ruthless
1-84416-136-6 • £5.99 • $6.99

ABC WARRIORS

The Medusa War
1-84416-109-9 • £5.99 • $6.99

Rage Against the Machines
1-84416-178-1 • £5.99 • $6.99

ROGUE TROOPER

Crucible
1-84416-111-0 • £5.99 • $6.99

Blood Relative
1-84416-167-6 • £5.99 • $6.99

NIKOLAI DANTE

The Strangelove Gambit
1-84416-139-0 • £5.99 • $6.99

DURHAM RED

The Unquiet Grave
1-84416-159-5 • £5.99 • $6.99

The Omega Solution
1-84416-175-7 • £5.99 • $6.99

NEW LINE CINEMA

Blade: Trinity
1-84416-106-4 • £6.99 • $7.99

The Butterfly Effect
1-84416-081-5 • £6.99 • $7.99

A TOUGH PLANET

Cellular
1-84416-104-8 • £6.99 • $7.99

Freddy vs Jason
1-84416-059-9 • £5.99 • $6.99

The Texas Chainsaw Massacre
1-84416-060-2 • £6.99 • $7.99

FINAL DESTINATION

Dead Reckoning
1-84416-170-6 • £6.99 • $7.99

Destination Zero
1-84416-171-4 • £6.99 • $7.99

End of the Line
1-84416-176-5 • £6.99 • $7.99

FRIDAY THE 13TH

Hell Lake
1-84416-182-X • £6.99 • $7.99

Church of the Divine Psychopath
1-84416-181-1 • £6.99 • $7.99

JASON X

Jason X
1-84416-168-4 • £6.99 • $7.99

The Experiment
1-84416-169-2 • £6.99 • $7.99

Planet of the Beast
1-84416-183-8 • £6.99 • $7.99

A NIGHTMARE ON ELM STREET

Suffer the Children
1-84416-172-2 • £6.99 • $7.99

Dreamspawn
1-84416-173-0 • £6.99 • $7.99

THE TWILIGHT ZONE

The Twilight Zone: Memphis/The Pool Guy
1-84416-130-7 • £6.99 • $7.99

The Twilight Zone: Upgrade/Sensuous Cindy
1-84416-131-5 • £6.99 • $7.99

The Twilight Zone: Sunrise/Into the Light
1-84416-151-X • £6.99 • $7.99

The Twilight Zone: Chosen/The Placebo Effect
1-84416-150-1 • £6.99 • $7.99

The Twilight Zone: Burned/One Night at Mercy
1-84416-179-X • £6.99 • $7.99

WWW.BLACKFLAME.COM